The Nightingales in
Mersey Square

LILLY ROBBINS

ORION

First published in Great Britain in 2020 by Orion Books,
an imprint of The Orion Publishing Group Ltd
Carmelite House, 50 Victoria Embankment,
London EC4Y 0DZ

An Hachette UK company

1 3 5 7 9 10 8 6 4 2

A CIP catalogue record for this book is
available from the British Library.

ISBN (Hardback) 978 1 4091 9199 5
ISBN (eBook) 978 1 4091 9201 5

Typeset at The Spartan Press Ltd,
Lymington, Hants

Printed and bound in Great Britain by Clays Ltd,
Elcograf S.p.A.

www.orionbooks.co.uk

The Nightingales in Mersey Square is dedicated with love to our old Newcastle college friends Anne and Phil Read

Chapter One

Stockport, Cheshire
June, 1940

Clare felt an elbow in her ribs, and turned towards her nursing colleague.

'Oh, he's going to kiss her!' Gaye said, her eyes wide with excitement. 'Isn't Laurence Olivier absolutely gorgeous?'

Somebody behind them made a loud tutting noise.

'Shush or you'll get us thrown out,' Clare whispered to her friend, before turning back to the breathtaking scene. Gaye was her closest friend in England, and she enjoyed her company and her quirky sense of humour, but at times like this she often wondered what had drawn them together. Gaye – tall and red-headed – tended to be impulsive and could be embarrassingly loud at times, while Clare, smaller and chestnut-haired, was naturally quieter.

Clare sat in enraptured silence, watching as Cathy wrestled out of Heathcliff's grip then lifted her billowing skirts to scramble higher up on the craggy rocks. Heathcliff halted for a few moments, looking moodily out over the desolate, windswept Yorkshire Moors, giving her enough time to think she had escaped him. Then, her laughter bringing a smile to his usually serious face, he quickly moved up and over the rocks to catch her again and pull her into a rough embrace. Clare's breath caught in her throat as she watched Cathy turn towards Heathcliff with teasing eyes. There was a breathless moment as he bent his head

I

towards her again – and then the large black-and-white screen suddenly froze. There were a few seconds' silence as the figures flickered into life again and then died off into complete darkness. Murmurs of discontent descended over the audience as they waited for the film to kick into action again.

Instead, the main lights came on momentarily blinding everyone, and then a calm, formal voice sounded over the cinema system. *We have just received a warning of an air raid over Manchester, and we would ask all our patrons to immediately leave the Plaza building, and make your way in an orderly fashion to the nearest air-raid shelter. This is situated to the right of the building and a short walk from the cinema entrance.*

'Bloody typical!' Gaye gasped, her Newcastle accent stronger than usual. 'The Jerries would have to turn up just when they are going to have a proper kiss. I hope they let us in free tomorrow night to see the rest of the film.'

'We better move,' Clare said, collecting her coat and bag from the floor. Everyone around them was beginning to rush out of seats and into the aisles. When she looked upwards to the balcony circle, she could see the audience there moving quickly too. 'It could be serious; Manchester is only seven miles from Stockport.'

Gaye rolled her eyes, and then stood up. 'It will be a drama about nothing, as usual. If they do decide to drop a bomb somewhere, it's not going to be in flamin' Stockport. They're only interested in big places like London and the places down south.'

'Manchester is a big city too,' Clare said. 'Oliver told me they have been warned about air raids over in Liverpool and that's not too far away from here. They could easily drop bombs in this area as they're flying over.' Oliver was Clare's older brother who had come over to work in England, leaving their home in Ireland several years ahead of her. He worked as a photographer for one of the Liverpool newspapers, and often heard news before it was publically printed or came on the radio.

'We're more likely to get killed because of the blackout than we are by any bombs,' Gaye said.

Clare had her coat and scarf on now, and was putting on her gloves. 'If we don't get out of here soon, the air-raid shelter will be mobbed and we might not get a seat.'

'Keep your hair on, bonny lass,' Gaye said casually, pulling her coat on. 'We're perfectly safe in here. One of the porters was telling me that the Plaza is as good as a shelter because it's built into a rock face. We could just stay in here and watch the rest of the film.'

'We can't,' Clare replied, 'and the film is gone off the screen anyway.' She watched anxiously as the other cinema patrons moved towards the exit.

Gaye pulled her felt cloche hat down over her red curly hair, and finally made a move towards the nearest aisle, Clare following closely behind. People were still moving out of the rows of seats, all heading towards the exit. Clare stopped to let an old lady with a walking stick out first. Then two young boys suddenly came running through the crowds, laughing and dodging around people as they went.

The old lady turned around to see what was going on, and one of the boys bumped against her, knocking her stick out of her hand. As she tottered sideways, Clare stepped forward instinctively to catch her, Gaye quickly behind her. Together they managed to get her into in an upright position again.

'Are you okay, love?' Gaye checked, her voice kind and caring, just as they'd been taught in their training classes when handling elderly patients. 'You take your time now, there's no rush. There will be plenty of room in the shelter.'

Clare looked at the old lady. 'I think you might be best sitting down for a few minutes, just to catch your breath.'

They guided her into the seat nearest the aisle.

'Those flamin' kids,' Gaye said. 'They should have better manners. I'd say that gave you a bit of a scare, didn't it?'

'It did...' the old lady replied. 'When I went to the side, I came over a bit dizzy like... I get that sometimes.' She looked around her now, a look of panic on her face. 'My stick – I've lost my stick...'

Clare cast around and saw it on the floor beside the row of seats. 'Don't worry, your stick is here,' she said, bending down to retrieve it.

A petite young woman with bobbed black hair glanced as she passed them by in the flow of traffic, then she stopped and turned back. 'Is there anything I can do to help?'

Clare looked at her, surprised that someone with such an upper-class accent would even think of stopping to help. 'Thanks, but I think she's fine now.'

'Thanks, love,' the elderly lady said, looking at the girl. 'I'm all right now, and we best be moving to the air-raid shelter.' She suddenly stopped. 'My gas mask...'

Clare looked down at the floor once more and picked up the box she found below the seat. 'It's here,' she said, with a cheery smile. 'I'll carry it with my own.' She looped it over her shoulder alongside her own.

'Thanks, love.'

The dark-haired girl stepped forward again. 'If you're sure there's nothing I can do?'

'I think she'll be fine,' Gaye said, still using the soothing voice the nurses had taught them to use when dealing with patients. 'We'll walk her over to the shelter.'

A male usher came quickly down the aisle, and the dark-haired girl stepped into a row of seats to let him by.

'I could see there was a bit of a commotion going on down here, and I said to myself, I'm sure that's Mrs Atherton.' He bent down towards her now. 'You all right, love?'

'Just makin' a fool of meself, Frank,' Mrs Atherton said. 'I don't know what came over me. One minute I was on me feet and the next minute I was tottering around.'

'It was those cheeky young buggers who knocked you over,' the usher said. 'If I find out who they are, they'll be barred.' He looked at the girls. 'I know Mrs Atherton. She comes here regularly, don't you, love?'

Mrs Atherton nodded her head.

'She loves all the old films. She lives down near the market with her daughter. They own the fish and chip shop there. They have a bit of a café area – a few tables – where you can eat in.' He studied the old lady. 'Would a glass of water help?'

'No, no ... I'll wait and get a cup of tea in the shelter. I'm fine to get up and go now.'

'Are you sure?' Gaye asked.

Mrs Atherton patted her hand. 'I would feel responsible if a bomb was to drop down on us and we all got killed.'

'Ah, I doubt it, love,' the usher said. 'The war will be over soon enough, and all the lads will be back home again.'

'I hope so,' Mrs Atherton said. 'I've two grandsons out there ...' She looked up at Gaye and Clare. 'I think I'll try getting up now, if you wouldn't mind giving me a hand.'

Then, very carefully, holding on to Clare's arm with one hand and leaning on the cinema seat with the other, Mrs Atherton stood up. 'Yes, I'll be fine,' she said, 'if I take it steady ...' She took her stick from Clare, took a few testing steps forward and then nodded her head.

'How do you feel?' Clare asked. 'Are you feeling dizzy or seeing double?'

'Maybes just a bit light-headed ...'

'Are you up to walking?' Gaye asked.

'I'll be all right, and we need to get out of here,' she said.

Glancing around the empty auditorium, Clare realised they were the only ones left, but she pushed that thought from her mind and tried to focus on keeping Mrs Atherton calm, happy and safe.

Slowly, they made their way up the aisle and out into the dimly lit foyer.

'You go on ahead, while I switch off the lights,' Frank told them.

With Clare taking Mrs Atherton's arm and Gaye carrying her crocodile-skin handbag, they slowly made their way out into the night air. They stood in silence for a few moments, getting used to the pitch blackness, and trying to make out buildings or any landmarks that would guide them along the street. There was no one else outside; everyone had already made their way to the shelter.

'I hate this bloody dark,' Mrs Atherton said, a tremor in her voice, 'and there's hardly a moon out at all tonight.'

'The shelter is only a minute away,' Clare reassured her. 'We just have to get across Mersey Square and walk down to Chestergate.'

'I'm glad I have your company,' the old lady said. 'I heard there are young buggers who are taking advantage of the black-out and robbing houses and shops and everything.'

'I've never seen any trouble here at all,' Gaye said reassuringly.

Clare stayed silent, as they had had several incidents with prowlers around the hospital at night. The older nurses had told them that the female accommodation block was a magnet for certain sorts of males, and it had definitely got worse since the blackout. The student nurses had been advised to go everywhere outside the hospital in twos where possible.

'Don't you worry,' Gaye said. 'I'll brain anyone who comes near us with your walking stick!'

'Good girl, I'm glad I met you!' Mrs Atherton said, and they all laughed, trying to dispel the sense of unease that was creeping over them now they were out in the pitch-black night.

'So, you live down near the market?' Gaye asked, keeping the conversation going and Mrs Atherton's mind off the danger of their situation.

'I do, it's only a few minutes' walk on an ordinary night when you can see where you're going. Where do you girls live? Are you here in Stockport?'

'Not too far,' Clare said. 'We're actually living where we work—' She halted abruptly, hearing heavy footsteps behind them.

'It's only me,' Frank the cinema usher said. 'I could hear Mrs Atherton's voice and followed you along.'

'You're as bad as my son with your sharp ears,' the old lady said, laughing, 'He's always telling me I talk too loud.'

They walked along now, Frank behind the women, and

everyone keeping a slow pace with Mrs Atherton. They crossed the road over to Chestergate and walked onwards towards the shelter.

'Thank God,' the old lady said, 'I'm dying for a cup of tea. I usually go down to the number six tunnel, and meet up with some of my neighbours there. They'll have kept me a place.' She gave a little sigh. 'I'm not sure there will be room in it for three more, but you never know.'

A car engine sounded from Great Underbank now, and everyone quickly moved in towards the safety of the buildings as the vehicle, its headlamps muted, went past.

'Those blooming cars,' Mrs Atherton said. 'Even in daylight they're a danger. My son-in-law has one, and I dread getting into it.' She took a few steps forward and then seemed to lose her balance again and fell against the wall. The girls caught her as she sank to the ground in a faint.

'Did she bang her head?' Gaye asked Clare anxiously as she knelt down next to the elderly lady.

'I couldn't see,' Clare replied, trying to keep her voice calm as her mind began to race. 'It all happened so quickly.'

'How can we get her into the shelter when she's like this?'

'We'll have to get her help,' Frank said. 'Some of the ARP should be around, and they have stretchers down in the Red Cross area in the tunnels.' He lowered his voice. 'Do you think it's something like a stroke or a heart attack?'

'It's hard to tell...' Clare said. She didn't want to start explaining about them being student nurses. While they were used to dealing with sick patients in the hospital, it was under the orders of the staff nurse or ward sister. It was a very different situation for them to make decisions on their own.

Mrs Atherton suddenly moaned and in the dim light they could see her eyes flutter open. 'What's happened?' she said, her voice thin and crackly. She lifted her head. 'Where are we?'

'You're okay, Mrs Atherton,' Frank reassured her. 'You just had a bit of a faint.'

Everyone froze as the noise of aeroplane engines suddenly sounded in the distance.

'We better move,' Frank said urgently. 'They're probably our own lads training out of Manchester, but you never know.'

'Can you sit up?' Clare checked, her heart racing now. They were constantly warned in the hospital and on the radio or in newspapers about the risks of being outside during an air raid.

Mrs Atherton moved into a sitting position. 'I'm just a bit shaky, like...'

'Take your time,' Gaye said, her voice gentle, but firm just like Sister Townsend's. 'We'll stay with you until someone comes to help you.' She flicked an anxious glance at Clare and whispered, 'You go on, I'll wait here with her until she's up to moving.'

Clare gulped. She didn't want to go out into the dark street alone. Trying to swallow her fear she took a tentative step forwards, her heart hammering, when she suddenly heard footsteps and voices echoing in the black night.

A group of three Red Cross members – two men carrying a stretcher and a woman carrying blankets – appeared out of the darkness to stand in front of them, accompanied by the dark-haired girl from the Plaza.

'I waited at the door of the shelter for you,' she explained with a smile, 'and when I heard the planes and saw no sign of you, I got worried and fetched the Red Cross.'

The two men quickly got to work, lifting Mrs Atherton onto the stretcher and wrapping her in blankets, and then everyone moved at a fast pace in the direction of the shelters.

Clare found herself side by side with the dark-haired girl, who was striding confidently ahead, seemingly calm despite the pitch-black night and the sirens still sounding across the sky. Clare couldn't help but be impressed by the kindness and concern the obviously upper-class girl had shown for the old lady.

When the air-raid shelter came into view Clare felt relief course through her, especially when the ARP wardens went ahead of the Red Cross, loudly telling people to clear a path for the stretcher and the accompanying group until they were all safely inside. She hadn't realised how terrified she'd been. Hadn't this been exactly the kind of situation her mother had feared? Stockport was supposed to be safe from the dangers, and this may well have been just a drill, but what if there had been a German bomber flying overhead? Clare shivered and then pushed the thought away as she watched Mrs Atherton be taken away into the makeshift Red Cross room.

After a few minutes, a kindly nurse opened the door and said, 'There's only room for one person inside, and she's asking for the girl with the red hair.'

Gaye glanced at Clare with wide eyes. 'Why would she want *me*?' she asked in a low voice. 'Shouldn't it be you?'

'Because you were so good with her,' Clare said, squeezing her friend's hand. 'You managed to keep her calm and feel safe. You did all the right things we were told to do in training.'

'We both did,' Gaye said.

'But I was absolutely terrified,' Clare admitted, 'and you were really professional. You carried on as if you were dealing with one of the patients in the hospital.'

'Get away . . .' Gaye laughed.

'You should feel proud of yourself for doing everything right,' Clare said. 'I hope I'm like you and not so frightened when anything like this happens again.'

'Thanks,' Gaye said, her voice emotional. 'That's one of the nicest things anyone has ever said to me.'

When Gaye went into the Red Cross room, the girl turned to Clare and smiled, then put her hand out. 'I'm Diana.'

'And I'm Clare,' she said, smiling back, inwardly admiring the girl's easy confidence.

The two girls found seats near the room, while Frank went to get them all a cup of tea. He had only just moved away when they heard a bit of a commotion further along the tunnel. Moments later, one of the wardens and a middle-aged man came into view, supporting a younger man with a panic-stricken look on his face.

'You're all right,' the warden said in a brisk manner. 'Just take a good deep breath and try to calm yourself down.'

'If he could get a good deep breath he would be fine,' the older man snapped back. 'Surely you can see that's what his problem is?'

'He'll be fine,' the warden said, guiding the young man into the sick bay. 'It's only claustrophobia, we get this all the time.'

Diana leaned in closer to Clare. 'Poor boy,' she whispered.

Clare nodded, feeling sorry for the young man, who she thought would feel mortified at his situation later.

Frank returned with their drinks and they chatted companionably for a while about the film they had all been watching, when the Red Cross door opened and Mrs Atherton and Gaye came out.

'You've all been very good,' the old lady said, evidently touched to see them waiting for her.

A smiling Clare immediately helped her take a seat. She was so pleased to see Mrs Atherton standing and with a rosy glow to her cheeks.

'I wouldn't have managed without your help,' Mrs Atherton said, reaching a hand out to Clare in thanks. 'And I believe you and the young lady from Newcastle are nurses up in St Timothy's?'

'Yes,' Clare said, 'but we're only student nurses, we're still training.'

Mrs Atherton smiled up at her. 'Two proper young Florence Nightingales helping me out, and I never even got your names...'

'Well, I'm Gaye Robinson, and she's Clare O'Sullivan.'

The elderly woman looked at Clare. 'You're Irish, aren't you, love? I thought it early on, I can tell by your accent.'

'Yes,' Clare said. 'I came over last summer.'

'Stockport must be a big change. Are you all settled here?'

'Yes,' she said, 'although I do miss home at times.'

'Course you do. It's only natural.' She then turned to Diana. 'And what about you, love? I didn't get your name either. Are you from around here?'

'I'm Diana,' she said quietly. 'I'm from Cheshire... out in the country, near Macclesfield.'

'Oh,' Mrs Atherton said. 'Out in the country. I'd say that's very nice?'

'I suppose it is.' She smiled. 'I'm staying with my aunt in Davenport now and I like it there too.'

Mrs Atherton nodded her head approvingly. 'Davenport is very nice. I go to the church there, if the weather isn't too bad.'

'My aunt goes to that church too,' Diana said. 'Maybe you know her? Her name is Rosamund Douglas.'

'Douglas...' the old woman repeated vaguely. 'Can't say the name rings a bell.'

'There's some cracking houses up in Davenport too,' Frank chimed in cheerily. 'Some of them are huge.'

'Well, it's certainly very convenient for buses into Stockport or Manchester,' Diana said with a smile.

'We're just down the road from you,' Clare said in surprise. 'We're in the nurses' accommodation in the hospital. Are you getting the bus home when we get out of here?'

'Yes, it's a bit far to walk, especially at night.'

'You can travel back on the bus with us,' Clare offered.

Diana's face lit up. 'Oh, that would be lovely.'

The sound of an accordion playing 'Danny Boy' drifted towards them from deeper into the shelter and the group turned towards the music as general conversation died down and everyone started to listen. Then, to Clare's surprise, people quietly began to sing along.

Clare felt tears come into her eyes as she listened to the mournful sounds of her mother's favourite song. Images flooded her mind: her parents and grandparents, her married sister and new nephew – who she had only seen photos of – and her two younger brothers and sister. She hadn't seen any of them for eighteen months. As a tear slid down her face, she searched in her coat pocket for her hanky, hoping no one would notice.

Gaye gently linked her arm with hers and then whispered, 'Are you okay?'

Clare nodded and forced a little smile. Gaye was used to her bouts of homesickness and although she teased her, she always gave a comforting smile or squeeze.

When 'Danny Boy' finished, people clapped and then they gave a loud cheer when they recognised the opening strains of the next one – Vera Lynn's popular 'We'll Meet Again' – and joined in singing with even greater gusto.

All three girls sang along, and as usual, people's heads turned when they heard the sound of Gaye's perfect-pitch, alto voice standing out from everyone else's. Diana looked at her in surprise, and then smiled and held her hands up in a silent clap of approval.

When the song ended, those sitting close by praised her voice.

'Not only are you a great little nurse, but you have the voice of a nightingale,' Mrs Atherton said, her eyes wide in wonder. 'We could do with you in our church choir or teaching the younger ones in Sunday School.'

'You should be on the stage,' Frank said. 'You have a cracking voice – you're as good as, if not better than, Vera Lynn.'

'Everyone in the hospital tells her that when she sings at parties,' Clare said with pride for her friend. 'I've told her she should be doing it professionally, on the stage or on the radio.'

'Get away!' Gaye laughed, flapping a hand at them all. 'I only do it for a bit of fun.'

'Where did you learn to sing like that?' Diana asked. 'Your voice is beautiful.'

Gaye shrugged, embarrassed, but Clare could just about see her flush with delight in the flickering light of the shelter. 'I was in the school choir,' she said, 'and I used to sing in church every Sunday.'

'Something told me you would be good helping with a choir,' Mrs Atherton said knowingly, 'and I was right.'

Gaye laughed. 'I hardly ever sing now, because I never go near the church since moving away from home.' She poked Clare. 'Not like this one, she's a right little angel, in the church every day, praying for everybody.'

Clare blushed. 'I don't have far to go, the Catholic church

is next door to the hospital, and all the Irish girls go to mass whenever they get the chance.'

'I sometimes go to church with Aunt Rosamund,' Diana said. She rolled her eyes and smiled. 'She keeps trying to get me involved in the Women's Institute too.'

'Not the Women's Institute!' Gaye laughed. 'Keep well away from that lot or they'll have you roped into all sorts. Me mam's a member of the one in Newcastle. You're far too young; it's all knitting and jam-making and boring stuff like that.'

'I like knitting,' Clare said, grinning at her. 'I find it relaxing and it gives me something new to wear.'

'Good girl,' Mrs Atherton said. 'There's nothing wrong with knitting, and there's truth in the old saying: busy hands are happy hands.'

Diana smiled at Gaye now. 'And I like sewing, so that makes two of us that are very practical, although some girls might find it a bit boring and mundane.'

'I don't think any of you girls are the slightest bit boring,' the old lady said. 'And if I had more time with you tonight, I'd be doing my best to persuade you to help up at the church.'

The siren suddenly sounded, signalling that all was safe outside again. The music stopped and people started lifting bags and putting coats and hats on.

'That's always happens,' one disgruntled middle-aged lady said. 'I was just startin' to enjoy meself and they have to go and spoil it on us, makin' them sirens go.'

'Never mind,' her friend said happily, 'there's always tomorrow.'

'Aye, there's always tomorrow,' an air-raid warden repeated loudly, as he made his way through the crowds. 'But tomorrow could be the day when they drop a bomb on Stockport, and none of youse would be singing and laughing then, would you? It would be a totally different tune then.'

The three girls looked at each other, then Gaye made a face behind the warden's back and they all stifled a laugh.

'I think,' Clare said, 'it's time we went for our bus.'

Chapter Two

'Here it comes,' Clare said to Gaye and Diana.

Diana looked into the distance and narrowed her eyes. 'Yes, I think you're right.'

Gaye turned to where they were looking, and after a few moments she saw the dim lights of the double-decker bus coming towards them. 'You always spot them before me.'

'You were used to having lights everywhere in Newcastle,' Clare laughed. 'In the countryside, you become used to the dark and you listen for any noises too.'

'Absolutely,' Diana said. 'Although it's surprising how quickly you adapt to new places. When I first went to live in London – I studied art there – I found the traffic and the Underground and all the people overwhelming, but within weeks I was trundling around it without a thought.'

The darkened bus drew to a stop now and they all boarded. Clare went first, and spied two empty seats near the front. They moved inside, then she and Gaye sat across the aisle from Diana.

Gaye turned eagerly to Diana. 'Did you like London? I've always wanted to go there.'

'I loved it. When you are a student, there is always something going on.'

'I would be terrified living in such a big place' Clare said. 'It took me weeks to find my way around Stockport.'

'Well, I was used to big cities like Manchester,' Diana explained, 'and I've often gone to London for weekends with my parents. Of course, it was rather different getting around on my own, as I was used to my father driving us to Oxford Street or to places for lunch or dinner.'

Gaye and Clare glanced at each other, both suddenly aware that Diana's world was a very different one to theirs. Clare had never even seen a black Dublin hackney cab until she was twelve years old, and Gaye had grown up in a terraced house outside the city.

'So how d'you find Stockport, like?' Gaye asked

Diana's brow creased. 'It's fine. I've only been here a month, so I'm still getting used to it.'

'I was very homesick when I first moved over from Ireland,' Clare confessed, 'but I'm used to it now, and the people here are very friendly.' Her face brightened. 'There are plenty of Irish girls working in the hospital too, so you get to know each other quickly.'

'Have you made many friends?' Gaye asked.

Diana's face flushed. 'No, not really. I think the other women in the factory see me as a little different.'

'What kind of factory is it?'

'Textile – parachutes and uniforms.'

'Are you a secretary?'

'No,' Diana said, 'although I was offered an office job, but I told them I really enjoy sewing. I preferred it to working in a munitions factory, and since I'm a bit squeamish with blood, I didn't think I would be much help in a hospital.'

'You sound as though you come from an upper-class background – couldn't your family get you something more important than factory work?'

'Gaye!' Clare gasped. 'There's a war on and everyone has to muck in the best they can.'

'It's okay, I don't mind,' Diana said, smiling. 'I was helping my mother run the estate at home, as most of the younger men who worked on the farms have gone into the armed forces. I was manning the phone, working in the stables and helping the housekeeper with the ration books – all those sorts of things. I even helped drive the tractors.'

'Didn't you prefer that to a factory?' Gaye asked.

Diana shrugged. 'I didn't fit in with the other girls. No matter what work I did and how hard I tried to fit in, the tenant farmers and their workers still saw me as the daughter of the estate family. They always seemed on edge, and I'm not very good at giving orders to men much older than myself and telling people what to do.' She pulled an anguished face. 'It was even worse when the land girls arrived to help out, and I knew they couldn't relax when I was around. They were expecting me to report them to the farmers, or even worse – my mother.'

'I suppose you can understand that,' Gaye said.

'I wanted to do a job that would make a difference, and making and packing parachutes is an important one. The airmen's lives depend on us checking every little detail.'

'But it must be hard,' Gaye replied, 'working with girls who aren't very friendly.'

'But it's me who's different,' Diana said, matter-of-factly. 'Most of them are local girls, and they have their own circle of friends to go to the cinema or dances with.'

'We're not local girls either,' Clare said, 'and the hospital has a mixture of people from all different places. You would be welcome to join our group of friends, wouldn't she, Gaye?'

'Of course,' Gaye said, grinning. 'We often work different shifts, and we're glad to have someone to go to the pictures with. And there's usually four or five of us from the nurses' home, when we go dancing in Stockport or into Manchester.'

Diana's face lit up. 'Oh, I'd love to go to a dance with you! It gets a bit boring listening to the radio with Aunt Rosamund every night.' She halted, thinking. 'There's a phone box outside the hospital, isn't there? You could ring me from there to make arrangements.'

'Yes,' Clare said, 'and we have a payphone in the nurses' residence too, so we can make calls and receive them. If we're working, you can always leave a message with anyone who answers it, and they'll pass it on to us or put a note under the door in our room.'

'That's terrific.' Diana lifted her handbag and took out a small notebook and a pencil. 'I'll give you my aunt's phone number, and I'll take your number down now too.' When she had finished writing, she tore a page out and gave it to Clare. 'I'm really excited now at the thought of going to a dance. My mother drags me to functions in hotels in Manchester, hoping to find me a husband, but I'd much rather go to a real dance hall with people my own age. You two sound as though you have a wonderful social life.'

'There's usually something going on, especially at the weekends,' Clare told her. 'We often have staff dances too, and every few months we join up for a big dance in the town hall with the staff from Stepping Hill Hospital.'

'It sounds fabulous,' Diana said.

Gaye's eyes lit up. 'Some of the doctors are really dishy, and a lot of them are good dancers.'

'Gaye is usually one of the first asked up on the floor,' Clare laughed. 'She's very popular.'

'I can imagine,' Diana said, smiling warmly at her.

Gaye shook her head and laughed.

The bus moved up past the ornate town hall and the two nurses got up for their stop.

'My stop is the one after this,' Diana told them.

'Do you want us to stay on and see you home?' Gaye offered.

'It's very kind of you,' Diana said, 'but I'll be fine.'

As the girls walked arm-in-arm across the road towards the hospital, Clare said, 'Well, that wasn't what we expected when we set out tonight, was it?' She laughed. 'And we didn't get to see the end of *Wuthering Heights* after all.'

'We can blame that on the Jerries,' Gaye said. 'And there wasn't a bomb in sight either.' She looked at her friend. 'Ah, we'll get to see the film another night. I'm glad the way it worked out, as it meant we were around to help that poor old soul.'

'You were very good with her,' Clare said. 'I only wish I had been half as professional as you.' There was a little note of regret in her voice, as she knew she needed to improve her own nursing skills in this area. 'You should be really proud of yourself.'

'We all did our bit, even the fella from the cinema and that posh girl, Diana.'

'You were really calm when the planes were heading our way.' She sucked her breath in. 'I was absolutely terrified...'

'Well, luckily our number wasn't up tonight.' They both laughed, then Gaye turned to her friend. 'What did you think of Diana? I was dead surprised that she had waited for us at the shelter.'

'So was I,' Clare said. 'I'd forgotten all about her by the time she appeared again. She was really concerned about Mrs Atherton.'

'You just don't imagine that somebody like her would have been so bothered about an ordinary old lady. Her being so upper class and everything.'

'She's seems very down to earth, and very practical.'

'She said she was an art student, and they're usually a bit on the weird side.'

'She didn't seem weird to me,' Clare mused. 'She's lovely looking, too, isn't she?'

'She has a beautiful little face,' Gaye said thoughtfully, 'although I'm not mad on her hairstyle. That black bob is a bit severe and old-fashioned for a young girl.'

'I think it suits her.' Clare thought for a few moments. 'It makes her stand out more, and you notice her eyes.'

'Well, there's no doubt she is beautiful,' Gaye conceded, 'and she is a lovely person. Though I thought it was a bit strange she's come over to Stockport when she could be living in a big fancy house in the country. I bet her mam is dead worried about her, in the middle of the town where she doesn't know anybody.'

'I thought that too,' Clare said. 'Although she does at least have her aunt. It was different for us, because we knew we were coming to train in a hospital with other girls all around the same age in our class.'

'Those factory girls sound like proper bitches, not asking her to join them for a night out, even if she is different.'

'I'm glad we asked her to join us,' Clare said, 'although God knows what we're going to talk to her about.'

Gaye started giggling again. 'Well, you were the one that invited her, so you'll have to sit with her.'

'Don't you dare leave me on my own all night with her,' Clare said, wagging her finger. 'I haven't a clue about art or the sort of things she'd be talking about. You're much better at making small talk than me.'

'I thought the Irish were meant to have the gift of the gab?' Gaye said.

'There's not an Irish person who could hold a candle to you!'

They both started laughing, falling in against each other as they went in the hospital gates.

Chapter Three

The following afternoon, Clare was having lunch in the nurses' canteen, having just told the others about the incident in the cinema, when Gaye hurried up to her excitedly. 'Some of the girls were telling me this morning, that the Co-op have some lovely new flowery dresses in, and I was thinking that we might go mad and buy one each. We should have enough coupons for them.'

'Flowery would be great,' Clare said, thinking of the rather limited choices she'd had before the last dance. 'And the different colours make it easier to match with cardigans and jackets.'

'They have lovely coloured bags in too,' Gaye said, glancing up at Clare through her eyelashes, 'big enough for our gas masks as well, which would be dead handy.' She knew that the sensible Clare would be more easily swayed by the practicality of the bags.

Clare shook her head. 'We'd never have enough coupons for bags as well, and I'm trying to save some of mine along with money to buy a new pair of shoes for work.' She looked down at her plain black, lace-up nurse's shoes. 'These ones won't last much longer.'

Gaye looked thoughtful. 'Maybe we could put our coupons together and buy one bag to share when we're on different shifts. What do you think?'

'Good idea,' Clare said, smiling. 'We'll go together to make sure it's one that suits us both.'

Gaye looked delighted that Clare was agreeable. 'What about tomorrow?'

'We have classes up in Stepping Hill.'

The nurses from the various local hospitals all went to the bigger hospital on specified days for their nursing lectures. They usually finished their class around four o'clock and were expected back in the hospital to help give out the patients' evening meal. They got the bus outside Stepping Hill and got off on Wellington Road, just outside a café, and the girls usually had a sneaky coffee break before going back to work.

'Instead of going for our coffee,' Gaye said, 'we could stay on the bus and go down to the Co-op. If we're quick, we could be back up at the café again and nobody would even miss us.'

Clare looked doubtful. 'We might be better waiting until we've more time.'

Gaye shook her head. 'I'm on late shifts this week, and you're on earlies. Those dresses are going to be gone if we don't get down there tomorrow.'

'Do you think we would make it back up to the ward in time?'

'We'll make sure we do.' Gaye's eyes lit up. 'I'd love a new summer dress. I've been wearing the same ones for the last two years.'

'Wouldn't it be great if we had a sewing machine? We could make dresses for half the price.'

Gaye rolled her eyes. 'I'm bloody useless at sewing. My mam banned me from using the machine at home after I broke the needle making a bag. Our Audrey is lucky, she can make any-thing.'

'Okay,' Clare said. 'We'll go down to the Co-op tomorrow, but it's straight in to the shop and back to the hospital on the next bus.'

'Fantastic! We'll be able to wear the dresses to the next dance.'

The next day the girls went on the bus up to Stepping Hill Hospital, with their precious coupons and money safe in their work bags. They sat through their class on Human Biology, and every time they caught each other's eyes, they both grinned at the thought of their shopping spree when they were finished.

As they queued with their trays in the canteen, Gaye told the other girls in the group what they were planning. 'We're going to rush like mad,' she said, 'so hopefully nobody will miss us.'

'What if the sister asks us where you are?' one of the other student nurses asked.

'We usually take about half an hour in the café,' Gaye said, 'so if you take an extra five minutes, then walk slow to the ward we should be back around the same time.'

'But what if something happens?' the girl persisted. 'Where are we supposed to say you are? We don't want them quizzing us, and then they might find out we were in the café, and it would spoil it for everyone.'

'She's right, Gaye,' Clare said, looking anxious. 'It's not fair, putting anybody else in an awkward position. We can't expect the girls to cover for us.'

Gaye thought for a few moments. 'Right,' she said. 'Just say we weren't on the bus with you, and that we must have got held up at Stepping Hill.'

The girls looked at her.

'I don't know what you're all worried about,' she said with a laugh. 'We're not going to be late in any case.'

As soon as the class was finished, Gaye grabbed Clare's arm and said, 'Right, we'll make a run for it out to the main road, and we might even catch an earlier bus.'

Their luck was in, as they came rushing out, they could see the red double-decker bus in the distance. 'God's on our side!' Gaye panted. They both took to their heels – hands on their hats and capes flying – and made a dash for the bus stop.

The Co-op ladies' department was very quiet, and as soon as they entered the area, two assistants came over to serve the girls. Gaye took charge and explained what they were looking for.

'They're going like hotcakes,' one of the women said when she'd returned with the girls' correct sizes. 'As you can see, they're lovely and bright, and a decent price. You won't get anything like them in the other shops in Stockport. You would have to travel to Manchester, and you might not be lucky there either.'

Gaye asked the other lady about the coloured handbags, and they were guided over to a corner where there was a display of bags.

There were several the girls loved and they would have looked great with their new floral dresses, but even with their coupons pooled together, it was still a stretch for just one bag.

'We'll think about it, thanks,' Gaye said, her voice heavy with disappointment.

While the woman was putting the bag back on the display stand, Gaye whispered to Clare. 'Some of the nurses said there's a fella who has a stall at the market on Saturdays, who can get things cheaper and without coupons. We might be better waiting until we get paid, and we can afford a bag each.'

'Do you mean the "black market"?' Clare said in a hushed voice.

Gaye raised her brows and nodded.

'But you can get into serious trouble for that.'

'Who's going to know?'

'I'm not sure,' Clare said. 'You've seen all the notices every-where about how we shouldn't buy anything without coupons.'

'Loads of people I know in Newcastle get stuff on the black market,' Gaye said. 'So why shouldn't we?'

'I don't feel right about it...I'd rather save up and buy some-thing.' She glanced down at her watch. 'Oh God, if we don't hurry we're going to be in trouble.'

'We're fine,' Gaye said. 'The others will still be in the café. You worry far too much.'

After they'd paid for their dresses, they rushed out of the shop up towards the bus stop at Wellington Road.

'Oh no, I don't believe it,' Clare said speeding up, 'that's a bus just pulling in.' Just as they made it across the square, the bus engine revved up and started to pull out. Both girls ran as fast as they could, waving and shouting at the driver to wait for them.

The bus gave a lurch and picked up speed. Gaye made a last, desperate effort to catch up with it, and then lost her footing, going over on her ankle and falling to the ground.

Clare immediately ran to help her. 'Are you okay?'

Gaye looked around her dazed and out of breath. 'I don't know what happened,' she panted, 'I think I've hurt my leg, I hit a stone...'

Clare got down on one knee, her bags thrown on the ground. 'Let me check.' There was a big hole in the knee of Gaye's thick black stockings, which revealed a bad graze with blood oozing from it.

Gaye tried to move and then moaned in pain. 'My ankle is bloody killin' me as well. I must have twisted it when I fell over.'

'Lean on me,' Clare said, 'and I'll try to help you up.'

Gaye tried to move, but it was too painful. Clare's heart was racing now. Not only was she worried that her friend had hurt herself, she was worried that they were now late, and were going to find it hard to explain away Gaye's injuries.

A young couple were walking nearby and when they noticed the trouble the girls were in, they moved to help Clare get Gaye back on her feet again.

Taking a few deep breaths, Gaye gave them a weak smile. 'Thank God, it's easing a bit now. I feel a total fool, having that happen to me.'

'We have to look after our nurses,' the young man said, grinning at her, and Clare was suddenly grateful that they were wearing their student nurse uniforms. 'If things get worse with the Germans, we'll need every nurse to be on hand.'

The kindly couple insisted on waiting until the bus came and then helped Gaye on board.

When they were finally settled in a seat, Gaye turned to Clare. 'Thankfully, my ankle has eased, although God knows what I'm going to say when we get in, and I'll feel terrible if I've got you into trouble as well.'

'I'm just glad you're okay,' Clare said, trying not to sound anxious, as she took another peek at her watch.

Walking towards the hospital gates, Gaye was still limping. 'It's Jimmy on the porter's lodge,' she said, sounding relieved. 'Quick, give me your bag with the dress.'

'Why?' Clare asked.

Gaye just tutted and grabbed the bag from her and limped as quickly as she could to the wooden cabin. 'Jimmy,' she said hurriedly to the middle-aged porter, 'would you do me a big favour? Would you keep these bags for us until I finish later? We haven't time to go back to our rooms and we don't want to carry them in with us.'

Jimmy looked doubtful. 'We're not supposed to ...'

'Ah, go on,' she said. 'We're going into Sister Bennett and she won't be best pleased if she sees them.'

'Sister Bennett?' His eyebrows shot up. 'I wouldn't want to get on the wrong side of her. Here, give them over.'

Clare's heart was racing now.

'One more hurdle to go,' Gaye said, as they carried on towards the ward, arms linked together to help Gaye, who was limping quite badly now. 'Now, don't you say anything, just agree with everything I say – all right?'

'You're making me really nervous,' Clare hissed.

'Try to relax and act normal,' Gaye told her as they entered the ward. 'Just keep a hold of my arm as though you're helping me along ...'

They passed the other student nurses, who were wheeling in the meal trolleys, and one of the girls whispered to them, 'Sister just sent somebody over to the residence looking for you.'

'Did you say anything?' Gaye checked.

'We said we never saw you.'

Then Sister Bennett came out of the office, and when she saw them she pointed and crooked a finger, beckoning them into the office. Clare's hand was shaking as she gripped Gaye's arm as they followed the Sister inside.

'Well?' Sister Bennett demanded, her trademark scowl in place. 'You're nearly half an hour late. What's your excuse?'

'Oh, Sister ...' Gaye said, her voice quivering. 'I had an

accident up at Stepping Hill...' She gestured toward a chair. 'Can I sit down please? I don't feel too well.'

'What's wrong with you?'

'She fell, Sister...' Clare said, hurriedly. 'If you look at her knee.'

Since there had seemed no objection, Gaye collapsed into the chair, moaning for good effect.

The sister bent down to look at the torn stocking and bloody knee. 'What on earth happened?'

'I was rushing,' Gaye told her. 'I didn't want to be late getting back here from our classes, and I went over on my ankle. I nearly fainted with the pain, and had to sit down. It's still killing me.'

'You need to get that cleaned up and bandaged straight away.' The sister sighed. 'I know we have to keep to times, but there's no need to run from one place to the other.'

'I'm sorry, Sister,' Gaye said, her voice still trembling. 'And poor Clare was late because she had to help me.'

'Well, I'm glad she was with you, because you gave yourself a sore one.' She made a clucking noise with her tongue. 'Get a bandage and gauze from the nurses' station, and then clean that knee properly and put a good dab of TCP on it before you put the bandage on.' Her voice softened to a tone that neither Clare nor Gaye recognised. 'Are you okay to walk back?'

'I think so.' Gaye leaned on the arm of the chair and then very carefully stood up. She gave a little shiver. 'My ankle is still paining me...'

'It should settle down when you rest it.' Sister Bennett looked over at Clare. 'Make sure she gets back to her room all right, and stay with her for a while. A fall like that can hit you harder afterwards. If we were at home, I'd even suggest a drop of brandy for the shock.'

'I will, Sister,' she said, nodding her head. 'And I'll bring her meal over to her room, too.'

Clare took Gaye by the arm, and they slowly made their way out into the corridor and outside.

As soon as they were out of sight, Gaye came to a standstill. 'Thank God we got away with it!' she said gleefully.

Clare looked at her surprised. 'Did you put the whole thing on?'

'No,' Gaye said, 'my leg *is* killing me. Even Sister Bennett believed me.'

'My nerves are in bits,' Clare said, as her heart finally started to return to its normal rhythm. 'I thought I was going to be sick when the sister took us into the office. I've never had anything like that happen to me before. That's what we get for telling lies.'

'We didn't tell lies as such. We just missed bits out.' A glint of devilment came into Gaye's eyes. 'At least we got our dresses, and now we've been let off doing evening meals.'

Clare's eyes went wide in disbelief.

'Come on,' Gaye said cheerily. 'We need to get to the porter's lodge to collect the dresses before we go up to our rooms. I'm so excited, I can't wait to wear mine on our next night out.' She looked down. 'Although I'll have to be careful with me leg for the next few days, so that it's all right for when we go dancing.'

'You are unbelievable . . .'

'And don't forget you've to bring me my tea up on a tray, and then you have to run down to the nearest off-licence and get me a drop of brandy.'

'Brandy!' Clare exclaimed and started to laugh. 'I know what I'd be doing with the brandy – hitting you over the head with the bottle.'

Chapter Four

Bit by bit, the noisy machinery ground to a halt, and the sound of the radio filtered through. Workers, dressed in overalls and turbans, all turned in their chairs to look towards the door expectantly.

'Not another bloody dignitary come to inspect us!' one of the women said in a loud whisper.

'This one is wearing all his necklaces and chains,' another one scoffed.

Diana looked towards the door and there stood their supervisor, Phyllis Hackett, alongside the mayor, bedecked in his robes and chains of office.

When all the machines were stopped, the supervisor held her hand up to silence the women. They were unused to being able to talk during working hours, and usually communicated by facial expressions and basic sign language. Two women from the office had come out to see what was going on, and the supervisor signalled to them to turn the radio off, and one went rushing back to do as she asked.

'Now, ladies,' the supervisor said when she had total silence. 'I'd like you all to be upstanding for our local mayor, who has taken time out of his busy schedule to come to see you all today. He would like to say a few words.' She simpered up at him and made a small curtsying gesture, then the mayor took a step forward.

'I won't keep you long, ladies,' he said, his voice echoing in the silence of the factory floor, 'because I know you have very important work to do. I came here today to say that I appreciate everything you are doing for the war effort. I know that's easily said to almost anyone, as everyone is contributing in their own way. But ... I want to recognise the very specialised area that the workers in this particular factory are engaged in. Work that means the difference between life and death for so many of our troops overseas.

'When I met up with your supervisors to arrange this visit, I asked them to talk me through the manufacturing of the parachutes.' He waved his hand towards the benches where yards of silk were laid out for cutting, then gestured towards the sewing area, and then over to the area where the parachutes were meticulously folded. 'I know that the making of parachutes is no easy task, and it is a big commitment to ask of you to come here day after day working these machines to make something very special.' He paused for effect, looking around officiously at the women. 'Make no mistake about it: your work in this factory is invaluable to the war effort. What you are manufacturing here saves the lives of our young men when they are bravely plunging from aeroplanes into the open skies.'

As Diana listened, she felt a stab of emotion at the picture this man was painting of the value of their work. She glanced around her, and saw that all of the women were now listening with a solemn intensity.

'And it is not just the making of the parachutes,' the mayor continued, 'the measuring and cutting, the careful stitching and attaching the strings or lines – it's also the packaging of them, the checking that every fold is meticulously in place before it is put into the package. And then the work that goes into testing them ...'

Diana could see that the women were impressed with the mayor's knowledge and understanding of the work they did. Most of the officials who made a visit on behalf of the local government gave a few stock phrases about 'keeping up the good work' and how the women were now the backbone of the country, leaving the workers with the feeling that they were just one factory in a chain of dozens of similar ones.

'I said I would not keep you back from your work for too long, so I just want to again congratulate you on the fine work that you are doing here – and to remind you that you are helping to bring home safely another woman's husband or another woman's son.' He paused again and in the ringing silence Diana could see that every woman was hanging on his words. 'There is no more important work than that – and I applaud you all for doing it so well.'

Phyllis Hackett started clapping and was quickly joined by all the other women. Diana had never seen such an enthusiastic response to the speeches that the visiting dignitaries gave, and she knew it was because he had reminded them all – including herself – that they were making a worthwhile effort to help all the brave men fighting for their country.

The machines were switched on once more and all the women turned back to their tables or machines, firm determination in their eyes, while the supervisor showed the mayor around each section. When they came around to the sewing area, they stopped at Diana's table. She turned off the machine as it was impossible to hear anything when it was running.

'Miss Thornley is one of the quickest and most accomplished sewers that we have,' the supervisor said proudly. 'On one day alone she completed five parachutes.'

'And what would the usual output be?' the mayor asked.

'Three would be the most in a day. You have to be very careful sewing the silk as it is so delicate, and we can't afford to have any wastage.'

The mayor rubbed his chin thoughtfully, while Diana felt her cheeks begin to burn red at being singled out. 'Five,' he said, 'that's an amazing output, and would make a huge difference to the timescale of getting the parachutes out to our young fellows abroad.'

After he left, Diana could see the other girls looking over at her and then turning to raise eyebrows to each other.

When break time came, Diana went to the canteen and got herself a cup of tea and a scone, and sat at a small table by the window on her own. The women serving her were always civil as they poured her drink – as were most of the other girls from the factory floor – but the conversations never went beyond superficial small talk.

She took out a little notebook and pencil from her overall pocket, then ate her scone and sipped the tea, while jotting down a few ideas for her art work. She'd started carrying the notebook at all times because she had often seen or thought of something that would be striking or unusual, only to forget it by the time she returned home.

When she first became interested in art, she had leaned towards delicate florals and landscapes in watercolours, then she had moved on to working with oils and had gone through a phase of still-life paintings. When she felt reasonably accomplished working with oil paints – and had built up a varied collection based on the gritty, realistic style of Caravaggio – she knew that art was going to be her life's passion. The more she learned, the more she realised she needed to study the subject in more depth. Her mother and father were concerned that she wanted to pursue a career in art when other girls her age were busy preparing for the 'coming out' season. Painting was very useful as a hobby and a talking point when meeting prospective husbands, and as a woman, there was no need for Diana to have a career. However, both had bigger issues to concern them: her father's ill health and her mother in trying to maintain the lifestyle she had enjoyed before the war had wreaked havoc with it.

Moving to London had opened Diana's eyes to a much bigger world both in daily living and also in the artistic field. She loved studying the history of art, and in between classes she spent hours in the library reading up on the lives of the famous painters, like Van Gogh and Rembrandt, studying their work in great detail.

Since embarking on her three-year art course, she found her interests in both art and life had changed quite dramatically.

She was now drawn towards artists who depicted real life in a variety of shades of grey, such as Wyndham Lewis and Paul Nash – as opposed to her family, who tended to see everything resolutely in black or white. She made friends easily with the other art students and was invited back to modest homes in other parts of England as far flung as Newcastle and the Cornish coast, homes that bore no resemblance to the houses her family moved between.

Seeing and hearing how other people lived made her realise that she had grown up in a small, protected cocoon in which she had assumed that most people had all the privileges in life that she had taken for granted. This led her to seek truth in both her work and in the people she mixed with, and she quickly found she was not alone in her search. Within months of moving to London she discovered like-minded students whose questioning of the class system had led them down a more political route. While she had not become involved in the party politics to the extent others had, Diana had been affected by it in a way that she and her family would never have envisaged.

After three years of living away and mixing with people of all backgrounds, returning to her family's estate in Cheshire had been almost a bigger culture shock to her than leaving had been. The daily routine of meals and socialising was suddenly unnecessarily formal, and she became increasingly aware of the different kind of lives that the owners and the servants of the homes she'd always visited led. She'd even given her parents a fright by broaching the subject with some of the staff whom she had known since she was a child, only to find that they too were baffled by her new attitude. It became quite clear to her that having and knowing their exact place in life was so entrenched that neither side of the class divide was concerned enough to make any great changes.

Added to that, the changing climate as war reared its head had left her feeling that she wanted to prove something to herself about her own individualism and integrity; and it was not something that she could easily do at home. When the farmhands had left to join the forces, the land girls had arrived from the cities and towns to work on the estate. She had relished joining in with them, as she had done with the other students in London, and much against her mother's will, she put on overalls and turbans like the other young women and went out into the field to work with hoes and spades and whatever implements were necessary for the job in hand.

Within a short time she began to realise that the other girls did not see the situation the way she did. Their natural position was to defer to her as they did with her mother, and when she explained to them that she wasn't comfortable in the role assigned to her by the class system, and that she wanted them to treat her as they would any other land girl, she thought they would happily agree. Given that the country was at war and all the women were being asked to pitch in, to Diana it seemed the obvious way to proceed in the new system that was now in place.

On the face of it, the young women did start off including her in the work schedules, and she was delegated the same duties as the others out in the fields and gardens. She dug and planted and lifted and carried whatever was necessary, the same as the others, and joined them in the estate farmhouse kitchen for tea breaks. And it was during those breaks that the difference between them became apparent, because the other women were silent and awkward when she was around. Eventually, when she went on ahead to make tea for the workers, the others stayed outside while one of them was delegated to tell her they did not want her to join them for breaks. They could not be relaxed and natural, the embarrassed girl explained, with the estate owner's daughter listening to every word they said.

Aunt Rosamund had unexpectedly come to the rescue when she took ill with shingles and needed someone to stay with her in Stockport for a few weeks until she had got over the worst of it. While there, Diana had come upon the notice looking for women to work in one of the big textile factories that had now been requisitioned to make parachutes. Helping her aunt had been the perfect excuse to get away from the oppressive lifestyle at home and yet feel she was being useful to someone at the same time. She had always loved creating things – drawing, painting, collage – and over wintry weekends the housekeeper in their home in Cheshire had taught her sewing and knitting. She had graduated to a sewing machine and found the time spent on it was both relaxing and rewarding.

Making parachutes, she knew, would certainly not be relaxing as it required total concentration to make sure every stitch, every seam was perfect and secure, but in a way it cleared her mind of everything else, and she left the factory each evening with a sense of satisfaction.

When she finished her tea, she made towards the ladies' lavatories before going back into her work area. There were half a dozen cubicles, all empty, apart from one at the end, so Diana went to the one at the opposite end. She thought she heard a sort of muffled retching sound of someone crying, and was unsure as to what to do. She had no idea who was in the cubicle and it seemed whatever was wrong, they wanted to keep it private. She came out and while she was washing her hands, she heard the sound again and stood for a few moments, uncertainly. When no one appeared, she shrugged to herself and then went back out into the corridor.

She walked a few yards and then slowed down, and then something made her go back into the lavatory again. There was a young woman there, holding onto the sink as though to steady herself. Diana recognised her from the cutting department: she was friends with the loudest group of women – a group who had never been particularly nice towards her.

'Are you all right?' Diana asked. 'I hope you don't think I'm interfering, but I was here a few minutes ago, and I got the feeling you might not be too well...'

The woman turned towards her, her face pale and her eyes wide and staring. For a moment she looked as though she was going to speak, then her eyes closed and she suddenly seemed to crumple. Diana caught her just as she slipped down onto the floor. Then, just as she was about to shout for help, she heard footsteps and the sound of laughter, and then the door opened and two workers came in. They stopped in shock at the scene in front of them.

'It's Judith!' one of them said. 'What are you doing? What on earth has happened?'

'I don't know,' Diana said. 'I heard her in the toilet being sick ... and I was worried about her and I came back to check. She looked very unwell, and then she suddenly fainted.'

The smaller girl looked at the other one. 'I told her not to come in,' she said. 'She was sick yesterday morning too ...'

The taller one shot her workmate a warning glance, then she moved to kneel at the side of her friend. 'Keep your voice down. Do you want everyone to know her business?' She looked at Diana. 'Did she say anything to you?'

Diana shook her head. 'No, she wasn't really fit to speak and then she just seemed to collapse ...'

As though she could hear them, the woman on the floor moaned and her eyes began to flutter.

'She's coming around,' the smaller woman exclaimed quietly, bending down in front of her friend's prostrate figure. 'Can you hear me, Judith? Are you all right?'

'What happened?' Judith said in a quivery voice. 'Why am I here?'

'It's okay, you've just been sick and fainted. Take your time.' She looked confusedly up at Diana who was cradling her head in her lap and then back to her friend. 'She'll be all right now. Hopefully, no one will have missed her ...'

'Hopefully not.' The taller girl stared at Diana, her eyes narrowed. 'We'll look after her now, and let you get back to work in case you're missed. The less people involved the better.' She knelt down, moving to take over from Diana, and together the two women eased Judith into a sitting position.

As Diana stood up she noticed blood on the legs of Judith's overall. She went to speak, then halted, not wanting to frighten her. She motioned to the smaller girl to come a little further away from Judith, towards the door. 'I've just noticed that she's bleeding,' she whispered. 'I don't know if she's cut herself or if it's... if it's her period or something.'

The girl's eyebrows shot up. 'Go back inside, and don't say a word to anyone.'

'What if she needs a doctor? Surely the supervisor will need to know.'

'Say nothing!' The woman moved her face closer, her eyes shining with malice. 'Do not go near the supervisor or anybody in the office. If any of the bosses finds out what's happened here, we'll all know who's to blame.'

Diana's breath caught at the injustice of it. 'I don't understand,' she mumbled, 'I'm only trying to help, and I'm worried that Judith...'

'You don't understand! You know nothing about the situation. You're too busy trying to be the fastest sewer, making the most parachutes, and showing the rest of us up.'

Diana looked at her. 'That is absolutely not the case.' She wanted to say more, but it was neither the time nor the place. Shocked and wounded, Diana turned to the door, giving a final glance back to see Judith being helped to her feet, her two friends crowding round making supportive noises. Realising that there was nothing more she could do, she went back out to the canteen, just in time to join the others returning to the factory floor at the end of break.

Soon the machines were whirring again, and every so often Diana glanced towards the cutting area to see if the women were back. At one point she saw the smaller woman coming in, along with the supervisor, but there was no sign of the other two. Judith had obviously not recovered enough to return to her work. Diana shrugged to herself, and turned back to her machine.

She wasn't quite sure why she was left feeling as if she had done something wrong. Would it have been better for her not to get involved? And yet she knew that would have been impossible. She could not have left the girl lying on the floor, and pointing out the blood stain might have been embarrassing, but it was obviously one of the reasons she had fainted. While she herself only got a fuzzy headache and slight stomach cramps, she knew other women suffered quite badly with periods. Were the other two so old-fashioned that they were annoyed she had brought it up, she wondered.

As she was in the queue in the corridor waiting to clock out that evening, Diana caught a glimpse of the smaller woman rushing out of the main door, and a sense of injustice washed over her. Was she forever to feel like an outsider in this place? She had always worked hard because she liked feeling she had accomplished something, and there was a part of her that was determined to prove she could work just as hard as the others. And yet she had now been accused of working too hard and showing up the other girls. Nothing she did was ever right. Maybe her mother was correct after all, she thought ruefully. Sticking to her own kind was easier than trying to mix with people from different backgrounds who did not accept you.

She punched her card in the time machine, slipped it back in her bag and strode angrily out into the fresh air. Taking in a few deep breaths, Diana slowed her steps to a more relaxed but steady pace. She would not let the situation in the factory get her down. So far it was no better than working with the land girls back home, but it was not any worse, she reminded herself; at least she got to escape from it all in the evenings. She just had to look at the bigger picture – remember the words that the mayor had said that very morning – and focus on how important her work was to the men out fighting for their country. Her petty problems were tiny in comparison, and she would not let the situation with Judith or the anger of the other women get her down.

Sighing, Diana looked about her and smiled. Things were looking up in other areas, now she had met Clare and Gaye and they had invited them to join her at a dance soon. Her thoughts flitted back to the night at the cinema and then to Mrs Atherton. She must call on the old lady some evening and check how she was doing. Then she remembered that she needed some new sketching pencils and suddenly decided to walk into Stockport.

It was quite close to the market area where Mrs Atherton's family had the chip shop, she remembered. Maybe she could call in and ask after her, then she would be able to give Clare and Gaye an update too.

By the time she had picked up her pencils and a new sketch pad from the local shop, the incident at work had faded to the back of her mind, and she was planning what art pieces she would work on later tonight. She didn't have the same range of materials in her aunt's house as she had back at home, but she was adaptable and had become used to drawing or painting in whatever circumstances she found herself.

When she moved to her aunt's in Stockport, her mother had managed to get petrol from somewhere, and Diana had packed the car up with as much of her art supplies as she could manage, such as canvases, two easels – one free-standing and a smaller one for a table – bags and boxes filled with paints, brushes, chalk pastels, charcoal, inks and pencils. She had also brought her old paint-splattered aprons and dungarees.

'What on earth are you planning to do with this lot?' her mother had asked, leaning against the car, smoking with an elegant cigarette holder.

'I'm not sure,' Diana had said, smiling. 'But I feel better knowing that I have everything with me just in case.'

In a strange way – which she could never have explained to anyone, especially her mother – having canvases and brushes at her fingertips made her feel more secure. It provided her with her own little imaginary world she could retreat to wherever she was, and regardless of what was going on around her. It made her feel more *herself*, in a way she could hardly explain in her own mind.

Her mother had sighed – but then her mother constantly sighed. 'Oh dear, Diana, you truly are a Thornley, and oddness runs through that family. Your father is the most normal of them all, at least he was when I first met him. I just hope you grow out of it and become more jolly and ordinary like our side of the family ...'

Diana had almost laughed. 'I'll let you know the minute I feel more ordinary,' she said, in a light tone. Her mother was far from ordinary and her idea of being jolly was more extreme than most people's – even in their own social circle

Her mother had shaken her head and given a rueful smile. 'Well, I suppose I can live in hope, can't I?' She walked towards the open boot of the of the car where Diana was juggling around with her bags and boxes, trying to make sure nothing got squashed or damaged on the drive. 'You do know I will miss you, don't you?'

Diana stopped what she was doing and looked at her. Their eyes met. 'And I'll miss you,' she said. 'And I'm sorry if you feel I am abandoning you.'

'I'll manage,' her mother said wearily. 'The world has changed, and like everyone else, I will just have to manage with the remaining estate workers and the land girls.' She moved forward to put her arms around Diana. 'I know I complained and tried to stop you going, but really, I admire you for sticking to your guns and doing what you actually want.'

Diana had moved back surprised. 'Do you?'

'Yes. I want you to be happy, and I know it's been hard settling back in here after living an independent life in London.' Her mother paused. 'I know what that feels like, and I don't want it foisted on you.'

As she walked along the narrow winding Stockport street now, with the bumpy cobbles, Diana ruminated over her mother's comments. She knew she was perhaps a little odd and definitely different. The girls in the factory certainly would have agreed with her – she was a square peg in a round hole.

London was the only place she had felt accepted. Maybe she should go back there. She shrugged to herself. For the time being she would just have to make the best of things, and concentrate on the positive things, like her new friends and visiting someone nice like Mrs Atherton. She turned a corner and there was the family chip shop in front of her. She smiled to herself at the thought of seeing the lovely old lady again.

Chapter Five

Clare pushed the door of the entrance hall of the staff residence open and went over to the pigeonhole cabinet where mail was left. Lifting out the small pile of envelopes for those names beginning with 'O', she sifted through them, smiling when she found a letter with an Irish stamp, her name written in her mother's neat, distinctive handwriting.

As she moved away, she glanced down at the box below and saw an envelope with Gaye's name written in block capitals, and stamped with a Newcastle-upon-Tyne postage mark. It was always nice to have a letter waiting for someone when their shift was finished. Her friend had been assigned to the accident and emergency department, and having done a shift there earlier in the year, Clare knew that if things were busy Gaye wouldn't get out on time that night. Having a letter waiting might just cheer her up. However, it did make her wonder how the hospitals would manage if Stockport or even nearby Manchester were bombed, as the A&E wards and the hospital were full to capacity already. So far, Clare was relieved that all the dire warnings of bomb threats and casualties had come to nothing. During her afternoon tea break she had even read in the newspaper that more of the children who had been evacuated from Manchester to the surrounding country areas were now returning home.

This week, Clare had been transferred to the children's ward for the second time and, as before, she was really enjoying it. It was much cheerier and livelier than the other wards, with the playroom and the classroom where the visiting teachers held their lessons. Like on the adult wards, she had struggled with the very serious side when a little boy or girl was diagnosed with one of the more dangerous diseases, like polio or diphtheria or even a case of scarlet fever. It was so much harder to see a child than a grown adult cope with the news. Yet today's shift had gone well, and since the weather was nice, the children who were fit enough had been taken outside to do their lessons in the sunshine.

When she got upstairs to her small single room, Clare took the letter out of her navy nurse's cloak pocket and sank down on her single bed. Holding the well-taped envelope up, Clare gave it a little shake, her brow creasing as it gave it a little metallic rattle. Coins, she wondered? Surely her mother wouldn't send her money. Curiosity got the better of her and after pains-takingly pulling the strips of brown tape off, she managed to finally open the envelope. She smiled and shook her head when the contents dropped out onto her bed cover. Three silver holy medals – a Miraculous Medal, a St Christopher medal and another depicting St Francis.

She quickly scanned through the four pages of Basildon Bond writing paper, making sure there was no bad news or anything that might worry her, then kicked off her shoes and curled up on the bed with the pillow at her back to read it again in a more leisurely fashion. Her mother's letters always contained the small details of the familiar, everyday life she had left behind in the farmhouse in County Offaly, Ireland. Her mother was sure to mention everyone in the family, from her parents and grand-parents to her brothers and sisters and even her new nephew. As she read, she pictured everyone at home going about their lives as if there were no war going on at all. While there was rationing in Dublin and the major cities, there hadn't been the same impact down in the country, where chickens and eggs and bacon were still freely available.

Although she was hugely relieved that her family was safe from the bombings – due to Ireland's neutral stance in the war – she saw a different side to things since coming to live in

England. Her heart went out to her nursing colleagues who were worried sick about their brothers and boyfriends, out defending their country in foreign places, with the real possibility that they might never return home again.

Like many other Irish people, she had always felt aggrieved about the British ruling classes who had dominated and divided their small country for centuries, but with most of the countries in Europe now at war, she felt this was not a time to look to her own situation. In the face of all these young men being killed defending their own country against Hitler and his army, her own patriotism was no longer uppermost in her mind. England had offered her the chance to train in her nursing career for free, which Ireland could not afford to do. For the time being it was also her home, and she felt a bond with all the people she huddled beside in the air-raid shelters.

There were a few paragraphs containing random news about neighbours, and school friends of Clare's who had got engaged or married or had recently had babies. When she eventually returned for a visit home – hopefully this summer if peace on the seas continued – she knew she would find a big difference as so many people's lives had changed, including her own.

The last page contained a prayer for peace in the world, which her mother had painstakingly copied out. She told Clare that all the family were reciting the prayer morning and night, in the hope it would keep Clare and Oliver safe during this terrible war.

Clare went back to reread the letter, pausing to take in certain sections.

You were wise not to come home, her mother wrote, *because we are hearing news every day about boats and ships being bombed abroad, and I would much rather you and Oliver stayed where you were and kept safe until this terrible war is over. Now, you know it is Oliver's twenty-fifth birthday in a few weeks' time, and your father and I were thinking that it would be nice if you were to meet up with him for the night, so he has some sort of family celebration. Stockport would be safer, your father said, because Liverpool is a bigger target for bombing, being nearer the sea. You might phone soon and make arrangements to see him. It makes us all at home feel better knowing that you two are only an hour away from each other.*

We pray for you both every night and offer our family rosary up for you. If we'd had any idea that there was going to be a war, we would never have let you go out of Ireland. Please God you will be home safe and sound when it is all over.

You are in all our thoughts and prayers,

From your loving mother

XX

She was just pondering over the letter when she heard quick footsteps outside and then a knock on the door. When she opened it she found one of the Irish girls who had a room opposite.

'You had a phone call earlier on from someone called Diana,' she said, holding out a piece of paper. 'She said can you ring her back as soon as you get time, and she gave me her phone number again in case you had lost it.'

Clare thanked the girl and went back inside, puzzling as to why Diana had phoned her. She had promised to ring her aunt's house next time she and Gaye were arranging a night out, and had explained that it would probably be towards the end of the week. Diana must be keen to meet up if she was calling so quickly.

Ten minutes later – changed out of her uniform into a navy skirt and floral blouse, her hair pulled back in a ponytail – Clare went downstairs to return Diana's call. A brisk, no-nonsense Stockport woman came on the line, who said she would get Miss Diana immediately.

A minute or so later, Diana came on. 'Oh, thank you for calling back, Clare. I hope you don't mind me ringing. I know you said you would be in touch when you were going dancing, but I have news about Mrs Atherton. I was down in Stockport after work yesterday, and decided to walk down to the market where her daughter has the chip shop and inquire after her.'

'Oh, that was good of you.' Clare exclaimed.

'It was a nice evening, and I had nothing to rush home for.'

'How is she doing?' Clare asked, kindly.

'Apparently very well – she was actually out at a church meeting,' Diana said, 'but her daughter was delighted I had called in. She said her mother had told her all about us, and that she would love to see us again. She asked if we would drop in some evening this week.'

'Oh, that would be lovely.'

'Well, I didn't want to speak for you,' Diana explained, 'but I hoped that if you and Gaye were free this week, that we might call down there.'

'I know Gaye is working on lates all this week, but I'm free tomorrow night if that's okay with you? Any time from half past six is fine.'

'Perfect!' Diana said. 'I can walk down to the hospital gates after my shift and catch you there, then we can walk into Stockport together.'

Later that night when the late shift had finished, Clare knocked on Gaye's bedroom door, but there was no reply. She was walking back to her own room, past the doors of the staircase, when she thought she heard Gaye's voice. Opening the doors and heading out onto the staircase, she could quite clearly see Gaye chatting to one of the other nurses. However, when she went down towards the entrance area, she noticed that Gaye was actually talking on the payphone.

Conscious of giving her privacy, she turned to go back upstairs when she heard Gaye say in a high voice. 'But we can't do that, it would end up in complete disaster...' There was a pause. 'You need to listen to me. I know exactly what will happen – I know them much better than you.'

Assuming that she had overheard some sort of family row, Clare went quietly and quickly back upstairs. If it was something serious, she thought, Gaye would probably come straight up to tell her all about it.

Clare waited half an hour, then went back down to knock on Gaye's door. When the door was opened, Gaye merely smiled as usual and welcomed her in, before returning to lounge on her single bed.

Clare sat on the wooden chair beside the dressing table. 'I called earlier, but you weren't here.'

Gaye rolled her eyes. 'I got held up on the ward; one of the night-shift nurses was late and we had to wait until she arrived.'

Clare nodded understandingly and went on to tell her about Diana phoning and the planned visit to see Mrs Atherton.

'Well, this week is out for me,' Gaye said wearily, 'but I'll visit her another time. Did Diana say how she is?'

Clare went on to relate what Diana had told her on the phone. 'Hopefully Mrs Atherton will keep the chat going in case I can't keep up with Diana's talk about art or London.' She smiled at Gaye, remembering their discussion about their new friend after they got off the bus.

Gaye nodded, but looked around the room slightly distract-edly, then gave a little yawn. 'I have a letter to write and then I think I'll have an early night.'

Clare suddenly realised that it was a hint that she should go, and stood up quickly, feeling a little embarrassed. 'Okay, I'll leave you to it.'

'I'll hear how you get on with Mrs Atherton when you get back tomorrow night.'

As she walked back to her room, Clare thought that Gaye hadn't seemed her usual self and wondered if it was something to do with the phone call. Since Gaye had not referred to it, she felt that she couldn't ask. It was the same with the letter from earlier, which she was glad now not to have mentioned. Gaye usually told her everything, but, she told herself, Gaye was perfectly entitled to her privacy and did not need to share her personal life with her. Also, Clare did not want to become one of those clingy girls who needed to know everything about her friend's business.

Hopefully there was nothing wrong, Clare mused as she prepared for bed, and that Gaye would soon be back to her old, cheery self before long.

Chapter Six

The following day, Diana was waiting just as she'd said outside the hospital gates for Clare, holding a bunch of red roses wrapped in coloured paper. Clare was delighted when her new friend gave her a cheery wave as she saw her coming.

'Those flowers are lovely,' Clare said, a little out of breath from rushing to be on time. 'Are they for Mrs Atherton?'

'Yes, I picked them from my aunt's garden.'

Clare bent forward to smell the dusky roses. 'Oh, they have a lovely scent, she'll love them.' She took a small package from her handbag. 'One of the patients gave me a nice little soap, so I've brought that.'

'She will be delighted. Soap is getting a little more difficult to buy nowadays.' The two girls turned towards town, both glowing a little with the delight of seeing each other again. Clare also felt relieved that so far she hadn't felt out of her depth.

'It's great to get out in the evening,' Diana sighed, as they walked onto Wellington Road, 'even if it is just to go and visit an old lady. You must think I'm a bit of a sad case, having no social life. I feel it myself when I compare it to the busy life I had in London.'

'Not at all,' Clare said, smiling. 'And I'm glad to have someone to go out with tonight, as Gaye and the other girls I usually go out with are all working or studying.'

As they walked down towards the market area of Stockport town, the girls' main topic of conversation was the same as for most people in the country – the news about British troops retreating from Dunkirk.

'Thank goodness they had the help of all the people who had boats. I was listening to it on the radio in the canteen at the break today and it was amazing hearing how they had helped to rescue all the soldiers. Sad, of course, that some of the soldiers died before the boats came, but it could have been so much worse.' Diana paused, as they turned into the road leading to Mrs Atherton's home. 'I heard that when the Germans realised what was happening, they targeted the rescue boats as well.'

Clare gave a deep sigh. 'It's awful, isn't it? Especially when we hear other nurses or patients who have husbands or sons in the midst of all the fighting, and they don't know whether they are going to make it home.'

'There are times when I wish I could do more to help, rather than just stitch parachutes. At least you're helping people in the hospital every day, and you know you're doing something worthwhile.'

'I keep thinking about the poor, wounded soldiers,' Clare said. 'And I wish I could help them in some way. Maybe I could do a stint in a military hospital. We haven't had any real war casualties in Stockport.'

'The bigger cities are the targets, or the ports, I suppose.' Diana responded thoughtfully.

'Yes...' Clare sucked in her breath. 'My brother, Oliver, is in Liverpool. He works as a photographer for one of the newspapers and is often in the middle of dangerous situations, working alongside the reporters. He feels it's his duty to get photographs that show exactly what's happening.'

'I'm sure he knows what he's doing,' Diana said soothingly, sensing Clare's anxiety.

'Oliver can be fairly determined,' Clare responded, pausing on the doorstep to Mrs Atherton's home.

'Good for him!' Diana said, giving her new friend a confident smile. 'It's important to have people out there looking to find out what is really happening. We need to hear and see the truth to understand it.'

Clare nodded, the weight of worry for her brother lifting ever so slightly in the face of Diana's confidence, before she turned to knock.

A small, slim woman in her mid-forties with curly fair hair opened the door to them. 'Oh, I'm delighted to meet you,' she said, after she greeted Diana and then turned to shake Clare's hand. 'I want to thank you for looking after my mother when she took ill. Wasn't she lucky to be beside two nurses?'

'As Gaye and I told your mother, we're only students,' Clare blushed.

'Well, you were all Florence Nightingales as far as my mother is concerned. She's told everybody about you, and is just de-lighted that you want to visit her.'

Diana smiled at Mrs Atherton's daughter. 'And how is your mother now?'

'Come in and see for yourself,' she said cheerfully, guiding them along the hallway, and into a quiet room on the left.

Mrs Atherton was sitting in a high-backed chair, her grey hair perfectly curled and wearing a bright blue twinset with three strands of pearls and matching earrings.

'Oh, don't you look lovely,' Clare exclaimed, as soon as she saw her. Diana complimented her too.

'When I heard you were coming I went to the hairdresser's to have it set to look nice for you,' the old lady said, patting her head.

The girls gave her the little gifts they had brought for her and she was so touched that tears came into her eyes. 'You shouldn't have done that,' Mrs Atherton said, taking a hanky from her cardigan sleeve to dab her eyes. 'You were kind enough to me the other night, and thank God I'm feeling all right now. I'm out and about again; even made it up for a meeting at the church in Davenport yesterday.' She looked over at her daughter. 'Catherine walked me to the bus stop and I got the bus up and down from Mersey Square.'

'I wasn't too happy about her going out so quickly,' Catherine said, looking serious. 'But there's no stopping her when she makes up her mind. She can be a very stubborn and determined lady.'

Mrs Atherton gave a dismissive wave. 'I know when I'm all right,' she said, 'and I don't want anybody babysitting me. You all have enough to do with running the shop and the kids and everything.'

Catherine rolled her eyes. 'Now, you can see what she's like.' She put her arm around her mother's shoulder. 'But she's always been independent and we wouldn't have her any other way.'

Mrs Atherton patted her daughter's hand. 'Be a good girl now and bring in the tea for us.' When she went out, Mrs Atherton turned back to the girls. 'I'm sorry that nice red-haired girl couldn't come with you.'

Clare explained that Gaye was working but she would come with them next time.

'Well, that will be something nice to look forward to,' Mrs Atherton said with a satisfied grin. 'She was a lovely, cheery girl – same as the two of you – and I was hoping the three of you would be here as I wanted to suggest something for you all. When I was up at the ladies' meeting in the church yesterday, we were told that we might be getting a crowd of evacuees coming over to this area from the Channel Islands – Guernsey seemed to be the one they were talking about.' She waved her hand. 'I don't really understand it all, but it's to do with that bloody little Hitler taking over France and they think he might be sending his Nazi gang over to those islands. I believe they are between France and England, so it would be a handy place for him to be to sail ships over to England to come over here.'

Diana nodded her head knowledgeably. 'It's a real possibility. They've taken over so many of the other European countries that it could be England next.'

Clare felt her chest tighten. 'But I thought that a lot of the children who had been evacuated from Manchester and Liverpool were back home. I thought that meant things were improving.'

'Things seem to be changing again after what happened at Dunkirk,' Diana said gently, sensing Clare's rising anxiety.

'Anyroads, Mr Lomas, our nice vicar, told us at the church that Guernsey folk are getting prepared to have the kids evacuated if them Nazis come any closer.' Mrs Atherton lowered her voice. 'It's all top secret, the vicar said, and we don't know any details, but it could be if things get worse over there, that they'll have to come over to England and Scotland. He says that places like Stockport could be asked to take hundreds of the children.'

'Goodness,' Diana said.

Mrs Atherton nodded. 'Yes, the vicar says that if they get definite word that they are evacuating, they will need to start organising the town hall and places like that to house them until they can sort out proper homes for them all.' She held her hands out. 'The church are looking for volunteers to help out – young people especially who would be good with children – and I thought of you three girls. You're all so clever and talented. What do you think?'

Clare felt her heart quicken at the thought of helping out in a Protestant church. Before she left for England, she had been warned not to get involved with Protestants by lots of people, especially the priests back home. By the end of her first day in Stockport, Clare had already disregarded the advice by making friends with Gaye and various other girls who weren't Catholic. So far she had found no great difference between them and her friends back home in Ireland.

She then discovered she wasn't the only one in the family to make up their own mind about people. When Oliver had come over to Stockport to visit her shortly after she arrived, he had warned her to ignore the narrow-minded opinions in Ireland.

'It's a different world here in England,' he'd said reassuringly, 'and in some ways it's better. It's only when you get to meet different sorts of people that you begin to question all the things that you just blindly believed in back home.'

Clare was taken aback to learn that her quiet, slightly reserved older brother had held such views, but she listened carefully.

'My advice,' Oliver had said, 'is that you should take every person you meet on their own merit, and only judge them on whether they seem a good or not-so-good person – and I've met plenty of both. I've got to know some very good people from all sorts of religions, countries and backgrounds. I've also met a good few atheists, and after talking to some of them, I have to say I respect their views very much.'

Clare had caught her breath at the word *atheist*, because it was one of the few things that was deemed worse than Protestants.

'One of the nicest and most intelligent lads I've met,' Oliver had said, 'is half-African with an Irish mother, and he grew up in a rough part of Liverpool.'

Clare took a few moments to digest this. 'Does he work on the newspaper with you?'

'He works in a café I go to most days, and he has a coffee with me when things are quiet, and we talk about everything. When I first moved to Liverpool he was one of the first people I got to know. When I went into the café he recognised my Irish accent and asked me where I came from and that kind of thing. He's a poet, and has had a couple of books published, but he can't make a living from it, so he works in the café and writes when he gets time.'

'I've never heard you mention him at home.'

Oliver had shrugged. 'There are a lot of things I don't mention at home. There's no point in telling them things they would only worry about. As time goes on, you'll find that keeping some things to yourself is the best policy with regards to the folks back home.'

Clare remembered Oliver's advice now as she listened to Mrs Atherton talking about the church and all the things they did to raise funds for various causes. In her letters home she had been more or less truthful about everything and everybody she had met so far. She had told her parents that most of the other nurses and the elderly patients she looked after were lovely, but she had tended to emphasise the people who were Irish and Catholic, as she knew that was what her mother wanted to hear.

Working with people of a different faith couldn't be helped, but socialising and getting involved with a Protestant church's activities was something her mother would never understand.

'Clare...' Diana suddenly said.

Clare looked over at the petite, dark-haired girl and realised that she had obviously said or asked her something while she was lost in her own thoughts. 'Sorry,' she said, blushing now. 'I didn't catch that.'

'I was just saying that maybe we could help out with the evacuees at the weekends.'

'I'm not sure about time off at the hospital,' Clare said. 'We work shifts and we only get certain weekends off.'

The door opened and Catherine came in carrying a tray with fancy rose-decorated cups, saucers and a matching teapot. Placing them down on the coffee table, she left the room again, returning a short while later with a large plate piled with jam doughnuts and custard slices. 'A little treat for you,' she said beaming, 'for being so good.'

'I told her to get something nice for you,' Mrs Atherton said, 'and we're very lucky because with her and Terry having the business, they can get stuff that nobody else can.'

'It's very good of you.' Clare was dumbstruck. She hadn't seen such treats in so long. 'We really weren't expecting anything.'

They sat chatting over their tea and the sweet treats, listening as Mrs Atherton talked about how she had been born and brought up in a small house in Portwood. 'Very poor we were,' she said, 'but my mother kept the house spotlessly clean. I was lucky then when I met my late husband, Stanley, at a dance, because he had a small terraced house in Heaviley that his aunt left him. Well, we got married, and moved into his house, and Catherine and her sister and brother were all born there.' She gave a little sigh. 'After Stan got killed in the war, me and the kids lived there, and when they were all grown up and married, I stayed on my own until a few years ago, and then Catherine insisted I moved down here to live with them.' She paused, a faraway look in her eyes. 'Anyway, I made a lot of nice friends up in Heaviley, and they helped me out after Stan died. I got a part-time job in a café in Wellington Road, and the neighbours took turns looking after the kids for me. I wouldn't have managed without them.' She leaned forward. 'I know people talk about sisters being close to each other and a great help, but I never had one, so I don't know. But I do know that having a few good women friends on your side makes all the difference, especially when you are young.' She smiled at both Clare and Diana. 'I'm glad to see what good friends you three all are.'

Clare wondered now if she should explain that she and Diana weren't really friends, and had only come to know each other by accident – in truth, because of the old lady's accident. But she realised that it would only disappoint her, and maybe embarrass her, if she knew that her little episode had been of such concern to total strangers. She glanced over at Diana, and when she caught her eye she could tell that she was thinking the same thing. There was no point in saying anything.

'So,' Mrs Atherton continued, 'I still go to the church up in Heaviley. I like to see all my old neighbours and I've always been involved with the Women's Institute and fundraising for the church and that kind of thing.'

'She never stops,' Catherine said, pride evident in her tone. 'She's always knitting and sewing for them as well.'

'I know your church,' Diana said. 'It's actually the same one that my aunt Rosamund attends. I think I told you the night of the air raid that I'm staying with her up in Davenport.'

Mrs Atherton's brow creased, and it was obvious that she didn't remember.

Diana tactfully moved on to describe her aunt, but the old lady still looked rather vague about it. 'She's involved in the Women's Institute – she's actually on the committee – although she doesn't get to all the meetings as she sometimes has health problems.'

'It's a big enough church,' Mrs Atherton said, nodding, 'and there's a lot of people who go there, so I might not know her. I'm not on the committee or anything important like that. Me and my friend Sally just do anything that needs doing. We do our bits and pieces of sewing and knitting and we help with the teas and the washing up and that kind of thing. And Sally's husband grows raspberries and blackcurrants and I help her to make jam for the Christmas and summer fairs.'

Mrs Atherton's daughter brought more tea and insisted that the girls finish off the doughnuts and custard slices. When it was time for the news, the radio was put on and, like every other household in Stockport, they listened in silence to the latest information regarding the war until the programme ended.

'My heart goes out to all them poor lads and their families,' the old lady said after the wireless was turned off again. 'When I think of my poor Stan and all his mates out fighting on the Somme ... I still have nightmares about it. Thank God our Michael wasn't picked to go this time. He works on the railway, in a reserved occupation.'

Catherine came over to put a comforting hand on her mother's shoulder. 'Hopefully it will all be over soon.'

Clare could suddenly see that Mrs Atherton looked tired and lifted her handbag and gas mask from the floor, prompting Diana to do the same. 'I think we'd better head back home now,' she said kindly. 'I'm on an early shift in the morning.'

'Before you go,' Catherine said. She rushed from the room and returned with a small paper bag. 'For your friend back in the hospital. Just a doughnut and cake for her as well, so she doesn't feel left out.'

'She'll be delighted,' Clare said. 'She loves anything sweet.'

When they reached the bus stop, it looked as though they had just missed a bus as there were no other passengers around.

'If you are not in a hurry, shall we just walk on?' Diana suggested. She glanced up at the sky. 'We don't often get such a lovely warm evening.'

Clare looked at her watch. 'It's only half past eight,' she said, 'and I'm not in any rush. A walk would do us good.' She found she was enjoying Diana's company, and no longer felt awkward with her.

As they strolled up towards the ornate Stockport town hall, they stopped to admire the lovely flower beds, in full summer bloom, which surrounded the building. As they moved on, Diana asked Clare about the dance halls and the bands that played in them, and then they chatted about their favourite music.

'Are the dance halls in Ireland the same as here?' Diana asked.

'God, no...' Clare said. 'They're much smaller back home, and we have to cycle out to them.'

'Do you ride a bicycle too? Oh, I love cycling.'

'Yes,' Clare said, 'but we only have one bike at home, and my mother uses it most of the time, but my friend used to borrow her brother's and she would bring me to the dances on the crossbars.'

'That's hilarious! But how on earth do two of you manage on one bicycle when you are all dressed up for a dance and carrying handbags? There are times when I've found it difficult getting in and out of a car without catching my stockings.'

The casual mention of a car suddenly brought Clare up short, as the differences in their backgrounds hit her again, but she just shrugged and gave an embarrassed smile. 'As the saying goes, "needs must when the devil drives". When you live out in the country in Ireland, you're glad to get a lift on a bike, and the handbags and gloves go into the saddlebags, you learn to be very careful with the stockings.'

'I love people who refuse to let obstacles hold them back. I would have done the very same thing.'

They carried on walking up towards the hospital and as the wrought-iron gates came into view, Clare began to slow down with the intention of crossing the road. 'I've really enjoyed the evening,' she said.

'I did too.' Diana suddenly halted by the side of the road and looked a little awkward. 'If you're not in a rush, we could walk up to Aunt Rosamund's. It's only another five or ten minutes from here, and you can get the bus back.'

'Won't your aunt mind?' Clare asked, wondering why Diana was inviting her back to her aunt's home.

'I've told her all about you and Gaye,' Diana said, 'and she suggested that I bring you back if you had time.'

'If you're sure?' Clare replied, but was secretly delighted to have been asked.

Ten minutes later, they turned into a gateway almost hidden by overhanging trees in Buxton Road. Clare felt her stomach tighten when she saw the size of the garden and the big rambling house behind it. The feeling of her and Diana being so different washed over her again.

Following her new friend through the tall gates and up the curving drive, Clare found herself standing in full view of the enormous red-brick Victorian house. When they stepped inside, she caught her breath at the size of the open hallway and wide mahogany staircase, her eyes drawn up to a large sparkling chandelier.

She was just taking in the wall full of paintings, and the gilt table decorated with lamps and a large vase of flowers, when a thin, delicate-looking woman came down the hallway towards them. She wore a green silk dress with a broad black belt emphasising her tiny waist, her hair drawn back into a bun. She looked, to Clare, like a ballerina.

'Diana?' said the petite woman.

Diana rushed forward to kiss her aunt's cheek. 'I've brought my friend to meet you, and to show her where I live.' Turning back, she beckoned Clare forward. 'Clare, this is my aunt Rosamund, Mrs Douglas.'

Her aunt smiled warmly and turned to Clare with her hand outstretched. 'How do you do, my dear?' she said in a surprisingly strong voice. 'And I much prefer to be called Rosamund. You are one of the young nurses that Diana met at the cinema, I believe?'

'Yes,' Clare said, smiling as they shook hands. 'The night of the last air raid.'

'Dreadful, dreadful,' Rosamund shook her head. 'It's a terrible strain not knowing when those awful Germans might decide to drop a bomb on us.' She raised her eyebrows, then swiftly changed the subject. 'And have you been training long?'

'I'm in my second year,' Clare told her.

'And do they teach you much about medicines? About the different tablets and so forth?'

Clare was taken aback at the question. 'We have covered basic illnesses and conditions that people come into hospital with, and we were given notes about the suitable medications for each one – penicillin, painkillers and that sort of thing.'

'I was thinking more about the stomach,' Rosamund said. 'I suffer with digestive problems, and the doctor put me on new medication for it, but I'm not at all sure that it's doing any good.' She held a finger up. 'I have the little bottle in the bedroom, I'll just go upstairs and get it now, and see if you might know anything about it.' She turned to her niece. 'Diana, take your friend into the drawing room and then ring for Mrs Brown and let her know whether you would like tea or cocoa. She might have some cake too; she was experimenting with a recipe involving carrots and dried eggs.'

Diana explained they had already had cake and her aunt went off to get her tablets.

'I should have warned you,' Diana said in a low voice as she led Clare into the drawing room, 'my aunt is a bit of a hypochondriac. She's obsessed with her health and medication.' She shrugged. 'She was absolutely thrilled when I told her you and Gaye were nurses.'

Clare's eyes widened. 'But we're only students, and still doing basic care work in the wards. We haven't learned much about medication yet; the ward nurses do all that.'

'As long as you have something to do with doctors, Aunt Rosamund will find you hugely interesting.'

Later, the girls sat sipping tea while Aunt Rosamund rummaged through a tin box containing bottles and little packets of medication, reading out the labels to check if Clare knew anything about them.

'I've been reading up on herbal remedies too,' Rosamund said, lifting a large book from a bag next to her. 'I've borrowed this from the library three times already to copy the recipes out of it.'

'I know a man who cures people back home in Ireland,' Clare said, eager to be off the subject of tablets and complicated medicines she'd never heard of. 'He grows herbs and makes them up into oils for the skin or a liquid medicine.'

'How fascinating!'

'He's the seventh son of a seventh son, and he can cure all sorts of things.'

'Seventh son of a seventh son?' Rosamund looked aghast. 'Surely people don't believe all that superstitious nonsense?'

In the small silence that followed, Clare felt herself flush, and wondered if she should drop the subject. But after a few moments she felt compelled to defend the nice man, who she believed was genuine. 'We know some neighbours and other people he has cured. Even the local doctors recommend him when the medicines they prescribe don't work, so there must be something in it.'

There was another pause, then Rosamund said, 'Would he cure stomach problems, I wonder?'

'I don't know,' Clare said, trying not to smile.

'Even if he does,' Diana said, 'it wouldn't help, since he is in Ireland.'

'Yes dear,' said Rosamund looking thoughtful, a faraway look in her eye.

Diana finished the last of her tea and placed her cup back in its saucer. 'I'm going to take Clare upstairs to my bedroom to show her my records.'

When they reached the top of the stairs, Diana turned to Clare. 'I'm really sorry about Aunt Rosamund... she's so obsessed with her health. I almost died when she was so rude about the healer in Ireland. I hope you're not offended?'

'Not a bit, I thought it was funny!'

'Really?' Diana said. 'You're not just being polite?'

'For a moment I thought she was going to ask if she could come over to Ireland to meet him.' Clare suddenly pictured herself introducing Diana's aunt to her mother and then to the healer, and had to bite her lip hard to stop herself from laughing.

Then she caught the look of laughter in Diana's eyes and they both started to giggle.

'Quick or she'll hear us!' Diana said, propelling Clare down another vast hallway. She wrenched open a door and they almost fell across the threshold inside, still laughing.

When Clare arrived back at her room in the nurses' block later that night, there was a note under her door.

Come down to my room when you get in. Can't wait to hear how you got on with Mrs Atherton and our posh friend tonight. Gaye xx

Clare smiled when she read it; Gaye sounded as if she was back to her usual cheery self. Throwing her gas mask and handbag on the bed, she lifted the bag of cakes that Mrs Atherton's daughter had given her for Gaye and headed to her room.

'Oh, I wish I had been able to go along with you,' Gaye said, after she'd heard the account of the night. They were both sitting together on Gaye's bed. 'Her daughter sounds like a lovely person. Imagine her sending the cakes for me.'

'Mrs Atherton spoke very highly of you,' Clare said. 'I think you're her favourite.'

'Get away!' Gaye said, her eyes wide in disbelief.

'You were very good with her during the air raid, when I was terrified.' Clare confessed.

'It was nothing, I knew they weren't going to bomb us.' Gaye paused. 'I'm sorry I was snappy last night. I wasn't feeling my best, and then my period came today.'

'I'm glad you feel better now.' She waited for Gaye to say something about the phone call she had overheard, but again, she didn't mention it.

Gaye unwrapped the cakes, and her face lit up when she saw the custard pastry. 'My favourite!' she exclaimed. 'I haven't had a custard slice since rationing started.' She got up from her bed to go to a small cupboard that held a few pieces of crockery.

'I've got to eat it now,' she said, lifting a side plate and a knife, 'or the icing will go soggy. Will you have half of it?'

'Believe it or not,' Clare said, 'I couldn't eat more cake. I just had cocoa at Diana's too, so I'm full up.'

Gaye started laughing. 'I can't believe it either.'

Gaye asked her all about the visit to Diana's aunt's house, and listened with great interest as Clare described everything that she could remember about the place and Diana's eccentric aunt.

'They sound very posh,' Gaye said, pulling a face.

'Diana is more down to earth than you would imagine,' Clare said, 'and she's great with her hands too, I can see why she wanted to work in the factory making parachutes, because she's a real natural at sewing. She had a full-sized tailor's dummy in the spare bedroom, and a sewing machine set up.'

Gaye was suddenly interested. 'What kind of things was she making?'

'A pair of pinstripe trousers.' Clare said, all the drama of the moment echoing through her.

'*Trousers?* For work?'

'Not just for work,' Clare replied excitedly. 'Diana said she likes wearing smarter trousers at the weekend with jumpers or blouses. I've noticed more women wearing them recently, they're much handier than skirts or dresses.'

'Yeah, if you're riding a motorbike or a horse,' Gaye said, laughing. 'I think trousers are awful on girls, they're not a bit feminine. It's amazing when you think that Diana's family have loads of money and she could have any clothes she likes and she picks *trousers* ...'

'We're all different,' Clare said, 'and she should wear what makes her happy.'

'How can trousers make any woman happy?' Gaye asked in wonder, a second bite of custard slice halfway to her lips. 'Unless there's a handsome man inside them.'

They both started to laugh, and Clare was relieved that all seemed back to normal between them again.

Chapter Seven

Clare looked in the small mirror above the sink in her room, and straightened her stiff nurse's cap. Night shifts in the geriatric ward were not as unpredictable as the early or late shifts. It depended mainly on the elderly patients and how well they were, and how well they slept. It also depended on who she was working with – especially the ward sister. Tonight should be good as she was on with Sister Townsend, who was excellent at her job, lovely with the patients, and nice to the student nurses.

The girls had been given a lot of variety, working with adults and children, and she had just recently moved on to the Ladies' A3 Ward, which she was really enjoying. She liked the elderly patients, and chatted to them in the same way she used to chat to her grandparents. The early-morning shifts went quickly as they had to get the patients up and ready to start the day, bringing them breakfast and helping those who were mobile into the bathrooms to be washed and dressed. Others had to be bed-bathed, and there were lots of mundane, busy tasks to be done, like changing bed linen and towels, and dispensing jugs of water.

The late shifts were busy too, spending time in the day room with the patients and filling in medical charts when the visiting period came around. Clare had got to know some of the patients' families, and since she was more approachable than others, they often waited until after visiting to have a word about their sick relatives.

She checked her large work bag before leaving, making sure

she had her knitting needles and enough wool to carry her through the breaks. All the nurses knitted or crocheted during their breaks or if they got a quiet spell during the night. It helped keep them busy and, more importantly, awake and alert.

Leaving the nurses' residence and heading out into the grounds, Clare took the path that wound its way past the numerous Victorian, red-brick buildings, enjoying the sight of the beautiful old structures. When she arrived at the ward she hung her cloak and bag up in the cupboard before heading to the main office. The nurses who had finished their shift were waiting to give handover information about any departures or new arrivals, recent changes in patients' medications and anything else deemed important.

When the handover was finished, Clare and the other nurses went with Sister Townsend on their ward rounds. Afterwards, she helped hand out cups of tea and toast for the patients' suppers, then a short time later, she went into the day room and brought the patients there back to the wards. Her next task then was to help the elderly ladies get changed and settled for the night. Clare loved the organisation of it, the calm and reassuring nature of the work, following the schedules.

Around one o'clock in the morning, when the six staffers were having their first break, the phone rang and Clare offered to run to the office to take it. Late-night calls always brought with them a sense of unease as most of the wards were quiet and settled at this point. She stiffened a little when she recognised the voice of the sister of the male ward on the opposite side of the corridor. Sister Bennett was an older woman who was regarded as being very strict and who had little patience with the trainee nurses. Clare was grateful that she had never worked for her, because Gaye had been on her ward for a couple of months and had hated it.

Clare came back a few moments later, and everyone dropped their knitting or crocheting in their laps to hear what she had to say. 'It was Sister Bennett,' she told Sister Townsend. 'She is looking for two staff to help out, as they've just had a sudden death on the ward. They've also had two staff call in sick, and had to send one of the male nurses' home earlier on after a bad vertigo attack.'

Sister Townsend immediately went to see what was happening, while the others finished their tea in silence, waiting for her return. When Sister Townsend came back to the staffroom, she looked grave and asked Clare and one of the qualified younger nurses, Nurse White, to come into the office.

'I've spoken with Sister Bennett and I think it would work best if you two could go over to help them out.' She turned to Nurse White. 'You're experienced and can help them with the medication, and Clare is very good with the patients, and quick with the practical early-morning work.'

Clare tried not to show she was taken aback. She had never worked on the men's wards at night, and the thought of being under the beady eye of Sister Bennett did not fill her with enthusiasm.

Sister Townsend looked quizzically at Clare, as though sensing her reluctance. 'You don't mind going over, do you?'

'No,' Clare said, her face flushing. 'Not at all.' Being a student nurse meant working in any sorts of situations, with all sorts of staff and patients. She needed to be prepared for these kinds of situations; it wasn't like she'd be able to choose if she was working in the war hospitals.

Twenty minutes later, Clare and Nurse White put on their capes and headed over to the other ward. They were met by Sister Bennett, who was eagerly waiting for them. Turning abruptly, she spoke over her shoulder in a stern voice, 'I'm glad you were able to have your tea break, you'll be lucky to get another for the rest of the night. We've had to keep going straight through, so when things settle down you can sit on the ward and give our nurses a break.' She pointed down the corridor. 'The laundry room is the second door on the right, and when you've taken off your capes, go and get sheets and pillowcases for two beds and a basin of hot water, some fresh washcloths and a towel. Bring them back to the ward and you'll be told which beds to change.'

Clare's heart sank as she thought of the long night ahead, but said nothing. She seemed that it was fine for the trained nurses to complain, but she had learned that the students were better off to keep their thoughts to themselves.

They collected the fresh laundry and basin and entered the ward. Two nurses came out from behind a curtained bed and moved quickly and quietly towards them. 'Sister Bennett is waiting for you at the far end of the ward, and she'll tell you what to do.' As they went quietly along carrying the sheets, Clare could sense a difference in the atmosphere compared to the female ward. Everything seemed very urgent and tense here. She wondered if it was because of the patient dying or whether it was always like that.

Sister Bennett led the girls along to the first patient – an elderly, frail man who hardly seemed conscious and was unable to communicate – and a wet bed that needed changing, and they quickly got on with the job.

They were just finishing when Sister Bennett reappeared silently at the end of the bed to check everything was done exactly as it should be. 'Good job,' she said, nodding her head. 'Now we have another one that needs doing a few beds along.'

They repeated the same process with the second patient and when the man was settled back in bed, they took all the damp bedding back to the laundry. Clare felt the usual small sense of achievement, knowing that she had done something good with the least fuss possible, which would make the patients comfortable and able to get back to sleep.

After they had spent time sorting out laundry and then writing up a few notes about the patients they had worked with, Sister Bennett told them to sit at the table at the end of the ward and if they heard any sound or movement from the patients, that one of them should go and investigate while the other stayed put.

'Keep your ear out for the phone as well,' she instructed. 'We might have relatives of the patient who died arriving. They are Catholics, and they gave us the parish priest's number to phone if their father took a turn for the worse, but it all happened so quickly he was gone by the time we phoned, so they might decide to wait until the morning. The priest said he was low on petrol, so he wasn't sure if he could bring them down anyway. If they do come, the priest will either phone you or will call from the porter's lodge if they decide to come on ahead. If you hear anything either way, one of you should come straight down and get me in the office or the staffroom.'

Clare felt a bit anxious at receiving any recently bereaved relatives. Last week she'd been on the ladies' ward when a patient had died, and the family were distraught. It had reminded her of her own family's upset when her grandmother died, and she had gone back to her room in the residence that night and cried herself to sleep.

Watching Sister Bennett disappear around the corner, Clare was surprised when Nurse White gave a disgruntled sigh and flopped down in one of the chairs. 'Well, there's no chance of us doing any knitting tonight,' she whispered. Bending down she picked up two magazines from the table and handed one to Clare. 'Hopefully, we might get another cup of tea when the others have finished their break.'

She glanced at the cover of her magazine and made a little derisory noise as she held it up for Clare to see. 'How to look like a Hollywood star!' she read out, in a voice mocking a radio advert. 'Fat chance of that when you can hardly buy any clothes and make-up with this strict rationing.' She shook her head. 'It's so ridiculous that we've all had to suffer with shortages on everything, when we've not really had any war over here in England. There's only been this stupid Phoney War.' She gave a loud sigh and then she suddenly started to laugh. 'I'm just listening to myself and realising that I've turned into an old Moaning Minnie!'

Clare looked at her in surprise, not sure how to respond.

'That's what happens when you do a few night shifts in a row,' the young nurse said, 'and then you don't get enough sleep during the day. I've never been good sleeping during the day, the least little noise wakes me up.'

'It's not easy,' Clare agreed, 'but I suppose we'll get used to it as time goes on.'

They chatted quietly for a while about the things they missed the most, then fell into a companionable silence as they read their magazines, punctuated only by the odd bout of coughing from the patients. Every so often, one of them would quietly walk around, checking each bed.

Over an hour later, as they were back sitting at the table, Clare thought she heard a voice from the top end of the ward. 'Did you hear that?' she whispered, and when there was no reply, she looked over to see Nurse White dozing with her head resting on her folded arms. As quietly as she could, she got to her feet and went to see if she could find where the sound had come from.

She was halfway down when she heard a voice calling, 'Nurse,' and turning to the bed she saw a middle-aged man lying flat on his back. Picking up his chart, Clare noted he was recovering from a small stroke and she remembered Sister Townsend had said he was in for respite care to give his wife a break.

Clare went to his bedside. 'Are you all right?' she asked, drawing the curtains around the bed so as not to disturb the others. 'Do you need anything?'

'A drink of water,' he said, pulling himself up into a sitting position.

As Clare lifted the jug of water, he said, 'You're new on the ward, aren't you? I saw you earlier going up and down with the other one.'

'Yes,' she replied politely, 'it's the first time I've been on the men's ward. I'm just helping out for the night.'

'You're Irish, aren't you?' he said. 'My mother was from Dublin.'

'I'm from the Midlands,' she said quietly, always delighted to meet someone with Irish connections. 'A town called Tullamore.' She handed him the glass of water.

'Do you get homesick?' he asked. 'It can't be easy being in a strange country, especially with a war going on.'

'Sometimes, but we're so busy working in the hospital and studying.'

He took a sip out of the glass. 'It's nice to see a friendly face for a change. The sister on this ward is a right oul' crab, isn't she? She runs the place like Hitler with the Nazis.'

'Shhhh!' Clare said, putting her finger to her lips, but there was a glint of laughter in her eyes. 'You shouldn't be saying things like that.'

'Well, you have to admit she is a bit of a dragon. The other nurses are terrified of her, aren't they? If she says, "jump!" they say, "how high?"'

'You need to stop,' Clare warned him mock sternly. 'You're not allowed to talk about any of the senior staff like that. If she comes along we'll both be in trouble.'

The man started to laugh then he put his finger to his lips as well. 'I won't tell if you don't.'

'Have you had enough to drink?' she said in a low voice, the humour of the moment drifting away as she remembered she'd left Nurse White asleep. 'I need to get back down to the nurses' station in case anyone else needs me.'

He held the glass out to her. 'I wouldn't want to get you in trouble.'

'Oh, I'll do my best to stay out of trouble.' Clare took the glass and smiled at him. 'I hope you get back to sleep.'

'I'll be having nice sweet dreams now,' he said, winking at her.

Clare felt slightly uneasy as she pulled the curtains back, and went quickly back to the other end of the ward. It wouldn't do for Sister Bennett to come in and catch her dozing. As she got nearer to the table, she could see that the nurse was still fast asleep, and then her heart almost stopped when she saw the distinctive sister's uniform turning into the ward from the other end of the corridor.

She watched as the sister took Nurse White by the shoulder and shook her, and then a wave of relief washed over her as she realised it was Sister Townsend.

'You're lucky it was me who found you,' she heard Sister

Townsend say. 'Now get yourself to the bathroom and splash some cold water on your face.'

Nurse White scrambled to her feet and went rushed to the bathroom.

'How are things, Clare?' the older nurse asked with a concerned look as Clare took a seat at the desk. 'Has it been very busy?'

'We were busier earlier,' she replied professionally, 'but most of the patients are settled now. Just one or two still awake.'

A sound came from the bottom of the ward again, and they both stopped to listen.

'I think it's the same man from earlier,' Clare said, concerned.

'What was wrong with him before?'

'Just a drink. He was a bit chatty, and I was worried he might wake the other patients.' She moved to her feet again. 'I'll go and check.'

Walking quickly down the ward, she arrived at the bed to find the man was half sitting up. 'I'm sorry, nurse,' he said, 'but I started coughing and when I reached for the water I spilled it over myself.' He indicated his bed covers and front of his pyjama jacket. 'I feel such a fool...'

'Don't worry,' Clare said calmly, checking for any damp spots. 'I don't think there was much in the glass, it's just the top blanket really, the sheets seem fine.' She took the cover off and rolled it up. 'I'll run down to the laundry and get a couple of towels to dry you and a fresh top cover.'

'And pyjamas,' he said, rubbing his hand to his chest. 'I got a bit of a splash on them too.'

Nurse White and Sister Townsend were sitting together at the station. 'A spillage,' she told them as she passed by. 'I'll get a fresh cover and pyjamas.'

A few minutes later she was back at the man's bedside. He had already taken his pyjama jacket off. She drew the curtains around the bed to give him some privacy and passed him the towel. 'Rub that over anywhere that got wet,' she said in a low voice. 'And then you can put your fresh jacket on.'

She went to the bottom of the bed to unfold the blanket, and as she did so, he said in a hoarse sort of voice, 'Could you give me a hand with this?'

Clare moved back towards him, and as she did so, he suddenly leaned forward and gripped her by the wrist. With his other hand he whipped back the bed sheets to expose his rigid penis. 'Just a quick rub,' he said, pushing her hand down on top of it.

Clare gasped in shock and with her free hand she pushed him back onto the pillows, and pulled her other hand away. 'You dirty, dirty thing!' she gasped out, as tears welled up in her eyes.

'I thought you were game for it,' he said in a wounded tone. 'You were all chat to me earlier...'

'You thought what? Are you completely mad?' She looked at him in disgust. 'Cover yourself up!'

'What harm would it do? Nurses are supposed to know about these things—'

Before she got the chance to think of a response, the curtain was pushed back and Sister Townsend stood at the end of the bed.

'What's going on here?' she demanded.

He quickly scrabbled at the bed sheets to cover himself.

'This man,' Clare said, her eyes filling up again, 'exposed himself to me and asked me to touch his private parts...'

The older woman's eyebrows shot up. 'Did he indeed?' she said in a low, ominous voice. She took a few steps towards the top of the bed. 'Did you ask my nurse to do something to you, that you would expect a prostitute to do?'

There was a deathly silence.

'Did you?' she repeated.

'I meant no harm,' he said, 'it was only a bit of a lark...'

'A bit of a lark?' Sister Townsend said in a high, mocking voice. She looked at Clare and shook her head. 'Can you believe it?' She then turned back quickly and moved her face close to the patient. 'Well, if you ask any of my nurses to do anything disgusting like that again, then you will have the pleasure of me doing it for you. I'm well experienced in dealing with the likes of you.'

Clare caught her breath, wondering if she had heard right.

'But believe you me, there will be no pleasure in it for you, because I'll put on the roughest pair of rubber gloves I can find, and by the time I'm finished with you, you'll be glad to keep that pathetic thing hidden under the covers. And it will be so raw, you won't be fit to do anything with it for a long, long time.' She whirled back to Clare, her eyes flashing. 'Now, Nurse, put that blanket on the bed now while I'm here to watch him, and then we can leave him to think over what I've just said. I think we should suggest to Sister Bennett that we might need to have a word with his wife.'

'Oh no, don't do that,' he said quickly. 'I'm sorry, Nurse, I was only teasing the girl. I can see now what I did was wrong. I didn't think ... I didn't mean to cause any offence.'

'What you did could be reported as an offence,' Sister Townsend went on. 'Young women working here on long nights and getting abuse from the likes of you: it could put them off their nursing career, you know.'

'It'll never happen again,' he said. 'I wasn't thinking straight – it could be the tablets I'm on. I'm a respectable man ... I'm very sorry.'

'Well, I think you need to say that to Nurse O'Sullivan.'

He dropped his head, 'I'm sorry ...'

Clare found she couldn't even look at him, the memory of his naked private parts was still too vivid in her mind.

'Get back to sleep now,' Sister Townsend said icily, 'and I don't want to hear another word out of you, or we'll be in touch with your wife.'

Clare gathered up the towels, pulled the curtains back from the bed and followed the sister silently down the ward. When they were halfway down, Sister Townsend stopped and turned to Clare. 'Are you okay?'

Clare took a deep breath. 'Yes,' she replied shakily. 'I'll ... I'll be all right.'

'Is it the first time anything like that has happened to you?' the sister asked, concern filling her voice.

Clare looked up and nodded.

The older woman put her arm around her shoulder. 'I know it's not nice, but we all have to get used to these things. Don't let that dirty bastard put you off. It's all part of the job, and it's all part of life. You won't think it now, but as you get older, you'll look back on it and you'll laugh. You'll realise how pathetic men can be, ruled by their urges.' She nodded her head. 'And believe you me, even the best of them can behave badly under the wrong circumstances.'

As they walked along, Clare tried to digest all that the older woman had said, and tried not to be as horrified as she felt about the incident.

Nurse White was sitting at the station, writing in the report book, and looked up anxiously as they approached.

'Well,' Sister Townsend said, 'is all quiet here?'

'I walked around and checked on everyone and they are all settled.'

'I'll get back to A3 now, and leave you to it. I'll see you at the end of the shift.'

When the ward doors swung shut, Nurse White turned to Clare. 'Thank God she didn't say anything else, I was terrified she might tell Sister Bennett that she found me asleep.'

'She's very good,' Clare said in a quiet voice.

'You both looked very serious. Did something happen?' she asked. 'You were gone a while, did one of the men take poorly?'

Clare took a deep breath then went on to explain.

'Oh my God!' Nurse White exclaimed. 'I've had a few awkward things happen, but nothing as bad as that...' She dropped her voice. 'We were warned in class that men can... they can react to you washing them or touching them, it's something they can't help, that nature takes over. I've found most of them are very embarrassed when that happens, but it doesn't sound as though he was in the least bit embarrassed.'

'He wasn't.' Clare shuddered at the memory.

71

'It would make you frightened of men, and make you wonder what they are thinking.'

When her shift finished in the morning, Clare didn't feel like going straight to bed. She went over to the canteen, where she found Gaye having breakfast with a group of other student nurses. Gaye was an early riser, unless she had had a late night out, and was often up and about before many of the other students.

Gaye pulled a chair out to let Clare sit beside her. 'How did your night shift go?'

Clare rolled her eyes. 'I'll tell you about it later, when we're on our own.' She had some toast and tea, listening to the others chatter about their day and the upcoming dance; and then gradually the other girls went, leaving the two friends on their own.

Gaye folded her arms on the table. 'Right, so what happened?'

Clare took a big drink of her tea and then she related the whole story in a low voice.

Gaye's eyes widened. 'The filthy bastard! Imagine asking you to do that.'

'It was horrible... I mean, I've seen men's...' she halted. 'Private bits, but never one that was...' She shook her head. 'You know...'

'That's terrible, especially being an older man. The very thought makes you feel sick.' She squeezed Clare's hand. 'Try not to think about it.'

'It would nearly put you off men for life,' Clare said, thinking of what Nurse White said. 'And make you wonder what to expect... you know, in the future if you get married. I never gave my wedding night much mind, but the thought terrifies me now.'

'It will be totally different when it's someone you love.' Gaye lowered her voice. 'Even women get feelings about sex.' She gave a little knowing smile. 'Surely you must have felt it when you're dancing with a fella that you fancy? You know, when you get that hot and bothered feeling where you're all flustered and don't know what to say to them.'

Clare thought for a few moments. 'I don't think I've ever really felt like that.'

'What about that lad, Steven, you went out with for a few months last year?'

Clare shook her head. 'No... I liked him, but not that way. I broke off with him because it was like going out with one of my brothers.'

Gaye laughed now. 'He wasn't a bit like your brother, your Oliver is a fine thing. I wish he lived over here instead of Liverpool.'

'I'm surprised you like him so much,' Clare said, 'because you and Oliver are totally different. I think you would find him a bit too serious and boring.' Clare did not want to encourage her friend, as the first time they met, Oliver had said he found Gaye giddy and immature. His opinion had obviously not changed much because they had met up several times when he visited Clare in Stockport, and he still rolled his eyes and smiled bemusedly when Gaye's name was mentioned.

'I can be serious too, you know.' Gaye flicked her red hair back. 'Mr Herbert up in Stepping Hill said I was mature for my age when we were on the tour of the laboratories a few weeks ago. Didn't I tell you?'

'I'm sure you can be very mature when you put your mind to it.' They caught each other's eye and exploded into giggles, then when they'd calmed down Clare said, 'Have you started your essay yet? I'm not even halfway through and we have to have it in for Friday.'

'Do you know what shifts you are on this week and next?'

'My brain has suddenly gone dead,' Clare said, feeling her eyelids grow heavy. 'I think I need to get to bed.' Pushing her chair back, she said, 'When I wake up later, I'll check my roster out and let you know.'

'I'm on a late,' Gaye said frowning. 'We're like ships passing in the night, aren't we? Anyway, you go and get a sleep and we'll work a day out to go down to Stockport and a night out with Diana.'

Chapter Eight

Clare woke with a start when she heard the knock on the door. She looked at her alarm clock and was surprised that it was four o'clock. She usually woke around lunchtime and then dozed on and off until about three. The door was knocked again, and when she called that she was coming, one of the nurses called back that there was a phone call for her. She ran downstairs to the payphone and when she picked it up, Diana's voice came on the line.

'I hope I didn't wake you,' Diana sounded anxious. 'The nurse I spoke with said she thought you had been on night shift.'

'It's fine,' Clare said hurriedly. 'I'm usually up at this time.'

'I'm so sorry,' Diana said, 'but I'm ringing with bad news. You won't believe it – I'm still in shock myself – but Mrs Atherton has died.'

'What?' Clare was shocked. 'Did you say, she's *dead*?'

'Sadly, yes. I spoke to her daughter this evening and she told me that she had a heart attack the day after we saw her and died shortly afterwards.'

'Oh no…' Clare's voice was choked. 'I can't believe it. Poor Mrs Atherton… She seemed fine when we saw her at her house.'

'I couldn't believe it either. I don't think I've ever had such a shock.'

'How did you find out?'

'It was a total coincidence. I was down at the music shop after work, picking up a new record I had ordered. The shop is on the hill on the way to the market, and as I passed the

74

chip shop her family owned, I noticed that it was all closed up, and there was a note taped on the window. Something made me go over to have a look, and the note said there had been a sudden bereavement in the family and they would be closed until further notice. I thought it might be a grandson or a nephew or someone who was abroad with the forces, then, just as I was turning to walk away, the door of the house opened and Mrs Atherton's daughter – you remember Catherine – came out. She started crying the minute she saw me, and I guessed straight away that it was her mother.'

'Oh, I feel really sad about it,' Clare said. 'She was a lovely old lady.'

'I know we were only with her a few hours in total, but I feel as though we'd known her for ages.'

'She was that kind of person,' Clare agreed, sadly.

'Her daughter said the funeral is next Saturday in St George's Church in Heaviley, and that the family would love us to attend. She also said they would be having a meal after the funeral is over in the Alma Lodge. Do you know where it is? It's not far from Aunt Rosamund's house.'

'I've seen it from the bus to Stepping Hill Hospital.' It looked fancier than any place she had been in, even grander than Aunt Rosamund's house, but she did not say that to Diana.

'Catherine said that her mother would be happy for the three of us to attend. Apart from her health incidents, she told the family she had a lovely night with us in the air-raid shelter, and kept talking about Gaye's lovely singing.'

Clare gave a little sigh. 'I feel sad that she thought a night in an air-raid shelter was having a good time.' She paused for a moment. 'I would like to go to the funeral, that's if you're going too.'

'Yes, I'll go. St George's is the church my aunt goes to every Sunday, so I know it well.'

'I'm sure Gaye will come too,' Clare said, 'and we can make arrangements to meet up and go into the church together.' She paused. 'Does it matter that I'm Roman Catholic? I've never been in a Church of England church before, and I'm a bit nervous about it.'

'The vicar, Mr Lomas, is very nice and makes everyone welcome.'

Diana had no idea how big a step going into a Protestant church was for an Irish Catholic girl, who had been warned all her life against mixing with other religions. But she would go. In her heart, she knew that going to the funeral was the right thing to do, and that Oliver would agree.

They hung up, having agreed that Diana would phone the following evening with the exact time of the funeral and arrange where they would meet.

Later that evening, Clare went along to Gaye's room to tell her about Mrs Atherton. Gaye sat on the bed while Clare sat on the chair by her friend's desk. Gaye was shocked and sad to hear the news, and looked as though she might cry when she heard that the old lady had told everyone about her beautiful voice and how she should be a professional singer.

'The poor old soul,' Gaye said, 'but I think it's a bit too late for me to do anything about a singing career. I'm too far into my nursing training to think of anything like that now.'

'Would you have liked to train as a professional singer?' Clare asked.

'My parents wouldn't have let me do anything like that. They wanted me to be a teacher like our Audrey. They don't think nursing is that great. My mother says it's only a step up from being a skivvy.'

'Sometimes it is!' Clare said, smiling now. 'But it's better than being called a prostitute, which is what Sister Townsend said to that man.'

Gaye's face lit up. 'Did she?'

'Yes, she said that what he had asked me to do is the sort of thing that men ask prostitutes to do.' Clare's brow creased. 'I must be very innocent, I never heard of anything like that before.'

'You are innocent!' Gaye said, laughing. 'I wish I'd been there to hear Sister Townsend and see the look on his face.'

Clare was glad to see Gaye back to her old self, and in a funny way, her laughing about the horrible incident with the man made her feel better, made it seem more normal somehow. She still shuddered every time she thought of it, but she knew she would have to get over it. They chatted a while longer, but then Clare noticed that her friend's mind had become distracted again. She had asked twice how Diana had heard about Mrs Atherton dying, and had checked again about the funeral arrangements.

'Did you say it's *this* Saturday?' Gaye asked.

'Yes, in the church up in Heaviley.' Clare's brow creased. 'You're not working this weekend, are you?'

'No, but I've already made arrangements to go somewhere that day.' She bit her lip. 'I'll see what I can do, but I might not make it.'

'You never mentioned you had plans this weekend.'

'I just made them today.'

'Have you been asked out on a date or something?' Clare smiled and clapped her hands together. 'Is it the junior doctor you met when you were on the medical ward? Dr Harvey?'

'It's nobody you know.' There was a silence, then Gaye said, 'I'm sorry about the funeral, but with different shifts and everything, we can't keep each other up to date with all our arrangements. I don't expect you to tell me every little detail about what you're doing.'

Clare caught her breath at Gaye's unusually forthright comment but tried not to let it show. 'If you can't make the funeral, it can't be helped.' She shrugged. 'It's not as if we knew Mrs Atherton really well or anything. It's just because of the circumstances...'

Gaye's face softened. 'I'm really sorry I can't make it, but I'll get a sympathy card for you to give to the family.' She paused. 'If you don't mind taking it for me?'

'Of course not.' Everyone had off days, Clare thought. She

looked down at Gaye's desk and noticed a letter with the address written in distinctive block writing. It was still unopened, and beside it was another envelope – opened – with the same handwriting.

'You got your letter then?' Clare said, touching her hand to it. 'I noticed you had one when I was at the pigeonhole collecting my mail the other day.'

Gaye moved quickly to the desk and snatched up the envelope. 'I hate the way our mail is open to the public in that flaming cabinet.'

'I'm not interested in your mail,' Clare gasped, wounded. 'I was only making light chat.'

Gaye took a deep breath. 'Look, I'm sorry, Clare. I didn't mean you. I've had an awful day and I don't feel great. The staff nurse in A&E had a right go at me over a form she couldn't find, and when I eventually found it under a folder for her, she blamed me. It happened in front of two doctors and a patient, and she made me look like a bloody idiot. I know it's not an excuse for being so snappy to you, and I am sorry.'

'It's okay, I understand,' Clare said. 'We've all had bad days that leave us feeling out of sorts. Is there anything I can do? Do you need a Beecham's Powder or anything?'

Gaye gave a weak smile. 'I think I'm just tired. I'm going to have a lie down for an hour before tea.'

As she walked back to her own room, Clare felt a little knot of unease in her stomach. This was the first time she and Gaye had clashed. She knew that the staff nurses and the ward sisters could be sharp with students, but she felt instinctively there was more to the situation than Gaye was saying. Her outburst about privacy had left her wondering if she had, unknowingly, overstepped a boundary regarding their friendship.

Back in her room she went over the scene again in her mind, trying to work out what she had said or done to cause offence. It had started with her asking Gaye about her plans for the weekend – something they had done more or less every week since they had become close friends. Gaye had often asked her the exact same question. The same with the letters. There were plenty of times when Gaye had brought letters for her with Irish stamps directly to the ward Clare was working on, knowing she'd want to read them immediately.

The more she thought about it, the more she realised that she had not done anything different to what she normally did. And while Gaye had brushed away her awkward mood and snappy comments, something didn't ring true. She hadn't said anything about her plans for Saturday and, oddly, had not even opened the letter that had caused the argument. Clare presumed from the postmark that it must be from her family or a friend from Newcastle. Clare wondered if Gaye was having more problems with her family.

Gaye had been open about enjoying her independent life in Stockport, away from the eagle eyes of her old-fashioned parents. She felt her parents favoured her sister Audrey, who was engaged to be married, and knew that they thought her sister's career choice of teaching was preferable to Gaye being a nurse.

'They got a shock when I didn't pick Newcastle for my training,' Gaye had told Clare on one of the first nights they'd worked together, 'but I decided I'm better off where they can't criticise everything I do.'

When the family came to visit for Gaye's twentieth birthday and invited Clare out for lunch with them at the Bluebell Hotel, Clare could see that her friend was not exaggerating. There was an obvious coolness between Gaye and her sister, and it seemed as though Audrey had been dragged along by their parents, to keep up the pretence of family unity.

Clare pondered things for a few more moments, then she went to the wardrobe for her light-blue coat and matching cloche hat, collecting her mother-of-pearl rosary beads from her desk drawer. She would walk up to the church, she decided: the exercise and the fresh air would do her good.

Half an hour later she left Our Lady and the Apostles Church feeling much lighter. She had selected three candles and offered up a prayer as she lit each one. The first candle was for her family back home, the second asking that the war would be over soon, and the third candle was asking for guidance with the situation between her and Gaye.

In the meantime, Clare decided, she would tread carefully and not assume anything of her friend. Instead, she would ring Diana and suggest they go to the cinema tomorrow night. If Gaye wanted to join them, that would be great. If not, Clare would leave well alone until she was back to her old self.

Chapter Nine

On Saturday morning, Clare crossed over the Buxton Road to the bus stop on the opposite side and caught the bus up to St George's Church in Heaviley. As arranged, Diana was there waiting for her outside the Scout Hall next door, dressed more formally than usual.

'You look lovely,' Clare told her. 'Your coat and hat are gorgeous.' Diana's outfit was impeccable and it really set off her beautiful face and emerald-green eyes, and the black-and-grey-trimmed hat elegantly framed her dark bobbed hair, making her look even more striking than usual

'The credit must go to my mother,' Diana said. 'She loves fashion, and is forever trying to make me more glamorous, even for occasions such as funerals.' She looked down at the black linen coat and the patent shoes with the little fabric bow. 'I feel much more comfortable in my trousers and a loose blouse or sweater.' She turned her gaze to Clare and smiled warmly. 'You look very stylish, yourself.'

Clare was wearing a plain black suit with a nipped-in waist, and a cream blouse with a pussycat bow. The outfit was further lifted by her two-tone court shoes and her best black-beaded satin bag. 'And I notice you have new stockings too.'

'Believe it or not, they came from Ireland,' Clare said. 'My mother somehow managed to get me two pairs for my birthday, and I keep them for special occasions.' Her face fell. 'So I'm wearing them today in honour of poor Mrs Atherton.'

'So sad, isn't it?' Diana glanced over at the church. 'It looks as though most of the people have gone inside. Shall we?'

'I have a sympathy card for the family, and one from Gaye.' Clare suddenly remembered.

'Oh, that was nice of her,' Diana said. 'Such a pity she couldn't make it as well.'

'She's coming to the dance with us tomorrow night, and she's looking forward to seeing you again.'

'I'm so glad I met you two,' Diana said.

Clare smiled now, as her new friend slid her arm through hers. Things were looking up all round, she thought. Gaye had come down to her room with the card the previous evening, and had apologised again. She had also brought her a present of a red lipstick, which Clare was delighted with. She would never have been brave enough to choose such a bright shade herself, but the glamorous Gaye knew it would suit her.

Just under an hour later as the mourners all filed out of the church, Clare thought how silly she had been, worrying about being in a different church. The service was easy to follow, the people were all very friendly, and the two vicars on the altar gave a warm welcome to everyone and made her feel completely relaxed.

As they stood outside the church, Mr Lomas, the younger vicar, came walking quickly towards the girls. 'Diana,' he said, 'I was hoping to catch you, as I need to round up as many bodies as I possibly can.'

Diana looked at him in surprise. He was fairly new, she'd told Clare in a whisper during the service, and she had only met him a few times. 'What is it?'

'We just had word this morning that we are to expect an influx of hundreds of evacuees from the Channel Islands – Guernsey to be exact – tonight or tomorrow.'

'Does that mean that the islands have been invaded by Germany?' Diana asked quickly, turning her big green eyes to Clare.

Clare immediately thought of the conversation they'd had with Mrs Atherton the last time they had seen her.

'If it hasn't already happened,' he said sadly, 'it looks imminent. All the churches and organisations like the Women's Institute have been notified and we have to get moving as quickly as possible.'

'When do they arrive in Stockport?'

'They are arriving down in Weymouth and will be checked before being quickly dispersed by train. They can only use the Great Western and Western Divisions of the Southern Railway, as all the others are needed for military purposes. So, they are sending them to what they have decided are neutral areas in northern England, and Cheshire is one of them. Stockport will be among the main towns, so we have to get things organised at the town hall as quickly as possible to receive the children and families, and then start looking for homes to take them all in.' He shook his head. 'It's not going to be easy with the huge numbers and at such short notice, so we need all the help we can get. I hope I can rely on you and your Aunt Rosamund's support?'

'Of course,' Diana said. 'I'll let her know when I get back home later.'

'Wonderful!' He looked relieved and smiled when he noticed Clare standing awkwardly next to Diana, feeling quite out of place. 'I don't think I've seen you at church before?'

'Oh, this is my friend, Clare,' Diana said quickly.

He shook her hand enthusiastically. 'Can I put you down to help as well?'

'I'd love to,' she said, 'but I'm not a member of the church, I'm actually Roman Catholic.'

'That's no problem,' he said, smiling warmly. 'Aren't we all equal in the eyes of the Lord? The last thing these little evacuees will be worrying about is what denomination any of us are. The help we need is purely practical, organising food and clothes and bedding for them initially. No one will be asking you to lead prayer groups or anything like that. I don't know much about Guernsey and the other Channel Islands, but I would imagine they have people from various denominations there too – presumably Roman Catholic as well.' He stopped now, thinking. 'Which church do you go to in Stockport?'

'Our Lady's, in Shaw Heath,' Clare said.

'You have a young curate there – Father Noah Gorman – and I've met up with him at Scout and Cub meetings, as we use the same camping facilities. I'm sure he will be rallying the troops down at Our Lady's as well.'

Clare smiled now, relieved to hear that her own church was involved. She desperately wanted to be part of the teams helping, and it made it easier to tell her family about the volunteer work she was doing when there was a link to the local Catholic church.

'Children under five will be accompanied by mothers or relatives, and teachers will be supervising their classes.' He shrugged. 'We don't know much more than that.'

'Do you think it will take long to get the children and families sorted into their new homes?' Clare asked.

'No idea. The voluntary groups will be needed at weekends when the children are out of school so they can meet up with the other Guernsey folk. We will probably run activities in the church halls on a Saturday and possibly on Sunday as well. That's where girls like you might be able to help'.

Clare remembered Mrs Atherton and the way she had talked about how her friends from the church had rallied around to help her out after her husband's death. She pictured the glow on the old lady's face as she had talked about the groups and the crafts and activities they had been involved with at the church. And, of course, it was Mrs Atherton who had first suggested they get involved in supporting the evacuees.

There was a silence now, and she realised that both the vicar and Diana were waiting to hear her response.

'Yes,' she said finally, 'I would love to help, and I think Gaye, my friend, would like to be involved too. We would have to work out our shifts at the hospital, and hopefully the ward sisters will help us juggle things around the weekend rosters.'

Reverend Lomas said, 'When everyone is back in the Alma Lodge Hotel, I will gather together as many of the local people there who might be able to help out, and we will work out a plan of action. It sounds like we are going to be busy all weekend preparing for the arrival of the evacuees. Some of the trains will be arriving late at night, so we will have the reception centres open day and night.'

He shook both of their hands warmly and strode off to speak with more of the mourners.

Diana turned to Clare. 'I'm so pleased that we'll be doing this thing together.' A beaming smile broke out on her face. 'I'm already starting to think of all sorts of activities that we could do with the children. Gaye will help too, won't she?'

Clare nodded, hoping her old friend was back to normal like she'd seemed. 'I hope so.'

Chapter Ten

Gaye stood in front of the wardrobe mirror, taking out the rollers from her long red hair. She stared at her reflection for a few moments, and a cold shiver ran through her as she wondered what on earth she had got herself into.

It seemed only weeks ago she was a free and easy nursing student with the world at her feet, and the possibility of a romance with more than one of the junior doctors. Now, she found herself in a situation she could never have envisaged, one that could have a serious impact on her future and might affect more people than herself.

She hadn't really considered it a romance; it had started out as a harmless flirtation that had helped pass away the boring evenings back home in Newcastle last Christmas. She did not think she had led him on *seriously* in any way; it had only been the odd little tease or joke, and then a harmless kiss under the mistletoe when they were on their own. Just little things that confirmed how attractive men found her, things that added a tinge of excitement to an otherwise boring afternoon or evening.

She had found – as far back as her school days – that a bit of light banter and the odd compliment or harmless double-meaning joke kept her popular with the opposite sex. Her easy, familiar manner had also helped her settle into her new life in Stockport with Clare and the other girls, and she knew she was a favourite with the hospital porters and the ambulance drivers. It was only recently she had got to know some of the doctors, but she could already tell that she was making an impact there too. At the last dance she had been asked up on the floor several times by Dr Harvey – a very good-looking lad from Durham – who had made it obvious he fancied her. He had joked along with her, imitating her Geordie accent and telling her silly jokes. Later in the night – after he had had a few more drinks – after dancing with her again, he took her hand and led her into a dark and quiet corner. There, he had kissed her passionately, and told her that if he didn't already have a steady girlfriend back home, that he would love to get to know her a lot better.

Back in the nurses' home that night – slightly tipsy and with shining eyes – she had repeated everything Dr Harvey said to Clare and the other girls.

'The bloody cheek of him!' one of the girls said. 'He should have told you about the girlfriend first before kissing you.'

'Are you upset?' Clare had asked, feeling sorry for her.

'Not a bit,' Gaye had laughed. 'I'm glad he didn't tell me, because now he knows what it was like to kiss me.' The girls all whooped and laughed. 'Next time he sees his girlfriend, he'll be comparing her kisses to mine.' She shrugged. 'Who knows? The romance might even be all off the next time he comes back from Durham.'

She had bumped into Dr Harvey on several occasions since the dance, and he always singled her out to chat to, and only last week he had brought his lunch tray over to her table to sit with her in the canteen. There had been no mention of the dance or the kiss, and no mention of his girlfriend. Instead, he had been serious and talked about the ongoing war and his fears that the conflict was moving closer to Britain.

'Who knows what will happen if they start bombing our cities?' he had said. 'More of the doctors might be conscripted into the forces, and there are soldiers being killed every day. It makes you wonder about everything – all the plans we make for the future might never happen.' He had looked directly at her then. 'Maybe we should just be making the most of every single day while we have the chance, instead of worrying about tomorrow.'

Gaye had just been on the point of asking him exactly what he meant, when one of the other student nurses had appeared at the table with her tray. Dr Harvey had quietly finished his shepherd's pie and trifle, and said he needed to get back to the ward. Gaye could have cheerfully killed her colleague, knowing that she might have got somewhere with the young doctor if they had been left alone for another five minutes.

A few days later when she was in the office where the medication cupboard was kept, there were two staff nurses there, discussing the doctors' roster for the coming week, and she overheard them saying that Dr Andrew Harvey was on leave and had gone back home to Durham.

'I was chatting to him yesterday before he left,' one of the staff nurses said, 'and you'll never guess what he told me about his girlfriend.'

Gaye hovered about at the cupboard, pretending she was looking for something. 'What? Have they got engaged?' the other nurse asked.

'No, nothing personal like that. You know he said she was working in a hospital in York, and we thought she was a nurse? Well, we got that wrong; she's training to be a doctor as well. She's actually a year ahead of him, and came top of her year in the summer exams. He says she's hoping to go on to be a surgeon.'

'No wonder he's never shown any interest in the nurses, he's obviously got his sights set on higher things.'

Gaye had quietly crept out of the office, her heart leaden at the news. Any hopes she had about a romance with him were well and truly gone. What doctor would choose a student nurse over a student doctor? And, she thought, his girlfriend would have to be clever enough to want to become a bloody surgeon!

The following day – while she was still feeling wounded over the news about Dr Harvey – Gaye had received a letter from Newcastle from another young man who was openly declaring his love for her: the last person in the world who should be doing such a thing. She had ignored the letter and a few days later another letter arrived – and then another. It was obvious that he was not going to give up. Afraid to reply in case anyone else saw her letters, she eventually went out to the public phone box over at the town hall and rang him during her lunch hour at work.

'Thank God you've phoned,' he had said, his voice full of relief. 'You didn't answer any of my letters. I was so worried, I was going to phone the hospital to ask if you were all right.'

'I'm fine,' she had told him in a low voice. She had then taken a deep breath. 'You know perfectly well that you shouldn't be writing those things to me, and it can't go on. There can be absolutely nothing between us – ever. I don't want any more letters or phone calls from you.'

'But I'm in love with you, Gaye, and I think I have been since the first minute I set eyes on you. I tried not to think about it, but I can't help myself. You're on my mind every minute of the day. It's you – only you.'

'Don't be so stupid,' she had told him sternly. 'You're just going to stop all this carry-on. I'm far too young to think of falling in love or settling down with anyone. I have my career to think of. And if I was going to settle down, it's not going to be with you. You need to get that into your head.'

'You know you don't mean it, Gaye,' he had said quietly. 'I know it's complicated now, but I promise you, I'll find a way through this so that we can be together.'

'That will never happen,' Gaye had been clear. 'Not in a million years – and you know exactly why that is.'

She looked into the mirror, brushing her gleaming red hair out, remembering how strong she'd been; and then she spent a few minutes putting on her make-up and lipstick. Afterwards, she checked her green polka-dot dress and her white cardigan in the mirror, and her white slingback sandals.

Lifting her handbag, she checked she had all she needed for her day out. She was going into Manchester to meet up with the man who was convinced he was head over heels in love with her. The man she had stupidly led on. The man who could destroy her reputation, destroy her relationship with her whole family and ruin her ambitions of meeting someone like Dr Harvey.

She was going to meet up with a man who was engaged to be married to someone else.

Chapter Eleven

When Clare got back to the nurses' residence around two o'clock, she made herself a cup of tea and took it back to her room. Sitting down at her desk to write a letter home, she found herself distracted, thinking about everything that had happened at the funeral. After they had eaten, the vicar had called for silence and then gave all the mourners the information about the evacuees coming to Stockport, possibly in the next twenty-four hours.

'There will be hundreds of children along with teachers and mothers of those under five,' he said, 'and the last phone call I had this morning said some of them had a very rough trip over the seas. Some of the poor souls had to travel in cattle ships, so you can imagine what that was like. From what we have been told, certain families have very little with them, as they had to leave quickly and were not very well prepared.' He had cleared his throat for silence, as the hubbub of worried voices had risen around him. 'Some of the families were not in good circumstances financially and did not have very much to bring. They didn't have cases or bags or spare clothes. We will need to provide food and drink for them, and items that could not be carried, like baby chairs and toys and books. Hopefully, we will get the older children settled into schools quickly, and that will help them acclimatise to their new situation.'

He'd gone on to explain that Stockport Town Hall was to be set up as the main centre, and the first thing that had to be done by the various church groups was to collect clothing, towels and bedding to have it ready for the children arriving. By the time the vicar had left the funeral, around twenty people had volunteered to start knocking on people's doors that afternoon to start the wheels rolling.

Clare had shied away from the thought of doing anything like that on her own. She hoped that Gaye and some of the other student nurses would help her with approaching people for assistance, as she didn't feel confident asking the local people on her own in case they didn't understand her Irish accent.

She turned back to her letter, and for the next hour lost herself in a different world as she commented on family goings-on and snippets of local news in her mother's last letter. Clare always kept her mother's letters beside her when writing so she could go back over the exact details.

Clare then wrote several pages about the hospital and any Irish nurses her family might have connections with, the sad story about Mrs Atherton, and then about the expected Guernsey evacuees and Our Lady's Church involvement in collecting all the household items necessary for the families settling in. She finished on a light note, telling them about her trip to the Co-op with Gaye, and then asked her mother if she could get her hands on any more nylons for herself and her friends, as they were still as scarce as hens' teeth in England.

After checking the time, Clare decided to walk down to the main post office in Mersey Square. She lifted her letter, bag and gas mask, and then took the stairs two at a time, feeling an urgency she hadn't felt in a while. Walking down Wellington Road, she reached the station and went to cross to the opposite side of the road, when she glimpsed something out of the corner of her eye. She halted, checking again. Ahead, she could see a girl sitting on the bench outside the station, and as she moved nearer she recognised the green polka-dot dress and the red hair tumbling out from under her hat. She was right, it *was* Gaye, and her whole demeanour told Clare that her friend was ill or upset.

As she went towards her, Gaye lifted her head, and stared off into the distance, seemingly oblivious to the people around her. Clare could see by her red, puffy face that she had been crying. For a moment she hesitated, afraid that she was interfering, but she knew she had to take the risk.

'Gaye?' she said, hesitantly. 'I saw you as I was walking down. Are you all right?'

Gaye straightened up, a startled look on her face, before turning away from Clare. 'I'm fine... I was just taking a little rest.' She lifted her handbag from the bench and went to stand up, but Clare reached her hand out and placed it firmly on her shoulder, easing her back down. Clare sat down beside her.

'I don't want to interfere, and you're entitled to tell me to mind my own business, but I'm worried about you.' She touched Gaye's hand hesitatingly. 'You haven't been yourself for a while and I thought it was best to leave you to yourself...'

Gaye made a slight nodding gesture, but she still kept looking straight ahead.

'I wouldn't be a good friend if I didn't say something.' Clare swallowed hard, trying to find the right words. 'You were so good to me when I first arrived here – when I was homesick. You invited me out with you and the other girls, and were always trying to gee me up when I didn't feel like it...'

Gaye shook her head. 'This is completely different.' Her voice was cracked and hoarse. 'I wish it was something ordinary like that...'

'I'll do anything I can to help. Anything at all.'

Gaye made a sudden little movement to lift her bag and then she took out her hanky and pressed it to her eyes. 'I've done something terrible. I've been stupid, stupid... stupid.'

'We all make mistakes.' Clare's voice was soft and gentle. 'You would never do anything that would hurt anybody.'

'And you wouldn't hurt anyone intentionally either, Gaye. I know you wouldn't.'

'Well, I have hurt someone. I've been stupid and selfish – I've gone and got myself involved with a lad who is already engaged to somebody else.'

There was a little pause as Gaye sniffed into her hanky, then Clare asked, 'Is it Andrew Harvey?'

'I wish it was... at least I wouldn't know his fiancée. I might feel guilty, but it wouldn't be as bad as this.'

'I promise I won't mention it to anyone else, and I'll do my best to help you sort it out.'

'No one can sort this out...'

There was a long silence and then Clare put her arm around her friend's shoulder. 'Is it a baby?' she asked in a low whisper. 'Are you expecting a baby?'

Gaye's head jerked up and she looked at her with wide, astonished eyes. 'No!' she said. 'I'm not.' She gave a short, bitter laugh. 'That's the only thing that could have made it worse... but, thank God, I'm not.'

'I'm glad,' Clare said, 'but I would have helped you if you had been pregnant. I wouldn't have let you face it on your own.'

Gaye's face softened. 'Thanks... that means a lot to me. I'm sorry if I've been a bit snappy with you lately. You're a good pal and I didn't want to drag you into this mess.'

'Surely things can't be that bad if you're not pregnant,' Clare said. 'That's probably the worst thing that could happen, and in the middle of studying.' She halted, looking at Gaye's strained face. 'What is it then? What's upsetting you so much? It really can't be as bad as you are imagining.'

Gaye turned her face away again. 'I've been seeing Laurence... that's who I was meeting up with in Manchester today.'

Clare looked blankly at her.

'D'you not remember? Laurence is Audrey's boyfriend. The lad my sister Audrey is supposed to be getting married to in a few months' time.'

'Oh my God...' Clare put her hand to her mouth. 'Oh, Gaye...'

Chapter Twelve

'I told you it was bad,' Gaye said.

'Was it very serious between you?'

'Not really, we were only on our own once ... and that was about six weeks ago.'

Clare's brow furrowed. 'But he's in Newcastle, isn't he? You're not going to have to see him.'

'Well, he was,' Gaye explained, 'but he got a job in Manchester and he said he's moving over to live here to be near me.'

'Did you talk about it before?'

'He's done it all without telling me. He handed his notice in at the office in Newcastle and he's moved to a new one in Manchester. He's a railway engineer, and they're often sent to different cities, so he told our Audrey his work transferred him and he had no choice.'

'Audrey doesn't know anything about you and Laurence?'

Gaye shook her head, more of her red curls escaping her hat.

'Are you in love with him?' Clare asked gently. 'If it wasn't for Audrey, would you want to be with him?'

'No, I don't, but he won't listen. It's all my fault for stupidly leading him on.' Tears came into her eyes again and started to run down her cheeks. 'It started off as just a harmless bit of flirting after he had a row with Audrey when I was home at Christmas. She was going on about the wedding and the guest list, and arguing about him wanting to invite this old couple he was fond of, who he'd known since he was a child. She shouted at him in front of everyone and told him that men didn't have a say in who was invited. She was being a right cow to everyone, and she started on at me again, going on about how nurses were only skivvies and saying it wasn't a proper professional job.'

Clare caught her breath. 'I know she's your sister, but at times she's not a nice person.'

'When I look back, I suppose me and Laurence were sympathising with each other about the way she treated us. He then started saying he was having second thoughts about getting married and that he'd love to be with somebody who was more easy-going and a bit of a laugh. He said he wished he had met me first as we were more suited than him and Audrey.'

'Didn't you get a fright when he said that?'

'That's the stupid thing ... where I made things worse. I've always told you he was very good-looking, haven't I? Everybody says he's like a film star, and I was flattered.' She shook her head. 'Looking back, I was bored being at home, I'd forgotten how strict Mam and Dad were, and thinking about Laurence fancying me added a bit of excitement. When he arrived at the house one afternoon and there was only me in, and I poured us a glass of sherry, with it being Christmas like. He started talking about Audrey again – all the same stuff as before. Then, for a bit of a laugh, he lifted the mistletoe that Mam had on the wall and kissed me. After that, we met up in town a couple of times – just in a small café for a cup of tea.'

'Oh, Gaye ...' Clare said anxiously. 'Didn't you think about all the trouble it could cause?'

'It was always at the back of my mind.' Gaye looked dismal now. 'But I suppose it all just went to my head a bit. I thought it would all fizzle out when I left to go back to Stockport. The last day I saw him, I told him to have a good talk to Audrey and to tell her that he wasn't happy, and I thought she would get a fright and make more of an effort with him.' She shrugged. 'I thought they would patch things up and everything would go back to the way it was, but then he started writing letters to me and phoning me at the nurses' residence. When I wouldn't speak to him on the phone, he left messages with the other nurses and

I was terrified he would say something to them. I've told him loads of times not to phone me but he won't listen. I just hope nobody has heard.'

Clare decided to keep quiet about hearing her arguing with him on the phone, as it would only make Gaye feel worse.

'He asked me to meet up with him in Manchester about six weeks ago,' Gaye continued, 'so I went to see if I could talk sense into him, but it obviously didn't work because he's starting work in Manchester next week and he was over today looking at digs.' She suddenly stopped, tears welling up in her eyes. 'Oh, Clare, I'm terrified. I don't know what I'm going to do if he comes here. I told him today that what we'd done was wrong and that we needed to put a stop to it before Audrey and Mam and Dad find out, but he said he didn't care. He said that we need to think of ourselves, that with the war on anything could happen.' She paused. 'I don't know if I told you, but he has an older brother in the navy and he's been missin' in action for over a year.'

Clare shook her head. 'I didn't know.'

'He's married with two little kids. Laurence talked to me about it, and when he had a few drinks he broke down in tears. I think it might have affected him more than he's been lettin' on to Audrey.'

'It's bound to have affected him,' she said, 'and it sounds as though he feels he can talk about it with you.'

Gaye started to cry again. 'I feel as if I don't know him any more – and that he could do or say anything and start all sorts of trouble.'

Clare noticed two women who had come out of the station staring over at Gaye. She looked at her friend now, feeling helpless. The situation was a serious one, and by the sounds of Laurence, he wasn't going to be easy to shrug off. She squeezed Gaye's hand. 'We'll think of something. He can't force you into anything you don't want to do – you're under no obligation to him. It's not as if you asked him to move to Manchester.'

'I can't believe I've been so stupid, and while our Audrey is a mean cow at times, what I've done is worse. She's my sister and I've betrayed her, and that makes me a bad and terrible person.'

'You're not bad,' Clare said. 'You're a great nurse and you've got a good heart.' She swallowed hard, trying to pick her words carefully. 'You're not the first to make a mistake and you won't be the last.'

'Well, it looks like I've got what I deserve. He won't listen, he said he's moving to Manchester and that everything will work out.'

'What if you say you're going to be too busy to see him?' Clare suggested. 'The families are arriving from Guernsey late tonight or tomorrow morning.'

'Are they arriving so soon?' Gaye asked.

'Yes,' Clare told her. 'And it's the perfect excuse to give to Laurence, as well as the truth. Explain that you're not going to have any free time because you will be helping out with the families from Guernsey. He obviously cares about his poor brother's children, so he should understand.'

'I doubt if he'll listen, but I suppose anything is worth a try...'

'It will do you good as well,' Clare said, 'working with the children will help to take your mind off him, and you'll feel better knowing that you're doing something good.'

Gaye gave a weak smile. 'I do need to get off my backside and start doing something useful, and singing always makes me feel better. When I was in the choir at school, I always came home cheery and happy after it.'

'Mrs Atherton kept going on about your lovely voice,' Clare said. 'She was very grateful to me and Diana, but the way she talked about you, I think you were her favourite.'

'I feel really guilty about not making her funeral today, and all because I had to see bloody Laurence to try and sort things out.'

'I didn't mention her to make you feel guilty,' Clare said. 'It's not as if we knew her really well. I was just reminding you how much she had praised your lovely voice.'

'She was a lovely lady, the kind you never forget.'

'She came through a lot during the last war – widowed with

young children. She said the women from the church helped her get through it all. I think that's why she was so anxious to help others in the same boat now.'

A determined look came on Gaye's face. 'Well, I'm going to do what she suggested, and help the evacuees. And Laurence can like it or lump it when I tell him I'm not going to have any free time, and I'm going to stop feeling sorry for myself and do things that are right.'

Clare stood up. 'We need to go and see Sister Townsend and ask her if she'll sort out the duty roster, so we can work with the families at the weekend and a couple of evenings during the week.' She reached her hand out to Gaye and pulled her to her feet. 'You'll get through all this; I'll make sure you do.'

Gaye threw her arms around her friend. 'I feel a bit better already. I wish I'd told you all this sooner. I don't deserve to have such a good friend.'

'I'm sure there will be times when I'm going to need you,' Clare said, smiling. 'As Mrs Atherton said, us Nightingales have to stick together.'

Chapter Thirteen

Diana watched as her aunt paced anxiously back and forth over the drawing room floor, her hand twisting her long strands of pearls. 'I'm too old to have a child living here,' she said. 'My nerves can't take it.' She waved a hand around the room, taking in all the delicate pieces, ornate lamps and crystal candlesticks. 'It's not really a house for children, and I wouldn't know what to do with them.'

'I'll help you,' Diana said, 'and you have Mrs Brown cooking and doing the laundry. We'll pick a child of school age, so they will be out all day.'

'There must be something else I can do to help,' her aunt continued.

'I think you will have to offer to take at least one of the Guernsey children. You're on the committee, and all the other members of the church and the Women's Institute are helping out. Some are taking mothers with young babies and two or three children. It will look very bad if you are asking all the others to take the evacuees in, but don't actually do it yourself.'

'Under no circumstances could I have a baby in this house,' Rosamund replied strongly. 'The crying would drive me over the edge. I couldn't tolerate it.' She shrugged. 'And what could I talk to a young mother about? Especially if they have a very different background, if they weren't used to talking as we do, if they didn't have the same social skills.' She closed her eyes. 'No, no – it's completely unthinkable.'

'You can't talk like that, Aunt Rosamund,' Diana said, her

voice patient. 'There's a war going on and everyone has to pitch in and help each other. And the Church would say that Jesus didn't turn people away because of their backgrounds.' She smiled. 'In fact, he came from a working background himself, and wasn't St Joseph a carpenter?'

Rosamund sank down on to one of the armchairs. 'What about the schoolteachers?' she asked. 'Couldn't we take one of them instead? I know they come from all sorts of backgrounds too, but at least we would at least know they were educated.'

Diana stifled a sigh. She knew there was no point in arguing with her aunt about the class system. Her old-fashioned attitude was the same as her parents'. The only ordinary, working-class people they encountered were their servants, or people in shops. They had no idea that the world was changing and that there was an intellectual movement towards people being viewed as equals. The previous war, Diana believed, had brought people from all classes together in a way that had not been seen before. And in the last few years, a significant group of educated young men had followed their principles by joining the Spanish Civil War in the fight against fascism. Living in London had opened her eyes and her mind to a very different world that was emerging compared to the one she had been brought up in. An awareness of this new world just hadn't reached her family yet.

The only chance she had of getting her aunt Rosamund to do something solid was to get her down to the town hall this morning, where she would actually see how much help the Guernsey families needed. Clare and Gaye would already be down there, working alongside the other volunteers, as the staff had done their best to adjust the rosters to accommodate them.

Diana looked at her aunt now, anxiously twisting her pearls, and decided to respond kindly – it wouldn't help to have her aunt all frazzled. 'Taking in one of the Guernsey teachers would help, I'm sure, as we're central for quite a few of the local schools. I know that the first groups were all allocated last night, and a new group were due early this morning.' She looked at her watch. 'I think we need to go down to the town hall straight after breakfast.'

An hour later Diana and a very wary Rosamund arrived in the packed hall to find crowds of children with name tags hung around their necks still waiting to be allocated to a family. Some had already been assigned to church groups who would provide them with temporary accommodation in church halls. There, beds and cooking facilities had been hurriedly set up, until families or single or elderly people who had room were willing to take them in.

Diana was delighted when she saw Clare sitting at a table with some of the ladies from the church she attended. Waving cheerfully at Diana, Clare got up and went over to speak to them. While Rosamund was talking to some of the ladies of the WI, Clare quietly explained that, before she had a chance to talk to the vicar, she had been commandeered by the Catholic Women's Association.

'A few of them recognised me from going to Mass on Sundays,' she explained, 'and they came rushing over to ask me to join them. I suppose it doesn't matter which group I'm involved with, as long as the families get the help that they need from someone.'

'Of course, and it's good to see the churches all pitching in and working together.' She glanced around. 'Is Gaye here?'

'Yes,' Clare said, smiling.

'Oh, that's great. She has been so busy lately, I wasn't sure if she would make it today.'

'Our ward sister organised for Gaye and I to get most Saturdays and Sundays off. It means we will have to do more night shifts, but we don't mind.'

Diana's face lit up. 'Oh, I'm delighted; it's great to have you both here.'

'Gaye went out with some of the other women to collect another tea urn for the kitchen, as one wasn't enough.' She gestured back towards the table she was working on. 'We've been making lists of the mothers who have travelled over with their own children, and checking them against the lists of local people who have offered to take families. It's a case of trying to match the right families with those who have enough space to keep them all together.'

'Oh, that's so important,' Diana said, 'especially the younger ones: they need to be with their mothers.'

'I pity the poor little souls that are only six or seven that have come on their own. It's probably the first time they have ever been away from home. Some are lucky to have older brothers and sisters, who are doing their best to look after them.'

'I hated going away from home to boarding school,' Diana said, suddenly remembering the fear she'd felt to be all alone, 'and this must be a hundred times worse.'

'Hopefully, the people they go to live with will be kind to them,' Clare said. 'They might even enjoy it, and even if it's not perfect, at least they will be safe.'

Diana bit her lip. 'I'm afraid I've had a bit of a hoo-ha at home with Aunt Rosamund. She's not confident about taking in children. She's just not used to them. She was married briefly during the last war, but her husband was killed soon afterwards, and they never had any children.'

'Oh, that's sad,' Clare said. She hadn't imagined Diana's hypochondriac aunt had a husband long dead.

'She's worried about having noisy children running around, but she said she might take in one of the teachers.'

'She might be too late,' Clare said. 'I think the ones that have arrived so far have all been allocated places.'

'Oh dear…' Diana glanced over to the group where her aunt was, and she could see Rosamund moving in their direction. 'She's coming over now, so I'll see if I can coax her into having at least one of the children.'

'I'll go and check the children on the list,' Clare said, 'and I'll see if there are any that might suit your aunt.'

When her aunt came back, Diana explained the situation regarding the teachers.

'Yes, I had heard that,' Rosamund said, giving a weary sigh.

'After listening to the other ladies about the terrible traumas some of the families have had on the boat journey, I can see that we will have to help out with the children.' She looked at her niece. 'I will be relying on you and Mrs Brown to help out. I just don't have the constitution for children.'

Diana was delighted with the breakthrough. 'We will have to pick someone now,' she said quietly. 'The longer we take, the less choice we will have.'

'I don't want boys. They're much too noisy and dirty.'

'We can easily make sure that they wash and teach them to be quieter . . .' She paused as she noticed a tall, thin girl of around eleven or twelve standing in a corner on her own. She was dressed in a drab, dark raincoat that looked as though it had been discarded by an adult. Diana could see the girl's eyes watching everything that went on, but every time anyone looked in her direction, the girl seemed to shrink further back into the corner. Diana wondered if she was waiting for someone, but as time went on, she realised that the girl was totally alone. Something about her made Diana curious, and she moved backwards a little where she could view her better. Once you got past the neglected appearance – the dull, straggly hair, the dirty looking boots and the awful coat – she realised that the girl was actually quite pretty.

She turned to her aunt. 'Have you seen anyone suitable yet?'

'I'm just worried about the germs these children might be carrying.' Rosamund took her hanky out of her pocket and dabbed her nose. 'I'm not being uncharitable, but I have to consider my health. I'd be no use to anyone if I died.'

Diana fought the desire to roll her eyes, when Clare suddenly appeared in front of them with two red-headed boys who looked to be around eight and six. One had angry-looking red spots around his mouth, and the other had a streaming nose. She asked the boys to stand to the side so they couldn't hear what was being said.

'I have two lovely brothers here,' she said quietly, 'and we need a house big enough to keep them together. We have notes from their teacher from Guernsey who said they are very well behaved.'

Rosamund's hanky instinctively came back up to cover her nose and mouth.

Diana noticed the gesture. 'We're not too sure about boys...' She looked over at her aunt and lifted her eyebrows meaningfully. 'It wouldn't work.' She gestured over to the corner. 'Do you know anything about that girl?'

'No,' Clare said. 'She wasn't one of the children I registered, but I will find out, and be back as quickly as I can.' She turned back to the boys and gave them a big smile, then she took them by the hand and disappeared off into the crowd.

Diana looked at her aunt. 'What do you think of the girl over in the corner behind you?'

Rosamund glanced over. 'Oh dear...'

'Would you prefer the boys Clare brought over?'

'Of course not,' her aunt said. 'I'm just concerned that the girl will feel like a fish out of water with us. Surely there must be someone more suitable, from a similar background to us?'

'Most of the children went to homes last night,' Diana said. 'I did warn you that this might happen – that if you didn't come down sooner that you wouldn't have a choice.' She paused. 'I think we should give the poor girl a chance. It might be very good for her, and it might be good for us. Compared to most people we are very privileged.'

'*Very privileged?*' Rosamund gasped. 'But you know that I live on a very small income. I can hardly afford to heat the house, and we have slates missing from the roof that could end up costing me a fortune.'

'Compared to other people, our problems are very small. We really are lucky.' She glanced again at the girl. 'She's almost my height, and I have some things that might fit her. If we sort her hair and tidy her up...'

Rosamund shook her head. 'This wretched, wretched war has turned all our lives upside down.'

'I agree,' Diana said, her voice patient. 'But it is much worse for the families who have had to leave their homes in Guernsey.' She saw Clare coming towards them now with a well-dressed little girl of around four years old with blonde curly hair. Then she turned to look back at the older bedraggled girl, and as she did so, their eyes met, and something told her that the girl was terrified. 'Shall we agree on the older girl?'

'I can't think straight,' Rosamund said, searching for her hanky.

Clare came to stand in front of them. Diana ruffled the little girl's hair and smiled at her, and the little girl giggled. 'We're waiting on Pamela's mother,' Clare explained. 'She has gone with one of the ladies from the church to look at a house in Edgeley that might suit the family. She took the baby with her, and asked me to look after Pamela until she comes back.' She leaned closer to Diana now, and said in a low, discreet voice. 'The older girl's name is Stella O'Keefe, and it would be great if we could find her somewhere to stay, because she slept on the floor last night after travelling all the night before on the train. She hasn't had a proper sleep since she left home.'

'The poor girl,' Rosamund muttered.

'It seems she got separated from her brother Gilbert before they got on the boat at Guernsey,' Clare explained, 'and she doesn't even know if he got away from there or not. It has happened to quite a few families. He could have been taken to Glasgow or somewhere like that; it's impossible to know.' She looked from Diana to Rosamund. 'What do you think? Could you help her out?' There was a silence. 'For even one night? We can work it out tomorrow.'

Rosamund's hand came up to her throat. 'What if her brother turns up?' she asked, her voice high with anxiety. 'I could not cope with boys...'

Diana placed a comforting hand on her aunt's shoulder. 'If we take it one day at a time.' She turned to Clare. 'Shall we have a word with Stella and see if she would like to come with us? It is up to her.'

Rosamund's eyebrows shot up in amazement, as the thought had not occurred to her that anyone might find her unsuitable.

A few minutes later Diana returned to her aunt with the girl following behind and introduced them. 'Stella would be very happy to come with us, and she has told me that she loves reading, knitting and sewing.'

Rosamund viewed the thin girl and her straggly hair, and somehow managed the vestiges of a smile. She held her hand out. 'How do you do, Stella?'

Stella suddenly went as still as a statue, and tears rushed into her eyes. Diana looked anxiously at Clare. Then, Stella slowly put her hand out and shook Rosamund's. 'Thank you,' she said, in an accent tinged with French, 'and how do you do too... madame?'

Rosamund looked flustered with the response. 'Well,' she said, 'let us all get back to the house and help to get you settled in.' She looked over at Diana with anxious eyes. 'You can walk with Stella and explain to her how we do things at home.'

'Of course,' Diana replied sweetly, smiling from ear to ear. 'We will get Mrs Brown to organise some food for Stella while she has a nice bath and gets changed into fresh clothes.'

Stella nodded, then caught her lip between her teeth and looked as though she might cry again.

Diana put her arm around the girl. 'I have a nice blue blouse and floral skirt that I think will fit you perfectly, and I might also have a pair of sandals that are a little tight for me. After we get you fed and dressed, we will come back down to the hall again, and see what else we can do to help.'

'We will all do our best,' Rosamund said stoically, 'and we will review the situation tomorrow.'

Chapter Fourteen

Gaye walked up the steps of the town hall carrying a heavy cardboard box filled with white cups, saucers, side plates and dinner plates. She swung her hip against the door and pushed it wide open, and held it until the two older women from the Women's Institute came slowly up carrying a big silver urn between them.

'Oh, thank you, my dear,' one of the women said. 'You have been such a help to us this morning.'

'And as strong as any man would have been,' the other said, smiling in gratitude.

When they were inside, Gaye moved to allow the door to close behind her, and then she went into the busy hall. After a fitful night's sleep worrying about Laurence, she had been grateful to get up and grab a quick cup of tea and toast in the canteen before rushing down to the town hall with Clare. Her friend had been right: so far they had been much too busy for her to think of Laurence, and consequently the morning had flown by.

The situation with Laurence did not seem to her to be quite so critical as last night and, as Clare had said, he had not actually moved to Manchester yet. It might take him weeks before he found suitable digs. Clare had done everything she could to help take her mind off things, and had even rung Diana up last night to come and join them at the cinema. It had been a lovely night, and apart from a few minutes of sadness when they talked about Mrs Atherton, they had all laughed until they cried at a silly Laurel and Hardy film.

Walking home in the night air, all three chatted about the work they might do the following morning in the town hall. They had had no real idea what would be involved, but guessed that it would be organising the basic living needs of their Guernsey refugees to help them settle in the Stockport area.

As they discussed the ideas they each had, Gaye realised she had become easier being around Diana now, as Clare had done. She had got used to the funny posh things she said, and was less self-conscious about their class differences and her own Geordie accent. She now talked to Diana the way she talked to Clare and the other student nurses, although she was careful to avoid the odd swear word that she sometimes came out with. She found Diana to be a good listener, and interested in Gaye's ideas for musical sessions with the children.

There were times, however, when she could not stop her mind from flitting back to the situation with Laurence. Each time, her stomach lurched at the thought of what she had done. At one point she felt like pouring it all out again, but she held back as she thought that the well-bred Diana might be shocked when she heard her story.

As she headed to the kitchen carrying the heavy box of crockery aloft, she spotted Clare over at the table and diverted to have a quick word with her. Clare told her about Diana and her aunt taking Stella home with them, and then explained that the vicar had asked the girls to come into one of the side rooms around two o'clock, along with some other volunteers, to help work out a programme for the following day.

'I'll take this lot into the kitchen,' Gaye said, 'and then I'm going to help make tea and baps for the families.' She smiled. 'One of the butchers from Edgeley dropped in four trays of baps and cold meat scraps to use up for the kids. Wasn't that good of him?'

'Absolutely,' Clare said. 'I heard some of the women saying that a farmer's wife from outside the town dropped in a box of six dozen fresh eggs.' She paused. 'When you've finished in the kitchen, do you fancy going to the café on Greek Street? The women said to take a break any time we like, and it might be best to have it before the meeting with the vicar.'

'Good idea,' Gaye grinned. 'Looking at all that food will make me hungry, and it would look bad if I started eating the baps that's meant for the poor bairns.'

Just before one o'clock, Diana returned to the hall and found Gaye washing up in the kitchen.

'Where's the young girl you took back to your auntie's?' Gaye asked, wringing out a cloth to wipe down the work surfaces. 'Clare said you were bringing her back with you.'

'That was the plan,' Diana explained. 'She had her bath and got dressed and then I brought her down to have lunch. After she had eaten, the poor girl suddenly dropped her head on the table and fell fast asleep.' She shrugged. 'I woke her and then took her upstairs to her bedroom and gave her a nightdress. I went into the hall for about a minute to let her get changed in privacy, and when I looked back in she was fast asleep again.'

She did not add that her aunt had been quite alarmed when she told her that she was going back down to join the other volunteers, leaving Stella asleep in the house with only herself and Mrs Brown to manage her when she awoke.

'Ah, the poor bairn,' Gaye said, wiping the cloth around the tap and sink now. 'She must have been exhausted after all that travelling.'

'Exactly,' Diana said. 'Some of them had to stand on the boat over to England, and apparently the crossing was rough; lots of them were dreadfully seasick. I imagine she will sleep for most of the afternoon, if not longer.'

Gaye lifted a towel and dried her hands. 'Have you any plans now?'

Diana looked at her little gold watch. 'I was just going to check where I might be needed next...'

'Clare and me are going to the café on Greek Street for fish and chips. D'you fancy coming with us?'

Diana's face lit up. 'I'd love to.'

A short while later all three slid into seats at a table by the window. A young waitress, dressed in a white pinafore and a starched cap, came over to them with menus.

'Thanks, but we don't need them,' Gaye said. smiling at her. 'We all want fish and chips.'

'I'm sorry,' the girl said, 'but we've not had any fresh fish in this week.' She shrugged. 'It's something to do with the war and the fishermen not being allowed out to fish in certain areas.'

'No fish?' Gaye repeated, looking at the other two. 'An' I was really looking forward to it as well.'

The waitress handed over the menus and there was silence as the girls checked down the list.

'Oh, not bean pies and lentil rissoles again,' Clare said. She looked at the waitress. 'Do you have any meat and potato pies?'

The waitress made a little face. 'Not today, but we've Wooten pie, and the cook says it's in a nice thick onion gravy.'

'You mean steak and kidney pie without any steak and kidney?' Gaye laughed. 'All that's in it are carrots and potatoes instead of meat.'

'It's not great, is it?' the waitress agreed. 'But everything is so hard to get.'

'We eat enough carrots in the hospital canteen,' Clare said. 'They seem to put carrots in everything.'

Diana felt sorry for the waitress. 'Well, at least the carrots will help us to see in the dark,' she said, smiling.

The waitress shrugged again. 'It's terrible, having no fish and chips for people. It's all they seem to ask for.'

'What about sausage rolls and chips?' Clare suggested.

'We have them, and we have ordinary sausages as well,' the waitress said.

Eventually, after another minute's debate, the girls decided to have sausage roll, chips and baked beans along with a pot of tea.

They were sipping their tea when another student nurse walked past the café. She glanced at the window and seeing the girls, she waved to them and then turned around and came rushing inside. 'I'm glad I spotted you two,' she said, 'I have some news.'

They introduced Diana to Ann Cannon, then Gaye said, 'Go on then, tell us what the news is.'

Ann raised her eyebrows and smiled. 'Well, it's about Dr Cumiskay. Do you want the good or bad news first?' Dr Cumiskay was a young, fresh-faced man with a dark moustache, who both girls had worked with on the geriatric ward.

Clare looked over at Gaye. 'The bad,' she said. 'Might as well get that over.'

'He's leaving in the morning,' Ann informed them. 'He's been called down to London to work in one of the hospitals with the wounded soldiers.'

'Oh no!' Gaye said, flopping back in her chair. 'That's bloody awful news. He's one of the doctors who is nice to the nurses, and treats you like a real person.'

'I don't know how there can be any good news about him leaving,' Clare agreed.

'There's a farewell party being organised for him in the hospital social club tonight, and everyone is invited,' Ann told them. 'You two are off this weekend, aren't you? You haven't anything else planned?'

'No,' Gaye said, perking up. 'We've got today and tomorrow off to help out with the kids arriving from Guernsey, so we're free tonight.'

'Well,' Ann said, raising her eyebrows, and giving Gaye a knowing smile. 'I thought you might be particularly interested to know that Dr Harvey is helping to organise the party, because they're good friends. He actually asked me to invite all the student nurses who weren't working to come, and, he asked for you especially by name.'

'Did he really?' Gaye asked. 'You're not having me on, are you?'

'Honestly, he caught me in the canteen and said don't forget to ask that Geordie girl with the red hair, because she's always good for livening things up.'

Gaye went to say something funny, but a picture of Laurence flew into her mind, rendering her silent and dampening down any high spirits she had temporarily felt. The awful situation she was in was now over-shadowing everything.

'We'll definitely come,' Clare said, delighted. 'We can't let Dr Cumiskay go off out to the war without giving him a good send-off.'

Ann looked over at Diana. 'You're very welcome to come too.'

Diana shook her head. 'I don't work at the hospital, so I wouldn't be eligible to go to the staff social club.'

'When it's something like this, we're allowed to bring friends.' Ann grinned at everyone. 'The more the merrier, isn't that right?'

'Absolutely,' Clare said, 'You will really enjoy it, Diana. There will be a band and dancing.'

Ann looked at Gaye again, her eyes laughing. 'Don't forget, Dr Harvey will be expecting to see you there.' They chatted for a few more minutes, then she hurried off to see if she could find more of the girls to let them know about the party.

'It sounds as though you have an admirer, Gaye,' Diana said.

'I don't know about that,' Gaye turned and looked out of the window. 'Dr Harvey has probably said that about half a dozen of the nurses, so I won't be letting it go to my head.'

Clare looked over at Gaye, noticing her flat demeanour, and guessed what was on her mind. 'Well, he didn't ask for me anyway,' she said light-heartedly, 'and I was only working with him the other day.'

Before anything further could be said, the young waitress appeared with three hot plates on a tray, and they all turned their attention to the sausage rolls and chips.

Afterwards, they ordered another cup of tea.

'I wonder how Aunt Rosamund is coping with Stella.' Diana gave a little sigh. 'Luckily we don't live too far away. I told her if there was any problem, for them both to catch the bus down to the town hall and we would do whatever we could to sort it out.'

'I'm sure they will be grand,' Clare said. 'Stella seemed a nice quiet girl.' She paused, picking her words carefully. 'From what I saw of her, she didn't seem to arrive with many belongings.'

Diana nodded. 'She had very little with her in the way of clothes and necessities, and what she had was in poor condition. But they left in such a rush, the families didn't have time to organise things. She looked a very different girl when she had bathed and washed her hair and was dressed in decent clothes.'

'It does make a difference,' Clare agreed. 'I'm sure your aunt will get used to her.'

'I hope so,' Diana said, 'because she's become a bit of a recluse over the last number of years. My mother tells me she was totally different when she was younger, quite carefree and adventurous – and then something happened and she became very anxious and highly strung.'

'Did she change after her husband was killed in the last war?' Clare asked, sympathetically.

'No, it wasn't that,' Diana said. 'Although I'm sure she must have been affected by his death.' She leaned forward, her elbows on the table. 'It was actually losing the love of her life – another man who she met later – that affected her more. Well, according to my mother.'

Gaye and Clare leaned in towards her now, intrigued by the story.

'She met him after her husband died and the war was over,' Diana told them, leaning conspiratorially over the table. 'Apparently, she decided to get away from home and do some travelling. She toured all through Europe, and while she was in Spain – in Madrid – she met an Englishman who was working as a diplomat there and they fell in love.'

Clare joined her hands together. 'Oh, that sounds very romantic, like something out of a book.'

'It does,' Diana said, 'except that it turned out to be more of a mystery story than a romantic one.'

'Why? What happened?' Gaye asked.

'They got engaged, but apparently it was too complicated to get married out there so they set up home together, and she was under the impression that when his stint in Spain was finished, they would come back to England together and get married.'

Gaye's eyes were wide with astonishment. 'So, your aunt Rosamund and this man were living over the brush together? You know, living as man and wife?'

'Yes, I believe it wasn't uncommon during and after the war, with all the disruption.' Diana said, quite matter-of-factly 'Anyway, they seemed to be living very happily together, and one day he suddenly disappeared. Aunt Rosamund came home and the place they were staying in was completely empty – all his clothes and belongings cleared out. He had just upped and left without leaving a clue as to where he had gone.'

'Oh my God!' Gaye exclaimed, 'I don't believe it. What did she do next?'

'She spent weeks trying to find him, and then somehow she found out that he had gone back to London, and she tracked him down.'

'What happened when she found him?' Gaye asked.

'She discovered he had been living a complete lie, that he was a married man, although without any children. Poor Aunt Rosamund was devastated, as you can imagine. But the story gets even worse. When she confronted him, he told her that he was sorry for disappearing and having deceived her, but his wife was an invalid, and he explained that he couldn't leave or divorce her in case the shock killed her. He also assured her that he was totally in love with her.'

'What happened then?' Gaye was hanging on to every word. She had never heard anyone talking so openly about such things, as most families kept disgraceful things like that a secret. As she listened, it made her suddenly feel much better about her own situation with Laurence. If something like this could happen to upper-class people like Diana's aunt, then anyone could make a mistake, she realised.

'Aunt Rosamund said she understood. She was impressed by his loyalty to his sick wife, and she still was in love with him – I suppose "obsessed" is more the word – and she decided to move to London. She took a small flat nearby where she could see him every day, although his job took him back to Spain quite often, so a lot of the time she was left on her own.'

'She must have been head over heels in love with him to do all that,' Gaye said. 'So what happened? What made her come back to Stockport?'

'His wife suddenly died,' Diana told her, 'and that was when the worst thing happened.'

'Go on, tell us,' Gaye was positively riveted now.

'He disappeared again. He stopped calling to the flat, and when she went around to his house looking for him, the people next door told her the house was sold.' Diana's voice lowered. 'It seems he had met another woman back in Spain, and when his wife died, he went straight out there and married her.' She shrugged. 'So he had been deceiving her for years.'

Clare sat in complete silence as Diana related the story about her aunt, growing more and more shocked with what she was hearing. She was even more shocked by Diana's seemingly casual attitude to it all.

'Your poor auntie,' Gaye said. 'She must have been heart-broken.'

'She was. My mother said she had a nervous breakdown and was in a rehabilitation place down in London. Then she came back home, bought the house in Stockport and tried to rebuild her life again, but she has never looked at another man since. She just lives quietly on her own, and her main concern in life now is the church and the Women's Institute.' She gave a wry little smile. 'And worrying about her health, of course.'

'It's terrible the way a man can ruin a woman's life, isn't it?' Gaye mused.

There was a pause, then Clare said in a quiet voice, 'Well, my mother always says that if there were no bad women, there would be no bad men.'

The two girls looked at her with shocked faces.

'Aunt Rosamund is a bit odd,' Diana said in a hurt tone, 'but she is not a *bad* woman. Falling in love with someone does not make someone bad. If we have never been in the situation, we can't judge other people who have.'

There was an uncomfortable silence and a red, self-conscious flush spread over Clare's face and neck. 'I didn't really mean it towards your aunt, and I'm sorry if it came out like that.' She took a deep breath, trying desperately to pick the right words, while staying true to her Catholic principles. 'I know it might sound old-fashioned but I think that if women refuse to sleep with someone before they get married, then a lot of these situations wouldn't happen.' She held her hands out. 'When you hear stories like your aunt's, you realise how going with men before you get married is very dangerous. You have to be very careful... and, well... make sure you pick the right sort of man.'

Diana nodded. 'Of course, there is sense in that, but people are not perfect and we all make mistakes. In this case, Aunt Rosamund was certainly deceived.'

Clare found it hard to believe that a woman who had gone to live with a man without being married should elicit any sympathy. She knew it was not her business, but since Diana seemed so cavalier about it, she felt she had to press home the point, describe the worst scenario. 'Can you imagine if she had had a baby and was left on her own?' she said. 'The poor little thing would have had to carry the stigma of being illegitimate.'

'Yes,' Diana said, her voice slightly higher than normal, 'that could well have happened, but thankfully it didn't. I think Aunt Rosamund has paid a high enough price for what happened to her.' She then raised her eyebrows, thinking. 'Although maybe she would have been a different sort of person if she had had a baby, and had someone else to worry about apart from herself.'

Clare bit her lip; she could not imagine any scenario where it would be right to have a baby out of wedlock.

'Well, I feel sorry for her,' Gaye said. 'She's a very nice lady, and people can't help who they fall madly in love with.'

'And it was different times just after the last war,' Diana agreed, 'and she knew what it felt like to lose one man she loved.' She looked over at Clare. 'I wouldn't want to offend you in any way, but I think your religion is very strict and judgemental. I know when you have been brought up with those beliefs that it must be hard to understand people who live by their own choices.'

'No offence, Clare,' Gaye said, 'but Catholics are very strict. You won't know, Diana, but my father's family were Catholic and they disowned him for marrying a Protestant. They didn't come to see me and our Audrey until I was five years old.' She shrugged. 'The sad thing is, my Granny and Grandad Robinson are nice people and me and Audrey love them. Me granny has told me since that she wished she'd never fell out with my dad and wasted all those years, but she said it was because the local Catholic priest told her she had to cut him off.'

'That's very sad,' Diana said. 'We have a mix of religions in our family, and thankfully it doesn't seem to have caused any major problems.' She turned towards Clare. 'I think religion in Ireland is a bit different, and I hope you don't think our comments are in any way personal, because I really do respect your views.'

'And I respect them, too,' Gaye said, 'although I don't agree with a lot of it.'

Clare knew she should say something to finish on a good note with her friends, but she could not think of a single word to say. She felt a little pulse in the side of her head begin to throb as she tried to digest the details of the conversation. In a way, what both her friends had said made sense, but it went against everything that she had been brought up to believe.

She felt almost overwhelmed and could see that if she pushed her own religious views further – tried to explain that God had given the Ten Commandments to guide people into the right way to live – it would cause a rift with both her friends. Diana, she instinctively knew, was a kind and good person. The incident with Mrs Atherton had shown that on the very first night they met. The old lady herself had also been very kindly, showing all the traits of a person who tried to do good by others, and so had the vicar and all the other volunteers that she met. No one had questioned her religion, and no one had minded that she had moved to join her own Catholic group of volunteers.

Noticing how upset she seemed, Diana reached her hand out to cover Clare's. 'When I go to church, I like to think that Jesus is a friend to all of us, whatever our religion. And he lived his life being tolerant and kind to everyone.'

Clare nodded. Her friend did not need to say another word. She knew all the stories from the New Testament about Jesus helping others – even women like Mary Magdalene. She thought about Diana's aunt, and she knew that Jesus would have been much kinder to the poor woman than she had been this afternoon.

She looked Diana squarely in the face. 'I'm sorry about what I said about your aunt,' she said. 'You're right; it's not for me or others to judge.'

'Don't give it another thought,' Diana said, smiling at her. 'People are entitled to their opinion about religion and politics, and we learn from each other by sharing our views.'

Tears sprung into Clare's eyes. 'I feel I've not been very nice to either of you.'

Gaye threw an arm around her. 'Aw, don't let it upset you, pet! We're all friends and we're not going to fall out over what your Church has to say about anything.'

'Thanks,' Clare said, dabbing her eyes with a napkin.

Diana suddenly looked at her watch. 'Gosh, it's quarter to two. We better get moving to be back in time for the vicar's meeting.' She pushed her chair back. 'And I hope Aunt Rosamund is not down in the hall with Stella, waiting for me.'

As they walked back to the town hall, while Clare was still brooding and confused about their heated conversation, Gaye felt much happier and lighter in herself. She wasn't at all bothered about Clare's strict views. Since she first met her Irish friend, she knew she was an old-fashioned Catholic, and had very conservative opinions about morals and religion. But she also knew that Clare was a good friend and a kind and understanding nurse to all her patients – regardless of their religion.

Gaye thought it was funny how things turned out. She could never have imagined that the upper-class Diana would be far more open-minded about human failings than most other girls her age.

Chapter Fifteen

The vicar stood in front of the group of around twenty volunteers, who would be organising activities for the evacuees billeted in Stockport Town Hall. They were seated in a corner, away from the busy tables at the other side of the room, which were being set up by the women's groups as a reception area for the families. A steady stream of helpers were going in and out of the kitchen, bringing boxes of donated food and all sorts of dishes and cooking and serving utensils that would soon be needed.

Reverend Lomas explained that the Sunday School and the Masonic Guildhall were involved in similar planning, as were some of the other Stockport suburbs such as Hazel Grove, Disley and Cheadle.

'Of course, our main objective is still to find suitable accommodation for the families from Guernsey. We still have several hundred living and sleeping in places like this town hall. The WRVS are continuing to search for permanent accommodation, and are going from home to home in the borough canvassing to find suitable places. Notices have gone into the local newspapers explaining that there will be a billeting allowance for each mother and a separate allowance for the children.

'We have so far managed to house a small number of families and individual children, and are working on this from morning until night. The situation here is only temporary, and is not suitable for more than a week or two.' He joined his hands together as though in prayer. 'If anyone knows any local people who can take a child or a family into their homes, please send them to us immediately. These poor families, who have been evacuated from their own homes and all that is familiar to them, need to be taken to the bosom of our town. If things were the other way around, and families had to leave Stockport, wouldn't we all be grateful for any help or kindness offered by strangers?'

Diana crossed her fingers as she listened, hoping that her aunt would find the patience and the strength to cope with the young girl in her house. She felt so guilty knowing that they had the space to accommodate several families, if only Rosamund had been a different sort of person.

'We also have to find ways to occupy the time for the children and families, and also keep them in touch with the other Guernsey people, whether they are here in communal accommodation or living with families.' He looked around the group, catching the eye of all the volunteers. 'Saturday and Sundays are the most important days for people to be available,' he explained, 'as the older children will be busy in school during the week and the mothers will be at home or here in the hall to take care of the younger children. As you can imagine, it will be very difficult to contain and keep children under control unless we have activities organised for them. Not only will it keep them busy, but hopefully they will enjoy the various groups and it will take their minds off their dire situation here and whatever is happening to the families they left behind in Guernsey.'

A young man with a beard held up his hand. 'I often work weekends, but I would be happy to give up a few evenings during the week to do football or cricket. The younger lads might need something to keep them occupied during the long summer evenings.'

The vicar gave a thumbs up. 'Thank you, Lance,' he said. 'That's a good point. As we go along we can work out whether there is a need for organised events for the children during the week.'

'If I can get time off at the weekends,' Lance said, 'I'll be willing to help with any of the other groups that are going on. I'm happy to do anything at all.'

'Good man, Lance!' the vicar said, winking at him. 'That's entirely the spirit we need.' He turned back to the group. 'Regarding the weekends, I already have a list of suggestions, and I'm going to ask the people who volunteered to organise these to come forward.' He looked down at his notes. 'We have a suggestion for a children's singalong group or choir type of thing, and the young lady who has volunteered to take charge of this is one of our local nurses, Gaye Robinson.'

Gaye's cheeks flamed as her name was called, and she was further embarrassed when the vicar beckoned her to come up to stand at the front beside him. The next name called was a middle-aged man, Jack Fairclough, who played the piano and was happy to work along with Gaye. The next activity called was the art group, and Diana was soon standing alongside her friend, smiling and happy to be involved.

Two other women – Hattie Brown and Lilly Bracken – were called along with Clare O'Sullivan to help organise knitting and sewing.

Gaye was pleased to find that one of the large rooms had an old, but decent, upright piano. Jack Fairclough ran his hands over the keys and said it was in tune, and would suit him fine. Gaye discovered that the cheery-faced Jack had played in bands for years, and had also been brought into schools for Christmas and end-of-year concerts. He knew the words of all the old popular songs, and Gaye felt more confident having his professional experience.

Another room was designated for the knitting and crocheting groups. Local women had donated needles and balls of wool and old knitted jumpers, which could be unpicked and unravelled and the wool used again. Sewing, it was decided, was too complicated to organise, as there was a shortage of material and organising spare sewing machines would be very difficult.

'I would love to have done a little sewing with the girls,' Diana said, 'but any sewing machines are needed at home for mothers to make or alter all the family's clothes.' She shrugged. 'We can do hand-sewing and simple things like sewing on buttons or taking up hems or adding new cuffs to jumpers. It will be easy enough; any ideas we need are in that useful little government pamphlet—'

Before she could finish, Clare and Gaye both chanted, 'Make do and mend!'

Gaye started laughing. 'The way you said that, Diana – and especially with your posh voice – you sounded like one of them government adverts on the radio.'

Diana raised her dark eyebrows as a disapproving teacher might, and then she burst out laughing too. 'Thankfully I am thick-skinned,' she said, 'and don't worry, Gaye, I'm sure I'll find a way to get my own back on you two soon!'

As they all giggled together, Clare was pleased that Diana had shown herself to be a good sport, and she knew Gaye now felt comfortable with her too. If she was working any night now, she knew that Diana and Gaye would happily go off to the pictures together or out with a group of their nursing friends.

Clare was also relieved that her own little outburst in the café about religion had not been held against her. Both Gaye and Diana had been kind and respected her point of view. In a way, their kind attitude had begun to make her question the strict Catholic dogma. Although she had always found religion to be a comfort and a mainstay in her life, she already felt a small change in her views, and she could now see how Oliver had found himself questioning things that the family had always taken for granted, drawing his own conclusions.

Walking back to the main hall, the vicar and Lance were working out where Diana's art class might be held, and debating whether a room above the Nag's Head bar would be suitable.

'The publican has offered it to us, as it's rarely used,' the vicar explained. 'It's just a few steps from the town hall and, while it's a bit shabby, it has tiled floors that could be easily cleaned if paint was splattered.'

Diana smiled at the two men. 'I think the Nag's Head function room sounds perfect. If we were in one of the lovely rooms in the town hall, I would be worried about making a mess.'

They then discussed how they would sort the children into different age groups for the various activities, and let them choose which ones they were interested in. Two hours were allotted for each session so that the children would all get to three different activities in the day, with time in between for tea breaks and lunch.

'A bit like school,' Reverend Lomas said, 'only hopefully more relaxed and fun for the children.' He looked at the volunteers, his eyebrows raised. 'All we have to do now is sort out the equipment needed for the activities, then turn up tomorrow morning and start dividing up the groups.'

A door banged and everyone turned around to see Diana's aunt Rosamund stride in, a determined look on her face.'

Diana's heart sank. 'Oh, no,' she whispered to her friends. She craned her neck to see where the young evacuee girl was. There was no sign of her. 'Please don't tell me she has brought poor Stella back...'

Chapter Sixteen

Diana left the group and went to her aunt. 'Is everything all right?'

'It seems we have been misled about our young evacuee,' Rosamund said, her voice in a low, conspiratorial tone. 'The billeting officers did not give us the relevant details about her situation back in Guernsey.' Her hands moved in an exasperated gesture. 'The girl could have ended up with the wrong people entirely.'

Diana's brow furrowed in confusion. 'What do you mean? Where is she?'

Rosamund indicated an area where a group of Guernsey people were waiting to be checked in. 'She's over there, with some of the officials from Stockport Council.'

Diana's shoulders slumped and she asked in a low voice, 'Have you brought her back to rehomed again?'

Rosamund looked startled. 'No, not at all. The poor girl has been through enough. We've come back to find out some more information about her brother's whereabouts.'

Diana's eyes narrowed. 'So, will you be bringing her back to the house afterwards?'

'Well, someone has to ensure the girl is looked after...' Rosamund said, tilting her head imperiously. 'I was just about to have a late lunch when she woke this afternoon, so I invited her to join me. She was initially very quiet, but when she overcame her shyness, she explained her circumstances to me in some detail. The clothes she was wearing yesterday gave the completely wrong impression about the girl. It seems another child vomited over her own decent clothes on the boat journey across the channel, and they had to be thrown away.' She wrinkled her nose. 'Those awful drab clothes she was wearing were all that could be spared from another family when she arrived at Weymouth.'

Diana cut in. 'So are going to offer her a home?'

Rosamund raised her eyebrows, as though the question was ridiculous. 'Yes, for the time being...' She took a deep breath. 'After all, I am on the committee and we all have to do our bit for the war effort. Also, Stella is the nearest we will get to having our own sort with us.'

'What do you mean "our own sort"?'

'It seems her father is one of the main solicitors from the Guernsey Islands. She's a very clever girl; she can speak fluent French and Spanish. And she can also play the piano well. She played a few tunes this afternoon for me and Mrs Brown.' Rosamund lowered her voice. 'It wouldn't do for her to be billeted in one of those awful, cramped terraced houses in the less salubrious areas of Stockport. It would almost be as bad as putting a child from the lower end in with us.'

Diana made herself ignore her aunt's classist attitude. 'You said you were looking for information about Stella's brother?'

'Yes; naturally she is anxious about him. When she was taken away in Weymouth to be cleaned up and have a change of clothing, apparently he was shepherded onto a different train.' She shrugged. 'The boy could be anywhere. From what Stella tells me, he is quiet and studious, and was hoping to become a lawyer like his father.' She put her hand on Diana's shoulder. 'I want you to speak to the billeting ladies and see if they can find out anything about him. I think it would help Stella to settle in easier if she knew where he was. He's two years younger than her, and she naturally feels responsible for him.'

Half an hour later Diana, her aunt and a quiet, anxious Stella stood in a corner of the hall. 'No one knows anything about Gilbert O'Keefe,' Diana said. 'They have checked all the places in Scotland. They think he could still be travelling as there have been difficulties with the trains and coaches.' She placed a comforting hand on the young girl's shoulder. 'We will just have to wait a little longer, and then I am sure they will find him.'

'In the meantime,' her aunt said briskly, 'I have offered my services to help sort out boxes of toys that have been donated. I thought Stella might help me...'

Stella looked at her with sad eyes. 'Of course.'

'I have to go now to organise art materials,' Diana said, pleased to see that they were rubbing along well together. 'So I will see you back at the house this evening. I will be out tonight, as I've been invited to a hospital staff party.'

'That's unfortunate, since it is Stella's first day,' Aunt Rosamund said, a note of reproach in her voice.

'I only found out at lunchtime. It's for one of the doctors who has been called to service with wounded soldiers.'

Her aunt gave her a long look. 'I hope the nurses are not going to be a bad influence on you, Diana. You were at the cinema only last night, and now you're out again tonight,' she gave a little sigh. 'I do hope you're not going to turn into a social butterfly like your mother.'

Diana gave an incredulous smile. 'I don't think there is any fear of that,' she said. 'But neither do I wish to become a total hermit.'

Chapter Seventeen

Gaye stood back to look at the seam she had drawn up the back of Clare's leg with a dark eyebrow pencil. 'Perfect – even though I say it myself!'

'I can't believe that I've laddered my last pair of nylons,' Clare sighed. 'I've been so careful with them, but I caught my leg on a splinter in the chair and it tore a huge hole in them. They're not even worth darning.'

'You can join the rest of us now, pet,' Gaye sympathised. 'I ripped my last pair weeks ago. Lucky the weather is good enough for bare legs.'

'I'd still prefer proper stockings,' Clare groaned, as she twisted to check out the drawn-on seam.

Gaye laughed. 'You could always wear your thick black work stockings!'

'I'd look lovely if I turned up in those,' Clare said, rolling her eyes. 'I was depending on my mother sending some stockings over from Ireland, but so far nothing has arrived. I was hoping to give you a pair if she sent two.'

'Ah, that's good of you to think of me,' Gaye said, patting Clare's head. She went over to the wardrobe mirror to check her reflection, turning this way and that. 'I think we both look dead glamorous in our Co-op dresses and sandals. The red lipstick and mascara makes a big difference, doesn't it?'

Clare went to stand beside her, and looked at her reflection. Unlike Gaye, she never felt confident about how she looked, as she knew there was nothing very striking about her. Compared to Gaye and Diana she was just average.

'Your hair is lovely too,' Gaye said. 'That little wave at the front really suits you.'

'Do you think so?' Clare asked.

'Didn't I just say it? You look brilliant tonight.'

Clare suddenly realised that in spite of all her recent problems, Gaye was still being cheerful and upbeat, while she herself was moaning about stockings and looking for any little flaws. She smiled at her friend. 'Thanks for doing my hair and my legs. And you're right, the wave does look better. I don't know how you manage to do your own hair, it looks amazing.' Gaye's lovely thick red hair was styled in long silky waves, with one side falling over her eye in the style of Veronica Lake.

'I used to spend hours in my bedroom at home trying to copy film stars' hairdos.'

'You could have been a professional hairdresser. Did you ever consider it? Hairdressers always seem really glamorous to me.'

'Funnily enough, I worked as a Saturday girl in a hairdresser's one summer in Newcastle,' Gaye said. 'I loved it, but me mam knew somebody that got me a Saturday job in Fenwick's department store instead, in the glove department.'

'And did you like that?'

'Aye, it was a nice glamorous place to work, but I knew it was only temporary until I went into nursing. I made up my mind that's what I wanted to do when I was a little girl.'

'I was the same,' Clare said. 'I went to visit my granny when she was in Tullamore Hospital for an operation, and I thought all the nurses were wonderful. I liked their uniforms as well: the cloaks, the caps.' She rolled her eyes. 'I had no idea what I was letting myself in for with all the long hours, the bossy sisters and heavy lifting.'

Gaye laughed. 'Not to mention the odd pervert patient!'

'Oh, don't remind me ...' Clare shuddered.

Gaye looked thoughtful. 'I actually wanted to become a nurse after reading a story in school about Florence Nightingale. She was a real inspiration to me.'

'I've heard of her,' Clare said, 'but I don't know the details.'

'She was a great woman – very brave and determined. It was back during Victorian times and her ideas were ahead of everyone else. We must go down to the library some time and get a book about her.' Gaye glanced at her watch and then lifted her fan-shaped straw bag from Clare's bed. 'We better get moving or poor Diana will be standing like a lemon at the door of the social club, not knowing anyone.'

'She's very confident,' Clare said, lifting her light-blue summer coat. 'Nothing seems to faze her at all, does it?'

'She was great speaking up at our meeting with the vicar, and then she went across to the Nag's Head on her own to chat to the fella that owns it to sort out the room for her art classes.'

'I would have died going into a pub on my own,' Clare said.

'Her and her auntie Rosamund are a right pair, aren't they?' Gaye said. 'They just say outright what they're thinking. They make me nearly laugh at times. But I really like Diana. You know exactly where you are with her.'

Clare looked directly at her friend and smiled. 'How are you feeling now? Are you managing to put Laurence to the back of your mind?'

Gaye sighed. 'Well, let's just say I'm a lot better than I was last night, but it's all there on me conscience.'

'Has he been in touch today?'

'No, thank God. I'm just hoping he comes to his senses after what I told him in Manchester, and forgets about the whole thing.'

'Tonight,' Clare said firmly, 'you are going to enjoy yourself and forget all about him.'

Gaye put her arm through her friend's. 'To hell with Laurence – tonight we're going to dance the whole night away!'

Chapter Eighteen

The girls turned the corner of the street where the hospital social club was, then they both looked at each other.

'Where is she?' Gaye asked, as they slowed down to a more leisurely pace. 'And us rushing in our heels to get here at eight o'clock for her.'

Clare turned to look backwards, 'She's usually early.'

Gaye fanned her handbag in front of her face as they walked along. 'I'm boiling – I hope I'm not sweating too much. I had a long bath this evening because I want to smell all lovely when we're dancing with the doctors.'

'You're fine,' Clare said. 'All I can smell is your nice Shalimar perfume.'

'Thank God for that,' Gaye said.

They heard a voice and they turned around to see Diana hurrying towards them down the road, her jet-black bobbed hair bouncing as she moved along.

'Doesn't she look lovely all dressed up?' Clare whispered.

'Gorgeous.' Gaye gave a little giggle. 'Thank God she hasn't got bloody trousers on.'

Clare dug her with her elbow.

Diana was wearing a long black fitted dress with three-quarter-length sleeves and panels in silk and rayon, which emphasised her tiny, boyish figure. She wore art deco earrings in gold, red and green and a dramatic matching necklace, and instead of a coat she carried a black velvet wrap draped over her arm. Her green eyes were rimmed with kohl and mascara, and she had the deep red lipstick she always wore in the evenings. A square handbag embellished with black beads, and sensibly big enough for her gas mask, hung on her shoulder, finishing off the ensemble perfectly.

It struck Clare that Diana would create a stir in the hospital social club because she looked so different – so artistic. Diana, Clare decided, was the most distinctive person she had ever met.

'I am so sorry for being late,' Diana said, for once looking flustered. 'I hope you haven't been waiting long? I was actually ready over an hour ago, so rather than get here early I went upstairs to work on a sketch I had started, and quite forgot the time. I should have known better; the time always disappears when I'm drawing or painting.'

'We literally only arrived a minute or two before you.'

'Oh good!' Diana looked them up and down appraisingly. 'You both look absolutely lovely! Your beautiful floral dresses and your hair... Did you go to a hairdresser today?'

Clare told her about Gaye's hairdressing expertise.

'Oh, you're so talented,' Diana exclaimed. 'I'm useless at doing hair. Thank goodness my hair is poker-straight and that it works for me cut short – plain and simple.'

'Your hair and clothes always look fabulous,' Gaye said. 'That dress is gorgeous.' Clare nodded in agreement. 'And your make-up suits you perfectly too.'

'Well, thank you.' Diana looked down at herself now. 'I was so tempted to come in trousers, but my aunt said I would be the only girl there dressed like a man, so I thought it best to put a frock on.'

'More girls are wearing trousers these days,' Clare said. She could see Gaye trying to catch her eye to make her smile, and deliberately ignored her. All three started to walk towards the social club door.

'So, what were you drawing before you came out, like?' Gaye asked.

'Oh, just a little project I'm working on,' Diana told her. 'I suppose you would say it's a collage of sorts. It's about gas masks. Different sizes, and layered over each other.'

'*Gas masks?*' Gaye repeated in a high voice. 'What are you drawin' bloomin' gas masks for? It's bad enough we have to carry the flamin' things without making them into pictures.'

'Gaye!' Clare hissed. 'She can draw whatever she wants.' She looked at Diana. 'Pay no heed to her. Artists work on all sorts of things, don't you?'

'We do,' Diana said, not in the least offended. 'It's expressing your own individual idea, just like music and literature or even fashion. It's about finding new ways to look at things.'

'I don't mean to be funny, like,' Gaye said, 'but bloody gas masks.' She made a face. 'Who on earth wants to hang a picture of something as ugly as a gas mask on your wall? Especially now we have a war on. We need something to cheer us up, like...' she paused to think '...a picture of a nice garden or maybes a vase of flowers or something like that.'

'I can perfectly understand that,' Diana said.

Gaye looked at Clare. 'What kind of pictures do you like?'

Clare felt pinned to the spot. 'I have to be honest, I think I would prefer something a little cheerier too. I don't think I could hang a painting of a gas mask on my wall either.'

'Well, it's not really meant to be decorative,' Diana said. 'It's a sort of document or statement about how people are living now. It's to make people stop and think. Tomorrow I might do a sketch of people standing in ration queues or of the air-raid shelter.'

'Why don't you go out to Lyme Park or up to Bramhall Hall or someplace nice like that?' Gaye suggested.

'There's a nice park at Cale Green, that's even closer,' Clare said. 'They have lovely flower beds and plants in fancy tubs.'

Diana was now smiling politely at the girls' suggestions. 'That might be a good idea,' she said. 'When I have some spare time I might take a trip out to one of those places.'

'There now!' Gaye said, nodding and smiling at Clare. 'You can ask us anytime you need some good suggestions.'

As they got nearer towards the club entrance, Diana's face lit up. 'The band are already on!' she said, glad to change the subject. They could all hear the lively, popular tune, 'We're Going to Hang out the Washing on the Siegfried Line'.

As Clare moved towards the door, Gaye tapped her shoulder and said, 'Don't forget to walk in all slow and casual, and we'll keep chatting to each other, as though we're not bothered what fellas are there.'

'Gaye,' Diana said, putting her hand to her mouth to stop laughing. 'You are an absolute hoot!'

'You're a hoot yourself,' Gaye laughed. 'You and your bloody gas masks!'

When they got inside, they stopped at the cloakroom to drop off their coats and Diana's wrap, and then they moved towards the hall, which was already pretty full. With the dim lights and the haze of smoke, the girls had to keep close together so as not to be separated, while keeping their eyes peeled for a table with three free chairs. Clare heard someone calling her and when she turned, she saw Ann Cannon beckoning them over to a table at the side of the dance floor. Clare steered the others through the groups of people over in Ann's direction.

Clare introduced Diana to the other nursing students, although it was hard to hear over the noise of the band and the talk and laughter which filled the hall. The waitress came around and a short while later all three were seated with glasses of gin and tonic with a wedge of lemon. As they chatted, the girls glanced around the room at the people standing chatting in groups, and the ones who were brave enough to get up first on the dance floor.

Clare and Gaye nudged each other, and indicated to the other student nurses when certain people such as ward sisters or consultants from the hospital came in. Even on a social night out, they always had to be on their guard – and look as if they were on their best behaviour. Thankfully, the more senior staff usually left early before any of the late-night revelling had begun.

'No sign of Dr Harvey yet?' Clare mouthed to Gaye at one point.

Gaye was lighting a cigarette, which she occasionally did on social occasions as she thought it looked sophisticated. She shook her red waves and then took a drag on her cigarette. They were halfway down their drinks, and feeling much more relaxed, when the band struck up Glenn Miller's 'In the Mood'. With whoops of delight, all the girls at the table got to their feet and headed onto the floor to join the crowd already dancing. Clare partnered up with Diana, while Gaye and Ann Cannon stepped out together.

Within a minute, Clare felt her shoulder being tapped, and when she turned around she was looking into the beaming face of Robert, one of the hospital porters she was friendly with. He was a lovely lad, and very popular with the patients as he was always cracking jokes with them, and nothing was ever too much trouble. He also had the knack of being able to remember everyone's name. His friend Adam, who worked as a gate lodge porter, stepped up and asked Diana to dance.

The girls stayed up with the porters for two dances, and when they returned to their seats they were laughing and breathless. The boys had been quite lively, leading them around at such speed. They had passed Gaye several times. She was dancing with one of the men from the accounts office, who she had previously turned down for a date, saying she found him boring. She gave Clare a knowing wink as she circled past them, her red hair swirling around.

'Oh, that was fun!' Diana said as she settled back into her chair. 'I haven't danced for months and I really enjoyed it.'

'Robert is a great dancer, and he said they'll be back later for another dance from us.'

'Well, if no one else asks us, I've had a lovely night already,' Diana said, taking a sip from her gin and tonic.

Gaye and the others came back, giggling and chatting about who they had danced with. The hall had become much more crowded now, and people were milling around and leaning over chairs to talk to the girls. Dr Cumiskay, distinctive with his dark moustache and spotted bow tie, made his way around all the tables, thanking everyone for coming to his farewell party, and asking how they had all managed to keep it such a secret.

After he left their table, Clare watched him go through the same routine with the next group he encountered. She wondered how he felt about going down to London to work with the soldiers, sailors and pilots who had been badly wounded during the recent evacuation of Dunkirk. She had heard many of them who had no visible wounds were suffering from shell shock, and her heart went out to them too. The nurses had been shown films of those traumatised in this way, and she thought it was every bit as bad as being physically hurt.

She wished she was finished her training, and hoped she would get the opportunity to work in a hospital to help the poor men who had been through so much to protect the people back home.

The band struck up 'On The Sunny Side of the Street', and the girls all got to their feet again. Before they reached the floor, Clare could see John Neil – one of the junior doctors with whom she'd been on the same ward on several occasions – making a beeline in their direction. She caught her breath. He was dark-haired, very handsome and quite upper class, and way out of her league. She moved towards the floor, her gaze straight ahead, planning to look surprised when he tapped her on the shoulder. A few moments later, she was glad she had not made a move towards him when he stopped in front of Diana and asked her to dance instead.

Clare watched them walk onto the floor and then move naturally into each other's arms and start waltzing around as though they had been partners for ever. As she partnered up to dance with Ann Cannon, she glimpsed them again, and could see Dr Neil's bent head as he listened intently to whatever Diana was saying. She smiled at her earlier foolishness. Of course he liked Diana, she thought, they had a lot in common. They were both from similar backgrounds and he had been to university in London as well.

Ann Cannon suddenly leaned in closer to Clare. 'Did you see Gaye's face when Dr Harvey came over to the table just there?' she asked. 'He came from behind and tapped her on the shoulder and she got the shock of her life. We heard he had been called away to an emergency on the geriatric ward, and we thought he wasn't going to make the dance at all.'

Clare looked around her. 'Are they on the floor now?'

'Yes,' Ann said, 'over there.' She gestured with her head. 'Don't let them catch us looking. They seem to getting on great; they've never stopped talking. I'd say Gaye will be over the moon!'

'She will,' Clare said, beaming. She caught a glimpse of the couple as they came closer, and could see they were still laughing and chatting as they circled around the floor. Gaye's gleaming auburn waves stood out among the other dancers, and her face looked absolutely radiant as Dr Harvey whirled her around the floor. While she felt relieved to see Gaye looking much happier than she had recently, Clare had a niggling doubt about her getting involved with another man who had a girlfriend. She hoped it was just a harmless flirtation and that nothing more serious would come of it. Gaye was one of the best people she knew, but Clare wondered if she had any common sense when it came to men.

'Oh, look!' Ann suddenly said. 'They're bringing the sandwiches and other trays of food out. They've already set up tea urns on the trestle tables, so it should be open for us soon.' As the music got louder, Ann moved closer to speak in Clare's ear: 'Nelly McCann said that she heard the social club caterers have managed to do sausage rolls and vol-au-vents as well, so it sounds like a good do!'

When the band finished the tune they were playing, they announced that they would be taking a break to allow people time to enjoy their tea and food. The girls rushed to join the queue and then came back to the table in twos and threes with their plates, in time for the waitresses to walk around with trays of tea. Clare, Ann and the other girls sat chatting, praising the band and the great range of music they were playing, and the lovely spread that had been organised for Dr Cumiskay's leaving do.

When Gaye arrived back at the table, Clare turned to ask her how she had got on with the handsome Dr Harvey, but suddenly noticed that he was standing behind her carrying their plates.

Gaye gave a beaming smile to the group of nurses and then shrugged. 'Ah, there's no room here for two of us,' she said. She batted her eyes in a funny, theatrical manner and then gave a little wave. 'There's some free seats over at the table where Andrew was sitting before, so I'll see you all later.'

When she was out of earshot, all the student nurses went into a frenzy of gossip about Gaye and the gorgeous doctor. Clare didn't get involved in the chat, and just laughed off any comments about how mad about each other the two of them seemed.

'I can't believe how starry-eyed Dr Harvey seems to be about Gaye,' Nelly McCann said, shaking her head. 'I know everybody thinks he looks like a film star, but he is actually quite a serious man, especially when it comes to work. Dr Cumiskay and Dr Anderson are a lot more outgoing than he is.'

'Sometimes the quiet ones surprise you,' one of the other nurses said knowledgeably.

Clare noticed there was a little silence and she wondered if they knew that Andrew Harvey had a girlfriend back home.

Ann leaned forward and said to Clare, 'Has Diana moved to a different table too?'

'I don't know,' Clare replied, with a bemused look on her face. 'I was just wondering about that myself.'

'The last I saw of her she was on the dance floor with Dr Neil, so she's probably gone back to sit beside him. Her and Gaye are lucky devils, having men running after them while we're all left sitting like blooming wallflowers.'

Clare laughed. 'Surely we're not that bad, are we?'

'Well, we're not exactly being rushed off our feet so far, are we?' Ann said, then suddenly grinned. 'Although the night is still young!'

'Ah, good for the two girls copping off already!' Nelly said. 'You have to enjoy life while you can, especially with this flaming war going on. None of us know what tomorrow might bring with that madman Hitler.'

One of the other nurses from Yorkshire joined in. 'If they start bombing places like London and Manchester, we'll have hardly any men left in this country at all. If one of those dishy doctors was interested in me, I wouldn't be wastin' any time or worrying about what people thought. Life's too short for that.'

Clare was just mulling over what the other girls had said, when Diana appeared at her side.

'Great!' Diana said, beaming at her, 'I thought my chair might have gone.' She placed a plate with two of the little sandwiches and a vol-au-vent down on the table.

'We thought you had disappeared off into the night with Dr Neil,' Nelly said, smiling gaily at her.

'I had a couple of dances with him, and then we chatted while we were queuing for something to eat, but he's gone back to join his medical friends.'

When no one else was listening, Clare asked quietly. 'Did you enjoy dancing with John Neil?'

'Yes, he's a lovely chap, but I think I talked too much about political issues and he became a bit bored,' Diana shrugged. 'I'm used to that happening. A lot of men are surprised when women have opinions on serious matters.'

'I thought you two would get on really well because you seem to have a lot in common. He went to university in London too.'

'We did have quite a bit in common, and he is a lovely man.' Diana gave another little shrug. 'But I didn't feel any real spark between us and, for me, that would come before anything else. I can't imagine being with someone day after day unless you have that real closeness.'

Clare lifted her teacup, trying to hide her surprise at Diana's statement. She had always been of the opinion that upper-class people didn't consider love to be that important when it came to marriage. The most important factor was finding someone of a similar background who had land and money in order to keep up their standard of living.

Diana finished off her sandwiches then sat back in her chair, looking around her. 'Everyone seems to be really enjoying themselves,' she said, smiling at Clare. 'Oh, and I saw Gaye on the floor with a very dishy young doctor earlier on.'

'Andrew Harvey,' Clare told her. 'All the girls are mad about him, but he seems keen on Gaye. She's over sitting at his table now.'

'They certainly make a very handsome couple, don't they?'

The waitresses came around collecting the plates and cups and saucers, and then the band returned to take their places on the stage again. Various young men came to the table to ask the girls to dance, and Clare noticed Gaye and Dr Harvey taking to the floor once again. She was just getting up to dance with Diana when one of the office clerks – an older Irishman called Tom O'Leary – came over to the table. He always talked to her when she was in the office since he discovered that Clare was from Tullamore, as he came from the nearby town of Mullingar.

He was a lovely, polite man and was renowned among all the staff as being a top-class dancer, even though he had a bit of a limp. Apparently, he had been shot in the leg during the Battle of the Somme in the previous war, but had recovered well, and the limp was hardly noticeable when he was dancing. He had been widowed in the last year, and the other girls had commented recently that he must be on the lookout for a new wife, as he was seen more often in the social club and in the dances around town.

He smiled at Clare, a slight uncertainty about him. 'Miss O'Sullivan, would you do me the honour?'

Clare smiled back at him. 'Thank you – that would be lovely.' He looked delighted, and moved towards the dance floor. She turned back at Diana and said quietly, 'You don't mind, do you?'

'Not at all,' Diana waved away her concerns.

Clare stayed up for three dances with him, and when he asked her for a fourth, she declined, saying, 'I don't want to leave my friend on her own any longer.'

He caught her hand, just before she could move away. 'I was wondering,' he said, 'if you would like to go to the Plaza one night next week?'

Clare froze. She had thought that he regarded her as a young, chatty girl who reminded him of his sisters or neighbours back home – but if he was asking her out on a date, that was obviously not the case. 'I'm not sure,' she said, easing her hand out of his grip. 'I'm working a lot of late shifts and we're helping out with the evacuees at the weekend...'

There was a silence and when she looked at him, she saw the disappointed look on his face and a feeling of guilt washed over her.

'Well, I'm sure I'll see you around,' he said, 'and we might arrange it for another night, when there's a good film on.' He smiled at her, but she could see the hurt and rejection in his eyes. For a moment she almost weakened. What harm could one date do? He was a good-looking, well-dressed professional man, and from all accounts was pretty well off with a nice house in Bramhall.

He might be almost as old as her father, but a difference in age was not regarded as a drawback in Ireland. In fact, her parents would be delighted if she brought someone like Tom O'Leary back home with her. Then she thought about what Diana had said about spending your life – day after day – with someone who you did not feel any romantic spark for. The thought filled her with fear.

She took a few steps back, then smiled apologetically. 'I must get back to my friends. I hope you enjoy the rest of the night.'

Chapter Nineteen

As she sat down at the table, breathless from dancing to 'Let's Fall in Love', Clare thought how odd it was that life could change from almost one minute to another. Before Tom O'Leary asked her to dance she had felt like a wallflower, and since then she had been asked up to dance five times in a row. Granted, one of the times had been with her porter friend, Robert, who had come around a second time as promised. The other times had been medical students or male nurses. All nice, respectable lads who had told her how lovely she looked, and they had chatted and laughed with her, and sang to the music as they danced.

More men seemed to be on the dance floor now or roaming about the hall chatting to the groups of girls. Drink, Clare thought, had made them braver as the night went on, and also made them more resilient to being refused. As they swirled around the floor, one of the junior doctors had also asked her out to the cinema, and again she had kindly and politely refused him. He was a nice young man, and she couldn't find anything at all wrong with him, but he was just not her type.

This time she didn't feel half as bad refusing him as she had done with Tom O'Leary, and he didn't seem quite so hurt with the refusal. She saw him later, up dancing with another nurse who seemed to be hanging onto his every word, which was confirmed when she saw them walking to the bar later, hand in hand.

Diana had been back and forth onto the dance floor as many times as Clare and the other girls. The band had just returned to the stage for their final round of the night when Clare saw Gaye heading over to their table with a stricken look on her face. Thankfully, none of the other girls had noticed, as they were all involved in a great discussion about one of the staff nurses, who had been led out of the hall in a drunken state.

'Are you all right?' Clare asked, wondering if Gaye had drunk too much as well.

Gaye shook her head, tears welling up in her eyes. 'The porter has just come over from the lodge to say that I've to phone home immediately.' She appeared quite sober, although her voice was wavery and she could hardly catch her breath. 'Both my mother and father have left messages for me, and they said I have to ring back whatever time I come in.' She closed her eyes and her hand came up to her throat. 'Laurence has left two messages as well.' She shook her head. 'It's Laurence, I know it is. He's gone out to the house and told Audrey and my parents what's been going on. Oh my God, Clare, I don't know what I'm going to do. I'm going to have to phone them, and I'm absolutely terrified. Our Audrey will be in a right state. They all will. They're never going to have anything to do with me again.'

Clare stood up and put her hand on Gaye's arm. 'Take a deep breath,' she said quietly, 'and we'll walk outside. The fresh air will do you good.'

Gaye looked at her watch, her hands trembling. 'My father told the porter that he would be at the phone box again at half past ten, waiting on me to ring. It's quarter past ten now, so I'd better go over to the residence now.' She shook her head. 'It's got to be something serious to phone at that time of night. They will have had to go out in the dark to the phone box at the end of our street, and neither of them would do that if it wasn't something bad. Maybe Audrey has gone mad and stabbed him or something like that. She has a terrible temper.'

'It's not going to be anything as bad as that,' Clare said reassuringly, although her own stomach was churning in sympathy. 'I'll come with you. I just need to check on Diana, let her know that we'll be back.'

Ten minutes later, they were making their way into the nurses' residence, having walked hand in hand through the darkened streets to steady each other.

As they pushed the heavy entrance door open, the phone started ringing.

'Oh my God,' Gaye whispered in a low voice, 'it's my dad on already. I think I'm going to be sick...'

'You'll be okay,' Clare said, trying to sound confident. 'It's better to get it over with.'

As Gaye put her hand out to lift the receiver, it suddenly stopped. She looked at Clare with anguished eyes, and then she lifted the receiver anyway. 'It's dead,' she said. 'He must have hung up.' She put the phone back down in the cradle.

It rang again, and this time she lifted it quickly. 'Hello,' she said. 'Is that you, Dad?' Gaye listened for a few moments, then, her face suddenly like thunder, she said, 'What the hell are you phoning me for? And what on earth have you done?' She went silent now, listening intently to whatever was being said.

After several minutes she said in a shaky voice. 'Is she all right?' Then shortly afterwards she said, 'What have you told Mum and Dad? They're going to be in a terrible state when they find out.' There was another pause, then Gaye said, 'I think it's best for Audrey that they don't know the full truth, and I won't tell them that you have already phoned me either – but I will tell Audrey you told me about the baby. I'll tell her that you were upset and needed someone to talk to. I'm not going to pretend I know nothing about it; she needs somebody she can tell the truth to or she'll go mad.'

There was another silence, then Gaye finally said, 'Laurence, you better do the right thing and look after our Audrey and, when this disaster is all over, don't ever contact me again. I don't care whether you are in Newcastle, Africa or Timbuktu. What happened between us was a terrible mistake, and I'll never forgive myself if anything happens to our Audrey. And you better do your damnedest to make it up to her as well.'

With that final word, she hung the phone up and then leaned her crossed arms on top of it, bent her head and started to cry.

'What's happened?' Clare asked. 'What's happened to Audrey?'

Gaye stood with her eyes still closed, taking in big gulps of air. 'She's in hospital seriously ill. She collapsed at home tonight and was rushed into Newcastle General.'

'Did he say what's wrong with her?'

Gaye turned to look at her with dull, dark eyes. 'A miscarriage.'

'A miscarriage?' Clare repeated. 'Did she know she was pregnant?'

Gaye shook her head. 'She was nearly four months gone, but she's always had trouble with her periods, so she didn't know.' She took a deep, shuddering breath. 'Laurence said she hadn't been feeling well all last week and had been sent home from school on two different days because she had fainted, but it had not clicked with her what might be wrong.'

Clare was staring at her friend, trying to take all this in. She knew that an unmarried schoolteacher becoming pregnant was an absolute disaster. Whether it was a church school or not, it would still be deemed an absolute scandal. 'Oh, Gaye...I am so sorry.' She shook her head, trying to find the right words to comfort her.

'When Laurence told her his news, she went hysterical and then collapsed.'

'You mean about moving to Manchester?'

'No – being drafted out to Africa!' She halted for a moment, holding the back of her hand to her forehead. 'Sorry, Clare – it's an awful lot to take in. I'm all confused myself. It seems that Laurence was called into his works office today, and they told him that he wasn't going to Manchester after all. The railway received notification from the government that Laurence and some of the other engineers are being sent out to Africa to work for the military.'

'But I thought he was in a reserved occupation.'

'So did he, but they need qualified engineers.' She shrugged.

'He said it was something to do with transport. To be honest, I wasn't really listening, I was more worried about Audrey. As I said, she wasn't well for the last week, and when he went round to tell her what was happening, she collapsed in the kitchen and fell against the table and chairs. They rushed her into hospital and when they examined her they discovered she was pregnant, and between the fall and the shock, she lost the baby as well.'

Clare put her hands up to her face. 'Oh, Gaye ... it's absolutely awful. I don't know what to say...'

The phone suddenly rang, startling them both. Gaye moved to lift it. 'Dad,' she said. 'What's happening?'

Clare waited while Gaye listened carefully to everything her father said. At one point, Gaye said, 'I'll come home tomorrow.' She paused, then suddenly said in a slightly panicked voice, 'I forgot it's Sunday and there are no trains. I'll get the first train on Monday morning.'

When she hung up the phone she turned to Clare, 'I've never had so many shocks in my life.'

'Is Audrey going to be okay?' Clare asked.

'I think so; she's just sleeping tonight after the anaesthetic.' She shook her head and sighed. 'My poor dad, I felt so sorry for him, he was dead embarrassed trying to tell me about Audrey bleeding and everything, and thinking it was just normal women's monthly problems. From what he said, it sounds as though she might have been losing the baby for the last week anyway, and didn't even realise she was pregnant.'

'What a shock for everyone ... and then the news about Laurence being sent to Africa.'

'I can't even bear to think about him,' Gaye said, 'because it makes me hate myself remembering about all that nonsense.'

'It's all over and done with,' Clare said. 'And you had made that decision long before this happened.' She put her arms around Gaye. 'What passed between you has nothing to do with that. Laurence going to Africa would have happened anyway, and the same would have happened to poor Audrey and the baby.'

'I would never have thought that would have happened to our Audrey. Not in a million years...not our Audrey.' Gaye started to cry. 'After all the fighting and arguing we've done over the years, I've just realised that I would be devastated if anything happened to her.'

'Well, hopefully she'll get all the help she needs in the hospital, and will make a quick recovery and get back to normal again.'

'I hope they treat her okay in the hospital when they realise she's not married,' Gaye said in a whisper, 'and I hope the school don't find out or she might lose her job.'

'They won't find out unless she tells someone,' Clare reassured her. 'The hospital won't give that information out to anyone.'

'I just wish I could have gone home tomorrow, just to see that's she's okay, and to let her know that I'll do anything I can to help her.'

'You can do all that on Monday,' Clare said. 'You won't have any problems getting time off when you explain you have a very sick sister in hospital and need to go home.'

Gaye straightened up. 'And if I'm not going until Monday, at least I won't be letting the kids down tomorrow.'

'If you don't feel up to it, I'm sure the vicar and everybody will understand.'

'Helping the families will make me feel I'm doing something good.' She bit her lip. 'I need to feel that I'm a good person again. After everything that has happened, I need to do some-thing good to make me respect and like myself again.'

'You are good,' Clare told her firmly, taking her friend by the arm to face her, 'and you will get over all this. You'll feel much better when you've seen Audrey and helped support her through her loss. Your parents will need you as well.'

Gaye nodded, thinking of all the difficult conversations that lay ahead of her in Newcastle.

'What do you want to do now?' Clare asked quietly.

'Bed. I couldn't face everyone else and pretend I was all right. It wouldn't be fair on you either, watching me to see how I was.' She hesitated. 'Would you mind explaining to Diana and

Andrew and any of the girls that ask where I went? Just say that I got news that my sister is in hospital and I didn't want to come back and be a killjoy at the party.'

'Are you okay going upstairs on your own?'

'I'll be fine.' She looked at Clare. 'Thanks for everything. Not just for tonight, or even for last night. I've not been the best friend to you recently, and yet you've stuck by me and I really appreciate it.'

'You would do the same for me.'

Gaye gave a teary smile. 'You're far too good and sensible. You're too busy helping everyone else to think about yourself.' She moved towards the stairs and then suddenly turned and threw her arms around Clare's neck and kissed her on the cheek. 'You're the best pal anyone could have, and I'll never forget you standing by me.'

When Gaye reached her room, she hung her dance dress in the small wardrobe, then had a quick wash in the small sink and changed into her pyjamas. Sitting at the mirror for a few minutes, brushing out her hair and then putting Pond's cold cream on her face, her mind was whirring. And when she was lying in bed, she kept going over the night's events, trying to take it all in.

To hear that Audrey was very ill in hospital upset her more than she could ever have imagined. As she replayed the phone calls in her mind with both Laurence and her father, at one point she felt physically sick. Audrey's pregnancy was the biggest shock of all, and it made her realise just what a rat Laurence was. He had sat with her, almost in tears, and running Audrey down to the lowest, saying how cold-hearted and demanding she was, when he had clearly taken advantage of her. She knew her sister well, and it had always been important to Audrey to guard her untarnished reputation as a schoolteacher. Any time Gaye had thought of loosening her own morals a little with some of the lads she had encountered, a picture of her sister had flown into her mind, as she feared Audrey's censure even more than her parents. She guessed that Laurence must have applied heavy pressure on her to drop those high standards – enough for the highly principled Audrey to become pregnant.

Many a girl could have had her head turned by the undoubtedly handsome Laurence, and Gaye had thought him a quiet, easy-going chap, happy to let Audrey take the lead in everything. That he, like Gaye, was the victim of an overbearing and unreasonable woman who would brook no criticism. Gaye shivered now, thinking how easily he had duped her.

She turned the light off and then she lay for a while, trying to think of other things, and eventually she fell asleep. It must have been after midnight when she suddenly awoke, hearing voices outside in the corridor. It was, she presumed, the other girls coming home from the dance. She recognised Nelly McCann's voice and she wondered what she was doing on this floor, as her room was downstairs. Then, she heard a light tap on her bedroom door. She moved to support herself on her elbows, and could see the shadows of two people against the hall light under her door. She held her breath, thinking, and then she lay down again. She didn't want to talk to any of the other girls, who would ask her what had happened and why she hadn't not come back to the dance. Then, she heard one of the girls say, 'She's asleep, we'd better leave her', followed by muffled laughter.

She moved to sit up in the bed, and as she looked towards light under the door she heard more whispers; then she saw the shadows at the bottom of the door again and watched as a folded piece of paper was slid under it. She heard the footsteps and giggling move away and down the corridor again. She waited a few more minutes and then she got out of bed to retrieve the note.

She tiptoed back across the floor and came to sit on the edge of the bed. She put her bedside light on and then she unfolded the paper. She read down it, and then she sat staring ahead, in a state of surprise. She pondered over it, and at one point she put the note on her bedside cabinet, got back into bed, and then lay there for several minutes deciding what to do. Then she suddenly moved and stripped off her pyjamas and quickly pulled on her underwear and dress again. Slipping her feet into her sandals, she brushed her hair again and dabbed powder over her face to blot the oily night cream she had just applied. A quick lick of red lipstick, cardigan over her shoulders, and she walked silently out of the room and down the stairs.

She stole quietly out of the main door and into the black of the night. She stood long enough to let her eyes adjust to the dark and then, when familiar shapes lit by the half-moon began to emerge, she went carefully in the direction of the porter's lodge. Before she reached it, she turned right on the path and headed towards the car park. She kept to the paved path, watching as she went and mindful of all the simple blackout accidents she had dealt with in accident and emergency.

There were brief instructions in the note as to where exactly the car was parked. As she walked along, she thought over the decision she had made to come out. While her mind was full of sadness and regrets about the very recent mistakes she had made, something drove her on: a little voice inside that told her that while there was the possibility that she was making yet another mistake, she might make a bigger one by not going.

Chapter Twenty

Diana was surprised and pleased at the interest her aunt had taken in Stella. Their relationship had grown a little warmer every day, and Stella was coming out of her shell and talking more about her friends and family back home in Guernsey. Diana going out and leaving them together in the house when she first arrived had been the best thing that could have happened. Mrs Brown had also taken to the girl, and was doing everything she could to help her settle in. She had brought Stella down into the kitchen this morning to have her breakfast with her, as Rosamund wasn't up yet, being an erratic sleeper. Diana had joined them at the scrubbed pine table, and they all chatted together as a lively music programme played on the radio, only falling silent when the news came on.

Stella had then walked down to the town hall with Diana, hoping to meet up with some of her school friends, teachers or neighbours. As they went along, the girl told her more about her aunt and younger cousins, who were still in Guernsey. Apparently they were all packed and waiting to board the ferry alongside Stella and her brother when her aunt suddenly took cold feet at the last minute and decided to stay in Guernsey and take the risk of the German invasion.

'I'm worried what will happen to them if the Nazis take over the island,' Stella had confided.

When they arrived at the hall, Clare and Gaye were already there, and Reverend Lomas asked to speak to the volunteers in another room about the news they had heard on the radio earlier that morning. 'The Guernsey people are very concerned that the British government has been forced to demilitarise the Channel Islands, which means that those left behind will be left defenceless. And there is news coming in that the occupation of the island by the Germans seems imminent.' He shook his head. 'All we can do is hope and pray that something happens to halt them before they cross the water into Guernsey.'

After a further detailed debrief, the volunteers headed to the kitchen to help those from the Women's Institute and other voluntary groups distribute breakfast to the families, taking a moment to sit and reassure them as much as possible.

As they were preparing the trays, the three friends caught up from the night before. Diana offered her sympathies to Gaye about her sister, and asked if she could do anything to help.

'Thanks, but it's too complicated,' Gaye replied in a quivery voice. 'When things have settled down, I'll tell you all about it.'

'No need to explain a thing,' Diana said. 'Every family has its difficulties. I could write a whole book about mine.'

'That makes me feel a bit better,' Gaye said, managing a weak smile. 'Most people pretend their families are fine and never have any problems.'

Diana reached over and squeezed her hand, and Gaye suddenly felt like giving her a big hug.

Clare sensed that Gaye was getting emotional again, and swiftly changed the subject. 'How is Stella?'

'Working out better than I could have hoped for,' Diana said. 'Aunt Rosamund has been amazing, and so has Mrs Brown. They have Stella playing pieces they like on the piano, and this morning she was explaining about the mixture of French and English that they speak in Guernsey, as Mrs Brown thought they all spoke Portuguese for some reason. I think it has given them a new lease of life having someone young about the place.' Her brow came down. 'Though I'm not quite sure what will happen when Stella's brother is eventually found, because my aunt is adamant that she can't cope with boys. If he is settled somewhere with a good family, then there is every possibility they might take Stella in too.'

'It's so sad,' Clare sighed. 'All the upset and upheaval having to leave their own homes, and then all the complications about finding them places to stay over here.'

The volunteers moved around the room, chatting to parents and teachers, and trying to help entertain the children. The ever-willing Lance went around distributing small toys that a kind shopkeeper had dropped in at the entrance hall. He told the girls that the owner had filled several boxes with play items that could be used in the confined space in the hall, such as hand-balls, bubbles and cardboard cut-out dressing dolls for the girls, and model soldiers and toy cars. She had also donated a variety of model aeroplanes and battleships, which were particularly popular with boys since the war had started.

'I'm going to set up a table for the model planes,' Lance said, 'and get all the boys together who want to make them, and it will keep them busy for hours.'

Clare sat for a while with May Tyrrell, a small, fair-haired woman a little older than herself, and her six-month-old baby girl, Margaret-Anne, who May explained had been named after her two grandmothers who were still in Guernsey. Clare rocked the little girl for a while to let her mother have a cup of tea. After chatting about general things, May told Clare that she was still in shock at the speed of the evacuation from home, and about leaving most of her family behind. She said it was like she was still in the middle of a bad dream, and when she woke, she kept hoping that she would be back in her own house in Guernsey, and in her own bed.

'The boat journey was rough and very uncomfortable,' she told Clare in a hushed voice, and with an accent similar to Stella's. 'The worst part was when I had to get on the train. We don't have trains in Guernsey, you see, so lots of us had never travelled on one before. Of course, we had seen pictures of them and watched them in the films in the cinema, but we had never imagined how it would be in reality.' She closed her eyes for a few moments, remembering it. 'The noise it made when it was arriving at the station, this big clanging, metal thing, and then all the clouds of steam. It was absolutely terrifying, and you can imagine what some of the children were like when they saw and heard it.'

'That must have been awful,' Clare said.

'We were travelling at night on the train with no idea where we were going. And we were warned not to open the blackout curtains.'

May explained how the train kept stopping at different stations and some of the other adults went to look out of the window to see where they were, only to find that the names of the stations had been removed. People were getting sick and mothers were struggling to feed and change babies on the crowded trains.

'I don't mean to complain,' May said, her eyes brimming with tears. 'And I know that people have been ever so kind to us. On the train up from Weymouth, there were people in the stations we stopped at who ran along the platforms to pass us sandwiches and drinks through the windows of the train.

'You must find everything very different here in Stockport?' Clare said. 'I know I did when I first arrived from Ireland.'

May nodded, 'It's hard getting used to the sound of the traffic and the trains.'

'I was the same; it took me a while to get used to things, but I'm happy here now,' Clare said, trying to give her hope. 'I come from a small town in Ireland – well, a mile outside the town, actually, in the country.'

May's eyes widened with interest.

'I grew up on a small farm surrounded by fields and cattle.' She smiled at May. 'We do have a train station in our town though, and my mother used to take us on the train to Dublin at Christmas and to Galway in the summer, so at least I was used to that.'

'But you have settled here?'

'Absolutely,' Clare said, rocking the child. 'I've grown to love

155

it here, and I hope you and all the other Guernsey people will, until it's time for you to go back to your own place.'

'My husband and both our parents are back there. They had never been off the island, and were too terrified to go.' Her eyes filled up. 'I miss everything about it. My family and my neighbours, and my friends from the hospital where I used to work, up until I had this little lady.'

'What did you do?' Clare asked.

'I was a midwife,' May said. 'And my best friend was a local children's nurse. We both qualified last year.' Her friend wasn't married, May said, and so she had stayed behind to see to the children whose parents had decided not to have them evacuated.

Gaye and Diana heard similar stories from the parents and teachers they spoke to. Stella introduced Diana to a teacher from the local school she went to, and to some of the other pupils. They went around the hall together and Diana assured anyone who knew Stella's family that the girl would be well taken care of.

At eleven o'clock, after the children had been given scones and a glass of milk, the volunteers took them off to the various rooms or to the playing fields for the planned activities.

Clare had rows of chairs set out for her group and was delighted when two brothers around eight and ten asked if they could join in. They explained they had been taught to do basic knitting at home by their granny and they wanted to make scarves to send home for Christmas. She made them welcome and got them to go around the group distributing knitting needles and colourful balls of wool.

Gaye and Jack Fairclough had the biggest group, and when they went to their allotted room, they organised the children to stand in several rows as a choir would, with the smaller children in the front.

'There's no sitting down in here,' Jack told them with a cheery smile. 'You have to be standing upright for your chest and lungs to work properly.' He then demonstrated, marching up and down and pushing his chest out and making all the children giggle and laugh.

Then, with Gaye conducting and leading them in the singing, they started off with a few simple well-known tunes like 'London Bridge is Falling Down' and 'Frère Jacques' to get their voices warmed up. After a bit, Gaye suggested that they might do the songs in a round, with one row starting off and the next chiming in after them. At first the rows got muddled as to when they were to sing their part, so there was a lot of stopping and starting and more laughing, which lifted Gaye's heart to hear.

Gradually, with Gaye and Jack prompting them, they all got the hang of the rounds of 'Frère Jacques', and began to sing in unison, with only the odd mistake. Gaye stopped singing to check how they sounded on their own. She walked back and forth, making encouraging gestures and waving her hands in time to the music. At one point she was standing still at the front, glancing around the fledgling choir at all the earnest little faces, when she felt a wave of emotion sweep over her. Those poor children so far away from home, she thought, and here in a strange town singing their little hearts out.

She took her hanky out of her pocket and turned away, pretending to cough so they did not see the tears that had suddenly filled her eyes.

Diana and two of the younger volunteers set off with their group to the Nag's Head. She was surprised and touched when she saw the balloons and bunting that the grumpy-looking publican had put up to welcome the children. He also gave her a big bag of toffees to share out.

Within half an hour, the children were settled at newspaper covered tables and busily drawing pictures of their new surroundings, which included the double-decker buses and trams, and the town hall building opposite. Diana went around each group, lending a helping hand and offering plenty of words of encouragement.

When the girls met up again at lunchtime, they all had similar stories about their groups. Clare was pleased to report that a lot of the older girls were already able to knit well, and they had each taken a younger girl to sit beside and help start them off by casting on stitches and then demonstrating how to do a row of basic plain stitches.

Gaye made them all laugh when she told them that Jack Fairclough had taught the children his own version of 'A Nightingale Sang in Berkeley Square'. He had not only changed some of the words to make it more fun for the children, he had also changed the title to 'A Nightingale Sang in Mersey Square'.

From the description of the music session, it sounded as though Gaye and Jack were a great double-act and kept the children entertained, as well as teaching them several new songs.

'The kids loved it,' Gaye told them, 'and they're now asking to go down to Mersey Square to see what it really looks like.'

Diana arched her dark eyebrows and smiled. 'I have seen both places, and all I will say is that Mersey Square is, in fact, very different to Berkeley Square.'

'I presume Berkeley Square is a bit posher?' Clare asked.

'It's essentially a very nice park encircled by some of the most expensive houses in London.'

'Well,' Gaye laughed, 'we'll have to make sure the kids don't get to see Berkeley Square, then they won't be too disappointed with Mersey Square!'

Chapter Twenty-One

On Monday morning, a serious-faced Gaye left Stockport, carrying her weekend case, to travel to Newcastle on the early-morning train. Sister Townsend had been very understanding when she heard about her sister having internal bleeding, and had told her to take the week off if necessary. Gaye was anxious about seeing Audrey and her parents, but worry for her sister dominated everything else.

Working with the families and singing with the children had distracted her the day before, and she had also been relieved to know that as she was travelling home to the north-east of England, Laurence was on a plane out to Africa.

'Not that I wish him any harm while he's out there or anything bad like that,' Gaye had told Clare when she left that morning, 'but I'm relieved I won't have to see him again.' She shrugged. 'And it's up to our Audrey what she does when he comes back home.'

'They were planning to get married anyway, weren't they?' Clare said, a little furrow on her brow.

'Yes, and I wish I could warn her what he's like.' Gaye lowered her voice. 'I hadn't a clue that he was so devious and capable of getting his own way. I wouldn't have believed he could get around our Audrey. I couldn't even imagine her doing it when she got married.'

After Gaye had left, Clare had gone to the canteen as usual for breakfast, and then walked down into Stockport to post a letter to her brother in Liverpool. She was looking forward to seeing Oliver in a few weeks' time for his birthday, and to catching up on all his news. She was also looking forward to telling him how involved Stockport was in helping with the Guernsey evacuees.

Oliver had been lucky that he had not been called up as yet, but being Irish he had not been approached. Apart from working for the newspaper, he often took photos for the police force and occasionally the government offices. Clare was grateful that her brother was in a safe location, and prayed every night that it would remain so. Like Stockport and Manchester, the war had so far not touched Liverpool city in a big way and hopefully it would all be over soon. Although all the major cities were still on alert, and sounded the air-raid sirens any time there was any likelihood of threat, nothing had yet come of it.

For Clare and Diana, the following week flew by, with Clare working late shifts in the hospital and Diana working up to twelve hours a day, as production of the parachutes had stepped up after Dunkirk. In fact, all the armament factories – those producing munitions, uniforms, army vehicles and bombs – had increased their output. Clare's heart swelled when she thought of all the people who had pulled together to help in any way they could; voluntary services were swelled to capacity in every sector.

Members of church groups and Women's Institute kept busy knitting socks and scarves for the soldiers. Even the evacuee families had joined forces with the locals, taking up spades to dig any available land for growing vegetables that were scarce in the shops.

While Gaye was in Newcastle, Clare and Diana used their free time during the day or evening to go down to visit the scores of adults and children still sleeping on camp beds in the town hall or the nearby Masonic lodge. Finding homes for them was slower than the local government had hoped, and the numbers that had arrived had far exceeded what was expected.

On Friday night, the three girls met up at the station when Gaye's train arrived in at nine o'clock, and together they all walked to a fish and chip shop near the hospital on Wellington Road.

Gaye was delighted to be home with her friends, appearing much more relaxed as she told them that Audrey was out of hospital and improving. 'I could have stayed the weekend in Newcastle. Me and Audrey got on great, but I felt it was better to leave while the going was good, and before we started niggling at each other again.'

'Do you feel a lot better after seeing her?' Clare asked, pleased to see her friend after such a long time away.

'Definitely,' Gaye said with a wide smile. 'But I wanted to get back to Stockport to be with the kids over the weekend. I kept thinking about last week and the happy look on their little faces when they were singing. I felt it would be a pity if I missed this week when they had just got going, and they might forget the words of their songs. Jack Fairclough is great with them, but he couldn't play the piano and walk around the room helping them at the same time.'

The waitress came to take their order, and they all laughingly commented on the fact that there was actually fish available on the menu.

Gaye flashed Diana a look. 'I've only told Clare the real truth about my sister, because I don't want any gossip among the other nurses.'

'Clare is your closest friend,' Diana said. 'It's only natural you would want to share a confidence with her.'

'I want you to know the truth as well.'

'No need to tell me a thing, if you'd prefer not to. I understand,' Diana said, waving Gaye's nervousness away.

'I want to tell you because you're very open and honest with us.' Gaye continued, stealing herself. 'What you said the day before I went to Newcastle, about all families having problems, made me feel much better.'

'Really?' Diana said, sounding surprised and touched. 'I'm glad if I helped even in a small way.'

'But it wasn't small, it really did help me, because sometimes you feel you're the only one with trouble, while everyone else's family are all getting on great.' Gaye leaned forward. 'Since I've got to know you properly, I've realised you're a very understanding person – someone I can trust – and I don't want to be sitting here making things up just to look good in front of you.'

Diana's face brightened. 'That is one of the nicest compliments I have ever been paid.'

Clare and Diana sat for the next ten minutes and listened as Gaye described what had happened to Audrey – how she hadn't been well for a week or so, her hysteria over Laurence being sent out to Africa, and then her fainting and hurting herself badly when she fell. As Diana sat with her hands up to her mouth, Gaye then explained that when the hospital doctor was examining Gaye, it was discovered that Audrey was carrying her fiancé's baby, which she subsequently lost.

'Oh, how sad!' Diana said, looking distressed. 'How awful for your poor sister. She must be in a dreadful state.'

'She's recovering physically,' Gaye said, 'but in herself, she's still in a bit of a state.'

'She must have been glad to see you and have someone she could talk to.'

Gaye shook her head. 'When I first saw her in the hospital – when we were on our own, like – she wasn't actually going to tell me about the baby. And when I told her that Laurence had phoned and told me about it, she still tried to deny it. It was only as I was leaving that she suddenly broke down and told me the truth.' She looked from Clare to Diana now. 'The thing is, she had only just guessed that she was pregnant, and was in a terrible state about it. She said she was waiting until the weekend to tell Laurence and say they would have to bring the wedding forward.' Gaye shrugged. 'But she never got a chance: as soon as he came in he told her that he was being sent out to Africa. He said that he didn't think it was fair to tie her to an engagement when he was going to be out in a dangerous place.' Gaye gave a great sigh. 'And that's when she went hysterical and told him about the baby – and then she fainted and fell, and hurt herself and the baby.'

'Oh, what a tragedy,' Diana sighed. 'A terrible thing to happen to a young couple.'

Gaye's eyes suddenly filled up. 'But there's more to it,' she said. 'And I'm hoping that you won't hate me when I tell you the whole story...'

She then went on to relate the whole sorry episode of her brief liaison with Laurence, and the fright she had had when he read far more into it than she had. 'I'll never, ever forgive myself.' She took her hanky from her bag and dabbed at her eyes. 'I was just selfish and looking for a bit of flattery and didn't think of where it might lead. It was terrible doing that to my own sister.'

'It's another sad situation,' Diana said quietly, reaching a hand across the table to Gaye. 'But it's all over and done with, and it's obvious that you are truly sorry, so you will just have to put it behind you.'

'I almost confessed it to Audrey, to get it all off my chest, but I decided at the last minute not to.' She hung her head. 'She's so devastated about the baby and Laurence going away that I felt I couldn't... I thought I'd better leave it until some other time.'

'Please don't tell her, Gaye. It might make you feel better, but she will never get over it.'

'Do you think so?'

'Just be kind and look after her. She needs you now, especially since she couldn't tell your parents about the baby. She needs you now more than ever.'

'But won't that make me a hypocrite on top of what I've already done?'

'Well,' Diana said, smiling kindly now, 'that's something that you will learn to live with. Confessing to make yourself feel better passes the burden of pain onto Audrey. I think it will be too much for the poor girl.'

'I think Diana is right, Gaye,' Clare said. 'I can see why you want to tell the truth, but it is kinder to keep quiet, and help Audrey to get over everything now.' She reached out and covered

Gaye's other hand with hers. 'The thing with Laurence was a silly mistake that got out of hand. Just leave it at that.'

Gaye nodded, sadness etched on her face.

'It's not uncommon, you know,' Diana said, 'for sisters and their boyfriends to be tempted. My mother told me a similar story about some of her aunts and a brother-in-law.' She rolled her eyes, laughing now. 'My mother is always telling me stories like that. She told me that if you learn about human nature early on, then it better prepares you for the world.'

'Well, I've certainly learned a lot from this,' Gaye said. 'It's given me the biggest fright of my life.' She looked at the two girls. 'Thanks for listening to me and for all the advice. I won't tell Audrey, I can see it would affect my mother and father too if we fell out, so I'll keep me mouth shut.'

Gaye looked from one friend to the other, feeling overwhelmed with love for them both. 'Thanks, girls – from the very bottom of my heart.'

The waitress appeared now with the steaming plates of fish and chips, and as they ate the conversation moved on to the everyday things of life in the hospital ward for Clare and in the parachute factory for Diana.

At one point Gaye asked Diana, 'Have things got any better with the girls in the factory. Are they nicer to you?'

'Not really,' Diana confessed, 'but I've got more used to it. Being left out doesn't affect me so much since I have made friends with you and Clare, and it's lovely having Stella to do things with at home. I just keep busy at my work, and at the breaks I read a book or make quick sketches in my art pad while the others are chatting.'

When Diana went to the ladies, Gaye turned to Clare. 'My heart goes out to Diana when I hear of the way they treat her in that bloody parachute factory. They haven't even given her a chance. They've just decided she's too posh for them, instead of getting to know her properly.'

'She's so kind to everyone, whatever background they come from,' Clare agreed. 'I saw her sitting with a little toddler on her knee and . . .' She made a little face. 'Well, to be honest, he wasn't the cleanest and had a dirty nappy, and she acted as if she hadn't noticed. She offered to take him to the toilet to change him, and afterwards she took him for a walk outside to give the mother a break. She's far more down to earth than those girls realise.'

They chatted for a few more minutes about Diana, then Gaye suddenly said, 'I've decided that I'm not going to see Andrew Harvey again. Even though I really like him, he's got a girlfriend back home, and I'm not going to make that mistake again.'

'You deserve better than someone who is playing the field,' Clare told her, 'and it leaves you free to meet a decent lad.'

'I think I've had my fill of them for a while,' Gaye said, giving a wry smile. She saw Diana coming towards them now. 'I didn't say anything about him having a girlfriend to Diana. She's heard enough bad things about me today, and I'm afraid it'll put her off me completely.'

'I doubt it,' Clare said. Then she caught Gaye's eye and smiled.

Chapter Twenty-Two

When the train pulled in at Macclesfield station, Diana stepped down onto the platform and joined the other passengers as they queued to hand their tickets to the guard. It was the first time she had been home in months, and her supervisor had been happy to let her have a few days off midweek, since she was still ahead of most of the other girls in speed and production.

As she walked along the platform, she spotted her mother standing talking to a tall, well-dressed young man. Diana wondered whether she actually knew him, or whether she had spied him and struck up a conversation. Annabelle Thornley had no inhibitions when it came to talking to men, especially handsome, younger men whom she knew she could impress with her upper-crust accent and sophisticated manner. When Diana had challenged her about talking to strangers, Annabelle had laughed it off, saying she was checking them out as prospective sons-in-law, but Diana guessed her mother enjoyed the male attention.

As she moved nearer she saw her mother's hands were moving in theatrical gestures, which made her heart sink. It was only seven o'clock in the evening, but it was a sign that her mother had already been drinking. Alcohol made her more animated and familiar with people. Diana stifled a sigh of despair as she handed her ticket in.

'Darling!' Annabelle called, when she saw her, waving a gloved hand. 'I have the car outside.' Most people would have been discreet about driving with the petrol rationing, but it would not occur to her that anyone might be curious about where her fuel came from. 'Diana, I must introduce you to this lovely young man, James Bailey, who has kept me company while I've been waiting for your train. I've been telling him all about you, and how we are as different as chalk and cheese.'

'How do you do?' he said, smiling and holding his hand out.

Diana politely reciprocated and shook his hand, wondering why on earth she was standing on the edge of the station platform making polite conversation with a total stranger. Why couldn't her mother just have waited quietly like a normal person and then driven her home, instead of dragging an unknown man into their lives.

'James tells me he is unmarried, and is travelling down to London to the War Office on what sounds like *very* mysterious business.'

Diana sucked in her breath as she saw her mother making eyes at the young man.

'I'm not sure it's so mysterious,' he said, smiling now. 'A bit of paperwork, when all is said and done. But everyone has to be careful when talking these days...'

'Exactly.' Diana raised her eyebrows. 'Most sensible people are acquainted with the saying, "loose lips sink ships" but, as you will have by now discovered, my mother thinks that rules don't apply to her.'

'Oh, shush, Diana!' Annabelle was laughing and shaking her head. 'I know what's required in the right circumstances and being wary of careless talk...' She waved her hand. 'But one can tell when you are on safe ground with certain people, like Mr Bailey. Can you believe that he went to the same boys' school as David and Charles? Although he was in a class between them, so only knew them slightly. I was just telling him how David is married to a newspaper tycoon's daughter in New York, and how poor Charles is exempt from the armed forces on account of his hearing problem.'

Diana felt herself squirm now as she imagined her older brothers' reaction to their mother flirting with an old school acquaintance of theirs, and then casually discussing their absence from the war effort.

'Of course, Charles is doing his bit for the country regardless. He has an estate to run in Northumberland, and he and his wife are busy as we are ourselves, with tenant farmers and land girls and so on and so forth. When will life ever return to normal?' She gave a bright smile. 'Although the hotels and restaurants are doing their best to keep going despite all the restrictions. Do you get into Manchester much in the evenings, Mr Bailey?'

'Not really,' he said, 'unless there are specific events I need to attend.'

'Thankfully, the Midland Hotel has managed to keep up standards in spite of all the rationing. We would be totally lost without it, wouldn't we?'

Before he could reply, large drops of rain suddenly began to fall.

Diana felt a wave of relief. 'It was lovely to meet you,' she said, then turned to smile at her mother. 'Shall we make a run for it before we get soaked through?'

Chapter Twenty-Three

Annabelle Thornley stood at the doorway, a cigarette in one hand and a glass of red wine in the other. 'How depressing!' she said. 'All those miserable people. Why on earth are you painting things like that?' She came into the large attic room that Diana had converted into an art studio when she started painting in earnest a few years earlier. Her heels tapped across the bare wooden floor until she came to stand by her overall-clad daughter and stare at the painting on the easel. 'What happened to all the lovely, delicate watercolours you used to do?'

'I've experimented with a variety of mediums since then,' Diana responded, without looking up. 'Oils feel right for the work I'm doing at the moment.'

'It's not the actual paint you're using, it's the subject and those awful dark, drab colours.' She lifted the sketch pad that Diana was working from, which had her original quick outlines that she would copy and develop later in paint. 'Oh, darling... these are ghastly. And the figures are sort of...' She paused, trying to find the right words. 'Well, I suppose *unreal* with almost stick-like forms and staring eyes.' She flicked through a few more. 'Gas masks! Why on earth would you paint those awful-looking things? Isn't it bad enough we have to carry them around with us, without having to look at drawings of them?' She shook her head, 'Most depressing. When I think of your lovely floral pieces...'

Diana turned to face her mother. She was not in the least perturbed by the criticism. Her mother had not the faintest idea about art, and her opinion was of no consequence. What mattered was that when she came home to their quite splendid country manor house, she had this spacious room all to herself, with natural light streaming in from windows either side, and a large ornate skylight in the centre.

'You did a series of still-life paintings in oils which I absolutely loved,' her mother continued. 'Don't you remember how well they sold at the charity auction a few years ago? I still have the one with the fruit and cheese in the kitchen.' She took a puff of her cigarette. 'There's no denying your artistic talent, but what on earth could you find interesting about these people and their circumstances?'

'Mother,' Diana said, putting her paint brush down. 'They are just ordinary people going about their ordinary lives during a very difficult time.'

'People queuing outside a butcher's shop with their baskets and ration books? People huddled together in air-raid shelters?' She flicked on a few more pages. 'A cinema packed with strange-looking people with big eyes watching Pathé News about Hitler invading France? Who on earth wants to see paintings of that dreadful man and his silly little moustache?'

Diana shrugged. 'I don't know,' she said, 'but I find it interesting, and I feel it's a period in time that should be documented in different ways.'

'We're reading it every day in the newspapers and hearing about it on the radio. That's more than enough for me.' Her mother suddenly smiled. 'What we need in our life now, darling, is light and laughter. We need bright colourful things – hats and gowns and flowers everywhere. Those land people have even commandeered the flower beds and planted bloody carrots and potatoes. Thank God we have managed to preserve the flower borders and our climbing rose bushes to leave us with a little reminder of normality.' She suddenly paused. 'Why don't you come with me to the charity ball at the Midland tomorrow night? You never know who you could meet there. Anyone helping out a charity usually has money to spare.'

'I'm not interested in meeting anyone at the moment.' She suddenly lifted her head. 'That's not strictly true. I met two very nice girls – nurses, actually.'

'*Nurses?*' Annabelle repeated. 'Do you mean voluntary nurses?'

'Real nurses; they are finishing off their training soon. I met them a few weeks ago when we had to evacuate the cinema. We all stopped to help an old lady, Mrs Atherton, who was knocked over in the rush, then we met up again with her in the nearby air-raid shelter.'

'How very kind of you all.' Her voice softened. 'Was she okay?'

'Well, at the time she was; the Red Cross were in the shelter and they took over. She seemed to have recovered and was chatting quite normally.' She gave a small sigh. 'Clare and I visited her at home the following week and she seemed to be hale and hearty. Sadly, we discovered a few days later that she took a sudden heart attack and died.'

'Oh, no!' Annabelle's hands fluttered to her throat. 'It's so awful to hear news like that, even if one doesn't know the person.' She closed her eyes and shook her head. 'I'm afraid these things happen only too often. You will discover as you grow older that life can seem very uncertain at times, and at the moment it is frightening enough with another war going on.'

'The family invited us to the funeral and after that, the girls asked me to join them for social nights out at the cinema and dancing. It's nice to have friends my own age to go out with in Stockport or Manchester. As you know, Aunt Rosamund is terrified of going out at night during the blackout.'

'And so she should be at her age. She's in her mid-sixties and not in the best of health.' Annabelle rolled her eyes. 'Well, her nerves are not in the best of health.'

'She has improved since Stella, the young evacuee from Guernsey, came to live with us.'

'Ah, the Guernsey people,' Annabelle said. 'You wrote about them in one of your letters.' Her brow wrinkled. 'I can't recall exactly what you said, something about helping entertain the children at weekends?'

'Art groups, and taking them to the park, that sort of thing.'

'Very good of you.' She gave Diana a sidelong smile. 'I hope you're encouraging them to paint pretty pictures, and not those depressing ones.'

'Of course not, they are only children and we're doing the sort of fun things that children love. Clare and Gaye are involved too, they're doing singing and craft work.'

A quizzical look came on her face. 'Clare and Gaye?

'The nurses I told you about. They are giving up their free time to help as well.'

'It sounds as though you haven't much time for yourself, with working in that awful factory and then coming home to evacuees in Rosamund's house, and then giving up all your spare time to voluntary work. I hope you're not going to wear yourself out?'

'Of course not,' Diana replied. 'Everyone is doing their best to help, and it's nothing compared to what our soldiers are going through fighting abroad, and the poor people in France and Poland who have had their countries invaded and taken over by the Germans.'

Annabelle placed her wine glass on a side table and then reached for Diana's hand, her eyes shining. 'That's why I want you to enjoy life to the full. None of us know what's going to happen, and that is so unfair when you are at the age you should be meeting a lovely young man and settling down.' She gave a small sigh. 'I wish we had organised a coming-out party and a month in London before the war, you might have been married by now.'

'You know I didn't want a party and I certainly don't want to be married.'

'You need to get out and about with bright, lively people – as I try to do even at my age. I might be heading towards fifty, but I still feel young inside, and I'm going to hang onto that feeling for as long as I possibly can.'

'That is your prerogative, Mummy, but you and I have different ways.'

Annabelle raised her eyebrows, then took a deep drag on her cigarette. 'Now, Diana,' she started, 'please don't fly off the handle, but I have to ask. You haven't developed a preference for other girls ... have you?'

'What do you mean?'

'You know ... you have been talking a lot about those nurses you are friendly with.'

Diana's eyes widened in shock. 'Mother! What a thing to suggest.' Her voice rose a notch. 'I can't believe you've just said that. Clare and Gaye would be horrified if they heard what you have inferred.'

'Oh, don't be so prissy, it does happen, you know.' Annabelle said, with a wry smile. 'Apparently it's quite the thing in certain circles in London. I just wondered if perhaps you had been swayed in that direction when you were at art college.'

'But I brought a boyfriend home several times when I was at art college. Don't you remember George? We were courting for over a year.'

'The communist law student?'

'George wasn't really a communist as such,' Diana said. 'He just had a social conscience.'

'Of course I remember him, but you haven't mentioned any other men since, and I thought that perhaps you might have decided afterwards that men were not for you.'

'But that still doesn't make sense.'

Annabelle picked up her wine glass. 'Well,' she said casually, gesturing with her other hand, causing cigarette ash to drop onto the large fringed rug. 'There's your short bobbed hair too, and the very masculine way you dress at times, in trousers and shirts. I will concede that your make-up is flawless and your eyes and lips always look rather striking.'

'I like my hair short, and I like wearing comfortable, practical clothes like trousers,' Diana said, 'but that does not mean I want to have love affairs with other women.'

Annabelle sipped her wine, eyeing Diana over the rim. 'You haven't met any nice men in Stockport, have you? You know ... eligible types who would fit in with our sort of class.'

'No, I haven't – and I haven't been looking for any either.' Diana said firmly, 'I'm perfectly happy being single until I find someone who is on the same wavelength as me.'

'You might be waiting a very long time, especially with the war going on.' Annabelle shook her head. 'And I'm afraid if you are waiting for the perfect man, there is every chance you are not going to find him. *Ever.*' Annabelle's voice suddenly wavered. 'Most of us never do.' She lifted her wine glass and drained it.

There was a silence now between mother and daughter.

'How is Daddy?' Diana eventually asked.

'Happy, I would imagine.' She took another drag of her cigarette. 'He's always happy when he is back at home with his dear sister in Derbyshire. Much happier than he is at home with me.'

Diana turned back to her easel. 'That's because they are so similar. Aunt Margaret is calm and quiet, just like Daddy. They like routine and things to be predictable.'

Her mother's eyes narrowed. 'I know the point you are trying to make, Diana. I know you think that I should be more like him, that I should just sink quietly into old age, pottering around the garden like Rosamund or Margaret.'

'I'm not saying that,' Diana said with a sigh, 'but I think he might be happier here at home if you didn't criticise him all the time. You just need to accept that he doesn't enjoy socialising as much as you do.'

'He wasn't like that when we first met, you know. He was the life and soul of the party; he enjoyed dancing and parties, and weekends in nice hotels. He loved all the same things I did, until that bloody war knocked all the stuffing out of him. He wasn't the same when he came back home. And now he never wants to go anywhere apart from visiting his sisters or the occasional trip to your brother's place.'

'How can you expect him to enjoy dances when he has such

difficulty with his leg? Have you forgotten that he had a bullet removed from it, and it was so bad he almost had to have it amputated?'

'Of course I haven't forgotten, and of course I don't expect him to be cavorting around the dance floor. It's the fact that he doesn't even like listening to the same music as me any more. It's all sober and classical and downright depressing.' She gave a theatrical sigh. 'I have tried to find things we can do together, but he just doesn't have any interest in anything I suggest. He'd much rather spend time horse riding with Margaret or helping her expand that never-ending bloody maze of hers.'

Diana looked at her. 'What do you want me to say, Mummy?'

Annabelle looked down at the floor, as though examining the pattern on the rug. 'Nothing,' she said in a low voice. 'There's nothing anyone can say.' She then turned and headed for the door. 'We're having chicken for dinner,' she said over her shoulder, 'and I asked Mrs Brown to make your favourite bread and butter pudding.'

'Thank you,' Diana said stiltingly as she surveyed her painting. She hated arguing with her mother, and afterwards always felt it was a waste of time. It only hurt them both and opened up a further distance between them. For all her mother was painfully open with her opinions and views, nothing ever changed.

Chapter Twenty-Four

When Clare walked into the town hall the next Saturday there was an air of despondency after the news reported that German aircrafts had dropped bombs on Guernsey and machine-gunned the harbour the previous night. Dozens of the islanders had been reported as killed or injured in the attack, leaving the evacuees in an anguished state, wondering if their loved ones were among the dead or if they had managed to escape.

This was news that the evacuee families had been dreading, as they had remained hopeful that their island would be left unharmed. Any lingering doubts the mothers and teachers had about evacuating the children to safety in Britain were instantly extinguished.

Then the inevitable followed, with grave radio announcements declaring that Guernsey was now occupied by Hitler's army and all communications from the island had been cut off.

'It's terrible news for our Guernsey friends,' Lance told Clare as they prepared tea for the evacuees that morning, 'and it's terrible news for everyone else. The Nazis are just across the Channel now, and that means Britain is the next target.' He shook his head. 'It's just getting worse and worse.'

'Thank God all the families got out to safety before this happened.' She closed her eyes. 'It just doesn't bear thinking about. It makes you realise that all the discomforts here, living on camp beds and waiting to hear if there is proper accommodation, are nothing compared to what the people in Guernsey are going through now.'

'I think it's just hitting them that this evacuation is not going to be as quick as they thought. The reports are that the Germans are settling in for a long haul.' He shrugged. 'It might not be safe for the families to return home until this war is over and done, which could take until next year.'

'The conditions here are getting worse,' Clare whispered over the clatter of teaspoons on saucers. 'There's no proper washing facilities and not enough toilets to cope with these numbers. Some of the mothers are already depressed, trying to manage children in camp beds with only a few belongings and not knowing where they are going to end up. They are all missing home so much, and hearing this news about the bombings on the island and that it's been occupied by the Germans . . .'

'It's a bloody nightmare right enough, but all we can do is just keep helping the families until they are moved out to somewhere better.' He nodded over to the table where the vicar was sitting. 'All the local churches are holding special services for the Guernsey evacuees tomorrow night, so we will be busy helping the families and children get out to the churches.'

Over the next few days, a mass exodus took place in Stockport and the surrounding areas when six hundred of the billeted evacuees finally got good news and were taken to new homes in rural Cheshire. Where possible, families were kept together and teachers went with the schoolchildren they had left the island with. In some areas, groups were all kept together to form their own separate Guernsey schools in the villages or towns they arrived in.

Each day afterwards, more and more of the islanders moved out, leaving a much smaller group in the halls scattered around Stockport town. Clare, Gaye and Diana found themselves spending much more time helping to smooth out the process for the families moving on, feeling almost sad to say goodbye to some of them. Even though it had been a bit of a squash, there had been a real sense of community and Gaye confessed she would miss having so many children in her singing group. It gave the choir a solid sound – and she was quietly disappointed when one of her best singers headed out to the country.

By the following Sunday afternoon, volunteers were busy cleaning up the hall, folding up camp beds and washing floors after many of the families had left. Later, there would be another meeting with voluntary groups to work out if it was practical to keep the weekend activity groups running for the children. Some of the families billeted locally said they wanted to maintain regular contact with the other Guernsey mothers and children, so arrangements were being discussed as to how that would be managed.

When they were in the kitchen making tea before the meeting, Clare turned to Diana and Gaye. 'Have either of you any plans for next Friday night?'

'I'm free as usual,' Diana said.

Gaye smiled. 'And so am I. I'm on earlies.'

'Great,' Clare said, beaming, 'because it's my big brother's birthday and he's coming over to Stockport.'

Gaye's eyebrows shot up. 'Oliver?'

'Yes,' Clare nodded.

'Lovely,' Gaye said, 'you can count me in.' She turned to Diana. 'Have I told you how gorgeous he is?'

'Gaye!' Clare said, in a mock severe tone. 'That's my brother you're talking about, and he's not gorgeous.'

'He is,' she said laughing, 'and he's a really brilliant photographer too. He's very brainy, always reading and talking about films and things.'

'Anyway,' Clare said, pretending to be cross with Gaye, 'My mother and father have sent money over for me to take him for a meal, and I wondered if you two would like to join us for a drink afterwards? I thought I'd book a table at the Alma Lodge, as it looked nice when we were at Mrs Atherton's funeral.'

'That would be lovely,' Diana said. 'The restaurant is very good too. I've been in the hotel bar on a number of occasions when my mother has been over to Stockport, and it's ideal for a little celebration.'

'A lot of the doctors from the hospital go there too,' Gaye said, giving a knowing smile, 'so it must be respectable.

'I'm glad you can come,' Clare said. 'I'll treat us all to the drinks, and it will make it more like a little party for him rather than just the two of us.'

The following Friday, when Clare finished work at two o'clock, she had a long soak in the bath and then she set her hair in rollers. She usually just tied her hair back or left it to dry in waves, but she always made a special effort for Oliver, as she knew her parents would ask him how she looked and if she was well. She lay on her bed for a while reading a magazine, and then she painted her nails with shell-pink polish and put on her make-up. She had arranged to meet him at the station at six o'clock, and they would walk to the main road and catch the bus up to the hotel.

Around five, Gaye called to her room. 'You look gorgeous,' she said. 'I'm glad to see you taking the government's advice that "beauty is your duty"! I'll be doing the same when I get myself dressed up later on to meet up with that brother of yours.'

Clare raised her eyes to the ceiling. 'You wouldn't last a week with each other, he's far too serious and boring for you.'

'D'you mean just like his sister?' Gaye retorted, grinning. 'How come we've stayed friends for so long?'

'Forget Oliver,' Clare said. 'Do I really look okay?'

'You always look fantastic in that floral dress. You should thank me for making sure you got it before they all sold out.'

'Well, I suppose I am glad I got it,' Clare laughed. 'Although my nerves would never let me go through all that drama again. No dress is worth that.'

'That's the difference between us,' Gaye smiled. 'I'd quite happily get a scabby knee if it meant getting a new dress!'

It was a beautiful evening, and too warm for a coat, so Clare wore her white cardigan over her shoulders as she walked down Wellington Road. Almost everyone she passed said hello or nodded in greeting, and everything seemed more normal than Clare had remembered in a long time. As she walked along in the evening sunshine, happily looking forward to seeing Oliver, the melody of 'On the Sunny Side of the Street' came into her mind. She hummed the tune to herself, and then pondered over the words, wondering if she would ever meet anyone special who would light up her day.

Since she had come to Stockport, she had had several dates with different lads and one romance that had lasted a few months, but none of them were right for her. Most of them had been Irish, and it was lovely for the first few dates talking about familiar things from home with them and enjoying the Irish banter. As time went on she came to realise, with each one, that if she had actually been back home, she would not have found enough in common with him to keep things going.

At times she questioned what she was actually looking for in a romantic partner, as the thought had not occurred to her before that she might be fussy. She knew she had always liked boys who were good dancers back home in Tullamore, and it was in the dance halls in Manchester that she had met most of the boys since arriving in England. After a while, she realised that when she got to know them well, she always found something lacking. While she had enjoyed the laugh and the few nights she had gone to a dance or to the pictures with them, there was never enough between them to move things on to a more serious footing.

She liked listening to music and reading, and since coming to Stockport she found she enjoyed the local art gallery and museums and taking the bus with some of the other girls to places like Bramhall Park or Lyme Park in Disley. Since visiting Liverpool to meet up with Oliver, she had become interested in learning about some of the other cities, and from what she had heard from Diana, she also would love to visit London. It was the wrong time now to think of going anywhere, but she hoped that when all the war business was over, she would get the chance to travel further afield.

Clare arrived at the station, checked which platform the Liverpool train was due to arrive at and, finding that she had a few minutes spare, decided to climb the stone stairs up to the platform and wait for Oliver there. She stood at the midway point of the platform, and as she waited, she glanced around her at the people waiting to board the train. Most of the women, she noticed, looked nicely dressed, and were taking the government's advice to keep British morale up. She smiled, thinking that if Hitler himself appeared around a corner, he would find the women defiantly dressed well, proving that the British spirit would not be crushed.

She heard the train engine in the distance, and thought that even just two years ago, she could not have imagined herself and her brother both being in England, and at the same time. When they were young, travelling up to Dublin for the day on the train was such a huge undertaking that it seemed strange to think that now she and Oliver travelled on buses and trains regularly without giving it a thought.

As the train slowed to a halt, Clare watched each carriage as it went past. Doors clanged open as people poured off the train, making for the exit.

She glanced down to the end of the train when she heard her name being called, and turning, she saw Oliver coming towards her; her tall, dark-haired, handsome brother, waving and smiling and looking less serious than he often did. Clare ran towards him, felling a little burst of almost childlike happiness to see his cheeky grin at long last.

Seeing him again made her realise how much she missed her older brother – missed all her family. When she got within feet of him, she threw her arms around his neck. It was uncharacteristic of her – and the O'Sullivan family in general – to show their emotions so openly. They usually made do with an awkward hug or quick peck on the cheek, but something about this week and all the terrifying news from Guernsey and the rest of the world had her throwing off her cautious attitude.

Oliver hugged her tightly, almost squeezing the life out of her in return, and then he stood back to view her. 'It's grand to see you. You look lovely,' he told her as she did a turn for him. 'Absolutely lovely! And so grown up. Where has my little sister gone?'

'Oh, I'm still here all right,' she laughed. 'And you're looking fantastic yourself. How is life treating you in Liverpool?'

'Fine,' he said, waving away her question. 'Fine.'

Swinging her bag and gas mask over her shoulder they started to move along the platform, leaning towards each other to block the noise of the train engine and the other people passing by. 'Still taking photographs?' she teased good-naturedly.

'Oh, indeed,' he said, turning to her slightly with a raised eyebrow. 'What else would I be doing?'

Someone bumped against her with a suitcase, causing Clare to step to the side and put her arm through her brother's. 'Anything special?' she asked.

'Out and about as usual,' he said, 'covering whatever I'm asked to. We're down a photographer on the paper at the moment, so I'm out one minute taking snaps of people at meetings in the City Hall and the next I could be out taking photos of car crashes.'

'Car crashes?' she repeated, awed.

'Liverpool city is the devil for crashes,' he said. 'They come flying around corners and it's worse, of course, at night in the dark.'

As she listened, Clare noticed – as though for the first time – Oliver's soft, clear Tullamore accent. As they came down the stairs to walk into the main station, Clare halted. 'You're booked in for the night at the Bluebell, aren't you?'

'I am,' he confirmed. 'I rang the place from the newspaper office before I set off today, just to remind them.'

'Do you want to drop anything off there, before we go out tonight?'

Oliver held out a Gladstone-style bag. 'I might as well carry it with me. I have my camera and gas mask in it with a clean shirt and a few other items. If they went missing in the hotel, I would be in big trouble.'

'As long as you're sorted out.'

'What about you? Are they keeping you busy at the hospital?'

As they walked out onto the main road, Clare told him about the different wards she had been working in, and the subjects they had been studying in Stepping Hill.

'Sounds like you're doing very well,' he said. 'And what a great opportunity to get paid while you're doing your training over here.'

'We could never have afforded it at home.'

'Have you given any thought to what you'll do when you're finished with your training next year?'

'Not really,' Clare said. 'I'm just concentrating on getting my qualifications and when the time comes I'll decide then.'

'Will you go home?'

She hesitated. 'I always thought I would...'

'But you're not sure now?'

'With the war and everything, there's so much going on it's hard to think that far ahead.'

'It changes you – being over here. It changes your outlook on life. You begin to see things differently, and when you know that, it's hard to think about returning to a much smaller place, to people who have never been away.'

'I'm just not sure what I'm going to do...'

'You're in no rush to decide.' He squeezed her arm against his. 'And maybe tonight is not the night for serious talk like that.' He gave a little chuckle. 'You told me on the phone that you were going to surprise me tonight.'

'Yes, I did,' she said, grinning up at him, relieved to be changing the subject, 'and I hope you'll like what I've planned. The last few times you were here we went to cafés in Stockport or Manchester, but since it's your birthday Mam and Dad said I had to treat you to somewhere a bit fancier, and they sent money over to cover it. I didn't want to say anything to you, so it would be a surprise.'

'Well, wasn't it lucky I made sure to put on my good suit and best shoes?'

'I never thought to tell you to wear a suit, because I thought it would give the game away, and you always look fairly decent.'

'Mam wrote to me,' he said, laughing. 'You know what she's like, she can't keep a secret. She said that you would be taking me somewhere posh, and that I'd better wear the best I had.'

'Ah, she means well, she wanted you to have a nice birthday. I think there are times she finds it very hard that we are both so far away.'

His face was suddenly solemn. 'It was kind of them to send the money, for they don't have a lot to spare. Ireland doesn't have the same free education system we have over here in England, and it's very hard on big families when they have to pay for books and pencils and everything.'

Clare was glad of the diversion as they stopped to cross the road. She could tell that Oliver was getting into one of his serious conversations. 'We're going on the bus for five or ten minutes. The bus stop is just up towards the town hall.'

In less than a minute they spotted the double-decker coming up the hill. As they boarded, Clare asked if he wanted to go upstairs so he could smoke.

'I've stopped,' he said. 'The cigarettes were getting too dear and too difficult to get, and when I saw the state some of the lads got into if they didn't have one, I decided it was best to stop before I got too dependent on them.'

'Good for you,' Clare said. 'We had a lecture about them from one of the doctors, and it seems they can be very bad for your health, especially the chest.'

'I don't know about that,' Oliver said. 'I know old lads who've been smoking for years, and they don't seem any the worse for it.'

The conversation flitted from one thing to the next as they both thought of things they had wanted to ask of the other.

'And how is your friend, the Geordie girl?' Oliver said.

'Gaye? Oh, she's grand, the same as usual.'

'She's a gas character, isn't she? As giddy as a kipper.'

'She sure is,' Clare laughed. 'But she has a great heart, and she's as clever as any of the other girls.'

'And is she keeping up with her studies?'

'Most of the time, although she's often down to the wire with essays.'

'As long as she gets them in,' he said, smiling. 'I'm often last minute with photographs for the newspaper.' He shook his head. 'The best stories often come in just as the paper is due to be put to bed.'

'Do you enjoy it as much as ever?'

'I do,' he said, 'but there are times you have to be careful about what you take pictures of, and the reporters are the same.' He suddenly halted and looked around at the people sitting anyway close to them, checking that no one could hear what he was saying. He continued in a low voice, 'There are things you see and hear ... things that certain people don't want made public.'

'What do you mean?' Clare asked quietly.

'Political things, stuff to do with the war.' He shook his head. 'You don't want to know, but you have to ask yourself the question – are you doing the right thing by keeping quiet?'

Clare suddenly felt a little shiver. 'I would hate to think you were in dangerous situations ...'

He squeezed her hand. 'Don't worry about me. It's the poor lads out fighting abroad we need to think about. I've seen a few of them who have come back injured, and when you hear what they have been through, you realise we know nothing about it.'

Clare was not sure what to say. She had hoped that this night to celebrate Oliver's birthday would be light and easy, but she knew it was unrealistic to think that anyone – especially someone so serious-minded as he – would go a whole night without mentioning the war. It was part and parcel of everyday life now.

They got off the bus and walked on for another fifty yards or so until the hotel came into view.

'Well,' Clare said, 'what do you think? Does this look like a good enough place to celebrate your twenty-fifth birthday?'

'Wow!' Oliver said, putting his hands to his mouth. He shook his head. 'Surely it's too dear for them to pay for? Mother already sent me a jumper she had knitted.'

'It's fine,' Clare said reassuringly. 'I've already been up and checked the menu, and we have more than enough and some left over for a few drinks later.'

Oliver put his arm around her shoulder and pulled her in towards him. 'You're a great girl, do you know that?'

'Go on with you!' Clare laughed.

'No, I mean it,' he said. 'I admire you for being brave enough to leave home and come over here, and for making such a good go of it. It's great to see women getting out and working and earning their own money and leading their own lives.' He nodded his head. 'I'm proud of how well you look too. Some lad will be lucky to get such a fine-looking, well-dressed girl. Have you one on the go at the minute?'

Clare was touched at the compliments, because she knew he was sincere. She shook her head. 'No, not a fella in sight. What about you?'

He gave a small laugh. 'Ah, there's one or two I see occasionally, but nothing too serious.'

'One or two?' she repeated. 'I hope you're not two-timing them or anything like that?'

'Not at all,' he said, winking mischievously.

As they walked up the wide, curving stone steps towards the front door of the hotel, Oliver asked, 'How do you know this place? I wouldn't imagine that student nurses could afford to come here too often.'

'Do you really want to know?' she said, raising her eyebrows. When he nodded, she said, 'At a funeral.'

'Whose funeral?' he said, opening the door for her.

'I'll tell you all about it when we get inside.'

They were met at the door by a smart uniformed member of staff, and when Clare told him about their booking, he led them through the busy foyer to the restaurant door. There were couples and small groups sitting at low tables lit pleasantly by candles, and a half-dozen smartly dressed businessmen were chatting animatedly, drinks in hand, over by the ornate fireplace.

'I can't believe how many people are out and about,' Oliver

commented as they passed through. 'I'm used to Liverpool being busy, but a small town like this is surprising. You wouldn't think there was a war going on at all.'

'It's Friday,' Clare told him, 'and I heard someone saying that they have a lot of weddings and business conferences here. Seemingly, there have been more weddings than ever since the war began.'

'I suppose life has to go on,' Oliver said. 'But I can't understand how people can even think of getting married under these circumstances. Who knows what changes take place when you're away for a long time? I've already seen how the first war changed some of the older men, and I'm sure some of the young girls regretted being in such a rush to get married. Being taken in by the romance and excitement of it all, not realising what a serious situation they might be getting themselves into.'

Although still slightly in awe of the glamorous surroundings, Clare was glad when the restaurant manager came towards them. She felt that the war talk was bringing out the serious side of Oliver again, and she so wanted his special birthday celebration to be light and fun. The way it would have been with all his family and friends back in Ireland.

They were escorted to a table for two over by the window. The manager moved to hold the chair out for Clare and then slid it neatly into position when she was ready to sit down. 'This is a nice, private, little corner,' he said, smiling at them. 'It's very popular with courting couples.'

Clare gave a small giggle. 'He's my brother!'

'Seeing your brother is still a special occasion,' he said, smiling. 'Would you like to see the wine list?'

Oliver looked over at Clare, and gave a little shake of his head, indicating that it was a step out of their league.

'Yes, please,' Clare said. She had already planned for this. She lowered her voice. 'Can you recommend a reasonably priced one please?'

'Of course,' he said. 'Red or white?'

Oliver shrugged, looking bemused by the whole thing.

'White,' Clare said, 'and quite sweet.' She had tasted both before at a party in the hospital, and she found the red too bitter.

'I'm sure I will find something suitable,' he said smiling at them, then he handed them a menu each. 'We have three courses for a special price,' he said, 'so take a little time, and I will take your order when you are ready.'

When the manager was out of earshot, Oliver leaned forward with his arms on the table. 'I can't believe you can afford wine on top of all this...'

'I'm treating you to the wine,' she said in a decisive voice. 'It's part of my birthday treat to you.'

'But how—'

'Believe it or not, I still have some of my savings from when I came over,' she told him. 'Daddy told me to put it in a post office account when I arrived, and only use it when I'm desperate, and that's what I did. If I have anything left over at the end of the week – even if it's only sixpence – I put it into the account.' She thought of her floral dress. 'Now, I'm not saying I have a lot in it, and I do treat myself every now and again.'

'Clever girl!' Oliver said.

Her face became serious. 'I always feel better if I know I have enough money to go back home at short notice. Enough for the boat fare and a bit over. When I first arrived, I was desperately homesick – before I became friendly with Gaye and some of the others – and the thought that I could just get up any morning and withdraw the money from the post office kept me going.'

'Do you ever feel like that now?' he asked.

'Occasionally,' she admitted, 'but not the way I used to. It's just as well, isn't it? Seeing that it's not safe to travel.'

The meal was lovely – melon decorated with thin slices of orange and a cherry; steak, well done with an assortment of vegetables; and a trifle like she had never tasted before. It was probably the best meal Clare had had in her whole life.

Oliver sat back in his chair and patted his stomach. 'Beautiful!' he said. 'What a feast. I haven't seen most of those things since the war started.' He laughed. 'And I had little occasion to enjoy or afford anything like it before. Any meals out back in Ireland were slices of ham, chicken or beef in gravy – and spuds, spuds, spuds!'

Clare laughed. 'I never realised how important potatoes were to Irish people until I came over here. I thought everyone talked about "lovely floury potatoes" and that everyone put lumps of butter on them whether they had gravy or not, and then I realised the girls were laughing at me. Not in a bad way, but I realised then that it was only the new Irish girls who talked like that.'

'Well, the English love their tea and their fish and chips,' Oliver pointed out, 'and they can be fairly opinionated over the best cafés for cod or plaice, especially in Liverpool.' He took a drink from his wine glass and then he gave a little shrug. 'But there is no denying that there is a kind of obsession in Ireland about potatoes, and is it any wonder? The whole country depended on potatoes, and when the famine came it was the biggest catastrophe that ever happened.' He shook his head. 'Weren't we lucky we never lived through that?'

'And here we are now in England,' Clare said, 'and I'm working with the nicest people who don't know anything about Ireland and our history. Wouldn't it make you wonder?'

'Exactly,' he agreed. 'We have to make the best of the situations we are in, whatever happens, and remember that people are people whatever country we are in.' He suddenly grinned at her. 'How did that serious conversation all come about because of spuds?'

They laughed, then Clare glanced down at her watch, thinking that the girls would be arriving soon. She had not mentioned them to Oliver as she knew he would say it was making too big a fuss of his birthday. Leaving it as a little surprise, she felt, was easier.

She noticed the manger over by the till desk, so she lifted her bag and said, 'I'm just going to the ladies, so you take your time and drink what is left in the wine bottle.'

'Don't you want some more?'

Clare shook her head. 'No, I enjoyed what I had, so you finish it.'

She went quickly across the floor and over to the desk, the wine giving her confidence. It was better, Diana had advised, to sort the bill privately than have the waiter come to the table.

The manager was nice and friendly, and went through the bill with her. When she paid, she left a tip for the waiter. She came back to the table smiling and with a sense of having accomplished something new. 'I thought we might go out into the bar for a drink, or maybe a tea or a coffee,' she suggested. She guessed that the two girls would be there by now.

'Only if I pay,' Oliver said, standing up. 'I can't have you buying anything more after the wine.'

'I won't argue with one drink,' she said with a laugh, 'but only if you don't mention the wine to Mum and Dad. They will think I've been completely corrupted in England if they hear that.'

'They have little to worry about, if a couple of small glasses of wine is the worst you get up to.'

When they went out into the sitting area, Clare was delighted when she spotted the two girls already seated at a table in comfortable armchairs. Turning to her brother with a big grin she indicated the table by the fireplace. 'Would you look who is here!' She gave the girls a cheery wave.

'It's your giddy red-haired friend,' he said, smiling at her.

She took his arm and guided him across the floor. 'I hope you don't mind,' she said in a low voice, 'but since it was your birthday, I thought it would be nice to have more than just the two of us.'

'I don't mind at all, it was kind of you to even think about it – and kind of your friends to come.'

Gaye was on her feet as they came towards the table and went over to give Oliver a hug. 'Happy birthday, handsome!' she said. 'Imagine you being twenty-five! Very mature and grown up.'

Oliver was unfazed by her exuberance and familiarity. 'Thank you, Gaye,' he said, giving her a peck on the cheek. 'I feel every day of it – in fact I feel thirty-five!'

Clare turned to introduce Diana. 'This is Diana, the new friend I was telling you about. The girl we met at the Plaza.'

When Diana stood up, Clare saw she was wearing her pinstriped trousers and her three long strings of pearls clinked cheerily. She had to stop herself smiling as she wondered what Gaye's reaction to them later would be.

Oliver's face suddenly looked serious as he moved towards her, his arm outstretched. 'Diana, I'm very pleased to meet you.'

'And I'm pleased to meet you, too,' she said, looking straight at him. 'And I would like to wish you a very happy birthday.'

'Now, before I sit down,' Oliver said, smiling at them all, 'I want to buy you ladies a drink, if you would be kind enough to tell me what you would like.'

'But it's *your* birthday,' Clare said. 'And I want to buy the drinks.'

'No argument,' he said. 'It's a gentleman's prerogative, and my pleasure, since I'm honoured to be in such lovely company.'

The girls had a quick discussion, then Clare said, 'Gaye and I are going to try a Martini.'

Gaye rolled her eyes. 'Diana said it is very popular among sophisticated young ladies, and we don't want to be out of fashion.'

'Martinis it is,' he said. He looked over towards the bar area, and as he did so, a waiter came straight over. He ordered the girls' drinks and a whisky for himself.

While the waiter fetched the drinks, he turned back to the girls to find three small, wrapped gifts on the table.

'Happy birthday again!' Clare said, lifting hers up and handing it to him.

'Oh, no...' Oliver shook his head. 'This is getting very embarrassing... I'm not used to this sort of palaver.'

'You're only twenty-five once, bonny lad,' Gaye reminded him, 'so if I was you, I'd milk it for all you can.'

He took the paper off, and then opened the small jeweller's

box to reveal a pair of silver cufflinks set with onyx stone. 'Ah, Clare, it's too much. How did you manage that, with rations and coupons and everything?'

'If you must know,' she told him, 'I sent the money to Mother months ago and asked her to get them in the jeweller's shop in Tullamore. It's easier to get things back home.'

He leaned over and squeezed his sister's hand. 'You are too good.'

'Now mine!' Gaye said, handing her small, round-shaped gift over. 'And don't get too excited, it's only a small thing, cos I never have enough coupons for myself.'

He opened it to reveal a small jar of Brylcreem. 'Oh, Gaye, that's very kind of you.'

'Well, I know what you lads are like with your hair, and it was either that or a bar of soap.' She looked at the girls. 'I didn't want to insult him with the soap, in case he thought I was suggesting he was dirty!'

They all laughed, and then Gaye spotted the waiter, 'Looks like our Martinis are coming!' She made a clapping gesture with her hands. 'I'm really excited to try it.'

The young waiter carefully put the tray down and distributed the Martini glasses, decorated with plump green olives.

Gaye sighed, 'I love the shape of the glasses and that fancy little pattern on the side.'

'They come in all different designs,' Diana said. 'But these are particularly nice.'

Clare raised her glass to her brother, 'Happy birthday, Oliver!' and the two girls did the same.

Gaye took a big sip of hers then suddenly stopped. 'Oh, God...' she said, pulling a face and putting her free hand over her mouth as she swallowed it down. 'Diana – what the... sorry, I mean, what on earth is in it?'

Clare looked at her, and then took a tiny sip from hers to discover it tasted nothing like she imagined. It was strong and very bitter. She put it back down on the table.

'Don't you like it?' Diana asked, her eyes wide and anxious.

'Like it?' Gaye said. 'It tastes like poison.' She lifted the glass to her nose and sniffed it, then she took another small sip. 'I suppose it's not as bad the second time, once you know what to expect...'

'I'm so sorry,' Diana said. 'I suppose it is a bit of an acquired taste.'

Gaye was examining the olive on the cocktail stick. She gave it a cautious lick then pulled a face. 'I thought it was a grape.'

'It's an olive,' Diana said. 'And they are rather bitter...'

Clare glanced over at Gaye and suddenly got a fit of giggles.

'Oh, no,' Oliver said, shaking his head. 'If I'd known what would happen when I offered to buy you all a drink.'

Diana bit her lip, 'It was my fault suggesting the Martinis,' she said. 'I should have explained what they were like. My mother has given me different cocktails since I was fourteen. When I first tasted them I thought they were absolutely awful, but she told me that you soon get used to different flavours. I won't make that mistake with anyone again.'

'Don't worry, Diana,' Gaye said, laughing, 'I'm getting used to it with every little sip I take.'

Diana gave her prettily wrapped gift to Oliver.

'But you've never even met me before...' he protested

'It's my pleasure, and there was no cost involved – just a little time, which I enjoyed.'

All eyes were on him as he carefully untied the thin ribbon and opened the delicate paper. 'Oh my goodness,' he said. He looked over at her and shook his head. 'Unbelievable... this is far too much.' He lifted out a navy silk handkerchief, then draped it over his hand to show the others. And while Clare and Gaye were exclaiming how lovely it was, he took out a maroon-coloured one and a black one with tiny red spots, and silently passed them over to the girls to examine them.

'I thought dark colours were better for you than white or something pale,' Diana explained. 'Clare told me you are out and about a lot with your camera, and then working in a dark room with all sorts of chemicals...'

He turned the navy hanky around between his hands, looking down at the tiny hand-stitching on the hem. 'And you actually made these yourself?'

Diana nodded. 'I find it soothing, and it gives me something to do in the evenings when it's too dark to draw or paint.'

'I wish I found sewing soothing; it takes me ages to even thread the needle properly.' Gaye said, taking another sip of her Martini and then looked at Oliver. 'So, anything exciting happening in Liverpool?'

'It's a busy city,' Oliver replied, tidying the hankies back into the wrapping. 'There's always something happening.'

'Have you taken photos of any famous people recently?' She looked over at Diana. 'He took a photo of Elizabeth Taylor last year.'

Oliver laughed. 'I suppose news about famous people helps to sell newspapers,' he said, 'so when the reporters hear any big names are coming to the city, they try to set up interviews and of course they need photos to go with the article. Most of the time, they just catch any film stars or singers coming out of the Adelphi or the theatres, and try to get a few words out of them. If they have a photo, then it takes up half the page.'

'There's such a lot going on in the big cities,' Diana said. 'It's much more exciting.'

'At the minute, everyone in Liverpool is talking about the war, and relieved it's not really come to anything yet. A lot of the kids that were evacuated have come back from the country, so that's a good, optimistic sign.' He looked at them. 'Not so good for Guernsey, though. Clare was telling me how you are all involved with the evacuated families.'

The girls went on to tell him about their voluntary work with the evacuees, about Gaye's singing groups and the crafts and art group.

When he heard that Diana was teaching art, he leaned forward, interested. 'What sort of art do you do yourself?'

She told him about the course she'd taken in London, and then said she just drew or painted anything that caught her attention. 'I'm glad you reminded me,' she said, and bent down to retrieve her handbag. She brought out an envelope that she handed to him. 'I made you a birthday card...'

He opened it and saw a plain white card with a perfect ink drawing of a camera that a press photographer would use, and the words, 'Happy 25th Birthday, Oliver!' written underneath.

'Wow,' he said, 'you got that perfectly.' He looked up at her, quizzically. 'How did you know the sort of model?'

'There's a photography shop down in Stockport,' she explained, 'so I went in and asked to see the sort of camera that a press photographer might use.'

'Clever girl!' Oliver said, shaking his head and laughing.

Diana went on to describe the various cameras she had been shown, while he listened intently, then Oliver told her the exact ones he used. Clare and Gaye eventually got bored hearing about cameras, and they moved on to discuss the following week's roster in the hospital, and a new make of lipstick that Clare had seen in a magazine, which apparently lasted hours longer than the usual one.

Gaye and Clare got up to go to the ladies.

'Okay,' Gaye said, when they were out of earshot, 'I'm buying us all a decent drink now. What do you fancy?'

'You know I don't have a clue about drinks,' Clare said, 'but let's split the bill: it's too expensive in here, and you'll leave yourself short for the weekend.'

'I fancy trying a gin and tonic,' Gaye said. 'I couldn't drink another of them Martinis if you paid me.' She laughed. 'Although at least I know now what people are talking about, and I can give an opinion.'

The young waiter came in from the dining room and Gaye waved him over. 'When you get a minute,' she said, 'would you bring a tray of drinks over to the table please?' She told him what they wanted and gave him a ten-shilling note, telling him to take sixpence for himself.'

'Remember I said I'll give you half,' Clare reminded her.

'I'm fine,' Gaye said, 'but if I get stuck later in the week I'll ask you for it.'

In the ladies they checked their hair and make-up while Gaye told her about a nurse on her wards who had just heard from her boyfriend, injured serving with the air force in France. 'He's in a hospital down near London,' Gaye said. 'She couldn't believe it when she heard he was alive.'

'It's so frightening, isn't it?' Clare said, 'but hopefully, it will all be over soon.'

As they washed their hands, Gaye turned towards Clare with a little grin. 'Well, what did you think of Diana's trousers?'

'They suit her,' Clare replied honestly. 'She looks lovely tonight, with that beautiful silk blouse.'

Gaye laughed. 'I was going to string you along and say they look terrible, but I'm actually coming around to them. In fact, I'm thinking of asking her to make me a pair as well!'

'Are you serious? You in trousers!' Clare giggled.

'They would be really handy,' Gaye said, 'and now I can see how nice they can look with a fancy blouse. I'm going to get some material when I get paid next week and get a pair made. What about you?'

'I think I'm the wrong shape for them,' Clare said.

'Well, Diana is smaller than you, and they're fine on her.'

'She's slimmer than me, and you're taller.'

'Get away! They'd be lovely on you.' Gaye dried her hands on the towel, 'So, has Oliver said anything about girlfriends? I'm surprised he's not got himself engaged or anything by now.'

'Nobody special, or no one that he's letting on about.' She halted. 'He's my own brother, and I think the world of him, but he wouldn't suit every girl. He can be fairly intense about politics and that kind of thing.'

'Well, most people listen to the news about the war every day and have an opinion on it.'

'It's more than that,' Clare said. 'He had friends who went out to fight in the war in Spain, and he still keeps up with what's going on out there, and he goes to meetings about it.'

'Once he meets the right girl, he'll lighten up a bit,' Gaye said. 'He'll be too busy going dancing or to the pictures to bother about things as much.' She paused. 'We should go over to Liverpool one weekend and get him out on the town to meet someone. What do you think?'

'I don't know...' Clare said vaguely. They walked back into the lounge and when she looked over at the table she saw that Oliver had moved to sit next to Diana. 'God,' she whispered to Gaye, 'I hope Oliver's not going on about the Spanish war or the fascists to Diana on what's supposed to be a happy night out. I know she's interested in those things herself, but he's only just met her.'

'Ah, leave the poor lad alone,' Gaye said, laughing. 'It's his birthday, and for all you know Diana could be boring the pants off him talking about the evacuees and her latest ideas for her art group.'

'At least that's interesting to listen to,' Clare said. 'Did I tell you that one of the older nurses is bringing me in a Moses basket for Mrs Brown's baby?'

'You're as bad!' Gaye said. 'You're always talking about the Guernsey people too, and you're calling your poor brother boring.' She put a finger to her chin as though thinking deeply. 'Thank God I never think about those kids.'

'What?' Clare said, mystified.

'And I'm definitely not setting my alarm to get up at eight o'clock tomorrow morning to finish copying out the words of the new song we're going to do.'

Clare started to laugh too. It was hard not to, with Gaye's sharp wit.

Gaye grabbed Clare by the arm. 'There's the waiter going over to the table now, and the other two don't know that we ordered the drinks.'

The rushed back to the table. When the waiter passed out the drinks, Gaye checked with Diana. 'Is the gin okay for you?'

'Absolutely! It's perfect, thank you.' Diana held the glass up in a 'Cheers' gesture.

Clare waited for Oliver to move back to his original seat, but he and Diana were still engrossed in whatever they were talking about, and when the waiter handed him his whisky and water, he set the glass down on the table beside him with no thought to move.

Clare slid into a seat next to Gaye and they started chatting about the student nurses' summer outing to Blackpool in the next few weeks. 'I hope my swimsuit still fits me,' Gaye said, 'because I can't afford a new one.'

'I won't need one,' Clare said, 'because I can't swim.'

'I love it,' Gaye said. 'We used to go to a caravan in Whitley Bay when I was young, and my dad taught me and our Audrey.'

'Have you any plans to go home to Newcastle soon?' Clare asked.

'I'll see what happens after my exams.' Her face grew serious. 'Audrey is getting back to her old self and my mam and dad seem fine, so I'm leaving well alone for a while.'

The manager came into the foyer now, and he went around the various tables. When he came to theirs, he told them that there was a band playing in the function room, and there were some spare tables if they would like to go in.

'Are people dancing?' Gaye asked.

'Yes,' he said, 'they were playing some Glenn Miller music and the floor was quite full.'

'What do you think?' Gaye said. 'Will we go in and have a look?'

Clare turned to ask the other two, and heard Oliver saying something about General Franco, and she felt sorry for Diana, guessing she would need rescuing. 'We were thinking of going in to hear the band in the function room,' she said. 'What do you think?'

'Oh, I don't mind,' Diana said. 'Whatever everyone else wants to do.'

Gaye leaned forward. 'What about the birthday boy? It's your lucky night having three gorgeous women here to choose from.'

She thumbed in Clare's direction. 'Even if one of us is your sister.'

'Why don't you two head on in, and we'll follow on. We're having a great chat... we've just discovered that we both have friends in common.'

Clare's brows shot up in surprise. 'How?' she asked. 'You don't know anyone from Stockport or Cheshire...'

'From when I was in London,' Diana said. 'People I knew when I was a student.'

'They came up to Liverpool to speak at a meeting I was at,' Oliver explained. 'It was back a couple of years ago.'

Gaye caught Clare's arm. 'Will we go in, in case the seats are gone?' She looked over at Diana. 'We'll keep you two places at our table.'

'Who would have believed it?' Gaye whispered as they walked down Buxton Road following Oliver and Diana. 'She's jumped in and pinched Oliver from under my nose. Maybe I should get a pair of trousers after all.'

'Maybe you should.' Clare gave Gaye a little friendly dig in the ribs. 'They do seem to be getting on well. I suppose it's because they know the same friends.'

'Well, friends or not, Diana has definitely grabbed your Oliver's attention. She's put my nose out of joint.'

Clare looked at her seriously now. 'You're not really disappointed, are you?'

'Not really,' Gaye said. 'I just like winding you up. Oliver is a lovely looking lad, but I couldn't be doing with all that political talk.'

'It doesn't seem to be bothering Diana. From what she said, she seems to agree with him.'

'I saw you talking to her when I was up dancing with him.'

'I was checking that Oliver hadn't got her pinned to her chair, and having to listen about his theories on fascism or whatever, and she told me she thinks Oliver is one of the most intelligent men she's ever met, and that she could listen to him all night.'

'The one thing he has going for him is his looks. Most of them intellectual types have terrible hair and big, thick glasses.'

'Oh, Gaye, you are awful.'

Gaye laughed and looked around her. 'Well, it's turned out to be a very different night from what I was expecting, although I've really enjoyed it, especially meeting those two lacrosse players.' She stopped. 'And now we're going down to Diana's auntie's house for another drink. I might have been a bit nervous, but knowing young Stella is living in the house with them makes it seem more normal. I'll just have to keep my gob shut, and talk slower so that Diana's auntie understands me.'

'I think even you would have trouble talking with your mouth shut, Gaye!' Clare said, grinning at her.

Five minutes later Diana and Oliver came to a halt outside the house, and when the girls caught up they all went up the driveway together. Clare wondered now if Gaye was right, and if there really could be a spark between her brother and her friend. They might have found some things in common, but their backgrounds were completely different, plus there were religious differences.

'All ready?' Diana said, turning back to the girls. 'I hope Clare's warned you about my aunt's hypochondria, Gaye. Just so you are prepared for her telling you all her ailments.'

'I've heard it a few times now,' Gaye said, 'and I've seen what she's like down at the town hall – so I'm all prepared.'

Clare watched as Diana moved nearer to Oliver again, and said something to him, and then he started laughing. He turned around and when she saw the relaxed smile on his face, she felt pleased that his birthday celebration had gone so well. The wine and the couple of drinks afterwards obviously would make him mellower, but she thought he looked happier than she had ever remembered.

As they went towards the door, Oliver placed his hand on the small of Diana's back, and she leaned towards him before they moved apart. It was a small gesture, but so easy and natural that Clare knew it meant something. Exactly what, she wasn't sure.

Chapter Twenty-Five

Clare and Gaye walked down towards the town hall together at ten o'clock the following morning.

'It turned into a much later night than we thought,' Clare said. 'It must have been around one o'clock by the time I got into bed.'

'When my alarm went off at eight o'clock, I didn't know where I was,' Gaye said. 'I think it was the two sherries I drank at Diana's.'

'I just had a few sips of one,' Clare said, 'because I felt a bit tipsy when we were walking down the road to the house after the mixture of drinks. I've never drank so much in one night before.'

'Don't mention that Martini and the bloody olive...' They both started giggling. 'Ah, it turned out to be a great night, and it was nice of Diana to invite us back to the house. I enjoyed listening to the records she played for us. It just finished the night off lovely.'

'And it was nice of her aunt giving us drinks and those little biscuits.'

'It was, but I can't stop laughing every time I think of her,' Gaye said. 'She's every bit as bad as you both said, and she's half-deaf; you keep having to repeat yourself. When I told her I had been working in the accident and emergency department, she asked about the worst cases that had been brought in, and then wanted to know what the doctors did. She didn't catch half of what I said, and I had to keep repeating myself.'

'Things seem be going well with Stella,' Clare said. 'They seemed relaxed with each other last night, and Diana said her aunt gave Stella some of Diana's old children's books and games.'

They crossed over the road. 'I wonder if Diana will be in the hall already,' Clare said. 'She usually goes down early to set out the art stuff. She was talking about doing collages with the kids today, as she had gone around to some of the local newsagents to get old magazines from them. She's always planning something, I don't know where she gets her ideas from.'

'And she doesn't make a big song and dance about it,' Gaye said. 'Talking of songs, I have all my music notes here.' She patted her bag. 'I was sitting at my desk this morning writing out the words to another song Jack gave me. It was driving me mad, because the carbon paper kept slipping and some of the bottom sheets were missing words, so I had to make extra. I've done twenty-five copies, so I hope it's enough.'

'It sounds plenty; if it's not they can share. I've plenty of wool and knitting needles now. One of the women from the church dropped a box of stuff in earlier in the week. She'd gone around the houses collecting.'

'The people in Stockport have been great helping out. Their hearts are in the right place.'

'In these last few weeks I've got to know more people than I've met in all the time I've been living here,' Clare said. 'Some of the families that have contributed haven't much themselves, but they gave anything they could afford.'

They paused at the entrance to the town hall. Clare said, 'I wonder if Oliver is up yet, or if he is having a lie-in. He said he was catching the train back to Liverpool around one o'clock, and that he would look in at the hall to see me before going.'

Gaye gave her a sidelong glance. 'Do you think there's any chance of your Oliver and Diana getting together?'

Clare shrugged. 'I haven't a clue. They seemed to get on well last night.'

'Get on well?' Gaye laughed. 'They only had eyes for each other. They have a lot in common, and Diana is a bit older than us. I suppose living in London and travelling abroad makes her more a woman of the world than us.'

'Oliver has lived in Liverpool and travelled to London a few times, but he's never been abroad,' Clare said. 'I think our families would be like chalk and cheese. Diana doesn't brag or anything like that, but I heard her and her aunt talking about her father's family estate.'

'That's enough to frighten anybody off,' Gaye mused, 'but your Oliver is very confident. I don't think he would be over-awed by anybody. He just chatted away to Diana as if she was the same as us.'

Clare shrugged. 'If he was living in Stockport then you never know what could happen, but he's going back to Liverpool later on, so it will be hard to keep in touch.'

Just as they approached the door, it suddenly opened and Mr Lomas came rushing out. 'Delighted to see you, girls!' he said. 'It's all hands on deck inside. We got a delivery of footballs and small handballs from one of the toyshops in Manchester, and they're sorting them out. I'm just rushing up to the school to borrow their skipping ropes and hula hoops.'

The girls went inside, where there were already a dozen or more people setting up tables and chairs and sorting out boxes of toys, clothes and household items.

'Looks like we've made it down before Diana,' Gaye said.

'I'm sure she'll be here soon.'

An older woman came towards them. 'Thanks for coming, girls,' she said. 'If you want to get a cup of tea before the kids arrive, there's an urn in the kitchen. Some of the volunteers are already in there now.'

'I'd love another cup of tea,' Gaye said. 'It might help my voice.'

They headed towards the kitchen, stopping to have a word with the other helpers as they passed by. Clare heard the sound of voices coming from the kitchen, and she smiled at Gaye. 'Diana is here, I've just heard her.'

'The late night didn't hold her back,' Gaye said, sounding impressed, 'if she's in there making tea for everyone.'

They turned into the half-opened kitchen door, and then froze when they saw Oliver standing beside her. They watched in astonishment as he caught Diana around the waist and pull her towards him. He said something to her and she laughed, and the next moment they were wrapped in each other's arms and kissing passionately, oblivious to the two onlookers. Gaye grabbed the stunned Clare by the arm and pulled out of sight.

'Oh, my God!' Clare gasped, her hands coming up to her face. 'I don't believe it... it's not a bit like our Oliver. I never imagined...'

Gaye raised her eyebrows and smiled. 'Well, you don't need to imagine any more, bonny lass. It was there, plain for anyone to see.'

'I can't believe it,' she repeated. 'Especially at this hour of the morning.'

'They probably don't have the faintest idea what time of the day it is.'

'I wonder if he even had any breakfast at the hotel.'

'That'll be the last thing on his mind.' Gaye patted Clare's shoulder. 'They don't have any time to waste, with him living in Liverpool, and not knowing when they'll meet up again.'

'Do you think they will?'

'From what we just saw, I would imagine they would.'

'What am I going to do?'

'Nothing,' Gaye said, steering her away from the kitchen. 'Nothing at all – it's not your business. They are two adults who are entitled to do what they want, and besides, they were only kissing.'

'But they hardly know each other, and I'll feel stuck in the middle if it all goes wrong.' *And*, she thought *if anything serious comes of it, I'll be blamed at home for introducing Oliver to a Protestant.*

'With this flaming war,' Gaye said, 'none of us know what's going to happen tonight or tomorrow.' She gestured around the hall. 'The families in Guernsey know what real problems are, and you worrying about your Oliver kissing Diana would make them wonder if you were right in the head.'

Clare gave a sigh, and then nodded. 'I know, I know...'

A short while later Diana came out, carrying two mugs of tea. Her face lit up when she saw them. 'Oh, you're here!' she said, looking pleased. 'Oliver arrived before you, he's in the kitchen. I've made some tea.' She held the mugs out. 'You can have these if you like.'

The girls took the mugs from her, and then all three stood in silence.

Gaye raised her eyebrows and smiled. 'Have you something to tell us, Diana?'

Diana's brow wrinkled. 'About what's happening today?'

'No,' Gaye said, 'about you and Oliver.'

A deep blush bloomed on Diana's face.

'We walked into the kitchen a few minutes ago,' Gaye said, a devilish look in her eyes, 'and saw the pair of you together. We didn't want to disturb you, like.'

Diana's face suddenly broke into a huge, embarrassed smile and she covered it with both hands. 'Oh no... I didn't know there was anyone around.' She turned to Clare, her hands clasped together. 'Please say you're not angry with me? I was awake half the night worrying about your reaction.' Her voice was trembling. 'Your friendship means so much to me, but I've never met anyone like Oliver before, and he feels the same. From the first moment we met...' She shrugged. 'It's almost as if we've been waiting to meet each other.'

Clare heard herself say, 'No, no... I'm not angry, I just... I just didn't realise.'

Something caught her eye at the kitchen door and she saw Oliver standing there, looking over at them. He had that same happy smile on his face that she'd noticed last night. The same happy smile that Diana had now. Clare closed her eyes. Who was she to decide what another person should have or feel?

What right had she to look for obstacles that might not even be there?

'We don't know how it's going to work,' Diana rushed on. 'But we want to see each other, no matter what. I know it's hard to understand in such a short time – but neither of us has ever felt like this before.'

Clare could sense everything that Diana was feeling – uncertainty, hope and determination. She clasped Diana's hands in hers. 'I'm very happy for you and Oliver, and I couldn't wish him to meet a nicer girl. Good luck to you both.'

Chapter Twenty-Six

Over the next few weeks, life fell into a different routine for the girls as Oliver travelled over to Stockport most weekends to spend time with Diana. She had talked her aunt Rosamund into letting him have one of the spare rooms and said how more secure they would all feel to have a man in the house at night during any air raids. Her aunt seemed to get on well with Oliver and was impressed by the fact that he brought his ration allowance with him, and anything else he could get his hands on, to share with everyone else in the house.

To Diana, she referred to Oliver as 'your Irish friend's brother' and had not seemed to catch onto the fact that he and Diana were romantically linked. The couple spent every spare minute together, and Oliver even helped with her art groups, going around the children, talking to them about what they were drawing and giving words of encouragement.

On one recent weekend, Diana had gone over to Liverpool to spend some time with him, and came back enthused about the beautiful buildings and the museums they had visited. Oliver had taken her to the theatre one night and they also had a meal in the Philharmonic Dining Rooms.

Clare could see that the romance was growing stronger by the day, and as Gaye commented every time she saw them, 'They're mad about each other and they both love talking about stuff that would bore us to death.'

Both girls had been rostered onto accident and emergency, which tested both their nursing skills and patience.

'I don't get how folk can be so stupid,' Gaye sighed to Clare as they walked back to the nurses' residence after their shift. 'Imagine getting so mortal drunk you can hardly walk and then going out into the pitch black. It's just asking for an accident, isn't it?'

'It is,' Clare agreed, then she suddenly laughed. 'Although some people are taking it to the other extreme. I was reading in the paper today that some farmer down in Devon painted white stripes on his cows so people wouldn't run them over.'

As July progressed, more homes were found for evacuees, with every conceivable building used, such as disused shops and new council estates which were in the final stages of building. Sometimes several families moved in together, and as time went on some of the mothers found part-time work in local shops, factories and cinemas or as conductresses on the buses, while others helped them with childcare.

The threat of Nazi invasion of Britain became more real to people as reports of air attacks on the British ports were heard and then, in August, raids were concentrated on the RAF airfields. The Home Guard came into force to act as a local defence group, and people were both alarmed and reassured to see soldiers with rifles around the nearby towns.

Life went on as normal and Clare and Gaye were relieved and delighted when they completed their two-year state enrolled nurse qualification and were now finally fully trained nurses. With things still in flux due to the war, both decided to stay put in St Timothy's hospital for the time being. They had a good group of friends and were happy enough in the nurses' accommodation. They still enjoyed their social nights at the cinema or dancing, when they were free, and if one was working they met up in their rooms or in the canteen to hear the latest news and gossip.

On a Thursday night when Clare was on a late shift in the women's geriatric ward, Gaye was rostered on accident and emergency. As usual, they were kept very busy with casualties of all sorts – babies with temperatures, lads who had been hurt on the football playing fields, old people who had fallen, and even a young woman who had collapsed at home and had been brought in by her two friends.

While they were waiting to see the duty doctor, Gaye had been sent out to take details from the woman. She had a high temperature and seemed to be in some pain, and was finding it difficult to respond. Her two friends had told her that her name was Marjorie Timmins, but didn't seem to be much help otherwise. Gaye had pressed on, though – it was crucial to get as much information as possible so she could let the doctor know if poor Marjorie was an urgent case.

'Have you any idea what's happened to her?' Gaye asked the two friends again, neither seeming keen to reveal their names.

The women looked from one to the other. 'We don't know,' the blonde woman said. 'She sent the oldest kid round to our house because she wasn't well.'

'Was her husband home?'

Again they looked at each other and the same one said, 'No, he's out abroad with the navy.'

'Did she say anything?' Gaye persisted. 'Give you any details at all?'

'She just said that she had stomach pains, like.'

'Was she being sick or anything like that?'

The women looked at each other. Then the other friend suddenly said. 'Look, it's nothing to do with us. We just brought her here ...'

'Was she able to walk?'

'No, we knew somebody on the street with a delivery van and he brought us.'

Gaye looked from one to the other, but neither of them would meet her eye. Then, she noticed that the blonde woman had her fists clenched tightly and she realised that they were both terrified to say anything. She wondered why, and then a little warning light went off in her head. If her guess was right, and Marjorie Timmins' friends knew more than what they were letting on, Gaye could understand their reluctance to get her or themselves into trouble

Suddenly, the sick woman slid off her chair and fell to the floor and Gaye waved at Robert, the porter she and Clare were friendly with, to help. He came racing over and between the two of them they got her into a wheelchair and whisked her out of the waiting room. They hurried down the corridor to where there was another area sectioned off by curtains, and then lifted her onto the bed there.

'Dr Harvey is on duty tonight,' Gaye whispered to Robert. 'Go and find him, tell him it's urgent.'

A few minutes later the fresh-faced young doctor came in. He looked from the woman to Gaye, expectantly. 'Do we have any notes as yet?' His manner was extremely professional, and there was nothing which suggested there had ever been anything romantic between them.

Gaye shook her head. 'She wasn't fit to say anything, and her friends didn't want to tell me anything.'

'Do we have her name?'

'Marjorie Timmins.'

'And is she a married lady?'

'According to the friends who brought her in, her husband is serving abroad in the navy.'

He pursed his lips together. 'Okay...' He looked thoughtful, then he looked over at Gaye and raised his eyebrows. 'Let's see what we're dealing with.' He went over to the side of the bed and gently lifted the young woman's hand. 'Marjorie?' he said, his voice kind and gentle. 'Can you hear me?'

When there was no reply, he put his hand on her forehead, and then he unbuttoned the top of her blouse and took his stethoscope from around his neck and placed it on her chest. He looked at his watch and listened intently. The woman made a little noise and moved her head, then she gave a moan of pain and brought her knees up to her chest.

'I'm going to have to examine her,' he said and Gaye pulled the curtains quickly for privacy, 'just to make sure. If you wouldn't mind placing the blanket over her stomach and legs.' He then went on to the lift the woman's skirt and within a minute, he put her clothes back in place.

He shook his head. 'If it's what I think it is, we need to get her straight into theatre.'

He beckoned Gaye outside where the woman – in case she became conscious – would not hear.

'She has all the symptoms of an abortion gone wrong,' he whispered. 'I'm just going to get Dr Lawson to get his opinion, he's far more experienced in this sort of thing.' His eyes met Gaye's and they held for a few moments. 'Stay with her until I get back.'

Gaye sat holding the young woman's hand, thinking that her initial assessment earlier had been right. Abortion was something that had been touched on in their nursing training. She had heard since that it was much more common than the student nurses had been told, and that there was someone in every town to help women get rid of babies they did not want.

She could understand the desperation young women must feel as there was a terrible stigma for both herself and the baby. Audrey had recently talked to her about this after she had had her accident, and said how lucky she was that she could have immediately married Laurence if she hadn't lost the baby. But other women did not have that option as fathers often refused to take any responsibility, leaving them to seek help where they could. The wealthier classes had more choice as they could pay privately, with qualified consultants to have the problem dealt with discreetly.

The best of the 'backstreet abortionists', as they were referred to, were doctors who had been struck off the medical register for malpractice and those who had had some training in midwifery. There were many with only minimal medical training or none at all, whose practice was to administer potions – which were supposed to bring on a spontaneous abortion – helped along by instruments such as hooks or even coat hangers.

Gaye knew that it was also common for young women to try

to cause a miscarriage by drinking large amounts of gin then sit in an almost scalding bath. She had even heard of girls who had thrown themselves downstairs. None of the practices were safe, and whatever available procedure was chosen, the risks were known to be very high. She looked at the young woman now, noticing the flushed skin and her rapid breathing, and felt a sense of anxiety. She hoped that Dr Harvey would be back very soon.

After Marjorie Timmins had been examined by the serious, middle-aged Dr Lawson, she was hooked up to drips and an anaesthetist was summoned. Within an hour she was rushed off to theatre. A weary Gaye went out to tell the two friends what had happened. Dr Harvey had also asked her to find out as much as she could from the people who had brought her in, and told Gaye to assure them they would not be involved in any investigations.

'The more information we can get to work out what has happened to her,' he explained, 'the better the chance she has of surviving.'

Gaye's heart had lurched. She knew it was serious but had not imagined the very worst scenario. She brought Marjorie's two friends to a private side ward and explained what was happening to her. They both sat, shoulders slumped, with tears in their eyes, as she explained that the doctors thought she had contracted some sort of infection, but they needed to do a thorough investigation under anaesthetic.

'Did you know she was pregnant?' Gaye asked in a low voice. 'And do you know what she did to try to get rid of the baby?' She halted. 'You don't need to worry about me saying anything – I promise to keep it confidential. It's just that anything you tell me might help the doctors.'

The blonde girl looked at her through lowered lids. 'You really promise not to say anything? We would get into terrible trouble too, and we don't need that. We're all working women – working in the local factories – and trying to do our best to manage and help each other.'

'I do understand,' Gaye reassured them, 'and I promise you won't be in trouble.'

'All I know,' the blonde woman said, 'is she'd been to some woman who gave her something to take to bring her monthlies on, and then she had to go back for the woman to make sure it was all gone. She said she put something inside her, to clear it all out like, and the pain of it nearly killed her.'

Gaye bit her lip. 'Has she other children?'

'A little girl.'

'And could she not afford to keep this one? You said her husband was away.'

The women looked from one to the other, and then the red-haired one said, 'That's why she did it. The baby wasn't her husband's. It was some fella she met at a wedding in Manchester. Her husband was at Dunkirk and he's in some navy hospital down south. She said she needed to get rid of it or her marriage would be over.'

'Or she would be killed,' the blonde woman said. 'Bert knocks her about something terrible. Marjorie is a decent woman. She made one mistake, and she's paying for it now.'

With that information, Gaye raced off to tell Dr Lawson, but despite the doctors' great efforts, five hours later Marjorie Timmins died.

Breaking the news to her friends had nearly broken Gaye, who had had to watch the two distressed women walk out of the hospital doors, holding each other up. She had looked to escape in the canteen, feeling her own eyes stinging with unshed tears, only to find a despondent Dr Harvey sitting in the far corner, staring into his cup of tea.

Gaye sat down beside him. 'You did your best.'

'It was too late. Dr Lawson tried everything, but it was too late.' He shook his head, red blotches on his cheeks. 'Another young woman gone because of barbaric, backstreet abortions. The butchers out there who are performing these procedures are risking women's lives every day. Something should be done to allow qualified doctors to deal with it – to make it legal and safe.'

'I agree,' Gaye said quietly, his anger soothing her own, 'but it's not going to happen until this war is long over and done with.'

There was a silence then Gaye stood up. She touched her hand to his shoulder. 'I'll leave you in peace.'

He suddenly caught her hand, and her heart leapt.

'I'm going home to York this weekend,' he told her, 'and I'm going to sort things out. I haven't been back since you and I spoke.' He sighed. 'It's the first time that Elizabeth and I have had the same weekend off.'

She looked at him, her legs suddenly felt shaky, so she sat back down. 'Are you sure about what you're doing? I didn't want to interfere or make things awkward for you. I've kept away like I said I would.'

'It's not been fair on you either.' He squeezed her hand. 'I'm going to tell Elizabeth face to face; she deserves that at least. I know it's been a long wait for you, but we couldn't organise time off before now. Both families will not be happy, because we've been together for such a long time – we were childhood sweethearts – and my mother has been hinting about an engagement soon.'

Gaye took a deep breath, scared to imagine that this handsome, kind doctor might feel something special for her.

Dr Harvey pushed his hands through his blonde hair. 'In some ways it would be easier to go along with it, but we've been growing further apart. All we seem to talk about is work. Who knows? She might even be relieved.'

Gaye could see the strain of the long shift etched on his face, coupled with the worry of the weekend to come.

'Since I met you, everything has changed, and I'm sorry if you thought I was using you to fill a gap, or whatever it was you said the last time we spoke about it.'

'I'm sorry too – I know it's not been easy for you.'

'I really care about you, Gaye. You do know that, don't you?'

'And I care about you too.'

Their eyes met, and she felt as though she could suddenly burst out crying, so she turned her head away.

'How have things been for you? We've hardly spoken apart from when we've been working together. Is your sister fully recovered?'

'Yes, thank God, she's back teaching and fine now. It was appendicitis and some complication with her falling.' This was what Audrey had told the school and anyone else who asked.

From what she had told Gaye in her letters and phone calls, she was still missing Laurence, and hoped he would get back for their wedding later in the year. She wasn't entirely hopeful as she had only received a couple of letters, all heavily censored so she couldn't read the names of any of the places he had been stationed.

'And you? Are you still helping with the evacuees?'

Gaye smiled. 'Me and the girls still have our groups going at the weekends, and we go out to visit the families during the week. We're just making sure they're settling in okay, because it looks like they could be here a while.'

He shook his head. 'This damned war.'

'I hope it's not too hard for you, when you go back home.' Gaye said as she stood once again, her mind in a whirl trying to process the poor death of Marjorie Timmons and now this. Yet she couldn't help but feel a glow around her heart at the thought of Dr Harvey choosing her, wanting to be with her.

He shrugged. 'It will be a weight off me.'

She touched his hand, daringly. 'I haven't been out much – at dances or anything like that. And I haven't looked at anyone else. I've just been waiting... and hoping.'

'Me too,' he said, his eyes meeting hers. 'After the weekend it will all be over – it will be all out in the open.'

Chapter Twenty-Seven

The women in the factory sat in silence in the canteen, their eyes glued to the screen as they watched a grainy, crackling film that featured young paratroopers learning their specialised skills from the Royal Air Force in a unit in Ringway, Manchester. The commentator explained how the gruelling training was necessary to prepare them for landing in enemy territory. The women watched as the young men started off jumping from wooden structures and learning how to roll to protect themselves, until they had graduated to leaping from steelwork towers and then barrage balloons. When they were competent, the film presenter explained, they then swiftly moved onto the final part of their training: jumping out of aircraft.

The women watched a parachutist standing by the door of an aircraft, waiting for the signal. Then they all held their breath as he dropped through the narrow hole in the plane and out into the open sky.

They watched him falling quickly for a few moments, their hearts in their mouths, and then a loud cheer went up as the silk canopy billowed open above his head. When he had gained his balance and was floating slowly and steadily, he turned to the camera and gave a thumbs-up, which elicited another roar of appreciation from the women.

Diana sat at the back of the room, her eyes riveted to the screen. The camera panned out to show the sky filled with dozens of silk parachutes all floating around like bubbles, bringing the brave servicemen safely to the ground.

There was another round of clapping and cheering as the film ground to a halt, and then there was silence.

Phyllis Hackett, the supervisor, thanked the man who had come with the projector and screen, and then she said, 'That was just a little reminder of the amazing work you all do in this factory every day. A reminder of all the lives we save by our careful measuring, cutting, sewing and packing.' She raised her hand into the air. 'You are all doing a fantastic job supporting our brave men, so give yourselves a round of applause.'

The film was followed by a tea break and free trays of sticky buns for all the parachute-makers, which definitely boosted morale among the tired and occasionally jaded workers.

Diana had just collected her tea and bun and was looking for a quiet place to sit by herself, when the supervisor made her way towards her.

'Bring your tea into the office,' Phyllis said, smiling at her.

Diana felt a little flutter in her chest as she followed her back out into the corridor, wondering if she had done something wrong.

Phyllis invited her to sit down, and then she lifted her own mug of tea and took a long, deep sip. 'Ah, that's better,' she said. 'That was a great film, wasn't it?'

'Fantastic,' Diana said, nodding. 'It really was uplifting and a great reminder of the work we are doing here.'

'Good,' the supervisor said. 'Although I must admit I'm not keen on standing up in front of the women and talking.' She shrugged. 'I always feel a bit self-conscious and think my mind is going to go blank, and leave me standing there looking like Piffin.'

'I think you did a splendid job.'

'Thank you, but I'm sure you would sound even better with your lovely eloquent way of speaking.'

'Not at all.'

Diana was surprised at the statement. There was a small silence during which she wondered again what she was doing here. Then, when Phyllis lifted a notebook from her desk, opened it, and ran her finger down some columns, she was even more confused.

'I have told you this before, Diana,' she began. 'You are one of the best machinists in the factory, with almost faultless stitching. You also have a very high work output.' She cleared her throat, then smiled. 'I have spoken to the factory owners, and we think it would be a good idea to have an assistant supervisor here, and I wondered if you would be interested in the position?'

There was a silence before Diana said, 'Oh, gosh . . . I certainly wasn't expecting this.'

Phyllis laughed. 'Well, I hope it is a good surprise?'

Diana's face remained serious. 'I'm sorry, but I couldn't accept that position. The other women wouldn't want me.' She shook her head. 'You must know how unpopular I am.'

'Surely it has nothing to do with being popular?' Phyllis said. 'It's all about fast, excellent work, supporting and helping the others to reach that standard. I think you are the perfect person for the job, and it would be silly to let others put you off.'

'No, I couldn't do it.' There was a note of determination in her voice. 'It's hard enough coming in day after day, knowing that people do not want to work with me.' She shrugged. 'I've got used to it, and I have very good friends outside of the factory who think well of me. That's what keeps me going.'

'People do think well of you, Diana,' the supervisor said. 'When you had time off recently, the difference your absence made was very much noticed. At one of the tea breaks the girls were discussing you, saying that they missed having you around to check things over. Some are certainly not as confident as you are at their jobs, and they know how high the quality standards are for the parachutes. They rely on you to give them the last check before they are allowed through.'

'I do understand what you're saying,' Diana said in a low voice. 'But if a machine could do my job, they wouldn't miss me at all. They just bring the piece they are working on to me, usually without a word, and stand while I check it or unpick and re-stitch it. They never say anything friendly or show any appreciation for anything, and that, of course, is their prerogative.'

Diana thought back to a recent situation where she felt very hurt, when one of the women took ill at home and died overnight. The woman was a bit older than her and married, and Diana thought she would like to pay her respects – perhaps send a sympathy card to the woman's family.

She thought about it, and decided to ask the woman she had helped in the toilet when she fainted, if she knew the deceased woman's address. She picked her because the woman had been a little warmer after the event, and always said a quiet 'thanks' if Diana helped to correct any of her work.

As soon as she mentioned the funeral, the girl looked taken aback and had muttered something about it being private. Diana later heard a group of the women making arrangements to call at the bereaved house, to deliver a card and a box with cakes and sherry to the family from her friends at the factory. No one had thought to include her or ask her to sign the card. She could relate this story now, to elicit her supervisor's understanding, but she did not want to think of the snubs she had endured – or recount them.

Diana lifted her head high. 'I am very grateful for the opportunity you have offered me, Mrs Hackett, but I think it best if you find someone else.'

Phyllis sat back in her chair. 'I'm so sorry you feel like that, and sorry that things have got so out of hand with the other women.' She pursed her lips together. 'In a way I feel I have some part in this – I should have been more observant and asked if you preferred to sit alone in the canteen or were you being excluded.'

Diana made a little waving gesture with her hands. 'Please, don't...' She took a deep breath. 'If we are to continue working side-by-side as equal workers then it doesn't matter what they feel about me – I just do my job, which I really like, and then go home. However, if I were to move to management, then I think it would be very hard for me to accept their attitude. I would have to interact with every one of the women for most of the day and I think I would find it too difficult.' She paused to still her breath, and because she had suddenly become aware that she sounded weak and whining. A picture of Oliver came into her mind, and she knew he would want her to stay strong and resolute in this situation.

'Look, Diana,' Phyllis said, 'we all know you could have chosen to go somewhere else, and that you could have had an easier time of it working with people of your own class.'

'I chose here because of the sewing, which I like, and because making parachutes is imperative for the war effort.'

'Well, it's obvious from your attention to detail how much you enjoy sewing, and for what it's worth, the women are all impressed that you have stuck it out here, given your background.' She raised her eyebrows and smiled. 'I admire you for having the guts to do what you want, and also for feeling that people should all be treated the same, regardless of background. It's the right attitude, but some people are more blinkered and don't feel comfortable with anyone who is not like them.'

Diana dropped her gaze. She had been warned by everyone that she would not fit in with the other workers in a factory, that the class difference was too great, but she had persisted nonetheless. The workers were only reacting to her class difference in the same way that Aunt Rosamund had reacted to the evacuee families and was only happy when she found Stella, who she felt fitted in. In this case, the workers had no other choice if she took the promotion. She was exactly what they did *not* want, and they did not feel comfortable with her.

If things had been different, Diana knew she would have been delighted to accept the assistant supervisor's post. She felt she was doing a good and worthwhile job that she was proud of, and deep down she knew she was the best person for the post, but under the circumstances, there was no way she could take it.

Chapter Twenty-Eight

The next weekend Clare went around the group of older children she'd been teaching knitting to for six weeks, checking if anyone needed help picking up dropped stitches or joining a new ball of wool onto the piece already knitted. Some of the ones aged around thirteen or fourteen were already fairly experienced knitters and were working on jumpers or cardigans. A girl at the back of the group put her hand up to say she had made a mistake and ripped a raglan-style sleeve out, struggling to get it back on the needles in the right order. When she was sure everyone was sorted out, she went to back to sit behind the table, and opened her notebook, checking the children's names off the list to see how many had attended today.

The numbers were down a little as it was a damp, miserable day and some of the mothers needed the older children to help with the younger ones at home. It was the same with Gaye and Diana's groups, although nobody minded as the smaller numbers meant more time spent with the ones who did come.

Her register checked, Clare went back to stitching up a pink cardigan she had knitted for May Tyrrell's baby girl, Margaret-Anne.

The mother and daughter had been housed up in Edgeley, ten minutes' walk from the centre of the town, sharing a house with another Guernsey woman with three children. Clare had started visiting her on her free nights. They had become friends of a sort, and Clare enjoyed her soothing company, as well as knitting her sweet daughter little gifts. It made her feel like she was giving back, not just here at the town hall, but by going that step further.

Although the servicemen out fighting for their country abroad were still the main radio news, very little had happened locally apart from the arrival of the Guernsey families. On the whole, in Stockport, things were still carrying on as they had been for the last few years, and the girls' routine of work, helping out the families and enjoying their nights out, hadn't changed.

Understandably, Gaye was spending most of her free time with Dr Harvey. Clare was delighted for her and didn't mind a bit. Gaye was thrilled that everything was above board and they could be open about their romance with her friends. Clare had been relieved when Gaye said that Andrew had done the decent thing and broken off with his girlfriend in York. Seemingly, it went as well as a break-up can, as Andrew had guessed correctly that Elizabeth too had felt they had grown apart, and that it would take a lot of effort to make it work. Both sets of parents were the ones who were most upset. Clare thought he must feel strongly for Gaye, to have travelled to York and done things properly in order to start officially courting her.

Clare could tell just by looking at them that they seemed very well suited to each other, and Gaye said she felt deliriously happy for the first time in her life.

'I just can't believe my luck,' she told Clare later that night over a cup of cocoa. 'I mean, imagine me landing a doctor! Never in my wildest dreams did I imagine that happening. I joked about it – the way I joked about your Oliver – but deep down, I never thought somebody like Andrew would ever be serious about me.'

'But you're lovely looking, Gaye,' Clare said, 'and lots of lads have asked you out.'

'But nobody like Andrew. He could have anyone he wants. His other girlfriend was a doctor too – I'm only a nurse.'

Clare's eyes widened. 'Nurses are important too, and we should be proud of our work.'

'And I am proud of it, I just meant that I'm more ordinary

than him. I'm not saying' I'm common or anythin', but Andrew is from a higher-class family and so was his old girlfriend.'

'You both work together, and you're friendly with a lot of the same people, and you are both Church of England. In that sense, you've a lot more in common than Diana and Oliver, and it's not holding them back.'

'You're right,' Gaye said. 'I think it's all those years listening to me mam and Audrey's disappointment that I didn't do a more professional job. It must have made me question it myself and think I hadn't done as well.'

'Forget about that,' Clare told her, 'and Audrey sounds as though she's improved in her attitude to things.'

'She is,' Gaye said. 'She's much better in every way, thank God.' She gave a slightly embarrassed smile. 'I know it's running ahead of meself, but I think if I ever got married, I might even ask her to be my bridesmaid – along with you, of course – and maybe even Diana, depending on the size of the wedding.'

Clare started laughing. 'Don't let Andrew hear your plans or you'll frighten him off.'

'I know, but it's lovely just thinking about it, and imagining how it could all be. The lovely dresses and the flowers.' Her face became more serious. 'Although, I must admit I'm terrified about meeting Andrew's family. God knows what they'll think about me, especially with him bein' an only child.'

'You'll be grand,' Clare said. 'Just be yourself and when they get to know you, they'll be happy for the pair of you. They won't want to fall out with Andrew, so it's in their interests to get on with you.'

'Do you think your family will be the same with Diana?' Gaye asked. 'They've seen each other nearly every weekend, either here or in Liverpool. And he's staying at Diana's auntie's house when he's here.'

Clare closed her eyes. 'I really don't know. It's so different with Irish families. It's all about religion. I just don't know.'

'Well, *you* don't need to worry about it,' Gaye said. 'Diana and Oliver will sort it all out. They're two very strong-minded people, and I suppose it will help that they're probably going to live in England.'

'I wouldn't imagine that anything too serious is going to happen between them for a while.'

'I'm so happy for Diana, because she's not had things easy at work. I felt so sorry for her when she told us about turning down promotion because of the way those girls still treat her. You'd think after all these months that they would have given her a chance and got to know her properly, wouldn't you?'

Clare nodded. 'She said they weren't nice even when she went to help somebody that had fainted in the toilets. That's just ridiculous.'

'And that business about the woman who died, and not asking her to sign the sympathy card for the family. They sound like absolute bitches to me.'

'I would ask for a transfer,' Clare said. 'I couldn't work in that atmosphere.'

The following Monday afternoon, Gaye called over to Clare's geriatric ward at the break. 'D'you fancy the three of us going to the Plaza tomorrow night? We're both off, and if Diana is doing a long shift, she could come straight from work. *A Yank at Oxford* is on and Ann Cannon says it's brilliant. She went with some of the others last night.'

'I'd love to,' Clare said. 'What about Andrew? You might want to go with him.'

'Oh, he's on lates this week, and he could be working until midnight or even after, depending on what's going on in casualty.' She sighed. 'I wish we had somewhere to go other than out to the canteen or the social club, or the pictures or a dance. It's awkward because we're both in the staff accommodation and neither of us are allowed in each other's block. I wish we had somewhere like an ordinary house where we could have a cup of tea, and sit and listen to the radio together.'

'That's what everyone our age complains about – no privacy.'

'Diana is so lucky, isn't she? Her and Oliver are in the same house together most weekends.' A glint came into her eye. 'Do you think they ever ... you know? He could easily sneak along to her bedroom when her aunt's asleep. She's half-deaf anyway.'

Clare rolled her eyes. 'I really don't want to think about it. It's weird when it's your brother.' She paused. 'Besides, I'm sure Diana wouldn't want to take any chances. She's an intelligent girl.'

Gaye looked at her watch. 'I think I better get a move on or I'll be late back to the ward.'

'I'm just thinking,' Clare said, 'would you mind if I ask May Tyrrell to come to the cinema tomorrow night? She doesn't get out much, and I know the woman she shares the house with will look after Margaret-Anne.'

'Not at all,' Gaye said. 'She's a canny girl, and it will help take her mind off what's happenin' back in Guernsey. It must be terrible for her and all the other people billeted here, not getting letters or phone calls, and not knowing if your family has been killed.' She sighed. 'One of the staff nurses on the ward got sent home today; her son is missing in action out in Egypt.'

'Oh, that's awful,' Clare said, she shook her head. 'Sometimes you forget there are servicemen abroad.'

'Last time I was speaking to Audrey, she said that Laurence is still out somewhere in Africa. She got a letter from him, so she was over the moon. He's safe enough, she said, because he's not involved in any of the fighting or anything like that.'

'That's good,' Clare said, then she tactfully changed the subject. 'I heard on the canteen radio that the navy and the RAF have all the coastline covered across from Guernsey, so hopefully the Germans won't come any further. Robert and some of the porters were chatting and they said there's been a lot of the Nazis killed in action, so they might decide to just be content with all the countries they've taken over and leave us alone.'

'I heard that too,' Gaye said, 'so hopefully it will all be over for us soon.'

Chapter Twenty-Nine

When the lights came on at the interval in the cinema, Diana turned to the others and said, 'It's my turn to get the ice creams.' She waited until the glamorous usherette came down the aisle in her neat uniform, her blonde hair tucked up under her fancy cap.

She stood up to join the queue, then stopped when she recognised two young women standing in the queue just ahead of her. Turning back to Clare, she asked in a low voice, 'Would you mind going down for the ice creams? There are two girls from work in the queue, and I don't want to have to stand next to them. They hardly speak to me at work, and I'd just feel uncomfortable.'

'No problem,' Clare said, who would usually be surprised to find Diana being afraid of anything, but knew how the way she was treated at work made her feel. 'Which girls are they?'

'The ones just at the end of the queue now.' She then gave a brief description of them, handed Clare the money and let her out into the aisle. She moved up to sit next to Gaye and dipped her chin in the hopes that the girls wouldn't turn around and notice her.

'Is everything okay?' Gaye asked.

Diana whispered the situation to her, and Gaye asked her to point the women out too. She sat forward in her chair, eyes narrowed, 'The ones standing right in front of Clare?'

'Yes,' Diana confirmed quietly, not wishing to bring May into the conversation as well.

'I would hate to work with awful bitches like that,' Gaye said, anger swelling inside her. She had recognised the two people Diana had pointed out, and the unfairness of it all sent her into a rage. 'You're the last person who deserves it, because you're always so nice to people.'

When Clare came back with the ice creams, the four girls chatted about the film, enjoying a debate about whether Robert Taylor was as handsome as Laurence Olivier.

'Maureen O'Sullivan is good, isn't she?' Clare said. 'I loved her in *Tarzan*.'

'You're only saying that because she has the same last name as you,' Gaye said, winking at her.

'Oh, be quiet, you!' Clare said, pretending to hit her, and the four of them went into fits of laughter.

May shook her head. 'I'm glad I came out with you to the film. I've laughed more tonight than I've laughed since we landed here last month.' She smiled at each one. 'It reminds me of being with my friends back in Guernsey, and it gives me a bit of hope feeling like my old self again – even if it's just for a few hours.'

The film came back on and they all relaxed into their seats. At one point, Gaye excused herself and slipped past Diana's seat to go to the ladies. She went quickly up the aisle, and when she got out through the main doors, she hurried along the carpet-lined corridor, her red hair flying as she went.

When she got into the toilet, two stalls were occupied, with several others vacant. She stood waiting, with her arms folded. At one point she turned to check her reflection in the mirror, and could see her face and neck had a reddish tint to them.

The toilet flushed and a woman came out and went straight to the sink without looking at Gaye. When the next door opened and the second woman came out, she glanced over at the red-haired woman and then did a double-take.

'How are you, ladies?' Gaye asked.

Both sets of eyes looked at her now, and then the blonde-haired woman said, 'I remember you ... you're the nurse that was in the hospital the night that ...'

Gaye nodded. 'I'm so sorry about your friend. That should never have happened.'

'It was terrible,' the red-haired woman said in a low voice. 'I've had nightmares about it since.' She looked at her friend. 'You're the same, aren't you?'

The blonde girl nodded, and tears welled up in her eyes. 'I'll never forget it, as long as I live. A girl hardly in her twenties... and leaving a little kid behind. She's staying with Marjorie's mam and dad. God knows when Bert will get back home, and from the sounds of him, he's not going to be much use looking after a little babby.'

'It's heartbreaking,' the other friend said. 'One night lettin' her hair down, having a few drinks and it all ends up like this.'

'It's a tragedy, and we see it happening in the hospital regularly,' Gaye confided. 'It's not just your friend, it's happened to other women as well. The ones who do this, the backstreet abortionists, should be hung, drawn and quartered. Most of them have no medical qualifications.'

The red-haired girl looked towards the door, afraid someone might walk in and hear them. 'This one was supposedly a qualified midwife. Marjorie checked her out – another one of the girls had her do an abortion on her just a month before, and she were all right after it.' She shrugged. 'Well, she had some heavy bleedin...'

The blonde nodded in agreement. 'And she did collapse one day in work, but after a few days she came around. Nowt worse than a heavy period.' She shrugged. 'She seems okay now, but you don't like to ask in case they don't want reminding about it.'

'That's understandable,' Gaye said. 'It's not somethin' you would want to keep thinkin' about.'

'She got a terrible shock when she heard about Marjorie. All the girls did, but it must have hit her the most, knowing the same thing could have easily happened to her.'

'You all sound like good friends, as if you all look after each other.'

'We do,' the red-haired girl said. 'None of us have it easy, most have kids and we're out workin' long hours in the factory.' She gave a little shrug. 'This is the first night we've been out since Marjorie died, and we keep talkin' about her, remembering that night.'

The blonde girl looked up at her. 'You were very good with Marjorie and so were the doctors. They were right kind to us, especially that young one. He never looked down on us or anythin' ...' She looked at Gaye. 'And you were very kind to us, especially when we were terrified about what had happened.'

Gaye nodded. 'We're all women,' she said. 'And it's not easy with the war and everything. We need to help each other.'

'That's what we all say in the factory, we women have to stick together.'

'Do you work in the parachute factory?' Gaye asked quietly.

'Yeah,' the blonde girl said, sounding surprised. 'How did you know that?'

'Because I have a friend who works there. A very good friend. A friend I would do anything to help.'

They both looked at her, then at each other. 'Who?' they both said in unison.

'Diana Thornley.'

Both girls looked shocked. They glanced at each other and then they lowered their heads.

'She's one of the kindest people I know,' Gaye said, 'although she is posher than all my other friends. You might not know, but Diana gave up a nice, cushy situation at home to come and work with ordinary girls like us. She felt it was only right she should do her bit for the war, same as anyone else.' She paused, letting the words sink in. 'But I hear she's had a bad time at the factory, people don't speak to her or include her in anything. It's been so bad she turned down a promotion to assistant supervisor, because she couldn't face going around the tables when no one will hardly look at her. Can you imagine that? She also went to help a poor girl who fainted and got the nose snapped off her from some of the other women, just for being kind.' She looked at them both firmly. 'It might have been that girl you mentioned earlier, the one who had been to the midwife.'

Their heads drooped further.

'Can you imagine how you would feel if it was one of your friends being treated like that?'

There was silence, during which Gaye stood her ground until the girls eventually looked at her again, shame-faced and cringing.

'We don't really know her,' the blonde said. 'And like you said, she's very posh ... she's always readin' books in the canteen, or writing in her notebook. She's so different, the girls don't know what to say to her.'

'Well, maybe you might think of something to say to her tomorrow,' Gaye said. 'Something nice. As I said before, I'm like you, I look out for my friends and I don't like seeing them unhappy.' She looked from one to the other. 'Do you agree?'

Again, neither of the women had anything to say. Then they both nodded.

When Gaye got back to her seat, the girls all turned and whispered to her, checking she was all right.

'You were gone ages,' Clare said. 'I was worried you were sick or something.'

Gaye shook her head. 'I met someone I knew, and we got chatting.' She sat back into the velvet cinema chair, satisfied with what she had done.

Chapter Thirty

One Thursday afternoon in the second week in August, Phyllis Hackett took a phone call and then came out onto the factory floor to deliver news. She directed that the machines and the radio be silenced, and then she called all the workers together.

'We have a problem with the silk,' she told them. 'We were due a big shipment tomorrow or the day after, and I have just received a phone call to say there's a problem over at the docks in Liverpool with some of the lorries, and Customs and Excise are not letting anything through until it's all been checked. It could take a few days before they get it over here to Manchester, and that means we're going to run out of material.'

There was an immediate buzz of conversation at the news, and one of the girls looked at Diana. 'What do you think has happened?'

Diana tried not to look surprised at someone else speaking to her on the factory floor. For some reason, there had been a gradual shift in the last few weeks, and a number of the women had started speaking to her. Two of them had even started to sit at her table in the canteen. It was strange now, after all these months, and having got used to her solitude she wasn't sure how to react.

'I don't know what could have happened at the docks,' she said. 'It could be anything.'

'It might be the Jerries,' the woman said. 'Lord Haw-Haw mentioned something about the Liverpool docks in one of his broadcasts.'

'Let's hope the delivery gets through soon,' Diana replied. 'There's only enough silk to keep us going for a few days.'

'Okay,' Phyllis said, clapping her hands together for silence. 'I've spoken to the factory bosses, and we've decided that we should use the situation to let people have a few days' break if they want. We only need a few people to keep the machines going, so if any of you want to take Friday and Saturday off while we're quiet, it's no problem.'

Diana suddenly felt fearful. 'But what will happen if we don't produce the numbers of parachutes that are expected?' she asked. 'Won't the delay in production cause a serious problem for the soldiers?'

'I was just thinking that meself,' one of the other women said. 'It would be terrible to think that some of the aeroplanes will be held up waiting on parachutes, when they're needed to join the other men fighting out abroad.'

'We have it covered,' Phyllis reassured them. 'The bosses have already been in touch with the other factories working with parachutes, and they are going to go on overtime over the weekend to make up for any losses. And we will do the same when the silk eventually arrives.' She smiled. 'So you can all enjoy your break without worrying.'

Diana's heart leapt. A chance to see Oliver while Liverpool was a little quieter on a Thursday, and she could stay until Sunday morning. He hadn't been able to make it over to Stockport for the last two weekends and she was really missing him. Stella had settled in well at home with her aunt, despite still being worried about her family and missing brother. Hopefully, with being at school during the day, she would hardly miss Diana for a couple of nights. She could ask Clare to take her to the cinema or maybe for an evening walk with May and little Margaret-Anne in Alexander Park.

Phyllis called again for quiet, interrupting her plans. 'You can have a ten-minute tea break,' she told them. 'Then those who want the time off, come and see me in the office.'

While the other women filed out to the canteen, Diana lifted her work bag and went outside, walking out to the factory gates where there was a public telephone kiosk. She rang the familiar Liverpool number and spoke to the receptionist, and a few minutes later an anxious Oliver came on the line.

'Diana?' he said, his voice breathless. 'Is everything all right?'

'Yes it is,' she said, a smile breaking out on her face at the sound of his voice. 'I'm ringing with good news. I've got two days' leave from work, tomorrow and Saturday, and I thought I might come over to Liverpool. I could come tomorrow or even tonight after I finish work...'

There was a moment's silence, then he said, 'That's absolutely wonderful news! Come tonight. It doesn't matter how late the train is, I'll be there to meet you.'

After her phone call, Diana went over to the canteen for her mug of tea and, smiling to herself, went to speak to the supervisor. As she walked past, a blonde-haired woman got up from her table and followed her out.

'That's a turn-up for the books, isn't it?' the blonde woman said. 'Being offered time off instead of having to beg for it.'

Diana looked around to see who she was talking to. When she realised it was herself, she looked back at her. 'Yes ... it certainly is.'

'What are you going to do? Some of the girls are delighted, and a few others with kids are just going to work on while it's quiet and take the weekend off as usual.'

Normally, she would have given no personal information away, but she was so excited about seeing Oliver, she said, 'I'm going to take the few days off and go over to Liverpool.'

The woman raised her eyebrows. 'Liverpool?'

'Yes,' Diana said, tilting her head and smiling, 'my boyfriend is there.'

She knew the information would cause gossip, but she didn't care. It would do them good to know that she had a real life outside of work with real people in it. She had overheard conversations in the canteen where the women were talking about their husbands and boyfriends, peppered with ribald comments about how often – or how little – the men looked for sex. It was as though they thought that it was something that existed only in their own domain.

'I didn't realise you had a fella.'

'Well, I do,' she said, 'and it will be lovely to see him sooner than I thought.'

Oliver was waiting for her at Lime Street Station when she got off the train at eight o'clock. He wore a smart dark suit and hat, and was carrying over his shoulder his large leather bag that held his camera and some basic equipment. He smiled in appreciation as the raven-haired Diana came towards him wearing a blue linen coat with a white straw hat, which had a matching blue band around it. Underneath, she wore a plain, cream jersey dress with long strands of black pearls and cream sandals and gloves. She was carrying a small beige case edged in brown leather, in which she had spare clothes and her gas mask.

'You look fabulous as always, my darling,' he said, wrapping his arms around her. 'And what a bonus having a few days midweek, and it has come at the right time as well.' He took her case from her.

'I couldn't believe it,' Diana said, her eyes shining. 'The best surprise ever.'

'I have a few little surprises for you as well.'

Diana's eyes widened. 'What?'

'You'll have wait and see,' he laughed, then gave her a quick kiss on the lips, 'otherwise it wouldn't be a surprise.'

They walked out of the station and into the evening sunlight, arm in arm and bringing each other up to date on news as they went along. They carried on down Lime Street, passing the lovely St John's Gardens on their right, a place they often walked when Diana visited.

They walked on a little further, then Diana slowed down and looked at him. 'Aren't we crossing over?'

'What for?'

'To call to my usual bed and breakfast, with Mrs Devlin.' She nodded towards her weekend bag. 'I want to drop the case off and get a key from her in case I'm out late.' Bridget Devlin was a lovely Scottish lady, whose husband had been killed during the previous war. She kept herself busy running a nice bed and breakfast in Rodney Street for commercial travellers and tourists visiting the city.

'Let's take a little walk down this way,' he said. 'I thought we might stop off for a drink since it's a nice evening.'

Diana looked at her watch. 'Sounds lovely.'

They walked a little further and then he guided her towards the Adelphi Hotel. 'I thought it would be nice to go in here,' he said. 'A bit of a treat for us.'

They found a table in a secluded corner where they could see everything going on around them but could chat privately. Diana took her straw hat off and then shook her head to make sure her black bob was perfectly in place. After the waiter took their order, Oliver turned to Diana, 'Would you mind if I just went to the main desk to check something out? I was here last week taking photographs for a new hotel brochure, and the manager said he would leave something for me at the desk.'

'Of course, I don't mind,' she replied. 'I'm happy sitting here. It's such a beautiful hotel.'

Oliver was back in a few minutes with the waiter following, carrying an ice bucket with champagne and two crystal flutes.

Diana sat up straight, a bemused look on her face. She waited until the waiter had popped the cork and poured the drinks, passing them one each.

Oliver held his glass up and touched hers. 'To us,' he said, 'and to a few stolen days.'

Diana took a mouthful of the bubbly, cold drink. 'Ah, lovely...' She sat back in the chair and then she looked at him directly. 'You have to tell me what on earth is going on. We ordered a glass of ordinary wine and the waiter has turned up with a bottle of very good champagne.'

'Can't a man treat the woman he loves?'

She reached across and covered his hand with her small gloved one. 'It feels too special. What's going on, Oliver?'

He took a long drink from his glass then he put it back down on the table. The waiter came forwards immediately, and Oliver waited until he had refilled both glasses. 'Okay,' he said, 'I will put you out of your misery. The surprise is that you are not staying with Bridget Devlin – we are both staying here for the next three nights.' He held his hand up. 'Before you say anything, it is a gift to me from the hotel, because of the work I did for them. The manager – James Morgan – was really pleased with the photos, and has asked me to do some staff portraits for him as well. I was down here this afternoon just after you rang, and I told him you were coming and we got chatting, and he offered me the room free in exchange for doing the staff photos and some private family ones.' He grinned at her. 'He made me an offer I couldn't refuse! Especially after our last conversation at your aunt Rosamund's.'

Diana closed her eyes and sat there for a few moments in silence.

Oliver's face suddenly became grave. 'You are happy, aren't you? You meant what you said about wanting us to spend private time together?'

When she opened her eyes, there were tears glistening in the corner. 'Of course I meant it,' she whispered. 'I have been dreaming about spending the night with you since we first met.'

His shoulders slumped in relief. 'Thank goodness for that.' A thought came into his mind. 'James is a broad-minded chap, and when I said you were joining me, he asked no questions.'

Diana lifted her glass and stood up. 'I would love to see the room now,' she said. 'In fact, I can't wait another minute.'

Oliver laughed and stood up too. 'That's exactly what I was hoping you might say.' He lifted his bag and her case, while she leaned over to pick up her hat and handbag.

The waiter appeared at Oliver's shoulder.

'I would be grateful if you would bring the bottle and glasses up to our room,' he said, showing the key with the room number on it to the waiter.

'Would you like me to call a porter to carry your luggage, sir?'

'No, we can manage grand,' Oliver told him.

A few minutes later they were in the room, the waiter having deposited the champagne bucket and glasses. Diana turned in a circle in the middle of the huge bedroom – a full suite with their own beautiful, marble-decorated bathroom, and a sitting area with a radio. They also had a private telephone, which was useful in case the newspaper needed Oliver to take photographs of something dramatic during the night.

Oliver hung his coat in the wardrobe. 'You should have seen the editor's face when I gave him the phone number of the Adelphi, and said to ring if he needed to get in touch.'

'I'm not surprised,' Diana said. 'I'm still in shock myself.'

'You told me you had lunch in here before with your parents when you were over in Liverpool shopping,' he said, 'and I've wanted to bring you here ever since.' He waved his hand around the room. 'I never imagined that we would have something like this, but they had a few spare rooms as it's a relatively quiet weekend, and the manager insisted that I have one of the best ones.'

'I feel as if this is all some sort of dream,' Diana said, perching on the edge of the bed.

Oliver sat beside her. He lifted her hand and kissed each of her fingers. 'Are you sure you really want this?' He gestured towards the double bed. 'If you have the slightest reservation, I'm happy to continue as before. No pressure. Not until you are ready or if you want to wait until . . .'

Diana looked up at him. 'Until what?'

He took a deep breath. 'Until we get married. That's if you would consider me.'

'Do you really mean that?'

'Diana,' he said, looking into her green eyes, 'I would love to marry you. I knew that almost the instant I met you.'

'And I knew we were meant to be together the night I met you,' she said softly, leaning her head against his chest.

'I've been afraid to bring it up because of all the difficulties... our class difference, our religion, living so far apart.' He shrugged. 'Me being Irish – that could well be another problem. I was going to wait a bit longer until we had time to talk properly about all these issues. How, if you were actually willing to marry me, we would handle all these things...'

'Well, I've actually been waiting on you saying something that would let me know how serious your feelings were,' she told him. 'In fact, tonight when you brought me here – when you said you had a surprise – and then I saw the champagne, I really thought you were going to propose.' She pressed her lips together. 'I shouldn't really have said that...'

Oliver held her out at arms' length and stared deep into her eyes. 'There is nothing in the world I want more than to spend the rest of my life with you. You are the single most wonderful person that I have ever met. Forgive me for being too careful – for not having the courage to do this the minute we arrived here.' Then, getting off the bed, he went down on one knee. 'Diana Thornley,' he said, his voice slightly hoarse, 'will you marry me?'

'Oh, yes,' she said throwing her arms around him. 'Of course I will!'

He stood up, gathered her in his arms and kissed her harder than he had ever kissed her before. Then, very slowly, he took her coat off and threw it over to land on a chair. Then he unzipped her dress, and Diana drew it down over her shoulders and let it drop to the floor.

'You're sure?' he said, lifting her up in his arms.

'Absolutely,' she whispered, reaching to pull his tie off and unbutton his shirt. She had never felt so sure about anything in her life. Oliver was everything she had ever dared to dream of and more. For the first time in her life, Diana felt like she was in the perfect place at the perfect time, and she wasn't going to waste a single moment of it.

Chapter Thirty-One

The sun slanting through a chink in the curtains woke Diana early on Friday morning. She took a few moments to get her bearings, and then she remembered everything – the surprise of staying in The Adelphi, the champagne, followed by the proposal then the most wonderful night of passion in Oliver's arms.

She turned over, and there he was. She could see the back of his dark head with the little curls she loved on his neckline. Reaching out, she gently trailed her fingers over the skin on the back of his neck, and then his bare shoulder. The touch woke him almost instantly and he turned around, a smile on his face.

'Can you believe it?' he said sleepily. He gathered her close into him, and then lightly kissed her on the tip of her nose. 'It's like I died last night and went straight to heaven.' He smiled. 'And now I'm awake again and I'm still in heaven.'

He started to kiss her again and within a few minutes he was on top of her and ready to start making love again. 'Are you sure you're okay?' he said, nuzzling into her neck. 'I'm sorry it was a bit painful for you the first time last night.'

'I'm perfectly fine,' she whispered, nipping playfully at his ear. 'After we got over the initial...' She paused, slightly embarrassed. 'The initial barrier, it got easier. The second time was very different, it was just wonderful.'

As he did the night before, he entered her and they moved together in unison for a few minutes, then he stopped, and reached for the contraceptives he had brought with him. 'I'm sorry about stopping for these blasted things. Talk about passion killer.'

'Not at all,' Diana whispered. 'The last thing we need is me becoming pregnant while there is a war on.'

'And I want us to be married before anything happens too. I want things to be right for us.'

When he had everything in place, Oliver moved over her again. As he entered her, he whispered, 'I'm going back to heaven!'

Diana gave a tinkly laugh, and then she moved her lips to meet his. 'Take me with you,' she said, 'and never let me go.'

Later, when they were lying in each other's arms, Oliver asked her if she would like breakfast delivered to the room.

She thought for a moment. 'No,' she said, 'I think I would feel as though we were flaunting our situation and I would rather keep it private. If we go down to the dining room, no one knows what our sleeping arrangements are, whereas if we are in the room together in dressing gowns, it is rather obvious to the staff.' She looked up at him. 'Does that sound silly and not very worldly?'

'Whatever you want, my darling,' he told her, in his soft Irish tone. 'Personally, I couldn't care less what anyone thinks, and where I eat breakfast is of no consequence.' He laughed. 'The fact we are going to have an actual cooked breakfast with no worries about rationing is just wonderful.'

'I can't believe I hadn't even thought of that!' Diana exclaimed. She started to giggle. 'Mr O'Sullivan, you have absolutely turned my head.'

'And you, my darling,' he said, taking her face tenderly between his hands, 'turned mine from the first moment we met.'

They went down to breakfast at half past nine and when they were finished, went out into the palatial lounge to have a last cup of coffee, in the same private corner where they had sat the night before.

'I never thought I would grow so fond of coffee,' Oliver told Diana. 'Tea is the big thing in Ireland, and the only coffee I saw before coming here was a liquid mixed with chicory. My mother used to make it with boiled milk and spoonfuls of sugar as a treat.'

Diana laughed. 'Camp Coffee! Mummy's housekeeper always keeps a bottle of that in the house for emergencies.'

'Sounds like the same thing,' he said, nodding his head. 'And that's all I knew until I came here to Liverpool, when I discovered that the stores sell all different kinds of coffee and even coffee beans to grind yourself.' He paused, then changed the subject. 'How are we going to tell our families about us? Have you given any thought to it?'

Diana shrugged. 'No, but I'm not concerned. Our family tend to do what they like, certainly my mother always has, so my attitude is they can like it or lump it. I don't really care.'

'They might be upset about me not being part of their English landed gentry,' he warned, 'and be horrified I'm from an ordinary Irish Catholic family, with not a lot to recommend me financially.'

'I'm not at all worried about my family's opinion,' Diana said, smiling. 'I have one brother living in America and the other in England is so busy with his own life, I hardly see him. Daddy doesn't get involved in anything, he leaves it all up to Mummy.' She rolled her eyes. 'She doesn't really like anything I do, especially my art, so it probably won't be a surprise for them to discover I have picked someone like myself.' She started to laugh. 'If her suspicions had been right, she would have had a lot worse to worry about than me falling in love with a decent, intelligent Irishman!'

'What do you mean?'

'She asked me once if I was a lesbian!'

He looked at her in amazement. 'Why on earth would she ask you that?'

'Because I often wear trousers, I get messy painting, because I am interested in how a car engine works, and because I don't want to go to fancy balls.'

He lifted his coffee cup. 'You kept all those details from me,' he said, mock-seriously. 'I shall have to reconsider my proposal.'

They laughed, then went back to discuss the difference in their families and what it would entail when they married.

'You know I've lost interest in religion?' he said. 'We talked about it that first night. So at least that won't be a huge problem for you. I wouldn't insist on a Catholic wedding or anything like that.'

'But it would matter to your parents, wouldn't it?' She held her hands out. 'It would mean something to them...'

He leaned across the table and took her hands in his. 'Apart from Clare, my family will be in Ireland, and highly unlikely to attend. They wouldn't need to know what sort of wedding it was.'

'Won't that be difficult for Clare?'

'I hope not.' He shrugged. 'We could leave her out of any preparations and then she could truthfully say she knew nothing about it. There would be no blame to lay at her door.'

The thoughtful look on Diana's face was suddenly replaced by glee. 'We could elope!' she said. 'Just quietly organise it ourselves at a church here in Liverpool or even a registry office. Wouldn't that be wonderful? It would save so many problems.'

'Really?' he asked. 'Is that what you want? Is it what you would want if you were marrying someone else?'

'I wouldn't marry anyone else,' she said simply. 'Not now I have met you. I would never have this with anyone else.' She squeezed his hands tightly and then sat back in her chair. 'And I am always happiest when we are on our own – just the two of us.'

'When?' he asked. 'When should we do it?'

'While it's still summer. We could walk in St John's Gardens afterwards, go somewhere nice for a wedding lunch and then spend the night here. What do you think?'

'Sounds perfect.'

Her eyes narrowed as she thought. 'When I get back to the factory, I'll work out when I can get another weekend off in early September. That's just a month away, and it should still be mild enough.'

'I think I should meet your family first,' he said, 'especially your father. I would hate to meet them afterwards; it would seem cowardly when it was all over and done. They might see it as a *fait accompli*. They might not forgive me.' He paused. 'We still have to work out where we will live and work, all those sorts of details. Are you ready to leave the factory yet? Will you come to Liverpool or should I look for work in Manchester?'

She suddenly could see his point. 'I think I just got carried away ... maybe there is no great rush.' Tears came into her eyes. 'I just want to have it official, so nothing and no one can come between us – ever.'

'We could start by buying you an engagement ring this weekend,' he suggested. 'That would be fairly official, wouldn't it? I can come over to you in a few weeks and we can go and see your parents and tell your aunt. We can also tell Clare, although I will ask her not to let my parents know yet.' He shrugged. 'When that's all sorted out, then we can plan our wedding date.'

'Where will we go in the meantime?' she asked. She glanced around the dining room, 'After staying here together – after sleeping together – it will be hard to stay in Miss Devlin's house while you go back to your single room in another street.'

'We'll sort something,' he said with a wink. 'Give me time.'

In the afternoon Oliver had to go over to the Walker Art Gallery to take photographs of an Impressionist art exhibition that had just arrived up from London.

'Come with me,' Oliver urged. 'I know you've been several times now, but you might find this exhibition interesting, and you can have a look around the gallery while I'm taking photographs.' He smiled. 'You might even get some inspiration for your own paintings.'

Since she didn't want to waste a minute of their time together, she agreed. 'I have my trusty little sketchbook full of ideas,' she said, laughing. 'But recently, I've been very sidetracked. Other things keep coming into my mind, I can't imagine why.'

Oliver looked at his watch. 'I think we have time to sidetrack you a little further, before we go out.'

Chapter Thirty-Two

On Friday evening, Clare and Gaye walked quickly back from the market, delighted with their purchases. They had been on an early shift, and afterwards had taken a trip down to the market in the hope of buying stockings, as some of the nurses had told them about a stall that had them in this week. After they had purchased them, they had dawdled around, looking at items they couldn't afford. Then, on a whim, had decided to walk down to have tea and a cake in the little café that Mrs Atherton's daughter owned.

She was delighted to see them and after she had served them, she brought her own cup of tea and joined them for a chat. 'I was talking to the vicar last Sunday,' she said, 'and he said that the Guernsey people are all settling in. My mother would have been delighted with all the great work people have done, especially you girls.'

They chatted a while longer and when they finished their tea, they rushed off as Gaye wanted to get back to have a bath and get ready for going out. Andrew was taking her to a restaurant in Manchester where they were meeting up with an old school friend of his who had come home after Dunkirk, and his wife.

'I can't believe we actually got the stockings!' Gaye said, holding aloft her bag with the stockings inside. 'They're definitely black market, I don't see how the woman on the stall could have got them anywhere else.'

'Oh, don't say that,' Clare said, sounding anxious. 'I always worry that a policeman or one of the Home Guard are going to suddenly appear and arrest us.'

'I don't care!' Gaye said. 'We do everything by the flaming book so I'm not going to worry about a pair of stockings. I think we deserve them after all the make-do-and-mend stuff. We haven't had a new dress since we bought those flowery ones, and I'm sick to death of wearing the same things.'

'What are you wearing tonight then?'

'An outfit Diana lent me.'

'Trousers?'

'No,' Gaye said. 'It's a lovely burgundy and black striped blouse with black pearl buttons down the front, and she's given me a matching burgundy turban. She said her mother bought it for her ages ago and she's hardly worn it. It has long, fluted sleeves, but because my arms are longer, they are three-quarter length on me and they look really nice.' She paused. 'If I had trousers I would have worn them with the blouse tonight; at least it would be something different.'

'Did you get material when you went to the market?'

'Yeah, Diana had promised to start on a pair for me this weekend, then when she got time off, she went to Liverpool instead.' She shrugged. 'I don't blame her one bit; I wouldn't give up a weekend with Andrew to sit at home on a blooming sewing machine.' She glanced at Clare. 'They've not wasted a minute since they met, have they?'

'No, and funnily enough I got a letter from my mother yesterday and she was asking if he had mentioned a girlfriend.' She shrugged. 'I'm not going to say anything until Oliver does. It's not my business.'

'I'm in the same boat, terrified to meet Andrew's mother and afraid she'll look down on me with my Geordie accent. I'm trying to watch how I speak now, so that when I meet her, she'll be able to understand me.' She gave a great sigh. 'Why is nearly everybody we know always worrying about pleasing their own parents or their boyfriend's parents? We're supposed to be adults and out workin' and helpin' in the big wide world, and yet we end up acting like kids that are going to be told off for pickin' the wrong sort of friends.'

'Are you going to meet them soon?'

'No, thank God, but Andrew has already mentioned us going to York together sometime. He said he's written to tell his mother and father about me.'

'Well, I wouldn't worry until the time comes. You might feel different by then.'

'At least my own parents are over the moon about it,' Gaye said. 'They can't get over me going out with a doctor.'

'That must make you feel better,' Clare said.

'I don't really care,' Gaye said. 'I'd like Andrew for himself, even if he was only a porter instead of a doctor.' She decided to change the subject, thinking Clare must be fed up hearing about her and Diana's love lives. 'So, what are the arrangements for the picnic in Lyme Park with the kids tomorrow?'

'We're all going on the bus in groups between ten and eleven,' Clare told her. 'And we're meeting up with the other groups outside the house at quarter past eleven. The ones that get there first can play around in the park. We've told them to bring raincoats just in case, as the forecast said there might be showers.'

'I'll remember that for myself.' Gaye said. She looked up at the darkening sky. 'And I think I'll need an umbrella tonight when we're going into Manchester as well.'

Once inside the nurses' residence, before they parted to go their separate ways, Clare said, 'I hope you have a great night in your fancy restaurant in Manchester.'

'So do I,' Gaye said. 'I hope I don't put my foot in it with Andrew's friends. Are you doing anything?'

'I'm going up to May's for an hour. She said she would come with us tomorrow, she's going to walk down from Edgeley with Margaret-Anne and get the bus along with us to the park.'

'Great,' Gaye called over her shoulder as she headed to her room. 'See you in the morning.'

May was pleased to see Clare, who had brought two carrot buns she had got at the baker's stall in the market. They sat in May's room, listening to the radio and drinking cocoa and eating the buns. They chatted quietly, so as not to waken the baby and the other three small children asleep in the room opposite, who May was keeping an eye on too.

Clare nodded her head towards the room where the three children were sleeping. 'What about Jenny?' she asked. 'She must be settling in well if she's meeting up with people.'

May bit her lip. 'I'm not sure,' she said. 'She just seems to want to mix with other Guernsey people who she knows from home. She's not happy mixing with the other neighbours here, and to be honest, I don't think she's too happy sharing with me. She has a sister who is in a house in Cheadle with a little boy, and that's where she's spending most of her time.'

'Couldn't she move in with her sister?' Clare suggested.

'There's no room, it's a big house, but there are four families in it already.' She sighed. 'I might be wrong, but I think she would prefer that I move out and let her sister move in here.'

Clare's heart sank. 'Are you okay?'

'Yes, but I don't want to swap and move to Cheadle or to a bigger house with lots of people. It can be noisy here with Jenny's three children, but it doesn't bother me. Edgeley is so handy for walking everywhere, to the shops or to church or to our meetings.'

'Something might turn up for Jenny,' Clare said. 'I'll have a word with the billeting people next time I see them around, although I know they are still trying to find accommodation for some of the families.'

May said that she had spoken to members of the Women's Institute who were in touch with the newly formed CIRC – Channel Islands Refugee Committee – down in London, which had become the centre of the evacuee community in Britain. She said they were aiming to keep the islanders in touch with each other, and were also offering help with clothing, relief and records.

Until local representatives had been organised, written applications could be made to the organisation's address in London for financial help or a grant. May had told the girls that she had applied for a sewing machine, and a Guernsey headmaster, who had taught her when she was young, had written a letter of support for her.

'I explained that if I had a machine I could make clothes for myself and help alter clothes for any of the other families that couldn't sew. Obviously I wouldn't charge them, because none of us has money to spare, but if they bring the things they need altering or bits of material, then it would help pass the time for me at night when Margaret-Anne is asleep.'

'Have you thought of applying for part-time or bank work in the paediatric ward in Stepping Hill Hospital?' Clare said. 'It would keep your hand in at your midwifery, and give you extra money.'

May looked over at the sleeping child in the Moses basket. 'I couldn't leave her.'

'They might have a crèche; I could find out for you. And, I could ask one of the student nurses to pick up an application form for you, when they have their next training day.'

'That's good,' May said, smiling gratefully. 'I'm not sure if I could leave her yet, she's all I have left... but maybe after the summer.'

They chatted, and then May went on to tell her about rumours she had heard that had shocked her. Apparently two of the married women who had come from Guernsey had been seen out drinking with local men. 'It's awful,' May said, 'one of their husbands is stuck with the Germans back in Guernsey, while the other is still abroad fighting for the British army.'

Clare was taken aback. 'That doesn't sound good, does it? How can they think of anything like that with all these awful things going on at the moment?'

'They told Jenny that they might never see their own men again, and God knows what they're up at home and out in foreign countries.' May shrugged. 'They're saying that life is really hard, and if they don't get out to the odd dance or for a drink they'll go mad.'

'Oh, God,' Clare said, shocked at the news. 'I thought things would improve when the families got more settled, but it seems that things can easily turn upside down again.'

Chapter Thirty-Three

Diana accompanied Oliver to the art exhibition, which she enjoyed immensely. As she moved around she took quick notes on the various paintings, and checked out the details of their techniques in the brochure. Afterwards they had an early dinner in the hotel, then they went out to a local golf club, as Oliver had to photograph the various teams and winners of their tournament.

While Oliver went around chatting to people and organising them into groups, Diana decided to take a late evening walk around the city centre, stopping to make quick sketches of buildings and places she liked, including one of the small areas with trees and plants in St John's Garden. They met up in the hotel bar for a nightcap and then went back upstairs to their own little world in the luxurious bedroom.

They were both sound asleep, entangled together, when the first bomb was dropped on Liverpool on Friday night. There was no siren warning, and the people in the Birkenhead area only knew what was happening when they heard the explosion. Shortly afterwards, sirens and warning bells rang out, alerting the area to the danger that was in the air.

Oblivious to what had happened just a few miles from the city centre, Oliver and Diana were up and bathed and preparing to go downstairs for breakfast on Saturday morning when the telephone rang. The newspaper editor asked Oliver to go straight out to a house in Prenton Lane, Birkenhead, which he said had been bombed the night before.

'Any casualties?' Oliver asked, holding his breath.

'Just one, thank God,' the editor said, 'a poor woman, a maid in the house, whose bedroom was up in the attic. Jerry bastards!'

They rushed breakfast and then set off together to cross the water over to Birkenhead. 'I hope this isn't the start of anything,' Oliver said as they walked down Prenton Lane. 'If it is, God only knows where it will lead to.'

There were groups of people standing outside the neighbouring houses in the area, and reporters from several newspapers were already there talking to them, trying to find any details of the tragic incident.

Diana stood at a safe distance away from the house, and after a while she leant her notepad on the short pillar in a gateway, and quickly sketched an outline of the scene in front of her – the bombed house with the tiles blown off the roof, the shattered windows and the gaping hole in the roof above the maid's bedroom. With deft movements she drew stick-like images of the people milling around outside the house, including Oliver with his camera held aloft.

Back in the hotel, he told her that so far no one had been able to find a single photograph of the poor woman who was killed. The newspapers had tried the house-owners, neighbours, local shops, but no one had any visual record of the poor maid who had died.

'This is why photographs are so important,' Oliver explained. 'Seeing the house in its bombed state says more than any words. A photograph of the maid who was killed makes it more human and drives home the seriousness of the incident and the loss of life.'

Oliver had another assignment for the newspaper mid-afternoon, so Diana said she would have a walk around some of the lovely Liverpool department stores. She liked John Lewis and Blackler's, and thought she might pick up a little gift for Stella if she had enough coupons. They arranged to meet outside the Philharmonic Dining Room for afternoon tea.

Oliver was already there when Diana arrived wearing a black blazer trimmed with white, a black top with strings of pearls and wide white trousers. It was one of her latest outfits, copied from a photo of Coco Chanel she had seen in one of her fashion magazines. Oliver lifted the petite Diana off her feet and whirled her round. He kissed her, then he stood back to study her. 'Look at you...'

'What do you mean?'

'You are bloody gorgeous, and I love the way you look. You would never blend in in a crowd.' He shook his head. 'What did I do to deserve you?'

She looked up at him. 'You're my other half – we were meant to find each other.'

'The ring,' Oliver said. 'I've been to the bank, so I thought we might go and have a look at some.'

'Are you sure?' Diana said. 'You haven't much time and I don't want you to spend all your money on me...'

'I have a bit saved,' he said, smiling. 'I live on the newspaper money and send a bit home to the parents, and the money I get from doing the private jobs I save in the bank.' He pulled her close and kissed the top of her head. 'I checked the main jewellers yesterday, and we should have enough to buy you a decent ring you can be proud of.'

An hour later they were sitting in the Philadelphia Dining Rooms, Diana wearing her emerald and diamond, art deco-style engagement ring. They had looked at numerous others, but after Oliver noticed that the emeralds were the exact colour of her eyes, they decided on it.

That night, as they lay together after making love, Oliver traced his fingers over Diana's profile. 'I hate to say it, but I will be relieved when you are on the train back to Stockport tomorrow morning. I'm worried in case the bombings in Liverpool get worse. The docks are a prime target and the city centre is very close to them. You'll be safer back in Stockport.'

'And what about you?' she whispered. 'I'm worried about you.'

'I'll be grand. There are thousands of people in Liverpool, so the chances of something happening to me is fairly remote. I'm concerned about you travelling on the train and going through the stations.'

'Maybe we should think of you moving to Stockport. I'm sure you would find work there in one of the newspapers.'

'I don't think it's as easy to find work as it was.' He looked thoughtful. 'Besides, we would have to think about where we would live. I have some money, but not enough to buy a house outright and I'm not sure how the banks are about lending at the moment. We might have to rent.'

She turned to face him, leaning up on one elbow. 'I have an idea. We could buy somewhere!' Her voice was high with excitement. 'I have a small legacy my grandfather left me – it's easily enough to buy a decent house in Stockport.'

Oliver's brow furrowed. 'I can't let you do that.'

'Why not? You've just spent a lot of money on a ring for me. When we are married, we will share everything.'

'There's a big difference between a ring and a house. Let's see what happens over the summer. You never know what might turn up.'

Chapter Thirty-Four

Earlier that morning, Clare and Gaye were having breakfast in the canteen, Gaye giving Clare all the details of her night out.

'I ended up wearing my old yellow dress again! Luckily, it was a bit cool last night, so I wore my knitted blue bolero over it. Andrew probably didn't notice it was the same old thing.'

'What happened to Diana's stripy blouse?'

'I must've put on weight since she gave it to me, as it was too tight on me.' She gestured with her hands. 'I couldn't get the blooming thing buttoned over me bust, and I was pulling at it so hard, I was terrified I was going to rip it.'

She went on to tell Clare how Andrew's friend George and his wife Doreen were lovely people, and she had got on well with both of them, but later she was surprised when Andrew said that he had been taken aback by the effect that Dunkirk had had on his friend.

'George had been in terrible pain with the injury to his back and leg, even though he's on strong painkillers,' Andrew had told her in the taxi travelling back home. 'But it's his state of mind I'm more concerned about. When we went to stand outside, the poor sod was in tears and shaking almost uncontrollably when he started talking about what happened at Dunkirk. Not just what happened to him, but the state the other men were in.'

Gaye explained to Clare, 'Doreen told me that George wakes every night because of the terrible nightmares he has. She said any of the soldiers' wives they meet up with who've been out abroad are the same.' She took a deep breath. 'Andrew said he is thinking of taking a transfer down to a military hospital down south for a few months, to help out with the soldiers there.'

'How do you feel about that?'

'Not very happy.' Gaye shrugged. 'What can I do? He told me he feels guilty he's not been in active service himself and thinks if he does a stint at one of the hospitals, helping the injured servicemen, that it will make him feel he's done something.'

'A lot of men feel like that,' Clare said reassuringly. 'I've heard Oliver saying the very same thing, and Ireland isn't even involved in the war.'

They stopped chatting as the news came on the radio, and then listened in shock as the newsreader reported on the bombing in Liverpool the previous night.

'They said it wasn't near the city centre.' Gaye put her hand over Clare's hand squeezed it. 'So Oliver and Diana will be fine.'

'Do you think I should phone the newspaper office?' Clare said, her hands shaking and her face white as a sheet.

'If it puts your mind at rest, but I think you're worrying too much. The news said there was only one person killed who was in the house, and anyone who was hurt was in that street.'

Clare nodded and decided to leave it as Oliver would probably think she was making too big a fuss, but as they walked down to the bus stop to meet May and the baby for the picnic, the bombing was still on her mind.

The day in Lyme Park went well, considering it drizzled on and off for part of the morning. The children, though, enjoyed the freedom of running around the huge park, climbing on fences to look over at the herds of deer, and later playing on the swings and slide. They were all relieved when the clouds cleared and the sun came out in time for lunch, and the groups could sit in the picnic area.

Clare, Gaye, and the other volunteers went around the groups, chatting and checking how the families were getting on. Most gave good accounts of local people still knocking on their doors to hand in blankets and spare pots and pans and other household items. They heard reports of how good the local schools were, helping the Guernsey children settle in.

Clare and Gaye listened to the sadder stories too, and had to comfort several of the women as they sobbed about not knowing what was happening back in their home island.

'If we could just hear that they are alive and well, I would be happy,' was the phrase repeated over and over.

When the children were gathering together at the end of the afternoon, to set off in relays again for the bus at the gates, some of them started to sing. They went through the usual nursery rhymes and some songs they learned in school, then one of the older ones started to sing 'A Nightingale Sang in Mersey Square'.

As it went along, some of the others joined in, and then Gaye went to stand in front of them, pretending to conduct as she did in the town hall. She was amazed and delighted to see how many of them knew the words of Jack Fairclough's cleverly adapted song off by heart.

Jack hadn't been able to make the picnic today, but Gaye knew he would be delighted when she told him how well they had done.

At the end of the song, all the other children, the mothers and the volunteers gave them a rapturous applause. When Gaye turned around, she saw around a dozen ordinary people who were just walking in the park had all stopped to listen to the singing.

'Well done!' a man shouted. 'They should be on the radio!'

When they got back to Stockport, both girls went straight to their rooms for a rest.

'I'm going to have an hour's sleep, or I'll never manage to do a nightshift,' Clare said.

'I feel I need a sleep too,' Gaye said, 'although thank God I'm not working tonight, I don't think I'd manage it. I'm on a late tomorrow, so I'll be down for my music sessions until one o'clock then straight to work.' She paused. 'The thought of it just makes me feel exhausted. I'm always tired recently. I feel I could sleep round the clock and still be tired when I woke up.'

'Are you out with Andrew tonight again?'

'He's working night shift too, and I'm quite glad as I'm going to have an early night. You'll probably see him on his rounds.' She halted. 'I meant to tell you today, and then I forgot all about it. There's supposed to be a prowler in the grounds. Some first-year student nurses were coming off the late shift and they said they saw a fella in the bushes. They shouted at him and he scarpered off over the wall.'

'That's terrifying,' Clare said. 'And to think I was walking back from May's around that time too. I could have run into him.'

'Well, we need to be careful. God knows what could happen.'

On the last night of their stay in the Adelphi, Oliver and Diana lay wrapped in each other arms, quietly talking and planning a future together. Discussing ideas such as a rambling house in the country, or maybe in a nice quiet street in a tall Georgian house off a city centre. Somewhere that they could both agree on. At various times they came up with ideas and they would almost start to plan it, only to be brought back to the reality of their life at present.

Oliver drew Diana close into him and kissed the top of her head. 'If things were normal,' he said, 'I think I might take you up on your offer of the house, and I would move to one of the Manchester newspapers. I might even set up my own photography business.'

'Why don't you? Lots of businesses are carrying on as normal.'

'I'm afraid to make any major changes until things are more settled. Until we know that Germany isn't going to try to invade us. Things seemed quieter since Dunkirk, and I thought that maybe they were satisfied that they have taken over most of Europe, and had reckoned up all their own losses, and decided to leave us alone. But now this bombing in Birkenhead makes me worried. It might be a one-off, but we don't know. We have to wait and see what happens.' He pulled her closer. 'It's only fair that I should tell you that if things did escalate, there's always the chance I could still be called up.'

Diana reacted as though a sudden jolt had gone through her. 'What do you mean? I thought Irish people were exempt.' She shook her head. 'And isn't working for the newspapers regarded as a reserved occupation?'

'After living in England for two years, Irish people are eligible for call-up.' He paused. 'I've been here longer because at one point – almost on the two-year mark – I went back to Ireland over the summer for a few months. I did some work for a Dublin newspaper, and then when I came back I registered as newly arrived.' He halted. 'At the time I was more politically involved, and against the war, and considered registering as a conscientious objector. I had very mixed feelings coming from Ireland and all the history about the English ruling us.'

'I'm not surprised,' Diana said. 'Ireland should have been left as a united country. No wonder they have remained neutral.'

He smiled at her. 'That's another of the things I love about you,' he said. 'You take the trouble to find out about things that are important to me, and then give me your opinion.'

She looked at him. 'There will be things we won't agree on,' she said, 'but the main thing is that we are always honest with each other.'

'Absolutely.'

'What will you do if you're called up?' she asked.

'My views have changed,' he said. 'The plan was that I would head back to Ireland if things got bad, but as time has gone on, and the way things have developed, I wouldn't feel right doing that. I've lived and worked in Liverpool for a few years now, and I feel part of the city. I know some fine and decent people who have similar political views about war, and they feel this is different too – that this German megalomaniac has to be stopped. We both know people who volunteered to go out to fight against Franco in Spain went to fight against fascism.'

'I don't want you to even think about this.' Diana said,

covering her face with her hands, feeling the engagement ring on her finger.

'We have to think about it. What will happen if he takes over Britain as he's taken over all the other places?' He tapped her hand. 'You're an intelligent woman, Diana, you must know the monumental changes it would bring if we were to be occupied like France or Poland.'

Diana sank back into the pillow. 'I can't bear to think about it.'

'Nor me, my darling, but I'm just laying out the situation, and why we have to wait a bit longer before making any serious plans.' He lifted her hand and kissed the emerald and diamond ring. 'But in the meantime, I am the happiest man alive. To know that at some point – months or maybe a little longer – we will be man and wife, will help us get through whatever happens.

Diana turned to him, tears streaming down her face, and he brushed them away with his fingers. Then, he bent his head to kiss her and she pulled him towards her with a force that was surprising for such a small, delicate thing.

When they made love it was different, more urgent, quicker and almost with a touch of desperation. And when they both reached the height of their passion, they clung to each other in a way they hadn't before, as though afraid that something outside in the pitch black would reach inside and separate them.

Chapter Thirty-Five

Back in St Timothy's, just after four o'clock in the morning, Clare and some of the other nurses were having a tea break when they heard Sister Townsend's footsteps coming along the corridor on her mid-shift rounds.

She came into the staffroom where the women were either drinking tea, smoking or knitting, the usual things to help them keep awake. She sat down on a chair at the door. 'I went across to one of the other blocks,' she said, looking around the group of nurses, 'and on my way back I called at the porter's lodge to check if there was any sign of the so-called prowler.' She raised her eyebrows and sighed. 'Those student nurses get hysterical about anything. It was probably only a cat or a fox or some-thing.'

'So you don't think there was any truth in it?' the staff nurse asked. She looked at the other nurses. 'Well, we're all glad to hear it. We were talking about it earlier and saying we need to make sure we are always in twos.'

Sister Townsend sat down and took out her cigarettes. 'Now, there's no point in painting it any other way,' she told them as she took one out and lit it, 'you are always going to get men sneaking about where there are all-women residences. It's human nature, and it has always happened, and it always will.' She took a drag on her cigarette. 'Most of them are oddities – peeping Toms – who are hoping to catch a glimpse of naked female flesh. Pathetic men who wouldn't know what to do with a woman if she offered herself to them on a plate.' She tapped the side of her head. 'It's all in their minds.' She laughed. 'Or in their hands. I caught one of them a few years ago on the worst night you've seen, windy and freezing rain – everything. I was coming back from the geriatric ward after checking on a death, and there he was, with his trousers around his ankles, staring over at one of the windows and enjoying himself.' She made a gesture with her hands.

The nurses started to giggle.

Sister Townsend rolled her eyes, enjoying shocking them. 'A skinny little runt of a thing. Well, I took my umbrella, and I gave him the biggest wallop around the head with it, and sent him sprawling into the bushes.' She looked at Clare, her face serious now, and she closed one eye. 'I don't think he would chance his luck around this particular hospital again.'

Clare had her hand up at her mouth now, laughing along with the others.

'So we've no need to worry?' the staff nurse said.

'Just carry an umbrella and you'll be fine. Be careful, mind,' she said, as she took another puff of her cigarette. 'There's always the chance it could be a maniac.'

They all laughed and then Sister Townsend said, 'When I was talking to the porter he told me that he heard there have been more bombings in Liverpool in the last hour or so.'

Clare's heart stopped. 'Where?' she said. 'Did they say which part?'

'I think the porter said Wallasey.'

Clare clasped her hands to her chest and closed her eyes. 'My brother is there, in the city centre.'

Sister Townsend sat up straight. 'Go and get your cloak,' she said, 'and we'll go down to the porter and listen to the news in the lodge.'

The two nurses and the porter listened to the radio account of the bombing, but due to the time of night and the fact they were still trying to put fires out, there was little or no information as to what had had actually happened. As before, Clare had to content herself with the knowledge that the bombs were confined to a specific area and Oliver and Diana were unlikely to have been over that side of Liverpool city.

When she finished her shift at eight in the morning, she went back to her room tired, and with a heavy heart. Things were definitely changing and not for the better. She got into bed, but she could not sleep with everything whirling around in her mind. She eventually dozed off, but was awake again in twenty minutes, then repeated the pattern.

At eleven o'clock, when she awoke again, she decided to get dressed and go down to the town hall to see how the groups were getting on. Hattie and Eileen were there with the group who were knitting, and they also had Stella there helping them. The group was small this Sunday. They fluctuated week to week depending on the weather and depending on whatever plans their parents might have. As they got to know more people and other Stockport families, they were becoming less dependent on the initial groups.

After chatting to the others and checking they were all happy enough, Clare said she would sort the drinks and scones for the children, and she took Stella along with her. Once they were in the kitchen, she turned to Stella to ask, 'You've heard about the bombing? Did Rosamund hear anything from Diana yet?'

'Yes,' Stella said, nodding her head vigorously, 'she rang this morning to say she was fine, and that the bombs fell a few miles away from the city centre.'

Clare's shoulders slumped in relief. 'Thank goodness, I've been worried sick.' Then, when she saw the anxious look on the young girl's face, she smiled and said, 'I think I'm just tired after working night shift and I was making a mountain out of a molehill.'

'It's easy to worry when serious things happen,' Stella said. 'I worry about my brother all the time... and everybody back home in Guernsey.'

Clare felt a wave of guilt flood over her. The poor girl had enough worries on her young shoulders to last a lifetime. She went over and put her arm around her. 'No news of Gilbert yet?'

'Not yet, but the women have told me that he is not the only one, and they have already found some. They are trying every single place that they know evacuees have gone to, but they said it's difficult trying to keep track of thousands of children.' She looked directly at Clare, a determination in her eyes. 'But I won't give up. I will keep asking until I find out where he has gone. He's only a little boy, and I promised my mother and father that I would look after him.'

'I'll speak to the women in the WRVS again, and see if there's anything else we can do.'

'Miss Thornley has told them they have to try harder,' Stella said. 'She said she is determined to help me find him.'

Clare wondered if Stella knew that Rosamund was still adamant she would not have a boy in the house. If Gilbert was found, Stella might be sent to join him wherever he was, in order to keep the brother and sister together. 'How are you getting on with Diana's aunt?'

'She's very nice,' Stella said, 'when you get to know her. She took me a little while to get used to...' She shrugged, picking her words carefully. 'But she is kind, and she and Mrs Brown and Diana have made me very welcome. We listen to music and the radio, of course, and she helps me with my piano playing. I like helping her with things.'

'Oh, and what do you do together?'

'Well, she's very strict about certain things, making sure we are all doing our bit for the war effort. She is great at saving and salvaging; she comes into the kitchen every day checking that Mrs Brown and I save every tiny bit of paper and cardboard, and any empty containers. She and I help Mr Chesterton in the gardens too, which I love, especially when the weather is nice. We have added to the vegetable plot, growing our own lettuces and spring onions and mustard and cress.' Her face grew serious. 'I wish I could write to Mummy and Daddy and tell about all the new things I've learned. I've written lots of letters to them, but I've no way of sending them. They're still not allowed to write or phone.'

'I'm sure things will change soon,' Clare said, 'I heard that the Red Cross are working on a way to exchange mail with the Channel Islands.'

'That would be wonderful.' Stella sighed and Clare realised how lucky she was to be able to exchange news with her family and to be able to ring up Oliver's newspaper whenever she needed news. She reached out and squeezed the young girl's hand and then diverted to a safer subject.

'It's fantastic that you're learning all about growing things in the garden,' Clare said.

Stella's face brightened again. 'We went down to the library to learn about growing our own herbs,' she said. 'Mr Chesterton had the well-known ones like parsley, mint and rosemary, but Miss Thornley has become very interested in herbal remedies and has been reading up on them, and she wants us to grow other ones that we can make into medicines.'

Clare tried not to smile. 'Well, that does not surprise me.'

Chapter Thirty-Six

When Diana got off the train, she walked down to the main road, and then turned left to catch the bus out to the parachute factory. After a few steps, she turned back and walked up towards the Nag's Head, curious as to how the weekend had gone, especially with the outing to Lyme Park. She was in no rush going into work. When she told Phyllis that she was going to Liverpool, she had told her not to worry what time she came back on Sunday morning, as she could make the time up with a few hours' overtime.

Diana knew all would be fine with Lance and the other volunteers who were working with her art group, as they were well used to the routine after all these weeks. She had left all the materials for the session set out on tables.

When she popped her head in the function room everyone stopped what they were doing and rushed over to her. The children came milling around her, wearing painting aprons she had made for them with donated scraps of materials. Some of them jostled against each other, trying to get her to look at what they were making first. Diana held her hands up, a broad smile on her face. When she got their attention she asked them all to sit down, and then she went around the group to look at each individual piece.

Afterwards, she chatted with the group leaders and said she would be in the following weekend on both Saturday and Sunday, then she went to the door and gave the children all a big wave and went back downstairs. She crossed over to the town hall to see what was happening, and when she got inside and heard the singing, then Gaye's voice calling to the children, she was delighted. She had hoped to catch her first.

Diana went down the corridor to where Gaye's room was, just around the corner from the craft room. She tapped on the door and then stuck her head in. Gaye looked over with a beaming smile, beckoned to her, then made an apologetic little face over to Jack, who smiled and signalled to her it was no problem. Gaye took a few minutes to distribute sheets with the words of 'Let's All Go Down the Strand' to her singers and instructed them sit and quietly learn the words off by heart.

'Don't you worry,' Jack called. 'I'll keep my eyes on them.'

Gaye came out into the corridor, closing the door behind her. 'Well, how did it go? Thank God you weren't anywhere near the bombs.'

'No, no, we were a few miles away, thank goodness,' Diana said, 'but Oliver had to go out to the place the following day to take photographs for the newspaper, and I went with him. As you can imagine, it was awful. He was going out to Wallasey today, to photograph the area the bombs went off in last night.'

'It must have been terrifying'!'

'Both bombings happened at night when we were asleep. We only knew about it when Oliver got a phone call to our hotel room the next morning.' She suddenly stopped, and a flush came on her face.

Gaye's eyes lit up. 'The *hotel*? Were you staying in a hotel?'

There was a small pause then Diana nodded. 'Yes, the Adelphi, in the centre of Liverpool, and the bombings were across the Mersey in Birkenhead and Wallasey.'

'You're a dark horse!' Gaye said incredulously, much more interested in the personal details than the bombings. 'You never mentioned you were havin' a romantic weekend in a hotel.'

Diana looked mortified. 'I honestly didn't know anything about it until I arrived; Oliver had kept it as a surprise. He was given a few days' stay as a gift for some photography he did for the hotel.'

'Things definitely sounds serious now,' Gaye said. 'You and Oliver have been going back and forward between Stockport and Liverpool like a fiddler's elbow for weeks now, and he even stays at your aunt's. You can see you are both mad about each other.' She clasped her hands together. 'Do you think he's the one?'

Diana looked at her and smiled, then she held out her left hand.

Gaye was, for once, utterly speechless. Silently, she examined the ring. 'I don't believe it...' she eventually whispered. 'You've gone and got engaged!' She threw her arms around her friend. 'I am so pleased for you!'

'What about Clare?' Diana said, moving out of Gaye's embrace. 'How do you think she will react?'

Gaye looked at her. 'You know she thinks the world of you, and she's glad you and Oliver are getting on so well...'

'It's different now we're engaged,' Diana said. 'It has made things official, and I think Clare might be worried about the differences in our religion and how her family might react to our news. You and I both know how much it means to her.'

'At the end of the day,' Gaye said, 'it's not really her business.'

'Oh, it is, Gaye. She's Oliver's sister.'

'What did he say about it?'

'Oliver said I can tell Clare about our engagement, but he doesn't want her to say anything to their family in Ireland just yet. In fact, he probably would have preferred if I waited until he came over to tell Clare himself.'

'Maybe that's a good idea...'

Diana shook her head. 'I couldn't do that. I knew Clare before Oliver. She's been such a good friend to me – meeting her and you completely changed my life. I would feel awful if I did anything to hurt her.'

Footsteps sounded and they both turned to see Clare in the doorway. 'I know you would never do anything to hurt me, Diana,' Clare said, coming towards her with tears trickling down her face. 'I'm sorry for eavesdropping, but I didn't realise it was

266

you and then I heard Gaye's voice all excited...' She put her arms around her friend's neck. 'I'm so delighted for you and Oliver – and so relieved that you're okay. I was worried sick until I heard you weren't near the places that were bombed.'

'Thank you,' Diana said, her voice croaky and strained. 'That means everything to me...'

Clare hugged her for a few more moments, then they moved apart, both still filled with emotion. 'Times like this,' Clare said, 'when there is so much to worry about, all the uncertainty about what could happen. It makes you realise what a waste it is to worry about people who love each other. Does it matter where they come from or what they have or what they believe in? If they decide they can make a marriage work, then surely it is up to them? Let them get on with it, without anyone else interfering.'

'I couldn't have said it better meself,' Gaye said, 'and I think I might bring you with me to York if Andrew ever decides to introduce me to his parents!'

'Oh, Gaye... you are the limit!' Diana said, laughing.

Clare smiled and looked at Diana. 'So, congratulations to you both on your engagement – and I will do everything I can to make things easier with our family when the time is right.'

Diana got off the bus, and walked to the factory feeling happier than she could ever remember. She felt as though nothing or no one could touch her any more. Whatever happened, she had Oliver. Any problems she envisaged with the O'Sullivans had evaporated, now she knew she had Clare on her side. They would weather any difficulties together.

Chapter Thirty-Seven

Diana opened the heavy factory door, and for the first time went in without taking a deep breath. The place was a hive of activity, all machines whirring noisily, as she went in to hang up her jacket and pull on her overalls and turban. She took her work card out of her handbag and then went over to the clock-in machine. The silk had been delivered and everyone was hard at work in the various departments, making up for lost time.

She then went down to the office to let Phyllis Hackett know she had arrived in, but there was no sign of her. She came back to the work area and stood at the front, looking around her, but couldn't see her, so she decided to just go to her machine and wait until she came back. As she went down through the aisle of machines, she noticed some of the girls glancing at her, but she was so used to it that she carried on. There was a pile of cut silk pieces by her sewing machine, so she knew that the production line would be waiting on her to get on with the sewing of them.

She had started the machine up, checked she had enough thread on the spools, and was ready to start on the first piece when she heard the other machines rattling to a standstill. She turned around to see what was happening and saw Phyllis standing in the middle of the floor staring down at her – then she gestured to Diana to turn off her machine. Diana did so immediately and swung back to hear what was obviously going to be an announcement.

Instead, Phyllis came down the floor towards her, stopping at the side of her chair. 'I just wanted to say how everyone in the factory got a shock when they heard you were in Liverpool this weekend, and we were all anxious, waiting to hear if you were out of harm's way when the bombs were dropped.'

Diana looked at the supervisor and was surprised to see the concern on her face, and then was more surprised when one of the women said. 'We heard about the second bombing on the radio in the canteen this morning and then Phyllis told us you were over in Liverpool, and we got a bit of a fright.'

Diana felt very strange suddenly being the centre of attention. Her face flushed and her throat tightened, as she could see they were all waiting for her to say something. She cleared her throat. 'We were a few miles away,' she said, directing her words at Phyllis, 'but I did go with my friend down to the first house that was hit – the one where the woman was killed.' She paused, thinking it might sound as though they were just there because of some macabre curiosity, as certain types of people did. 'Oliver is a photographer,' she explained, 'and he was asked to go down to take pictures of the house for the newspaper.'

'Well, thank God you were all right,' Phyllis said. 'Everyone here was worried about you, and we are all relieved to see you back in Stockport safe and well.'

'Well, thank you ... and I'm glad to say there was no need for any concern.'

'You were missed over the weekend, Diana. The lorries with the silk got through quicker than we thought, and we were running at full scale yesterday morning.'

'Oh, I'm sorry if I left you short-handed. I had no idea the delivery might come earlier than today.'

'Maybe it was no bad thing. You know the old saying, you don't miss the water until the well runs dry?' She turned and looked around the factory floor at all the women sitting behind machines and standing at the cutting tables. 'Well, I think there are more than a few people here now who have come to realise how much we depend on you, Diana.'

There were murmurs of agreement, then one of the women

stood up. 'We've all been talking this morning, and we thought it only right to tell you that we'd rather you took that assistant supervisor's job than have anybody else. There's no one else fit for the job.'

Diana's eyebrows shot up. Her eyes moved from the woman who had been speaking and back to Phyllis, but she said nothing. She was not in any way prepared for this, nor had she considered any ramifications of taking on a more senior position. Oliver was her only consideration now.

The woman looked at Diana. 'If you take the job, we want you to know that you'll have the full co-operation of everybody here. There will be changes.' She swallowed a few times. 'And we're all sorry if we weren't as friendly as we could have been.'

Diana could feel tears pricking at the back of her eyes but she fought them back. She would not let these women who had ostracised her see her cry. She tilted her head up, staring straight ahead.

There was no doubt in her mind that Phyllis Hackett had called a meeting and put the situation plainly to them. They needed her expertise and speed on her own machine, and they needed her unique skills and knowledge of all the other areas to maintain quality control. In short, for her to change her decision about the assistant supervisor's job, they would have to be nice.

It was all too late, Diana thought; the damage was done and she could not imagine trusting the women again. She also doubted how genuine the apology was, and whether they would have realised how hurtful their behaviour had been, without the supervisor's intervention. Only time would tell.

She looked up. 'Thank you all again for your concern about me when I was in Liverpool. With regards to the assistant supervisor's position – I'm afraid I am still not inclined to take it. I'm sure someone else here will do a perfectly good job on it.' She turned to a disappointed Phyllis. 'I think I should get on with my own work now.'

At lunch break, Diana waited until the women had gone into the canteen, and she got her bag and went out of the factory, and down to the public phone box. From what Oliver had told her of his day, he was due in the office to do a few hours developing photographs. A woman came on the line and asked Diana to hold, and then in a few moments she was put through. They caught each other up on their personal news, Oliver bringing Diana up to date about his work, and the newspaper's reaction to the bombings, and then Diana telling him about her journey back to Stockport and the girls' reaction to the engagement and her beautiful ring.

'That's all good to hear,' he said, 'and I'm especially glad about Clare's response. It's what I hoped for. And how is work?'

Diana told him about the turn of events with the factory workers and her declining the assistant supervisor's post again.

There was an unexpected silence, then Oliver said, 'Do you feel better about it now? Do you feel it was the right thing to do?'

Diana paused. 'I feel the other women were probably coerced into it. Considering the way they have been, I just didn't feel I could do a complete turnaround, and act like we were all great friends.'

'Maybe you don't have to be, maybe you could all just find a way to work better together and get those parachutes out.' He lowered his voice. 'I know it has been hard for you, my darling, and you didn't deserve the cold shoulder that they gave you, but you know better than those women.'

'What do you mean?' she asked.

'You're intelligent and you know exactly what to do in your work. I think you should rise above them, remember why you went to the factory in the first place. You went to use your skills to make a difference.'

She thought back to the situation back at the family estate with the land girls, and her heart sank. She was back in a similar situation again. 'What do you think I should do?'

'Take the promotion, darling,' he said. 'You are the best person to do the job and that's what's needed now more than ever. From what we know, all the forces are working on building up armaments, getting ready for what might be coming across the Channel. They are going to need thousands of parachutes – perfect parachutes that save lives. And you are one of the people who can make sure that everything is done to the highest safety standards.' He paused. 'Things can only get better with the women, and the supervisor is on your side...'

Diana remembered how she had felt the day they watched the film about the soldiers in action using the parachutes, and she knew Oliver was right. 'Thanks for listening,' she said, 'and thanks for the advice.'

'I don't know if I've been of any real help...'

'You have,' she said, 'You absolutely have.'

They chatted for a few minutes longer, then, just as she went to hang up, Oliver said, 'Are you wearing your ring?'

'Yes, of course,' she said, 'under my work gloves. Although every moment I get, I have a little peep at it, to make sure I'm not dreaming.'

Oliver laughed. 'Show it to your supervisor,' he said. 'She might be inclined to let you have a little more time off if she knows you have a fiancé far away in Liverpool.'

As she walked along to the canteen, Phyllis came towards her, carrying a mug of tea and a sandwich. She had a weary look about her, from all the hours trying to catch up on the delayed delivery.

'Can I have a quick word please?' Diana asked.

'Come into the office.'

Diana shut the door behind her. 'I have thought things over,' she said, 'and I've decided to accept the assistant supervisor's position.'

Phyllis's face lit up. 'I am delighted and relieved to hear it – and the women will be too. What I said earlier was genuine, they all want you in an official position so they can ask for help without feeling they are imposing on you.' She became more serious. 'I've spoken to them and they all know they have a lot of ground to make up with you. They won't give you any trouble.'

Diana moved her head up and down. 'Well, I'm happy to just get on with things.'

Phyllis leaned her folded arms on the desk. 'You and I will work hand-in-hand,' she said, 'and I will back you in any decisions you make regarding work and the other women.'

'Thank you,' Diana said. She turned back to the door.

'Can I ask you what made you change your mind?'

'I spoke to Oliver just now, and we talked things over.'

'Oliver?'

A picture of him came into her mind and Diana found herself smiling. 'My fiancé,' she said. She took her glove off and held out her left hand. 'We got engaged at the weekend.'

Phyllis examined the ring, exclaiming over the lovely emerald and diamonds. 'Very classy and individual.' She looked at Diana and gave her a friendly wink, 'just like yourself.'

When she went home that evening, Diana decided to take the bull by the horns, and after dinner she asked her aunt if she could have a quiet word. They went into the sitting room on their own, leaving Stella to help Mrs Brown clear the table. Diana explained that her friendship with Oliver had developed into a romance, and that over the weekend in Liverpool, they had become engaged.

Rosamund looked stunned for a few moments, then she held her hands out and said, 'Of course I knew there was something going on between you, but I wasn't quite sure what.'

'Well,' Diana said, her voice anxious, 'what do you think? And what do you think Mummy and Daddy will think of Oliver?'

'I could list out all the faults they might find in him, if that's any help? Just to warn you?'

Diana's heart sank.

'Naturally, being Irish is the biggest hurdle,' Rosamund said, 'and then he's not exactly top drawer, is he? And then his job, a photographer—'

Diana stood up. 'Stop!' she said, 'that's absolutely insulting and I don't want to hear any more.' She would never have broached the subject with her aunt had she any idea what she might hear.

'Now, Diana, please let me finish,' her aunt said. 'I was simply going to prepare you for what they might say – but that doesn't mean they won't accept him.'

Diana took a deep breath.

'The thing is,' her aunt went on, 'we've had all of those ingredients before in the Thornley family, and those marriages haven't fared any worse than the so-called family matches.' She smiled. 'In my opinion, Oliver is a decent young chap, and I wouldn't have any hesitation in recommending him to your parents. He has been a gentleman while he has been here.'

'Really?' Diana said, surprised. 'I didn't think you noticed that we were more than friends.'

'Well, one doesn't like to make assumptions. I've seen that happen before. In life there is often nothing going on when people presume there are all sorts of shenanigans. And the opposite is true. Often the last two people you would imagine would be in any sort of relationship can be the ones who are conducting the steamiest of sexual liaisons. I've seen it happen time and time again, in all sorts of combinations – not just the class divide as in *Lady Chatterley's Lover* – different ages, different nationalities, even people related to other people. Nothing would surprise me about people when it comes to relationships.'

Diana was taken aback. She hadn't imagined her aunt would have read the controversial book. It was the sort of thing her mother loved to say to shock people, but she thought her aunt – while having had her own experiences years ago – was long beyond thinking of such things.

'So, you don't envisage any great difficulties with Mummy and Daddy?'

'Not really, but might be best to warn them in advance,' Rosamund suggested. 'Let them mull it over and argue with you on the phone, and by the time they meet him they will have got it all out of their system. Believe me, I know. I've been through it myself.' She smiled. 'And both your parents are too caught up in their own lives to dwell on this situation for very long.'

Diana pressed her hand to her chest, relieved. 'I will ring Mummy later tonight,' she decided. 'And let her know about Oliver and organise when we should visit. The thing is, Oliver was hoping to do it the traditional way – ask my father for my hand in marriage – but after what you have said they might feel, I don't want to drop a surprise on my father as he might say no.'

'He might well be relieved. In one of our recent conversations, he had more alarming concerns about you.'

Diana's head jerked up. 'Daddy was worried about me?'

'Yes. Your mother had him almost convinced you were a lesbian.'

Diana closed her eyes and sighed. She thought her mother had only voiced that to her; she might have guessed she could not keep it to herself. Then, she thought her mother had actually done her a favour. Her father would be so relieved that he would find her being engaged to an Irishman much more palatable. She smiled to herself. She would ring her mother later and arrange a Sunday lunch where she would introduce their future son-in-law.

The following day, Diana rang Oliver to bring him up to date about her having accepted the promotion and to organise a day to meet her parents.

'I'm so sorry, darling,' he told her, 'but meeting with your family will have to wait. I actually have some news myself, I start training this week with the Home Guard.'

Diana listened as he explained how he had registered for active service, and was waiting to be called for training at Osterley Park down in London. 'It's being run by people who did voluntary service out in Spain, and were part of the anti-fascist movement. They are brave people who have survived terrible conditions themselves, and they will be teaching us all the techniques they learned for dealing with an invasion.' He paused, then lowered his voice. 'There are various special units as well, and there's a possibility I might be recruited for one of these.'

'It sounds very serious,' she said. 'I thought the Home Guard was involved in less dangerous activities – patrolling the streets and check points and mainly protecting civilians.'

'It's that too, but there is a lot of other work involved,' he paused. 'I do need your support with this, Diana, because it means we might not see each other as much as we have been doing. I'm still going to be busy with the newspaper, but by the sounds of things, and with the threat across the Channel getting closer, this may take up all my spare time.'

Diana swallowed and told him, with a forced cheeriness in her voice, that of course she would be on his side, even as her mind whirled with worries. Worries about the increasingly bad news reported on the wireless, about the devastation caused by the bombings that they had witnessed together in Liverpool. With Oliver by her side it seemed as though they could deal with anything, but with the thought of them being far apart, everything seemed suddenly changed. It was as though she had found love only for it all to be torn away from her.

Chapter Thirty-Eight

As August wore on, a pattern developed through the various strands of the girls' lives. Clare and Gaye continued their work in the ever-busy hospital and helped in their spare time with the evacuees.

At times, Gaye could not believe her luck as her romance with Andrew flourished, and she was thrilled when he took her for a weekend to Manchester for her birthday. They stayed in the Midland Hotel in the city centre, and the grand old place made her feel that their romance was somehow more official. Up until then, she had made do with the occasional stolen night in his room at the doctors' residence, when they knew there was absolutely no chance of being caught.

Clare's friendship with May had grown as they both enjoyed talking about the similarities in their backgrounds, coming, as they did, from small communities where everyone seemed connected to everyone else. May also had brothers and sisters, and Clare loved hearing about the things they had got up to as children, and recounting her own family stories, which she felt were a little boring for Gaye and Diana. She was delighted when May told her that a neighbour, Mrs Hartley, a retired nurse who lived a few doors down, had offered to mind Margaret-Anne if she wanted to do some part-time work. As the baby was content and thriving, May had filled in her application form and was hoping something suitable might come up.

'If I got enough money,' May said, 'I'll find a room in a quieter house and move out and let Jenny's sister move in with her.'

She shrugged, resigned to the situation. 'We'd both be happier, as we're different sorts.'

When Clare told Gaye about May's plans, she said, 'I wish I had a place of my own too. I'm getting fed up of living in the residence. It would be nice to have a real life outside of work.'

'Do you ever miss Newcastle? You used to say when you were qualified you might go back there to live.'

'Not now. I've got used to Stockport and I feel it's more my home.' She rolled her eyes. 'Besides, our Audrey is still planning to marry Laurence when he gets back home later in the year, and I'd have to see them every week. According to Audrey, he sends her all these lovey-dovey letters, so he seems to have got over all that nonsense, thank God. I think what happened gave him a fright, and him going away has made her realise that she needs to be nicer to him. But even so, I definitely don't want to go back to Newcastle. I'd much rather be here in Stockport with all you lot.'

'I feel the same too,' Clare said, smiling at her. 'I love Stockport, and it's lucky I do, because God knows when I'll get back to Ireland for a visit. I would be terrified the boat would be bombed on the way over, and my mother is even worse than me.'

'I'm even afraid on trains in case they get bombed.' There was a small silence, then Gaye gave a sigh. 'The other thing for me, of course, is that I'm hoping things will become more serious with Andrew, you know – like Diana and Oliver. He tells me he loves me and everythin', and can't imagine life without me, but he's got this thing about waiting until the war is all over. It's like everything is in limbo.'

'A lot of people feel like that,' Clare said. 'It's all the uncertainty. Imagine what it's like for the people from the Channel Islands having their homes invaded.'

'I suppose people just learn to cope,' Gaye said.

'Nice things happen too,' Clare said. 'May told me that one of the single teachers is going out with a vicar from Macclesfield.

He's just newly ordained, and he's friendly with our vicar and they were introduced.'

'Ah, that's lovely,' Gaye said. 'That will help them settle more if they're meeting new fellas.' She paused. 'What about those other women that May told us about? The married ones that are gadding about?'

Clare shrugged. 'She hasn't mentioned them recently, I think she's embarrassed about it, in case someone might think that all the women from the island are like that.'

'Any we know are behaving decently,' Gaye said, 'and you'll always get women who'll go with fellas who'll buy them drinks and show them a good time.' She shook her head. 'That's life and you can't change it.'

Diana settled into a routine in the parachute factory, a place she now felt happier in as the icy working relationship towards her had melted away to an easier and very respectful one. The women included her more in their talk and asked her about Liverpool and any plans she had when Oliver visited Stockport. They also showed great interest in her involvement with the Guernsey families.

A number of the women had taken a particular interest in what Diana told them about the evacuees, and they started collecting bits and pieces from their neighbours, and bringing into work anything they could find for her to pass on. Phyllis found a large box for them and they put it in the corner of the canteen so people could drop off any donations for the children or families any time.

Every few days Diana looked into the box and when she saw their donations, her heart lifted time and time again at the kindness of the women. There was everything in the box: hand-knitted garments, child-sized hankies, hair ribbons made from scraps of the discarded parachute silk or old dresses, knitted baby clothes, and blankets crocheted from squares of different coloured wool. In a way, the box became a symbol of the changing relationship she had with the women, and gradually it helped to heal the wounds left from their earlier behaviour.

The machines were all working at full tilt, with the women often doing twelve-hour shifts and more, to get the parachutes packed and out to be tested before being sent to storage in case the threats from across the Channel suddenly developed into a reality.

Diana's visit to her parents with Oliver had not materialised due to his work with the Home Guard and her own increased hours at the factory. She remained hopeful that they would find a spare day to take a trip home. In order to prepare her mother, she had rung her to explain that she had become close to her friend's brother.

As predicted, Annabelle had sighed and tutted when she mentioned his nationality and his profession. 'Well, I do hope you are not going to be silly and allow it to develop into anything serious. I'm glad you are getting out and about and enjoying yourself, but do be careful. Life is much easier when you are both of the same sort.'

'We are actually of the same sort,' Diana told her. 'We have so many things in common. He's also very settled in England, and he's recently joined the Home Guard. Oliver's work is fascinating, it's actually very similar in a way to my art.'

'Well, just be careful.' Her mother's voice was vague now, and Diana could tell she wasn't really listening. Annabelle had then gone on to tell her of the troubles she was having with the land girls working on the estate. 'I wish you could come back home and help me organise things, like most other daughters would do. We could go to dances together, and it would give you the chance to mix with the right sorts.'

'I can't come home, Mummy,' she said, 'and I am actually doing very important work at the factory. I've been promoted to assistant supervisor, and I have to check the machinery and every stage of the manufacture of the parachutes.'

'Oh, dear,' Annabelle said, distractedly. 'I just wish this tedious war was over, and that everything was back to normal.'

As the last few days of August came in, and the evacuees were preparing to return to school to begin a new term, they awoke to the news that Portsmouth had suffered a massive bombing attack, killing a hundred people and injuring another three hundred. As shock waves went through Britain, a few days later another serious Luftwaffe attack on Liverpool came, with a hundred and sixty German bombers attacking the city. This assault continued over the next three nights.

Diana and Clare were both in shock and worried for Oliver's safety. Thankfully, he rang Diana to tell her that he was fine and the damage had mainly been to buildings. When Diana asked if she could come and visit him, even for an overnight or a day, he had said, 'I am going to be particularly busy, darling, as I have to photograph all the bombed-out buildings and then I am travelling down to London for training with the Home Guard the week after next.'

Gaye also had felt the shock of unexpected news the following week. The first was when Andrew took Gaye out for a meal to a local restaurant and then took her hand and quietly told her that he was leaving in two days' time to start work down in a military hospital in Cambridge.

'They are not reporting it in the news in case it affects morale,' he told Gaye, 'but there is an influx of servicemen into the military hospitals due to injuries in the air attacks.' His hand moved to cover hers. 'I've applied to train with a surgeon who works with servicemen who have suffered severe facial wounds.'

'I wish I could come with you,' Gaye said. 'Do you think they would let me?'

'I would love that,' he said, 'but let me get down there and see what's happening. With all the recent bombings of ports and docks, I think you're safer here for the time being.' He squeezed her hand. 'If I think it's at all suitable, I promise I will organise for you to join me.'

Gaye's face had suddenly fallen. 'What if you meet someone else?'

Andrew's eyebrows shot up in amazement. 'Are you serious?' He shook his head. 'I would never look at anyone else,' he told her. 'Not in a million years.' He lifted her hand and kissed it. 'It's knowing that I have you waiting for me that will keep me going. This part of my life is exactly how I want it – it's so different to how it was with Elizabeth – and I'm not going to risk it by getting involved with anyone else.'

'You promise?' she said.

'Absolutely. The reason I'm going is to fulfil a part of me that doesn't feel right. I've explained before that I need to be properly involved in the war effort – and I feel that now more than ever. Do you understand?'

'I suppose I do understand,' Gaye said. 'But as long as we get together properly as soon as we can. If I can get a transfer down to Cambridge, I'll be straight down to join you.'

'As long as you're safe, that's my main concern.' He paused. 'Should I ask you the same question?'

Her brow furrowed. 'What?'

'What happens if you meet someone else while I'm gone?'

'You must be joking,' Gaye said. 'I've no interest in anyone else but you.'

She looked across the table at the handsome, sensitive Dr Harvey, wondering how she had got so lucky. After the awful time with Laurence and then Audrey and the baby, she had thought life would never go back to normal again. Things had not only settled down, but they had improved beyond her wildest dreams.

When this blooming war was over, Gaye thought, she would marry him with Clare and Diana by her side, and she would be the happiest and most grateful bride ever.

Chapter Thirty-Nine

All the waiting for the worst to happen was finally over.

The weekend after Andrew departed for Cambridge and Oliver went down to London for his training, the first attack on the London dock area by Hitler's air force finally came in spectacular form.

The Luftwaffe changed their strategy of bombing the British air force and the docks and airfields. Since they were not winning the battle in the skies against the RAF fighters, they resorted to bombing London and its people in a bid to demoralise the country.

At four o'clock in the afternoon, the air-raid sirens screeched out their warning all over the capital city, and shortly afterwards over a thousand German planes circled in the sky and started their relentless attack on the city. People ran for shelter as bombs came raining down and buildings exploded, sending glass and fragments of brick and stone into the air. When they had done as much damage as possible, the planes departed as quickly as they came, only to be replaced by another murderous entourage, who continued bombing until the early hours of the following morning.

By the end nearly two thousand people were killed or wounded, in London's first night of the Blitz.

Diana heard the news on the radio in the factory, and it took the heart out of her and the other workers. She hoped and prayed that Oliver's training base was nowhere near the flight paths. She rushed home as quickly as she could and waited until a call came through from him at nine o'clock that night to assure her that he was nowhere near the major bombings.

'You can see now,' Oliver told her, 'why I had to get involved. This has been coming a long time, and I'm glad I will be ready and prepared to do my bit, if anything more comes to Liverpool.'

Gaye was in the same boat as Diana. When the porter came to the accident and emergency department to tell the staff about the severity of the London bombing, she immediately asked to be allowed to leave the ward to phone the hospital Andrew was in. Trying to keep calm, she rang the hospital reception to ask if the bombings had reached their area. A friendly but anxious receptionist told her that their area seemed to be in no immediate danger, but they had been warned and were all on alert and ready to evacuate the patients to shelters if there was any sign of attack.

'It's terrible what's happening in London,' she told Gaye. 'It feels as though the world is coming to an end and there's nothing we can do about it.'

Gaye ended up trying to reassure the poor receptionist, who told her to call her Kathleen, saying, 'Don't you worry, Kathleen, our RAF boys will soon have them on the run.'

Gaye went back to the ward, feeling more reassured, having asked the nurses she saw in the residence to listen for the phone and let her know if any calls came through. When she had finished her shift later that night, a call came through from Andrew and again he told her not to worry, that all was well where he was working.

He also told her that all the upheaval moving down to Cambridge had so far been worth it. He was making a difference, he felt, being there to assist and learn from the doctors working with these brave, damaged and disfigured servicemen.

'It's helping other people now,' he said, 'and the training will help me in the future, as there is every possibility we could have hundreds more of these cases all over the country if things get worse.'

The London bombing continued for the next few nights, and

then the news came that shocked the country: the Luftwaffe had made another serious raid on London, inflicting heavy damage on St Paul's Cathedral and Buckingham Palace. Again, the people of London and the rest of Britain picked themselves up and continued their lives as best as possible with the attitude of 'business as normal'.

Clare, Gaye and Diana met up the following Saturday for the first regular meeting with the Guernsey evacuees since school had reopened. They all went to their various places to knit, paint and sing, and during the breaks caught up with any news from the Guernsey mothers and teachers, and the voluntary group. The vicar, as usual, read out any announcements or news about the people from Guernsey in other parts of Cheshire. Afterwards, he led everyone present in a prayer for the families who had been affected by the bombing in London, and then added the usual prayer for the families and friends back on the island.

'They are always in our thoughts and prayers,' he said, 'and we all look forward, with unstinting faith, to the day when everyone from Guernsey will be reunited.'

Diana had glanced over at Stella when the prayers were finished, and her heart went out to the brave young girl. She had still heard nothing about her younger brother, and Diana knew that a heavy burden of guilt lay on the poor girl's shoulders for not being able to keep him with her. And yet she carried on with her daily routine, up early for school during the week and helping Mrs Brown and her aunt out in any way she could.

Diana was also pleased to see that Stella was using the lovely notebook that she had bought her on her last visit to Liverpool. Diana had suggested that she use it as a sort of diary, where she could write up all that had happened to her since arriving in England.

Stella was delighted with it. 'That's a great idea. It means when we go back home, that I won't forget to tell Mum and Dad everything that we've done here, because it will all be written down.' Her face grew solemn. 'And I will be able to tell Gilbert too, whenever the authorities eventually find him.'

'The WRVS are still trying everywhere,' Diana had told her. 'They are receiving replies every week from all parts of England and Scotland and Wales.'

After the children had been collected by their mothers or older brothers and sisters, the three girls stood chatting about a party they had all been invited to that night in the hospital social club. It was a joint birthday party for three of the nurses, which had been planned before the raids on the country had started.

'The last thing I feel like doing is dancing,' Gaye grumbled. 'And it seems wrong to be out celebrating when hundreds of people have been killed.'

'I feel the same,' Diana said, 'but it's not easy sitting at home by the radio, listening to every report on the bombings.' She closed her eyes and shook her head. 'Those poor people . . . and then I worry about Oliver being so close to London . . .'

Clare put her arm around Diana and gave her a reassuring squeeze. 'We can't keep thinking like that, and Oliver has rung and assured us that he's fine.' She felt much more worried than she was letting on, but she knew if she gave into her feelings that she would find it hard to lift herself out of it. 'I think it would do us all good to go out for an hour,' she said. 'What else are we going to do? Sit around the radio and feel sick with worry. It might take our minds off it for a bit.'

Diana nodded stoically. 'You're right, and at least we can talk and comfort each other about what's happening in London. I feel I have to hold it all in at home for fear of worrying poor Stella and Auntie Rosamund. And if I go upstairs to do some sketching, I find myself staring into space, imagining the worst scenarios.'

'Don't forget the great British motto,' Clare said, smiling now, ' "Business as usual!" ' She said it in the way a sergeant major might do to his men. 'We've been told not to let those Jerries get us down!'

Gaye looked at her as though she had gone mad. 'Okay,' she said, 'we get the point you're making, and we'll go.'

Diana held up her hand. 'Presents?' she said. 'We can't go to a birthday party without bringing something.'

'I never gave it a thought,' Clare admitted. 'With everything going on...'

Gaye shrugged. 'Maybes we shouldn't go after all.'

'I have a remnant of some lovely floral material I found at home,' Diana said. 'It will only take me half an hour to run up three make-up bags.'

'That would be brilliant,' Clare said. They chatted a while longer, then made arrangements for what time they would meet up.

When Diana set off home with Stella, the nurses walked back to their residence.

'I'm going to have a lie down for a couple of hours,' Gaye said. 'Although lying down seems to make this heartburn worse.'

'Did you speak to a doctor about it?' Clare asked.

'No, I feel stupid,' Gaye said. 'He's going to say it's only heartburn and indigestion. They've enough on their plate without me turning up with a trivial complaint.'

'You've been complaining about it for weeks,' Clare said. 'You're a nurse and you won't go to the doctor. You should know better. The stuff you are buying from the chemist obviously isn't working.'

'I think the bicarbonate of soda has helped a bit,' Gaye said, 'but it makes my stomach swell.'

Clare looked at her. 'No wonder. Isn't that what is used in baking to make things rise?'

Gaye looked at her and then suddenly started to laugh. 'Oh my God,' she said. 'Have I been taking the wrong thing? She put her hands over her stomach. 'I must have made it worse.'

Clare started to laugh now too. 'You are unbelievable!' she said. 'Only you would do something as stupid as that without checking.'

They were both giggling like mad now. 'My heartburn was so bad I would have tried anything,' Gaye laughed.

They walked in the door of the residence, and Clare said, 'You should go over to the medical ward and see if any of the chemists are around and they might give you something. I know they're not supposed to, but some of them will give you a couple of tablets just to tide you over.'

Gaye stopped. 'D'you know, I might just do that, because I don't want it bothering me tonight at the party. First chance of fun we've had in ages. I'll see you later.'

She turned back and went over to the medical block. When she got upstairs to the laboratory area was, she met one of Andrew's colleagues, Dr Patricia Galvin, who worked on the medical ward. She was a cheery, down-to-earth Irish girl who Clare and Gaye got on well with. Patricia asked how Andrew was getting on at the hospital in Cambridge and they chatted for a few minutes about it, and then went on to discuss the current situation in London.

When they had finished with the personal chat, Patricia asked Gaye if she could help her, and Gaye had no hesitation explaining the situation, since she felt so comfortable with her.

'How long have you had the problem?' Dr Galvin asked.

'Weeks,' Gaye said, 'especially at night.'

The doctor then asked her what she had been taking it for, and Gaye laughingly told her about the bicarbonate of soda that she had been taking.

'It's an old wives' cure,' Patricia laughed, 'but I wouldn't recommend it, especially over a period of time.'

'Can you give me anythin' for it?' Gaye asked.

'I think you could do with getting checked, just to make sure where the discomfort is.' She put her head to the side, thinking. 'It could be acid reflux or gallstones – although you're a bit young for that.' She motioned with her head. 'Come on down to the examination room with me, I'm between rounds at the minute and I'll do a quick check on you.'

'Are you sure?' Gaye said, feeling like she couldn't believe her luck. 'I feel a bit stupid and I know it's not serious or anything but it's flamin' uncomfortable, like.'

Dr Galvin got her to hop up on the table, and then she felt her stomach through her clothes. 'If you don't mind, Gaye, I think it would be best if you let me check you out properly, so if you could lift the dress up.' After a few moments of gently pressing Gaye's stomach and then feeling around it with both hands, she took her stethoscope from around her neck. 'I want to check for any digestive sounds, just to see if there's anything out of the ordinary.'

'I hope that bicarbonate of soda hasn't made it all gurgly,' Gaye said, then she started to giggle.

Patricia started laughing along with her, then after a minute she said, 'Come on now,' putting the ends of the stethoscope in her ears. 'We'll see if there's anything out of the ordinary.' She moved the sound piece around Gaye's chest and heart, nodding as she did so, then she moved down along the digestive tract to the middle of Gaye's stomach. She listened for a while, her brow creased, and then she moved on further down.

Gaye lifted her head up. 'Is it very bubbly and gurgly?'

The doctor motioned with her hand for Gaye to stop talking as she listened, then moved the stethoscope again.

Gaye lay back wondering if the cause of her discomfort was anything obvious, like the food she was eating, or had it started back as far as the night she drank the Martini when she was out with the girls? That was the only strange thing she could remember. The doctor lifted the stethoscope and hung it back around her neck.

'Did you hear anything unusual?' Gaye asked her.

There was a small pause. 'I think I heard a heartbeat.'

'Do you mean an extra heartbeat?' Gaye felt a pang of alarm. 'Do you think there's something wrong with my heart?'

'No,' Dr Galvin said, 'but I think you might be pregnant.'

Chapter Forty

Gaye lay on the examination table in stunned silence.

'Had you no idea?'

'I can't be,' she said, 'I've had my periods regularly, in fact, I'm due one again soon. You must have made a mistake.' She moved to sit up, and as she did so, for the first time she noticed the discomfort in her breasts.

'I don't think so, Gaye,' Dr Galvin said, taking her arm to help her sit up. Gaye quickly adjusted her dress. 'I heard your heartbeat up in your chest; this heartbeat is much lower down.' She shook her head. 'I also noticed that the swelling in your stomach is actually pretty firm, it doesn't move around the way it would if it was digestive or wind or anything like that.' She paused. 'You know that some women still have light periods when they're pregnant, don't you? And heartburn is a very common sign of pregnancy.'

Gaye's mind flashed back to Audrey and how she had made that exact same mistake. Her hands came up to her face. 'Oh my God!'

'You had no idea at all? Did you not notice you had put on a little weight? Have your breasts been tender or anything like that?'

Gaye remembered the blouse that wouldn't button and the bras that seemed a little tighter, but none of it had registered. It was only once with Andrew, she thought, just that one night in the car when they hadn't been careful. The night she was upset after she'd had the call about Audrey. After that, they had always used something.

She looked at the doctor now, her eyes wide and full of fear. 'How far on do you think I am?'

'I can't be sure, but at a guess, with the strength of the heart-beat and everything, I reckon around three months – or maybe a bit less.' She looked at Gaye sympathetically. 'Are you okay? I can see you've had a bit of a shock.'

'I'm just trying to take it all in, work it all out. I can't believe I didn't know.' She shook her head. 'When I think now, I can see all the symptoms – I have put weight on my stomach, and now I realise why certain blouses that fitted me before are now tight at the bust. It was the periods, that's what had me fooled.'

'It happens,' Patricia said kindly, 'more often than you would think.'

Gaye looked at her. 'You won't say anything?'

'Of course not. Even if I wasn't tied by patient confidentiality, I wouldn't dream of telling anyone's private business to anyone else.'

'Thank you, I'm grateful for that.'

'You should go to your own doctor on Monday,' Patricia said, 'and she'll refer you to the antenatal clinic in Stepping Hill.'

Gaye paused. 'You're sure about how far on it is?'

'It's hard to tell, but I think you're a few months anyway, from the strength of the baby's heartbeat and the size of your stomach – probably anything up to three months or even a week or two more. Have you felt any movement yet?'

'I don't think so...'

'Work back your dates,' Patricia suggested, 'and see if you can see when your periods got lighter or when you might have had any other symptoms.'

Gaye went towards the door now. 'Thank you.' She held her hands up. 'It's the last thing I expected, and to be honest I'm totally in shock...'

'I understand.' The doctor smiled. 'Well, you have a very nice, decent boyfriend in Andrew, and I'm sure he'll do the right thing by you.'

Gaye ran back to her room, her mind and heart racing. She lay down in the bed and buried her face in the pillow. After a few minutes, she got up and went over to the desk where she kept her diary, and with trembling hands she opened the drawer.

There was only a slight chance she would have written any personal information in it, but she knew she had often tried to work her periods out by marking the likely dates of the month it was due. She flicked quickly through the pages, then she stopped to look at one page in June and ran her fingers down the page. She had had a normal, but fairly heavy period back in early June. She remembered it from a night shift when she had to leave the ward to run back to her room to get extra sanitary pads. It wasn't because of those personal details that she remembered the night. It was because an elderly woman, in the accident and emergency where Gaye had been working, had died that same night. She had noted the time and date of the death in her diary, in case she needed to write a report at a later date.

It was, she calculated now, the last two periods that had been light and gone very quickly. She went and got a pencil then she sat down on the chair, staring down at her diary and trying to work it out. Her brain was so muddled, she could hardly think straight. All she knew was that, due to a lack of privacy, she and Andrew had only had full sexual intercourse on a few occasions. And of those occasions – in the hotel in Manchester, the few stolen nights in Andrew's digs – she was sure that he had used a protective sheath. Was she further on than Dr Galvin had estimated? Her heart sank at the thought.

She dropped the diary on the table now and put her head in her hands. None of it worked out, none of the dates made sense.

She looked at her watch and thought of the party in the hospital social club later tonight. She couldn't face it. She closed her eyes. She couldn't face anything. She wished she could go back to a time when she was carefree and not constantly worried about the war and an impending invasion, not worried about causing trouble in her family. Not being the only one among her friends that seemed to make all the mistakes. She wished she could go out tonight and have a few gin and tonics as she used to do, and then laugh and enjoy herself as she danced the night away.

Tears trickled down her face now as she thought of all the stupid and thoughtless mistakes she had made. She was not even twenty-one, and she had managed to make a mess of everything. She thought of her and Andrew dancing in the club the night of Dr Cumiskay's leaving party. Would she ever dance the night away as carefree as she had that night, until she had received the phone call about Audrey?

Then, out of nowhere, a memory came into her mind. A memory of that very night that had changed everything. Much later in the evening, after she had picked up the note that had been slipped under her door.

Like a film running on a screen in her head, Gaye replayed the incident. How, after reading the note, she had quickly dressed and put a touch of lipstick and perfume on, and then she had silently gone out of her room, and walked in her bare feet along the cold, tiled corridor to the entrance hall. There, she had slipped on her shoes and opened the heavy main door and gone outside into the cool midnight air.

After adjusting to the dark, she had quickly and carefully picked her steps across to the car park – to find the dark-coloured Vauxhall car that was waiting for her. When she recognised it in the dim light, she ran over and there he was, waiting for her – Dr Andrew Harvey.

'Are you okay?'

As he spoke, Gaye had caught the faint smell of brandy and beer, and it reminded her of the wonderful time she had had dancing with him that night, and discovering how they both laughed at the same things and just seemed to fit so easily to-gether. She wondered also if the drinks she herself had drunk had made everything seem so completely hopeless. 'Yes,' she said, 'I'm a bit better now.' It was the truth. Being with Andrew

Harvey made everything seem better. Made her feel better about herself.

'I'm sorry if I disturbed you – especially when it's so late. I was just so worried about you when you didn't come back. Your friend explained about your sister, and I wanted to check if there was anything I could do?'

Gaye had then poured out the story she had rehearsed, about Audrey not being well, the fall and hitting herself and being taken to hospital. 'I was just upset and worried about her,' she explained. 'And I had to wait by the payphone for calls from my father and... my sister's fiancé. Everyone is so worried.'

Andrew had gathered her into his arms and kissed her hair. 'It will all be okay,' he said. 'I am sure they will sort it all out.'

They had sat talking about this and that, and how the war was dominating everything in everyone's lives and how no one knew what would happen. At one point, Gaye looked at her watch, trying to make out the time in the darkness of the car, and she said she should really go.

'If anyone comes by and sees us...'

'They won't,' Andrew said, 'no one is using the cars now, because they have no petrol. Please don't go,' he had said, 'stay for a little while longer. Don't leave me.'

'You have a girlfriend, Andrew,' she reminded him. She thought of Laurence and the trouble all that had caused, and then she thought of poor Audrey lying in a hospital bed.

'Elizabeth,' he said, 'she's a lovely girl but the thought of spending the rest of my life with her is... well, it's not what I imagined I would feel.'

'What do you mean?' Gaye held her breath.

He shook his head and when he turned to look at her his face was troubled. 'It feels like it was all planned for us since we were at school, that we made a natural couple and we just sort of drifted along with what both our families expected.' He shrugged. 'I'm so fond of her, but she's not the love of my life. I didn't know any different until recently, didn't know that that it was possible to feel so much more... and that is so necessary, especially if you are getting married. All those years together, there has to be something special to make it work, to be able to get through things – all the difficult times in life.' He shook his head. 'I know I need to do something about it, but finding the right way to do it, is just not easy.'

Gaye looked at him in the dim light and thought he looked almost as sad as she felt inside. They were, she thought, like a pair of lost souls.

She put her arms around him and he nestled into her, laying his head on her breast almost like a child. She touched his face with her hand and felt a surge of emotion run through her that made her feel like crying again.

'This feels right,' he said. 'When I'm with you, Gaye, I'm the person I should be. I can be truly myself.' He looked up at her and smiled. 'I could never imagine being like this with Elizabeth or anyone else.' Then, he pressed his lips to hers.

Gaye held back, afraid of making yet another mistake. 'It's late,' she said. 'I should go ...'

'Don't,' he said, 'please don't leave me yet.' He gently pulled her closer to him, and reached to kiss her again. His hands moved to caress her face and then her shoulders and then moved to the back of her neck. His touch was so light and tender and the most loving feeling she had ever felt.

A wave of passion swept over her; then, as Andrew's lips caught hers again, warmer and more inviting, she felt her resistance crumbling. As they kissed, she could feel all the reasons, all her resistance, beginning to dissolve. And then, an inexplicable feeling came over her that suddenly made sense of everything. A little voice that told her that being with Andrew in this pure and honest way would free her from the mistakes she had made. It would replace wrong with right, and wash away her sins with Laurence.

Gaye sat bolt upright now. Everything was falling into place and finally making sense to her. The memory of that passionate night had erased all doubt in her mind. The dates fitted perfectly, and the realisation that Andrew – Dr Andrew Harvey – was absolutely, and without any doubt, the father of her baby filled her with the most unimaginable joy. She put her hands to her mouth to muffle what could easily have been a scream of relief. It could so easily have been the biggest disaster yet.

It could have been Laurence's baby.

After that first drunken night together, when they had consoled each other, they had met up secretly again on several occasions. He had said he had been careful, and stopped before any accidents could have happened – and she had believed him. But when she got the shock today about the baby, she doubted everything. She had fully expected the dates to add up, and that Laurence would continue to overshadow her life.

Gaye sank to her knees and said a prayer of gratitude. Andrew, who she loved with all her heart, was her baby's father, and she was over the moon with the news. She did not care that the child had been conceived in the back seat of a car. She did not care about not being engaged or married to him yet – a quiet wedding with just the girls and a few of Andrew's friends would quickly be arranged. Now they were in this together, she felt totally confident, knowing that he would stand by her no matter what.

She would work out any difficulties with her family or his. Wait until they visited them, and say they had been married a while, but wanted to tell them face to face. And when the baby was born, if they questioned her pregnancy dates, she and Andrew would just say the baby came early. Shotgun weddings were nothing new, couples did it all the time – especially now with the uncertainties that the war had brought.

Gaye silently thanked God that for once she was not being made to pay for her mistakes. The incident with Laurence she would put firmly to the back of her mind as she had done before. Not one person knew, and she would keep it like that. As Diana had advised her, what was the point in telling truths which would only serve to make other people suffer? Tears streamed down her face.

It was a secret she would take to the grave.

Chapter Forty-One

Clare, Gaye and Diana walked into the entrance of the hospital social club. Since they were all wearing cardigans or blouses and carrying their handbags and gas masks over their shoulders, they bypassed the cloakroom and went on into the function room.

They paused at the doorway, all looking in at the half-empty dance floor.

'There's not many here,' Gaye said, 'maybe we shouldn't have bothered coming either.'

Clare gave her a friendly dig in the ribs. 'All the more reason we should have come,' she said. 'It's not that quiet, it's a big hall and three-quarters of the tables are already gone. Anyway, the poor girls have gone to all the trouble of organising a band and they have saved up for ages to pay for the finger buffet.' She craned her neck. 'I can see them all up at a table near the front, so we'll have to go up and wish them all happy birthday.'

Gaye pointed to a table in the corner. 'Let's sit there, away from the band, so we can talk in private, and without being deafened.'

They went and sat down, and when they were settled, Diana suddenly said. 'The birthday gifts!' She lifted her bag and brought out three small parcels wrapped in white tissue paper and tied with pink string, which she had made by soaking twine in beetroot juice. She also had a handmade card for each one with painted flowers and their names beautifully written underneath in Diana's distinctive handwriting.

'They are gorgeous,' Clare said. 'What do we owe you?'

'Not a penny,' Diana said, 'The make-up bags are made with odds and ends of material and lace, and I always have pieces of card I can use.'

After they had given their gifts and birthday wishes, the girls came back to the table, and for the first few minutes they sat, talking about the latest news from London and watching the half-dozen couples waltz around on the dance floor. When the music stopped a waitress came and took their order for three gin and tonics, which had now become their staple drink. They all paid for one round each and the three drinks lasted them all night.

As soon as the waitress had gone, Gaye put her hands on the table. 'I have somethin' to tell you, and I know you're both going to be shocked. But – before I say it, I want you to know that I am really, really happy – and I want you to be the same.'

The two girls looked at her, then at each other.

'I'm expecting a baby – Andrew's baby.'

Clare's heart almost stopped, then her hands instinctively came up to her mouth. 'Oh God,' she said in an anguished voice, 'Oh, Gaye...'

Gaye gave an awkward smile. 'It wasn't the bicarbonate of soda after all. I'm nearly three months gone.'

'Three months... how did you not know?' Clare asked.

'I had light periods for the last two months, so it never dawned on me.' Her voice dropped to a whisper. 'It must run in the family, because that's what happened to Audrey, if you remember.'

There was an awkward silence as the girls cast their mind back to the incident, which they had all tried to forget.

Clare's eyes narrowed as she studied her friend. 'Are you sure? You haven't really put on any weight. Maybe it's a mistake.'

'I have put on weight: I noticed weeks ago that I couldn't button some of me blouses, and I'm beginning to struggle with my skirts. Dr Galvin was almost positive... she could hear a strong heartbeat.'

Diana took a deep breath. 'If you are happy about it, then I'm going to say, "Congratulations!"' She moved out of her seat and went over to give Gaye a hug. 'I wish you and Andrew and your little baby all the luck in the world.'

Gaye suddenly felt all emotional and she clung to her friend. 'Thanks, Diana, that means a lot to me.' When they moved apart, Gaye said, 'I only found out this afternoon, so Andrew doesn't know yet, but I needed to tell someone. I know he's going to get a shock too, but he's already told me he loves me and wants to get married when the war is over. We'll just have to bring the wedding forward, like other couples have done.' She looked over at Clare. 'Are you all right? You're totally shocked, aren't you?'

Clare nodded. 'I don't know what to say ... I'm just really worried for you.' She took a deep, shuddering breath. 'It's not just that you're not married – honestly, it's not. I'm just worried with the war going on and with you having just got your SEN qualification, and I suppose I'm worried about how other people will react.'

'It's none of their business,' Gaye said, 'it's only mine and Andrew's.' She put her hand on Clare's arm. 'And I don't want you worrying about me. I know it's not going to be easy, I know all the problems it's going to cause with the families and work.' She paused. 'There's nothing I can do about it now, and anyway, I really meant it – I'm happy about this baby. I love Andrew and he loves me, and that's all that matters. As long as I have him and my friends, I honestly don't give two hoots about anyone else.'

'I'm really glad to hear that,' Diana said, 'and we will do all we can to help you, won't we, Clare?'

'Of course,' Clare said.

'I had to tell you,' Gaye said, 'but I'm tellin' no one else until me and Andrew are married. Dr Galvin said she wouldn't tell a soul.'

'Are you going to tell Andrew on the phone?' Diana asked.

'I'd prefer to do it face-to-face, but I don't know if he can get the time off to come up here. He said it would be a few weeks before he knew what his roster was, and when he can get time off. We were supposed to be going to visit his parents some time too, but we just can't work the time off.'

Diana nodded. 'Oliver and I are the same. I'm finding time off harder to get now that I'm supervising the other women. We need more parachutes than ever with all the fighter planes going out every day.' She shrugged. 'It's the same with weekends, I'm not making as many of the art sessions with the evacuees as I would like, but it can't be helped. Luckily, the other volunteers are used to it now, and know what to do if I'm not there.'

'We're the same with hospital rosters,' Gaye said. 'Some of the other nurses who have kids have said they need some weekends off too. When it gets nearer the winter, they won't need the groups so much.'

'Well, we can bring it up with Mr Lomas tomorrow,' Diana said. 'But, I think we should still keep some involvement with the groups if we can. I think it's been as good for the mothers as it has been for the children.'

'And it's been good for all of us,' Gaye said. 'It's made me feel I did something really useful for once, and I've enjoyed every minute with the choirs.'

Clare agreed, and was relieved to move on to more normal conversation, because she did not know what to say to Gaye about the baby. She didn't know any girls of their age who were single and who had become pregnant, and she could not be falsely happy for Gaye in a situation many people would think was disastrous. Her mind was filling with all sorts of anxieties for her friend. What would happen about her nursing career? What if Andrew did not marry her? What if her family turned their backs on her? All these fears were very real.

'So,' Diana said, 'any other news?'

Clare affected a bright smile. 'May has been accepted for nursing work in Stepping Hill. It will make a big difference to her money-wise and help get her out of the house more.' She could hear herself babbling a bit, but kept going. 'A neighbour is going to help her with Margaret-Anne.'

'That's great news,' Gaye said.

'She's been told they can give her a night a week to start, to see how she gets on.'

Clare was relieved when the waitress came with the drinks, and then the band started up again, playing an old-time waltz. One of Andrew's friends came over to talk to Gaye and ask her how he was getting on, chatting about the hospital in Cambridge and the bombings down south. He sat down at the table behind, and Gaye moved over so she could hear him better over the noise of the band.

Diana touched Clare's arm and then leaned closer. 'Are you all right?' she asked. 'I know the situation is upsetting for you.'

Clare's eyes filled up. 'I'm just so worried for her...' She searched in her handbag for a hanky. She dabbed it to her nose and then she swallowed hard a few times. She glanced over at Gaye and was glad she was occupied, as she didn't want her to see how upset she was.

'It's not an ideal situation,' Diana said in a low voice, 'and I think the reality of it may not have hit her yet.'

Clare looked at her quizzically. 'But I thought you were happy for her too – you congratulated her...'

'That's what she needed to hear,' Diana said, 'and truthfully, I *am* happy for her, and happy she wants this baby so much. She's going to have it anyway – she doesn't have a choice. Isn't it better that she accepts it, rather than be in the depths of despair and have the poor child brought into the world unwanted?'

As she listened, Clare could see the sense and kindness in Diana's words.

'Of course you're concerned about Gaye,' Diana continued, 'and I am too, but there's no point in worrying her tonight. When she gets over this initial excitement, the reality of her situation will hit her, and I think she will find it all harder than she imagines. She really will need us then.'

'Oh, Diana,' Clare said, 'you always make me feel better. You're much more capable of handling things than I am. You're so understanding, you always manage to make complicated things seem simple.'

A pink tinge appeared on Diana's cheeks. 'I'm not sure about that,' she said, giving her friend an embarrassed smile, 'but I have learned that it really helps if we try to put ourselves in other people's shoes. I have to do it all the time with my own family or they would drive me mad.'

Clare smiled too. 'Everything you say is always right and kind, even when people don't deserve it. When Gaye and I first met you, we were a bit anxious that we wouldn't have much in common. We could see you were a really nice person, but we thought that...' She shrugged. 'With you coming from such a privileged background, we wouldn't know what to say to you. We couldn't have been more wrong.' She gave a wry smile. 'I don't think I'm explaining myself very well – I hope we don't sound like the women you work with in the factory.'

'Not at all,' Diana said, an understanding tone to her voice. 'Most people are like that when they mix with others from different backgrounds. I feel anxious about meeting the rest of your family, and what they might think of me marrying Oliver.'

'I'll do everything I can to make them understand. It's difficult for them, because it's the way most people think in Ireland. They feel the Church has the answer to everything, and if people just follow their rules everything will fall into place.'

'I will do everything I can to understand and respect your family's point of view, so hopefully they will accept me. I'm going to try not to worry about it, as things often have a way of working themselves out.'

'Let's hope things work out for Gaye, too.'

The door opened and everyone turned to look as a large group of people of all ages came in, singing and laughing. The band started to play 'If You Were the Only Girl in the World', and two young men whom Clare did not know came up to ask them to dance. Neither were particularly good-looking, but they were cheery lads, and since males were becoming fewer on the ground at social events, due to being involved with ARP or Home Guard duties, they were grateful to be asked to dance.

As they circled around the floor, the one Clare was dancing

with explained that he was a brother of one of the nurses who was involved in the birthday party. He and his friend were both miners in Yorkshire, and had travelled over for the celebration.

Clare bent towards him trying to hear what he was saying, and trying to avoid his feet as he was not the most practised dancer.

'We need every bit of enjoyment we can get out of this flamin' war,' he said, 'cos none of us know what the next day is going to bring. It's gone completely mad down in London, you can't keep up with the news there's so much happening. Nothing is sacred any more – the Jerries have even bombed Buckingham Palace.'

'My brother is down in London,' Clare told him, 'although he's outside the city centre. I hope he's all right.'

'I don't know if any of us are safe,' he said, 'I've heard they're coming up north soon, and then we'll all be like sitting ducks. You're Irish, aren't you? Your country is neutral, you could be home and safe from all this. Do you not think of going back home?'

'Stockport feels like my home now.'

'Good for you. England is the best country in the world, and we're not going to let those Jerry bastards take us over.' They moved around the floor, Clare trying to avoid his clumsy feet. As the dance came to an end, he bent his head towards her and said. 'Are you going out with anyone?'

'Well,' she said, trying to think quickly, 'there is a lad . . .'

'No problem,' he said cheerfully. He glanced around the hall, with narrowed eyes. 'No point in wasting my time with a girl who's taken, when there's plenty of other fish in the sea.' He winked at her. 'That's one of the good things about the war, there's not so much competition with so many of the lads away.'

Clare went back to join Gaye and Diana at the table. She told them what the lad had said and they both laughed incredulously, then Diana told them that his friend has also asked her out and she was glad she could show him her engagement ring.

They watched the couples taking their places on the floor for the next dance, and then Gaye said, 'There they go again, your two lads, they're heading over for the far wall. Let's see who the lucky girls are.'

'That's Ida and Irene,' Clare said, smiling in amusement.

The three girls kept them in their sights then Gaye started giggling. 'Poor Ida has just had both feet tramped on,' she said, 'that lad has the worst two left feet I've ever seen. That's lads from Yorkshire for you!'

The girls ended up staying longer at the party than they planned, enjoying the music and the jovial atmosphere which distracted their minds from more serious thoughts. It was after eleven when they finally left. The party was in full swing now as other members of staff coming off the late shift had come to join in. The girls stopped off at the porter's lodge to check if there was any other news.

'It's all about Italy invading Egypt now,' the porter told them, 'and the usual bombing in London. There will be nothing left of the place at all if it keeps up.'

When they got out onto the main road, Diana was sure she saw a bus slowly coming up the hill, and she rushed as safely as she could to catch it.

Clare and Gaye carried on the short walk to the nurses' accommodation, still talking about the dance. When they reached the nurses' residence, Clare said, 'Get a good night's sleep and make sure you don't do too much lifting at work from now on.'

'I was just thinking about that earlier.' Gaye's voice was noticeably flatter. 'There's going to be a lot of changes that I hadn't thought about. I'm just hoping that as soon as Andrew knows, everything will fall into place.'

'It will,' Clare said, smiling at her. 'But you take care of your-self, and Diana and I won't breathe a word to anyone.'

'Thanks,' Gaye said. 'I'm going to try to put it out of my mind until I can talk to Andrew, and hopefully get this wedding organised. I might have to tell him over the phone, because it could be weeks before I see him.'

Clare put her arms around her friend. 'Sleep well, and I'll see you in the morning.'

Chapter Forty-Two

The following week, Diana woke early in the morning to the sound of rapping on her bedroom door. It took her a few moments to realise what was happening and then she looked at her bedside clock. It was only half past six, and she didn't need to be up for another hour at least. The rapping came again, more urgent this time.

'Yes?' Diana said, throwing back her bed covers.

'There's a phone call for you,' Stella called. 'It's Oliver and he said he's in a hurry.'

Diana moved quickly out of bed and across the floor, grabbing a dressing gown to pull on over her nightdress. She ran downstairs to the hall, where the telephone receiver was lying on the small table. Breathless, she picked it up. 'Hello, Oliver?'

'Yes, darling, it's me.' His voice seemed a long way off down the phone line. 'I'm so sorry about the time, but I'm travelling down south and I wanted to catch you before you left for the factory.'

'When are you coming back?' she asked. 'I thought you were only going for a week or so?'

'Things have changed with the London bombings,' he told her, 'and I have been conscripted to do some specialised work.'

'What kind of work?'

'Some of it involves my photography,' he explained, 'but there will be other work that I have to be trained for.' He paused. 'It's confidential, so I can't really talk about it, but I wanted you to know that I'm moving on to another training place at a location further south.' Again, there was silence on the other end of the line. 'I don't know if I will have access to phones, but as soon as can, I promise I will write.'

Diana felt bewildered by the change of events. 'You're not in any danger, are you?' There was crackling on the line and she could not hear his reply. 'What?' she said, in a louder voice.

'No more than the average person,' he repeated, 'and the training has been very useful.'

'Be careful, Oliver,' she pleaded. 'And keep away from London.'

'I can't guarantee where I'm going to be based, but I promise you that I will be extremely careful.'

Diana felt her mouth go dry. She had not imagined him close to the middle of the city where the continuous bombing was. She had seen pictures in newspapers almost daily – the burned-out homes, the fallen-down buildings, the fires, the rubble every-where. People being rescued from piles of bricks and mortar, and being carried on stretchers out of the absolute mayhem. So far, the one thing she had not seen was the dead bodies.

She thought back to the pictures that Oliver himself had taken that morning in Liverpool – but compared to what was happening now in London, the damage had been minuscule. The onslaught on the capital city was like the end of the world. To imagine that Oliver might find himself in the middle of all this tore at her heart.

'I've got to go now.' Oliver's voice was surprisingly upbeat. 'I promise I'll be in touch very soon, and I will be thinking of you all the time. In the meantime, Diana, keep up your art, keep up the war sketches and paintings. Just like my photographs, they will all be needed at some point in the future, and you will have the everyday man's story captured in your sketches. When you have time on your hands or are anxious, use it for your art. It's more important now than ever.'

'I will get on with my work,' she said, 'it will help the time pass and keep me from worrying about you.' She took a deep breath. 'Hopefully, you will be ringing soon to say you are on your way back to the north and back to me.'

'I cannot tell you how much I love you,' he said. 'You are in my thoughts from the moment I wake each morning, and are with me all through the day.'

Tears rushed into her eyes. 'I love you too ... and cannot wait to be in your arms again.'

When the line went dead, Diana stood there in the hallway, holding the receiver to her chest as though by putting it down in the cradle, she would be relinquishing this last little part of him. She stood for several minutes and then one of the creaky stairs sounded with footsteps and she looked up.

'I hope it wasn't bad news,' her aunt said, looking over the bannister, 'at this early hour of the morning.'

Diana shook her head. 'I don't think so ... I hope not.' She put the phone back down in its cradle. 'It was Oliver. He's been delayed down south; he's being moved to another branch for training. He couldn't say any more.'

'Your fiancé is an intelligent young man,' Rosamund said, 'and perfectly capable of looking after himself, so try not to worry.' She paused to look out of the hall window. 'It's not a nice morning – raining and windy. I think we should go back to bed for another hour or so.'

'Yes,' Diana said. 'I'm just going to have a drink of water, and I'll be up in a few minutes.'

She walked down into the kitchen and found a glass. She turned on the tap and half-filled it with water. She drank some and poured the rest down the sink, then she went to stand by the rain-splattered window. The sky was a solid dark grey, and as she looked out over the garden which her aunt, Stella and Mr Chesterton had been working on, she thought everything looked dark and gloomy. More like December than mid-September.

She felt a shiver run through her and she tightened the cord on her dressing gown, then she turned to pad barefoot across the cold stone floor to make her way back upstairs. She lay there for fifteen or twenty minutes, unable to sleep, and then she got up and went over to her desk, where she had left her small sketchpad. She sat down and put the lamp on, and flicked through the pages. She stopped when she found the sketch she did in Liverpool the morning after the first bombing.

She propped the small notebook up, and then went to the box which held her larger sketchpads. She selected the size she wanted, and then she lifted her box of graphite pencils. She did not know whether it would just be a sketch or whether she would go over it in oils or charcoal. That would come later.

Still in her dressing gown she started on her drawing, her hand moving across the heavy paper at times quickly, and other times very tentatively. She paused a few times to tuck a wing of her dark bobbed hair behind her ear, and then eventually got up to find a hairband to keep it back off her face.

She worked away, her pencil moving across the large sheet of paper, using her fingers and an eraser to soften or remove marks she had made. She paused when she heard doors on the landing and then the rattle of the old pipes told her that someone – Stella, she guessed, getting ready for school – was up and in the bathroom.

She glanced down at her watch and was startled. She barely had time to get washed and dressed before running out the door to catch her bus down to the factory. She quickly pulled on fresh underwear and a light, short-sleeved jumper. She then put her dressing gown back on, lifted her toothbrush and ran downstairs to the small toilet by the kitchen, to relieve herself and wash her face and clean her teeth.

There was no time for breakfast, so she went into the kitchen and buttered two slices of a fruit loaf Ivy Brown had made, and wrapped them in greaseproof paper. She would have them on the bus or walking along to the factory to save time. She rushed back upstairs to pull on her overalls and lifted her spotted work turban.

She had gathered all her essentials into work bag, and was making for the bedroom door when she turned back to her desk to take one last look at her drawing.

Her eyes moved over the picture of the bombed house – the fire-damaged roof, the shattered windows, and the debris scattered all around. She had included several people she remembered standing further down the street, and small random details such as a stray black cat walking past the house. Then her gaze came to stop at the back of a tall figure, a young man, facing the bleak house, his press camera held aloft.

She lifted the sketchpad and gently pressed her lips to the page. Then, tears glinting in the corner of her eyes, she rushed out of the house.

Chapter Forty-Three

Clare bent down to take a candle from the metal container below. She held it out to the flames of another candle, and when it was lit she placed it on the rack. She went through the same procedure until she had four candles in a row, all burning.

She went to sit at a nearby pew and then knelt down, saying her four prayers of intention – for her family in Ireland, for Oliver that he would keep safe, and for Gaye that her wedding would be organised quickly and very soon. The last candle and prayer was for herself. The actual intention was vague, but she knew there was something not quite right, something that she couldn't put her finger on. Recently, she had felt unsettled and sort of adrift.

She was still confused about the situation with Gaye and the baby and felt angry that she could not find it in herself to be comfortable with it. Until Gaye and Andrew were married, she just couldn't join wholeheartedly in the secret discussions about the baby. Her enthusiasm was forced when Gaye mused about whether it might be a boy or a girl, who it would look like, and what names for the child might be suitable.

A week had passed since they found out about the pregnancy, and Gaye had still not managed to pin Andrew down to a date when he was free to come up to Stockport. The hospital was unbelievably busy, he explained, and they were admitting wounded soldiers and pilots almost every day. She had told Clare she was going to phone him again today, and if he still couldn't manage a day off to come to Stockport, she would tell him about the baby.

'I've even thought of going down Cambridge,' Gaye had said, 'but when I called down to the station to see how I would do it, it was too difficult to travel in one day.'

'What about staying in a bed and breakfast?' Clare suggested.

'I'd need two days in a row off, and I'd have to give a good reason for it.' She sighed. 'I'll need to work something out soon.'

Clare prayed now that things would work out for Gaye. She stayed a little longer, and when she had finished all her prayers, she came out of the pew and then knelt to genuflect in front of the altar. She was walking down the aisle, her brow knitted in thought, when she noticed the elderly parish priest, Father Mackle, dressed in a black soutane at the back of the church. She had seen him on the altar on numerous occasions and also in the hospital when he was visiting patients, but she didn't really know him to speak to. The priest was sorting some holy pamphlets in a wooden stand.

She suddenly thought she might have a word with him – ask his advice about the situation with Gaye. For some reason she felt she needed official advice, some sort of Church guidance that would take the onus off herself.

He looked up as she came towards him and smiled. 'Can I help you, my dear?' He looked at her with narrowed eyes. 'You're one of our young Irish parishioners from St Timothy's, aren't you?'

'Yes,' she said, 'I'm Clare O'Sullivan, and we met on the geriatric ward one night, when one of the elderly ladies passed away.'

'I remember you now,' he said, nodding.

'I wondered if I could ask your advice on a difficult situation that I'm caught up in?'

He guided her over to a side pew, where, he said, if anyone came in to pray they would not overhear them.

Clare outlined the situation, explaining that her friend was not only pregnant now, but had been in a precarious situation with someone else before. 'I'm very fond of her, Father,' Clare said. 'She's like a sister to me, but I know at times her behaviour and attitude is not what the Church would approve of – and it's definitely not what my own parents would approve of. But, apart from that, she is a very kind and good person, and would do anything to help anyone else.'

The priest looked at her, his lips pursed tightly. 'You've answered your own question. You know that this person is not living by the teachings of the Catholic Church, and not in a way you feel comfortable about.'

Clare nodded. 'She is not a Catholic herself.'

'Ah,' said, raising his bushy eyebrows, 'that changes the situation, because you are dealing with someone who has been brought up with a different set of values from you. If she is from a different church, or no church at all, then you can't compare her values to ours.' He paused. 'But yet, from what you say, you obviously see a lot of good in her. And of course, you have to mix with all denominations in your working day.'

'I have a difficulty about knowing whether by continuing to be friends with her, that I'm condoning her having... well, having relationships outside marriage, and going against everything the Catholic Church teaches us.'

'How long have you been living away from home, Clare?'

'Almost three years.'

'Well, you're as much a woman at this stage as you're ever going to be,' he said, 'and you're living in a different country, so you can't keep going back and forth to check everything with your mother and father, so you have to listen to your conscience and decide for yourself. Make your own choices. Isn't that why God gave us free will?'

'But what about the Church's rules?' Clare asked. 'Aren't they fairly black and white about these things?'

'Yes,' he said, 'I suppose they are. But there are times when we have to think about what Jesus would do, and look back to the advice he gave. Do you remember him saying, "He that is without sin among you, let him cast the first stone"?'

Clare nodded. 'Are you saying that I should ignore what the church rules say about fornication and having children out of wedlock?'

'What I'm saying is that you are a member of the church and as such, should abide by the rules to the best of your circumstances. But, you are only responsible for yourself. Oh, you can try to advise and point out where people are morally wrong, but let me tell you it's a never-ending job doing it.' He stabbed a finger to his own chest. 'That's what the clergy are supposed to be here for, to keep everyone in line and get them to do all the right things, as is laid down by the church. To remind them that missing Mass on Sunday is a sin, to go with your neighbour's wife is a sin, to steal from someone is a sin.' He smiled at Clare. 'But that's not your responsibility. Yours is to care for people in the hospital and try to make them well again, and to do those things for anyone regardless of their circumstances – just as Jesus would do.'

Clare looked at him, trying to take it all in.

'Basically,' he said, 'my advice to you is to live your own life and do as much good as you can. None of us can live other people's lives for them, they alone are responsible for their own choices. Me, you, your friend, and your mother and father. We all have to choose our own way, and hope that all the good we do will lead us to God at the end of it.'

She nodded. 'Thank you, Father, I feel better for having spoken to you. In a way, I actually feel a bit silly for asking you something I should have worked out for myself.'

'Clare, from what you've told me about yourself, I would say you were a very obedient daughter, and abided by your parents' rules.'

'I tried to be,' she said. 'But it was a lot easier at home in Ireland. Everything was much more straightforward, and everybody seemed to think the same way.'

'Life is very different here,' he said, 'especially now with the war on.' He paused. 'Do you know how many mothers and fathers and wives I have coming in to see me, devastated after their son was blown to bits at Dunkirk or their husband was shot down when flying one of the fighting planes in the battles over the channel?'

'It's terrible,' Clare said. 'I suppose you must see a good few families who have been affected.'

'Every single day,' he said. 'And there's very little we can do to help those poor families get over their tragic loss. All we can do is listen to them, comfort them and pray for them. And sometimes the poor souls are so distraught they won't let you offer any kind of comfort. They want to know why God has done this to them, taken their loved ones in such a horrific way. What kind of God is he, who would allow such terrible atrocities in the world? What kind of God would allow all the terrible things that Hitler and his henchmen have done in their mad obsession to take over the world?' He looked directly at her now. 'Do you think we have answers to those questions? I can't find any words that truly comfort them. Who can blame them?'

Clare closed her eyes and shook her head. 'It must be terrible.'

'Doesn't your problem seem very small compared to those poor people's?'

Clare nodded. 'Yes,' she said, 'it does.'

'Well, my advice to you is to go to your friend and listen to her, comfort her and – when you can't do anything else – pray for her.'

Chapter Forty-Four

Gaye put her clipboard down on the reception desk. 'That's the report for the last admission,' she said to the nurse who was taking over from her. 'A fourteen-year-old boy rushed in with appendicitis. They're preparing him for surgery now. All his details are in the notes.'

'That's great,' the nurse said. She looked around the waiting room. 'It's busy enough for the middle of the week.'

'Nothing very serious apart from an elderly man who was brought in with severe breathing difficulties, coughing and a high temperature. The doctor is already in with him now.'

'Sounds like pneumonia.'

'It does,' Gaye agreed.

They chatted for a few minutes longer about the admissions and then as Gaye went to collect her cape and bag, the nurse asked, 'How is Andrew doing down in Cambridge? Any news?'

'I spoke to him at the weekend, and he's fine. Long hours and hard work.'

'Same as here then?' The nurse rolled her eyes.

'More or less,' Gaye said, 'but the military cases are a lot more complicated. Andrew said there are lot of cases with burns, and that involves complicated facial surgery.'

'Oh God, the poor men...'

Gaye went out of the main entrance of the casualty department and down to the phone box on the corner of the next street, as the payphone in the nurses' block was not private enough for such a personal call. She opened the heavy door of the kiosk, and was immediately hit with the stale smell of cold metal, cigarettes and dried urine. She felt her stomach turning, and took a moments to fight back the nausea she had become almost used to.

She put her bag up on the shelf, and then searched inside for her purse with the coins she had collected for the call. She put them in a stack and then took a deep breath and dialled the Cambridge number. When the receptionist answered, Gaye explained she needed to get in touch with Dr Andrew Harvey as she had some urgent news for him.

The receptionist, Kathleen, remembered the friendly, chatty Gaye from her calls before. She knew she had difficulty catching Andrew recently, as he was in theatre a lot of the time. 'Good news. He's actually in the canteen now; I was on my break and I saw him,' she told Gaye. 'So, if you hold on, I'll run and get him for you now, and you can have a private word with him on this line.'

Gaye waited, her stomach churning and her emotions running from excitement to feelings of dread. Finally, his voice came on the line, clearer than most of their other calls, both using public kiosks.

'Gaye!' he said, 'is there something wrong? The receptionist said it sounded urgent.'

'Can anybody hear you?' she said in a low voice.

'No, I'm on my own. Kathleen went to get a cup of tea. Is there actually something wrong? It's lovely to hear your voice, but you have me worried...'

'I'm pregnant, Andrew... I just found out.'

There was a stunned silence. 'Are you sure?' Then his voice dropped to a whisper. 'We were careful each time, I always used something.'

'Andrew, I am absolutely sure.' Her tone was adamant now as she had no time to lose. 'I was told last week, but I went to my GP a few days later and had a proper examination done and I'm over three months.' She paused. 'I know exactly when it happened, it was the night in the car, and we didn't use anything.'

'Oh God...' he said. 'I'd completely forgotten about that.'

She waited for a reaction, and then she heard a strange muffled noise, as though he might be upset or even crying. 'Andrew?' she said. 'Are you all right?'

'Yes,' he finally said. 'Gaye, I can't believe it... I am... I am so happy! It's wonderful news.' His voice cracked, and as he went on, she realised he was actually crying. 'I've had the most awful, bloody morning in theatre with a nineteen-year-old soldier who lost half his face, and another one who has lost an arm and a leg.'

Gaye again veered from feeling ecstatic at his response about the baby to concern about him. 'Oh Andrew,' she said, 'that's awful for you...' She gulped. 'But you're sure you're happy about the baby?'

'I'm over the moon,' he said. 'You know I want us to be together, and the thought of us having a lovely little baby is just the most wonderful news with all this horrific stuff going on around me here.'

Gaye felt her heart swell with relief and gratitude, then common sense prevailed. 'We need to get married quickly,' she said, 'because I found out about the baby very late. I've checked and we can get a special licence if you come up here two days before the wedding. You need your birth certificate and stuff like that.'

'Of course,' he said, 'I always carry all those documents with me, just in case there's ever a problem. I've been working non-stop since I arrived here, and a few days off should not be a problem.'

'If it's okay with you,' Gaye said, 'I think it should just be the two of us, and a best man and bridesmaid.' When he didn't argue, she continued with her plan. 'I think we should leave the families until it's all over. The wedding, the war and maybe even until the baby is born. We can go together up to Newcastle and then York and tell both the families. Make out we did it on the spur of the moment, as we didn't want people travelling with the war. They will have heard all the news reports saying that people should only travel if it's urgent, as they need the trains for the military.'

'We don't want people taking unnecessary risks anyway,' Andrew said, 'so I've no problem with that.'

'And we can even say that we got married earlier, so nobody thinks we were forced into a shotgun wedding,'

'You know how I feel about you, Gaye, and nobody would have to force me into anything. I want to be married to you, and I know it's the right thing for me.' He halted. 'I never even asked, are you okay? Is the pregnancy going well? Any morning sickness or anything like that?'

'I'm absolutely fine,' she said, laughing with relief at the way everything had worked out so easily. 'Just a bit of nausea now. In the beginning I really had no symptoms at all apart from noticing that my bust was getting bigger.'

'Well, that's certainly not a problem for me,' he laughed.

'Oh, Andrew,' she said, 'I'm so relieved, so happy that you're okay with everything.'

He reassured her again, and then he said, 'I'll organise the time off as soon as I finish in theatre this evening – probably after eight o'clock. As soon as I know what's happening, I'll ring you.'

'I'll be in my room all night,' Gaye said, 'and when it comes near eight o'clock, I'll be listening for the phone ringing.'

Gaye rushed back to the nurses' block to tell Clare her good news, and was disappointed when she knocked on her door and there was no answer. It was too early to ring Diana as she wouldn't be home from work yet. She turned back to go down to her own room, when she met Clare coming along the corridor.

'I was just looking for you,' Clare said, smiling at her. 'I've some news to tell you.'

'Which room?' Gaye asked. 'Yours or mine?'

'Why don't we get changed out of our uniforms, and I'll call down for you in ten minutes and then we can walk down to the café?'

'Brilliant idea.' Gaye couldn't wait. She looked around her to check there was no one who might hear. 'I've got some news too. I've told Andrew and he's delighted. We're getting married in the next week or so!'

Clare's face broke out in a beaming smile. She threw her arms around Gaye. 'I am delighted for you. It's the best news I've heard for ages.'

Gaye put her finger to her lips. 'I'll tell you all about it when we're outside.'

As they walked down towards the café, Gaye brought Clare up to date on their plans. 'It's only going to be a tiny wedding, with no more than six. I want you and Diana to be my bridesmaids,' she said, 'and I'm presuming Andrew is going to ask his friend, George, from Manchester to be the best man.' She went on to explain that they were saying nothing to either family until it was all over, and then they would tell a white lie about the date of the wedding, so their parents were none the wiser about when the baby was actually conceived.

'It sounds as though you have it all worked out,' Clare said. 'You just need to get your wedding dress and our dresses sorted, then decide where you'll have the wedding ceremony and breakfast.'

Gaye laughed. 'Well, you know I've had it all worked out since I started going out with Andrew! But I didn't expect it to happen so soon or like this. We have to get everything organised in very short time. I'm hoping Diana will help us out with making the dresses,' Gaye said, 'if we can get hold of some material.' She suddenly paused. 'Do you think there's any chance your Oliver would make it to the wedding too? I'd love him to come.'

Clare's face became serious. 'I've no idea, because we don't know where he is. He went on some Home Guard training down near London, and he's now been moved on to some other specialist place for more intensive training. I know Diana is worried, although she's trying hard not to show it.'

'Oh God, and I was thinking of phoning her later to tell her my good news, and ask her about the dresses.'

'Do phone her,' Clare advised. 'Your lovely news will cheer her up and take her mind off things.'

They were settled in the café with their milky coffee and a bun each when Clare said, 'I've decided to do a three-month nursing placement in a military hospital out near Knutsford.'

'Have you?' Gaye's eyes widened in surprise. 'I saw that pinned on the noticeboard the other day, saying they were looking for SEN-trained nurses to volunteer.' Her face fell. 'I'm going to really miss you...'

'It's only for three months,' she said. 'I'll be back for Christmas long before the baby's due.'

'What on earth made you decide to volunteer for that?'

'I've said loads of times that I want to do something for the war effort,' Clare reminded her, 'but there's nothing really I can do around Stockport. I know some of the other nurses have gone down to work in London and hospitals like the one in Cambridge where Andrew is, but I'm not brave enough to go that far on my own.' She shrugged. 'I'd find London too big and frightening for me even if there wasn't a war going on; I'd never survive. The place I'm going to is out in the country, somewhere between Macclesfield and Knutsford, so it's not that far. I'll get back to Stockport every few weeks.'

'I'll really miss you,' Gaye repeated, her face dismal. 'Especially with the baby coming.'

'To be honest, I need a change,' Clare told her. 'I feel I'm in a rut... I've been doing the same things for ages. I've been in England a few years now and I've stayed in the same little spot, and I just need to try something different. Just for a while.'

Gaye took a sip of her coffee. 'I've not gone very far either.'

'But your life has totally changed, Gaye: you have Andrew now and in the next six months you'll have a baby. It's the same with Diana, she has Oliver and she can go between her aunt's house and her big family home, and in her spare time she's busy with her art work.'

'You might meet somebody too,' Gaye said. 'There's a few of the doctors you didn't really get to know.' She halted. 'I could ask Andrew to introduce you to some of his old medical student friends from Manchester or York.'

Clare smiled. 'It's nothing to do with meeting a man. If that's going to happen it will. This is something I want to do for myself, I need to spread my wings.' She touched Gaye's hand. 'I promise I'll get back as often as I can, and I'll be finished for Christmas and back here.'

'You know I'll have to move out of the nurses' accommodation,' Gaye said. 'I'll have to look for a place for me and Andrew and the baby. I've just realised all the changes we'll need to make.' She gave a sigh. 'I'll get the wedding all sorted and then after that I'll start looking for something to rent near work.'

'Edgeley is handy for the hospital,' Clare said. 'And there are plenty of terraced and semi-detached houses. May was looking into renting a small place for her and Margaret-Anne, but she was told the Guernsey women aren't allowed to rent unless they can prove their husband is in the forces.'

Gaye nodded. 'I know, one of the WRVS women was telling me last weekend, that a lot of the families are in terrible accommodation, like old, closed-down shops and houses that were boarded up. She said they don't like to complain because they know how lucky they were escaping Guernsey, but it's really difficult managing little bairns in places that don't have proper washing facilities.' She thought for a moment. 'May will miss you too, and talking of the Guernsey people, what about the weekend activities?'

'It's got a lot quieter now since they're all in their own areas,' Clare said, 'and Mr Lomas said that we would be taking a break over the winter.' She shrugged. 'We're not needed as much now the children are settled in schools and doing their own activities there.'

'Oh...' Gaye said, looking disappointed. 'Me and Jack were saying that it would be nice to organise a Christmas concert for the kids. We were thinking that it would be a great way to raise funds for the new groups the Guernsey people are trying to set up.'

'Well, I'll be back the week before Christmas,' Clare said. 'So you can count me in for any help you need.' She gave Gaye a sidelong glance. 'Be careful you don't take too much on. Don't forget you'll be over six months by then.'

Gaye's face brightened up at the mention of the baby. 'Don't you worry,' she said, patting her stomach, 'This will be my number one priority along with its gorgeous father.'

'I'm really happy for you, and I know everything is going to work out fine for you.'

'It's like a fairy tale come true,' Gaye said, beaming. 'I can't believe it's actually happening myself!'

When she arrived home from the factory after another twelve-hour shift, Diana was delighted when her aunt handed her an envelope with a London postmark on it, and Oliver's neat, slightly slanted handwriting.

'Mrs Brown said she left your evening meal in the oven, covered with a plate.'

'I'm going upstairs first,' Diana told her. 'I want to get out of my overalls. I'll be back down soon.'

She took the stairs two at a time, desperate to be alone in her room to read her letter. She quickly tore the envelope open then threw herself down on the bed to read it. She felt an initial wave of disappointment that it was only one sheet of writing paper, and was slightly happier when she saw he had written on the other side as well.

My Dearest, Darling Diana, she read, smiling at the alliteration,

It was wonderful to hear your voice on the phone, and I feel so much better for it. I am so sorry that I have had to stay longer down south than I expected. To explain a little more to you, the training for the Home Guard went well very well, and some of the men were selected to go on to do a more in-depth training. It has been fascinating and I've learned things I would never have imagined. Some day, I will tell you all about it.

In the meantime, I am missing you very much. As I have told you before, I think of you first thing in the morning when I awake and you are there in my mind until I my last breath at night.

Any spare moments I have, I go over the time we had together in the Adelphi. I loved every single minute we spent in the hotel and walking around the city, but most of all, I loved our time in the lovely room together – and especially our time in bed, wrapped in each other's arms. That particular memory is etched in my mind, like a brightly coloured photograph of the pair of us.

I still can't work out what I did to make me deserve a woman such as you. How do I describe you? Beautiful, of course, but also individually striking, in a way that is hard to find the right words to define. Your face, your eyes, your beautifully shaped hands and feet, and that gloriously soft skin that I could spend my whole life kissing and touching.

I want you to know that everything about you enraptures me and has filled every little void in my life. All the little parts that I did not even know were missing. Meeting you has made me complete in a way I have never been – nor ever will be – in my life again.

You are my everything,

Your loving fiancé,

Oliver

When she finished reading, Diana closed her eyes and held the precious letter to her heart.

Chapter Forty-Five

Dr Andrew Harvey got off the train in Victoria Station, his case in his hand, his gas mask – like for hundreds of other men – slung over his shoulder, and strode on down the platform to have his ticket punched, marking the first leg of his journey.

He had not told Gaye that the only train he could get to arrive in Stockport on the Tuesday evening – for the wedding on Wednesday – meant a change in London. There was no point in worrying her, as she had been telling him how concerned both Diana and Clare were about Oliver doing a training course near the capital. Apparently, they were also disappointed that the specialised Home Guard training meant that he could not get the day off to travel up for the wedding either.

These things seem to mean much more to women, he thought. Men just shrug and understand that there are more important issues in life, especially in the current climate.

He had only met Oliver a few times, but he liked what he had seen of the Irish chap, and he had told Gaye that they would have plenty of opportunities to socialise together as soon as the damned war was over.

Andrew walked through the station, heading for the London Underground, where he would have a couple of changes to get him out to Euston for the train northwards. He had almost an hour and a half to spare when he reached Euston, so being in no great rush he decided to take a look outside of the station, to see what that particular area looked like now. Coming into Victoria on the train, he had been shocked to see the shattered houses and burned-out buildings. He didn't know why it shocked him, because there were photographs of the city's devastation in every newspaper he had seen over the last few weeks, and he had heard vivid descriptions of it on the radio morning, noon and night.

Instead of heading straight to the Underground, he walked in the direction of the main exit. He had just stepped outside when he saw the evidence of the bombing straight across the road from where he stood. The fronts of several shops had been blasted out and the accommodation above them destroyed. A pub that had stood there for over a century had had the whole of the outside structure blown away, leaving the bar area, with alcohol bottles, shattered mirrors, fireplaces and upstairs living quarters, naked to the full view of the travelling public. Dust and debris was everywhere, covering piles of brick and stone, slates and plaster, and men were already out, roping areas off while they worked at clearing the rubble to make it safe for pedestrians heading for work and to the station.

He walked up to the main road to see a similar story in the surrounding streets – gaping roofs and shattered windows. He crossed over and walked down one street that looked less damaged and then down another until he emerged into a street of tall Georgian houses that stood in pristine normality, quite separate from the destruction only a few hundred yards away.

Pure luck, Andrew thought. Had the bombs been dropped only seconds later, this prestigious street of houses could just as easily have been laid bare into rubble like the others.

He walked on for a few more minutes, looking around him, and then he spied a café at a corner opposite which looked open and functioning. He thought it would probably be better than anything on offer around the station, so he crossed the road and went in.

He came out twenty minutes before his train was due, replenished after the egg and chips and tea, and walked smartly back to the station and down into the Underground. It struck him, as he went along, that despite the damage to residential buildings and businesses it was indeed business as usual in the capital city. Men in smart business suits and bowler hats passed him by, as did women carrying bags of shopping, all with an air of normality in contrast to their surroundings.

Andrew went to the ticket window and double-checked his route, as it was a while since his last trip to London, and was told by the clerk to take the Victoria Line straight to Euston.

When he arrived in the station, there was a notice on the board saying that the train had been delayed by another hour. He stifled a sigh and then suddenly thought he had time to buy a newspaper from one of the kiosks, find a local pub and have a glass of some London brew.

Two pints later, and feeling more relaxed, he came out of the pub and gazed around him. Further down the street he noticed an elderly, heavy-set woman with a barrow filled with simple bunches of garden flowers tied with rough string. As he passed the display, it struck him that he had never bought Gaye flowers in the few months they had been a couple. The thought had not crossed his mind, and yet he had bought them for Elizabeth every time they met up again in York at the end of each university term.

Gaye was modest in her expectations of him. It was another trait in the woman he was going to marry that he admired. She was not only beautiful, vivacious, talented and funny, she also put few demands on him. Since they had been together officially, she had been happy to go along with any suggestions he made about where they went and what they did, and had looked for nothing from him, apart from his company. She had charmed his friends and, once they got to know her, he knew she would do the same with his family. She may not have had the same educational status as the quieter, more sensible Elizabeth, but her big heart and cheery nature more than compensated for that.

Andrew stopped in front of the barrow of flowers, wondering what she would like. He had a few words with the woman, and then he pointed to the largest bunch of red roses mixed with delicate sprigs of gypsophila.

'Lucky lady, they's me best flowers this week,' the old woman said in a cockney accent, lifting the bunch from her cart. She touched her hand – covered with a tattered, fingerless glove – to a stem of the white flowers. 'The baby's breath is very popular with the young ladies, very romantic they look when they're mixed with the red roses.'

'Baby's breath?' he said. 'I've never heard them called that.'

He was tickled with the idea. It was very apt that the first bouquet he gave Gaye should have a reference to the new life that would make them a family in the spring of next year. He would remember the name and tell her when he surprised her with the flowers.

He took the bunch from her, and was just checking his trouser pocket for the half-crown to pay for them when the air-raid sirens suddenly screeched and everyone stopped and looked around them to see what others were doing.

'It's never gonna be an attack at this time of the day,' the flower-seller commented knowledgeably. She halted as the ominous drone of a jet engine mingled with the loud city noise of cars, buses and trains. The sound became louder as Andrew and the flower-seller looked up into the sky, shielding their eyes against the sun.

'It is! It's them Jerry bastards again!' the old lady suddenly shrieked. 'We'd better get over to the Underground quick.'

'I'll pay you when we get there,' Andrew told her, his heart racing at the thought of the impending danger. He moved quickly to cross the road, then, when he got to the station side, he heard a cry. When he turned around he saw the old lady sprawled on the ground, having tripped over a wooden crate lying beside her cart.

Without hesitating, he ran back towards her. He dropped his bag and the flowers onto the pavement and then as she scrabbled to get to her knees, he caught her under one arm to hoist her up. She was heavier than he realised, and she sank back down to the ground, so he had to reposition himself behind her and try again, this time gripping her under both arms.

'God bless you, sir,' she panted as she struggled to her feet. She said something else but it was lost in the sudden roaring of a lone bomber plane which appeared above them and hovered just long enough to discharge a stick of bombs on the street below.

The blast took the flower cart and the blooms fifty feet into the air before they scattered down again in colourful shreds. It shattered glass in the surrounding shop windows and cars nearby. A hole was gouged in the middle of the road where the bomb had landed, and lying beside it were two bodies – those of Dr Andrew Harvey and Mrs Ruby Dodds, one London flower-seller.

By the side of the road lay the bouquet of red roses and baby's breath, surprisingly intact.

Chapter Forty-Six

Gaye waited anxiously on a phone call from Andrew. Every time the phone rang she ran out of her room and down the corridor to answer. And every time she expected to hear his voice, explaining how the train had some sort of engine problem and was delayed. It was also possible, she reasoned, that the train had set off from Cambridge, only to get stuck at some railway station where they were waiting for a platoon of soldiers who were being moved from one army barracks to another. The platoon may have been delayed, and the train dared not go without them. There were a number of other scenarios that could have caused Andrew to be late, and she allowed each one to run through her mind.

Clare, who had been on a late shift, came over to the nurses' residence at ten o'clock expecting to be greeted by an excited Gaye, only to find her white-faced with worry over her groom's whereabouts.

'He could appear any time,' Clare said, trying to think of things to reassure her. 'I've heard of cases where they're afraid of anything happening the trains, so they pull up at one of the stations and there's a coach to take them the rest of the journey.'

'That's true, with this flaming war anything could delay him.' Gaye agreed, glad to grasp at anything that would validate Andrew's absence.

'He might even be in on the milk train early in the morning,' Clare said. 'The wedding isn't until one o'clock, so he has plenty of time yet.' She turned to look at the wedding dress hanging outside the small wardrobe. 'You have everything organised, don't you?'

'Everything I can think of,' Gaye said, smiling now. In just over a week she had miraculously managed to sort out wedding dresses for herself and two beautiful bridesmaid dresses for Clare and Diana.

When May Tyrrell had been brought into the secret of the wedding plans, and heard of all the arrangements they were trying to make in a week, including a wedding dress, she immediately thought of her elderly neighbour. Mrs Hartley had recently shown May her beautiful lace dress, preserved for the last twenty-five years in the original box and carefully covered with tissue paper. The retired nurse had told her that she always hoped it would be worn again, but she had never had a daughter, only three sons whose brides all wanted to pick their own wedding outfit.

When May approached Mrs Hartley about the dress, the older woman was delighted to loan it to Gaye. She also found in a small, separate box a piece of the original material that had been cut off at the hem when the dress was altered and a pair of white lace gloves.

'Somebody good with their hands might be able to make some kind of a head-dress,' Mrs Hartley had said, 'and it would just finish it off perfectly.'

May had nodded and said, 'I know just the person who will be able to do that. A lovely lady who works with silk all the time, sewing parachutes.'

Diana had come up with the two bridesmaid dresses. She had taken an overnight trip home during the week, returning on the early-morning train in time for work, and had begged two lovely plain evening dresses from her mother – one pink and one pale lilac. She had then spent an evening making two sashes to go around the girls' waists, in a mixture of pink and lilac silk, the exact colours of the dresses. She had made them from remnants of the white parachute silk, which she had been given by Phyllis. She had painstakingly dyed the pieces overnight in pastel colours, to give the two bridesmaid dresses a decorative link. Diana's mother surprised her by coming downstairs with two lovely pearl bracelets, which she loaned Diana and Clare for the wedding.

The wedding breakfast was booked at the Alma Lodge, and now had been expanded for eight people, who included Diana and Clare, May and Mr Lomas and Andrew's friend George – who was to be best man – and his wife, Doreen.

'Well, you don't have a thing to worry about,' Clare said, 'apart from getting your groom here on time.'

Gaye had looked at her with wide, frightened eyes. 'You don't think he would jilt me, do you? Just not turn up without telling me?'

'Not at all,' Clare said. 'He thinks the world of you, and he's too decent to do anything like that.' She stood up. 'I'll go down to the kitchen and make us a cup of cocoa, and you can keep an ear out for the phone.'

The phone rang several more times, mainly for other nurses in the block, but on one occasion it was Diana, checking all was well. She went off very quickly when she realised Andrew might be trying to get through, after wishing Gaye well for tomorrow and saying that she was sure Andrew would turn up soon.

Eventually, it was after midnight and the phone had stopped ringing. There was still no word or sign of Andrew.

It was after nine o'clock the following morning, and there was still no news of Gaye's groom. Diana came over to the hospital and the three girls sat together in Gaye's small bedroom with a plate of egg sandwiches that Clare had brought over from the canteen. The door of the room was ajar so they could hear the phone at the end of the corridor. It was normally quiet at this time of the morning as most staff had gone out on the early shift and those coming off nightshift were now in bed.

Somehow, Gaye had managed to keep the wedding a secret from all the other girls. It was easier than she thought it would be, as the ones they were friendly with were often on different shifts, and any time they met up, they were more interested in asking about Clare's impending move to the military hospital out in Cheshire, which would happen a few days after the wedding.

Gaye had confided about the wedding to Sister Townsend, since she needed someone to help make sure Clare had the same day off for the wedding, and that Gaye had the following day off too. The sister had congratulated her and said she had got a good catch with the lovely Dr Harvey. Gaye suspected that the older nurse had looked at her and guessed she was pregnant, but she had not said anything outright. In a few weeks' time it would make no difference what people thought as she would have the ring on her finger to ward off any comments.

'You have to eat something,' Diana told Gaye, who had not touched anything apart from the tea. 'It's not good for you or the baby.'

Gaye took a quarter of a sandwich and took a few bites out of it. 'There's something wrong,' she said. 'I know it...'

Her fears were confirmed at eleven o'clock in the morning when a phone call came for her from the hospital in Cambridge that Andrew had been working in. It was Kathleen, the receptionist who had always been friendly and kind to her.

'I'm so glad I've managed to reach you, Gaye,' Kathleen said, her voice slightly breathless. 'We only heard this morning, and I had to go through the phone records to find your number.'

'What's happened?' Gaye said. 'There's something wrong with Andrew...'

'I'm sorry to tell you,' Kathleen went on, sounding very anxious, 'but he was involved in an incident at Euston Station in London yesterday evening. A bomb was dropped a few streets away and he was caught up in the blast.'

'But it can't be him,' Gaye said, 'Andrew wasn't in London. He was getting the train from Cambridge.'

There was a silence and then Kathleen said, 'I'm so sorry to tell you such bad news, but it is Dr Harvey. There's no doubt. The police and the hospital he was admitted to have his identity papers and he even had his birth certificate with him.'

'How is he?' Gaye asked, a hysterical note in her voice. 'Is he all right?'

'I'm so sorry... but he's very badly injured. The hospital have been asked to contact his relatives, and they found the hospital details in some of his documents as it was written down as his current place of residence.'

'Tell me what hospital he's in, and I'll get down there as quick as I can.' She held her hand to her mouth and then she started shaking and crying. 'We were getting married today, Kathleen,' she told the receptionist. 'He was supposed to be here last night...'

'I'm so sorry, Gaye,' Kathleen said again, now crying herself. 'He's been taken to a hospital in Watford. All the others nearby were full, and he needed immediate surgery.'

Gaye closed her eyes and shook her head. 'Oh God... oh God...'

'They said to come as quick as you can.' She gave her the name of the hospital and the directions, and Gaye called them out to Clare who wrote them down.

'Thanks, Kathleen,' Gaye sobbed. 'I don't know how I'm goin' to get there, but I'll get to him if I have to crawl on my hands and knees.'

Chapter Forty-Seven

Within an hour, Gaye and Diana and Clare were all in Reverend Lomas's Austin 10 car and heading down to the hospital in Watford. Gaye was in the front passenger seat, and the girls in the back. The vicar had driven them around three garages in the Stockport town centre – owned by his parishioners – who gave him as much petrol as they could without being in serious trouble. By the third garage he had a full tank and two full containers in the boot, enough to get down to Watford and hopefully back up.

Gaye, in her anxiety, kept thanking him and saying she hoped he wouldn't get into trouble with the petrol rationing being so strict.

He waved away her concerns. 'I have no qualms about bending the rules in this situation.' There was a silence and then he said. 'Besides, you young ladies have given your time to the church and the evacuees, and there are times when the church has to give back too.'

Although the vicar went as quickly as the car would allow, the journey seemed to take ages. Every so often someone would point out an interesting building or some lovely scenery, or make a comment on the sunny weather, but more often the car was quiet, with everyone staring out of the window, minds numb from the shock of what had happened Andrew.

Occasionally, one of them dozed off, and Diana and Clare were relieved when they heard light snoring noises, and realised Gaye was in a deep sleep. She had had little or no sleep the night before, and they hoped that an hour or two would help sustain her through the long hours that lay ahead.

As they drove along, Diana's thoughts drifted between her fears for Andrew and her own private fears for Oliver. She had not spoken to him since he rang at the beginning of the week to tell her that it was impossible for him to travel back north for Gaye and Andrew's wedding.

'I am in a suburb of London,' he had told her in a hushed voice, 'in a safe area away from the city centre, so please don't worry about me. I'm in a big old house, with several others, and we're part of a surveillance operation. You don't need to be at all concerned, darling, because I'm only doing what I do in my everyday life – taking photographs.'

'What of?' Diana asked. 'What kind of photographs?'

'I can't go into that,' he said, 'but one day soon I'll explain it all to you and you will understand. I am so sorry to miss the wedding. Hopefully, this will all be over soon and we will be having our own wedding.' His voice had lowered. 'I think about you night and day—'

She cut him off. 'Oliver, I miss you so much...'

'When you miss me, I want you to read the letter I sent you and remember me telling you all these things.'

'Please try and get back home, back to Liverpool,' she pleaded. 'I worry so much about you, not knowing where you are or when I will see you again.'

'I will be back at some point,' he said, 'but in the meantime, I can't guarantee getting out to a phone at the times you're at home.'

'But what if something happens, not just to me but your family... or just if I need to get in touch?'

He was silent, thinking. 'I'm going to give you a number,' he said, in a low voice. 'But only use it in a real emergency. It's someone in the training unit who can get the message out to me.'

When she had heard the news about Andrew being in Watford this morning, and the decision was made to travel down with Gaye, she realised that she was going to be within a short train journey of London. She was going to be within a short distance from her beloved Oliver.

She knew, of course – more than ever – the danger there was in the city, but from the recent newspaper reports, the day bombings had been greatly reduced. Andrew was one of the unlucky few who seemed to have been hit by a random air strike. What the chances were of that happening again, she did not know. All she knew was that if the circumstances were at all in her favour – if the situation with Andrew allowed for it – she would do her utmost to see Oliver.

She sat back in the car, planning how she would organise the trip to see him if things were right. She would say nothing for the time being. Andrew was the main concern and then supporting Gaye through this horrendous time.

Clare was evaluating her own situation, and trying to work out what she could do to help Gaye today and in the days to come. She had not imagined when she accepted the short post in the country in Cheshire that the world would suddenly turn upside down for poor Gaye. She had not considered that her friend might need and depend on her so much. If need be – if Andrew was in a really serious condition – she would withdraw from her posting at the military hospital. Gaye came first. Whatever happened, she would be there to support and comfort her.

Eventually, in the late afternoon they saw signs for Watford, and then Clare took out her piece of paper and directed Reverend Lomas to the hospital. They woke Gaye as they were just a mile or so away from the hospital. When she realised where she was, she started to cry, terrified as to what she was going to find. The girls and the vicar did their best to comfort her and she was easier by the time they arrived.

When they pulled up at the reception, the vicar strode on ahead to the main entrance, while the two girls waited until Gaye had composed herself. Slowly the three of them walked arm in arm into the hospital.

The vicar rejoined them, and then they were taken into a side room and a grave-faced doctor came in and closed the door behind them. He asked who was the person closest to Andrew, and Gaye lifted her heavy, red-rimmed eyes and said, 'I am... today is our wedding day... at least it was supposed to be.'

The doctor took a deep breath. 'I'm afraid Andrew – Dr Harvey – is seriously wounded. He has multiple fractures, but the biggest problem is internal bleeding. We have managed to block some of the sources, but there are some we cannot access.' He paused, then his voice softened. 'I want you to know that he is comfortable, he is coming around from the anaesthetic, and has been given morphine for the pain.'

Gaye nodded, but part of her looked like someone in a trance. 'That's good he's coming round after his operation so quickly. Can I see him?'

'If you could give me some time, I will go down and see his nurses and we will see what we can do.'

Over an hour later, Gaye was allowed into the room to see Andrew, who was lying in the bed, heavily bandaged and attached to some sort of ventilator. He also had drips in both his arms, and he seemed in a deep sleep.

Gaye looked down at the handsome man she loved lying in the bed, his body crushed and broken, and her legs suddenly gave way. The doctor and the vicar moved quickly to lift her up and settle her into the chair beside the bed. She moved nearer to him and she gently placed a hand upon his. After a few minutes, she felt his hand move and then she saw him turn his head towards her.

Gaye looked over at the doctor. 'He's awake!' she said, her eyes shining. 'He's conscious...' She gripped his hand a little tighter, and could feel him moving it in response.

'It's early days yet,' the doctor said guardedly, 'but it's a good sign.'

She turned back to Andrew, but he appeared to have fallen back into the same heavy sleep. 'It will do him good,' she said to the doctor, her voice lighter and more optimistic. 'Sleep is healing and he will be the better for it tomorrow.'

After a while the doctor left, saying he would be back when he had finished his reports, and Gaye checked if it was all right for Clare and Diana to join them.

'Of course,' the doctor said. 'I don't think he will be easily disturbed with the morphine he has been given.'

It was several hours later when he became conscious again. Clare and Diana had left Gaye with Mr Lomas while they went to get some tea and to bring some back for the others. This time, Andrew opened his eyes and turned towards Gaye, who had been dozing in the chair. He turned his head slightly. 'Gaye...' he whispered.

Gaye moved out of the chair and over to him. 'Oh, Andrew,' she said, 'thank God you are okay...' Tears spilled down her cheeks. 'I cannot believe what's happened, but thank God you're alive and getting better.'

He moved his head, and tried to lift it up, but he sank back into the pillows.

'Be careful,' Gaye said, her voice fearful, 'don't move too much in case you knock the drips or anything like that.'

'Come closer,' he whispered, and when she was as near him as she dared, he looked at her and said, 'I want us to get married.'

Gaye smiled at him, wiping her tears away. 'And I do, when you are better.'

Andrew closed his eyes. 'Now,' he said. 'I want us to get married now.' He swallowed and it took a minute or so before he could speak again. 'The vicar... ask him.'

Gaye looked at the vicar in shock. 'Can we do that?'

Mrs Lomas moved nearer the bed, so that Andrew could see and hear him clearly. 'I think we would have to check with the doctor. It might be best to wait until tomorrow.'

'Today,' Andrew said. 'Please...'

'I'll find the doctor, and I'll be back as quickly as I can.'

Half an hour later, Gaye and the vicar were on either side of the bed with the doctor and Diana and Clare around the bottom part. Gaye had all her official documents in her handbag, and

Andrew's were in his bag, which had been retrieved by the ambulance drivers at the time of his accident.

The vicar had gone to the office for paper and pen and had hastily written down a short version of the marriage vows, which ensured that Andrew had little to say and that he did not have to make any movement. The only difficulty was a wedding ring, which Gaye had left in her bedside drawer for Andrew to give to his best man, George. The doctor himself had come up with a substitute, which was a ring-shaped piece of grey metal that was used in the hospital laboratory.

Gaye held it out to show Andrew, laughing the way she always did about ridiculous situations, and she was delighted when he managed a faint, lop-sided smile.

The ceremony got started, and just as they were saying their vows, Andrew winced in pain. Gaye looked at the doctor in alarm but he gestured to her that he would be all right for a few more minutes.

The doctor turned and whispered quietly to Clare and Diana. 'If we give him the morphine now, he will be asleep in minutes. We'll give them a few minutes together when they're finished, and then we can give him another shot.'

They continued, and after both had repeated the necessary and monumental words, 'I do,' Gaye helped Andrew put the metal ring on her finger. The effort was huge for him, and everyone watched him make the small movement with great difficulty, then he leaned back into the pillow again.

Reverend Lomas then gave a beaming smile to all in the little assembly, before saying, 'Then I solemnly declare you man and wife.'

As Gaye bent to kiss her handsome young groom, he whispered to her, 'I love you, Mrs Harvey.'

Gaye heard the words she had longed for. She was now the wife of a brave and well-respected doctor, who was also the father of her child. Soon they would all be a proper, respectable family. She felt a surge of joy and pride, but it was tinged with sadness and fear. Never had she experienced such a bittersweet combination of emotion, and the memory of it would remain with her for the rest of her life.

Everyone left the room, including the doctor, giving the couple a little time on their own.

Clare turned to the surgeon and said, 'How long do you think it will take Andrew to recover fully?'

'I can't answer that,' he said, quietly. 'What happens over the next twenty-four hours will give us a clearer picture. The fact he is so compos mentis allows more hope than we originally would have thought possible.'

Reverend Lomas had gone down to reception to check about somewhere to stay for the night, and was given the phone numbers of two bed and breakfasts in the small village nearest to the hospital.

'We could drive into Watford where we would have more choice of places to stay,' he explained, 'but under the circumstances, I think we would be better placed to stay nearer the hospital in case of any changes. There is also the issue of petrol too.' He had then looked at the girls. 'I cancelled any commitments I have for the next few days, but I'm afraid after that I will have to think of going back up to Stockport for the weekend services.'

While they waited on Gaye, the girls took a walk around the grounds.

'If we have to wait here another day or even two,' Clare said, 'will that be okay with the factory?'

'It will have to be,' Diana said. 'We need to be here long enough to know that Andrew is all right, and to travel back with Gaye. If we're definitely not going back tomorrow, then I will ring them in the morning.'

'I'm the same,' Clare said, 'although I was due to travel over to the Cheshire military hospital on Thursday night for starting work Friday. Somebody was to meet me at the station in Knutsford and take me out to the hospital.' She sighed. 'I don't think there's any chance of us being home tomorrow in time for me to get the train over. I'll have to phone them.' She looked back at the hospital entrance. 'I'm sure they will let me borrow their telephone directory to look up the number of the hospital. I'm sure we passed a public phone box down at the gates as we came in last night.'

'I saw it too,' Diana said. 'I have a contact number here for Oliver, and I thought if I got the chance I would try to ring him. You never know, he might get time off to meet us...' She shrugged. 'When we are so close to London, I thought it was worth a try.'

'Oh do!' Clare said. 'If we could see Oliver or if you can even speak to him on the phone that would be a silver lining to all that is happening here.'

'I'll wait until I have a number to pass on to his contact, as we don't know where we are staying tonight.'

Eventually, a tired but happy Gaye came out of the room, encouraged by the doctor to go and get a good night's sleep. He had told her that Andrew needed to have a quiet night to continue his recovery.

'In the normal course of events, we would not have allowed visitors in this early,' he told her. 'He has used every ounce of strength he has and more today, so we need to halt things. I am going to give him a sedation and more painkillers tonight to ensure the healing process continues, and we will review the situation in the morning.'

Chapter Forty-Eight

The following morning, there was an optimistic air around the group as they sat around the dining table in the small village boarding house. It was often used by relatives of patients in the hospital, and the middle-aged couple who owned it were helpful and kind.

'Hopefully, when Andrew is well enough to travel,' Gaye said, already making plans, 'they'll transfer him up to Stepping Hill or one of the hospitals in Manchester, so I can go in to visit him every day.'

The vicar had placed a comforting hand over hers. 'I'm sure in time that will happen,' he said reassuringly. 'But one step at a time.'

When they arrived back at the hospital, the doctor had already been in to check on Andrew and he said that after a good night's rest, he felt his condition had stabilised. 'I feel more confident,' he told Gaye, 'everything has stabilised since yesterday, and in some cases improved. There's just a slight concern over his temperature, so we are bringing a fan in to help keep him comfortable.'

Around ten o'clock, Andrew came into consciousness again, and when he opened his eyes, Gaye was there right at his bedside. He smiled at her. 'Mrs Harvey,' he whispered, and she tenderly stroked his hand and then bent to kiss it. 'I've been thinking,' he said, 'and I agree that it would make things easier if you tell our families we were secretly married a few months ago ... we don't want anyone to think we were forced into it.'

Gaye smiled at him. 'I know it makes no difference to us, but it will make a big difference to them when they're telling other people.'

'Exactly,' he said. He paused to catch his breath. 'I don't want you worrying about anything else...' He halted, then he suddenly squeezed his eyes tightly together and then moved his head from side to side.

Gaye suddenly felt alarmed. 'Are you all right? Are you in pain?'

'My head's just a little hot and... sort of fuzzy...'

'Will I get the doctor?'

'No, no,' he said, opening his eyes again. 'I don't want more medication yet...' He was silent for few moments. 'I'm so sorry, Gaye, spoiling the wedding... I've given you so much trouble.'

'Shhhh,' Gaye said, 'that's nonsense. As long as you get better now, none of it matters.'

'I was buying you flowers,' he told her, 'when it happened. Red roses with little white flowers. The woman said they were called baby's breath, and it made me happy when I thought of you and our little one.'

'Aw, that was lovely of you.' Gaye bit her lip to stop herself crying. 'You can buy me the same flowers when you're up and about again. We've so many plans to make now, finding a nice place for us to live with a room for the baby.' Her eyes lit up. 'I might be imagining things, but I'm sure I felt the baby moving this morning.'

'Wonderful,' he said. 'I have enough money for a good deposit. It's in the bank at the top of Greek Street...'

'Don't worry about that now,' she said, 'we'll sort it all out when you're better.'

'When you leave here,' he said, 'I think you should take some time off and go to your mother's. You need someone to look after you for a while... they will be delighted when they know about the wedding and the baby.'

Gaye's forehead wrinkled in confusion. They had never talked about her family being involved before. 'I don't know,' she said, 'we'll see what happens over the next few days.' Andrew made a small noise and when she looked at him, he had his eyes closed and looked more peaceful now. She kissed his hand again, and when he didn't respond, she left him sleeping and tiptoed out of the room.

She went down to the waiting room and told the others how well he had slept and that she thought he was more 'on the ball' than yesterday.

'He's having a sleep now,' she said, 'so I'm going to give him a couple of hours before going back in. I think he's pushing himself more because I'm there, and there will be plenty of time to talk and make plans when all his injuries have healed up.' She looked at the vicar and the girls. 'I feel guilty you all hanging about here waiting for me. Why don't you go back to the boarding house and have a break or get something to eat in the village inn? The landlady said they do lovely meat and potato pies.'

Clare looked at Diana. 'You could see if Oliver has rung back yet.'

'I have a contact number and I rang from the phone box this morning,' Diana explained to Gaye, 'and I gave them the number of the bed and breakfast, and asked Oliver to ring me back. The landlady said it was fine.' She smiled. 'I was hoping he might be allowed to travel over to see us here.'

'Well, what are you waiting for?' Gaye said. 'Get over there and check. If he can't come, why don't you go and meet him somewhere? The landlady says there are buses going into London regularly from the pub in the village. Not the middle of London, of course, after what happened to Andrew – somewhere safe.'

'I couldn't desert you all,' Diana said, 'not until we know Andrew is going to be fine. That's our priority.'

'He *is* fine!' Gaye stated. 'He was chatting away to me earlier on, telling me I should have a few days' break back in Newcastle. I couldn't believe the things he was comin' out with, how he can even talk or think straight with all he's gone through.'

'He's certainly a brave man,' the vicar agreed, 'and the staff who are caring for him are amazed at his progress.'

'Go and make your phone call,' Gaye told Diana, 'and if you don't come back, we'll know you've gone to meet Oliver. Just leave a note at the bed and breakfast and we'll see you later on.' She looked at Clare and the vicar. 'We'll get something here in the canteen for lunch, won't we?'

'That's fine by me,' Clare said, and the vicar nodded his agreement. She would have loved to have seen Oliver, but she knew the chances of that were slight. She also knew that Diana and he would want to spend what precious time they might have on their own.

Diana stood up. 'I won't get my hopes up,' she said, 'if there's no news, I'll ring again, and if there's still nothing, I could be back in half an hour.'

The landlady was out in the garden, and when she saw Diana coming down the road towards the house, she rushed inside to get the piece of paper with the message for her. Diana's heart leapt when she read it, and as she went to go back out to the public phone, the landlady told her to come into the front room and use their phone in privacy.

A few minutes later, Oliver's voice came on the line. He immediately asked after Andrew, and Diana brought him up to date on his condition. He was delighted to hear of the improvement, and then then went on to discuss how feasible it was for them to meet up.

'I'm sorry I can't come out to Watford to meet you all,' he told her. 'I would love to see Clare particularly, but unfortunately I only have a few hours this afternoon. We could meet up if you feel Andrew is well enough for you to leave the others.'

Diana expressed her concern about the bombings. Oliver assured her that Andrew's incident had been the only daytime raid in the last week or two.

'I'm afraid nothing is guaranteed, darling,' he said, 'but if you caught the train to Ealing or somewhere like that it might be safer.' He stopped speaking. 'Damn, I think I heard something on the radio about that train line being closed for tunnel work.'

Diana thought quickly. 'I'll get the train to Euston,' she said. 'I'm sure lightning won't strike twice.'

'Are you sure?'

'Yes, I have a curiosity to see what is happening to the poor old city myself.' She quickly calculated the times the landlady had told her. 'I should make it in there for around one o'clock.'

'I'll check out somewhere safe for us to have lunch together,' he told her, 'and I'll be waiting on the platform for you.'

Chapter Forty-Nine

When Diana stepped off the train, Oliver spotted her and came running towards her, the camera and gas mask slung over his arm as usual. He lifted her off the station platform and swung her around, then kissed her passionately. 'I love you, love you, love you,' he said into her face and her neck.

'And I love you, my darling,' she told him. She stepped back to look at him. The smart suit, and pristine shirt and tie, the hat just on at the right angle. 'Now that I've seen you, and know you are all right, I can actually breathe properly again!'

As they walked through the station, she gave him the update on Andrew, and they both agreed to get out of the Euston area altogether. The last thing they wanted was to come across the site where the bomb that injured him so badly had gone off.

They took the Underground together out to Victoria – unknowingly walking part of the same journey that Andrew had taken – then strolled down a few backstreets until they came to a large, cheery pub bustling with office staff.

They found the more sparsely populated dining room and ordered their meals – Diana had chicken and roasted vegetables, Oliver steak and ale pie. After a quick discussion they ordered a bottle of French red wine, something they would never have done at that time of the day in Liverpool or Stockport. Today, they both agreed, was a stolen day and one to make the best of.

Over the meal and the glasses of wine, Diana managed to prise more information out of Oliver about his training and the current operation he was involved in.

'It was a combination of things,' he explained in a hushed tone, his face serious and tense. 'The training centre was asked to recruit a small unobtrusive team who could work together and use their skills and personal background to monitor certain people who may be collaborating with the Germans.' He took a gulp of wine. 'They needed a photographer practised in using long lens and they felt that my Irish status would make me more likely to go unnoticed.' He paused. 'They also had information about my political stance over the Spanish war...'

'How on earth did they know about that?' Diana asked.

'I had met one of the trainers at an anti-fascist meeting some time ago in Liverpool, and we recognised each other, and naturally spent time together talking. Some people then came to talk to a group of us, and outlined the programme they needed.'

As Diana listened, her concerns became etched on her lovely features and her eyes were filled with fear. 'Oh, Oliver... what will happen with your work for the newspaper?'

'It isn't a problem.' He shrugged. 'They notified the Home Guard and the newspapers that we were now fulfilling government business, and would not be available for the coming months.'

'*Months?*' Diana repeated. She lifted her glass and took a mouthful of the wine, swallowed it and then took another gulp. She needed something to dull the prickles of anxiety she felt over her neck and chest, and something further back in her mind which was akin to a feeling of doom.

'It could be finished sooner than that.' He leaned over and touched her face. 'Let's not waste a minute of today,' he said. 'It will help keep us going through the time we're apart. The time will fly by, you'll see. You're busy at work and with your friends. It might even be over in a few more weeks. After that, I'll feel I have done my small bit for this country and the others who are under severe oppression.' He looked into her eyes. 'What I'm doing is something we both believe in. It was one of the first conversations we ever had, about the Spanish war and the fascists and the class system and all those issues.'

'I know,' she said, 'and of course it was right and honourable and all about human empathy, but it was only talk. This is real, this is your life – our future – that could be in danger.'

He shook his head. 'I can't tell you any more, other than it's non-active surveillance work with my camera.' He shrugged. 'It's taking pictures, which I do every day in my working life. '

After they left the bar, they walked around the area and Oliver took photographs of the bombed-out buildings in Victoria, and while he did so, Diana made a few notes and did some quick sketches in her notebook. She had to fight back tears on a number of occasions when she saw the remnants of people's lives in the houses and shops. While she felt that meeting up with Oliver had almost been a miracle, she felt there was a mist of sadness in the surrounding London air that had wound its way between them.

All too soon, they stood on the station platform, their arms wrapped around each other, Oliver whispering all the loving things he had written and told her many times before. As she clung to him, Diana suddenly realised that if anything did happen to him, she would never find another man again who understood her so perfectly, and who she desired with such a passion. She would be on her own forever, for she instinctively knew that this kind of love only came once in a lifetime. The thought of losing him brought a tightness to her chest and tears once again welled up inside her.

She closed her eyes and buried her face in his neck.

Later, she sat staring out of the train window as she travelled back to Watford, going over all the changes that had occurred in her life that year. The move to Stockport, the factory, meeting Clare and Gaye and then all the involvement with the people from Guernsey. As she thought of the children and the art classes and Gaye's choir, and the mothers like May who they had helped settle into the area, a warm feeling came over her. They had done something good there, at least. However things turned out, she and the girls and the other volunteers had done something that made a difference to those lives.

And now, her beloved Oliver – who was the best thing that had happened to her that year – was called upon to do something that might help save lives. Although he would not divulge any great details, she knew that he was working on some sort of intelligence or espionage operation for the government.

When she arrived in the village, Diana called in at the boarding house to check if anyone was there. The landlady told her that no one had been back to the house at all that day. Diana was pleased to be offered tea or a cold drink, but she politely declined and said she would walk straight up to the hospital.

There was a lot of activity at the accident and emergency entrance to the hospital, with several army and Red Cross vehicles. Diana slowed up and watched as they went to the back of the vehicles and emerged carrying wounded servicemen on stretchers and then carried them inside the building. She paused for a few moments, taking in the details of the vehicles, the people and the surrounding buildings.

When she arrived in the entrance area, there was no sign of Gaye or the others. She saw a nurse who had been around the previous night and went over to ask if she knew where they were.

'I'm sorry,' the nurse told her, 'but I've not been down to those rooms today. We've had some transfers from one of the London hospitals and we're dealing with that.'

The nurse suggested she go to Andrew's room and check. 'You can look through the glass panel on the door, and you'll see if the others are still there.'

Just as she neared Andrew's room, Diana heard a strange sound – like an animal whining. She turned around to look at the window in the corridor which overlooked the gardens, but she saw nothing there. Then she heard a scream that was undoubtedly human and her heart stopped. She went towards the door of the room and through the panel she saw the vicar and the doctor struggling with Gaye, whose arms were flailing around in the air as she cried hysterically.

She opened the door and went in and Clare, who was standing

on the other side of the bed, turned around and looked at her with dazed eyes.

'Andrew's dead,' Clare whispered. 'It was just a few minutes ago.'

Diana stood rooted to the floor in shock. Her eyes moved across the bed and then she watched as Gaye's legs suddenly gave way and she crumpled in a dead faint on the floor.

Later, when they were in a side room, with Gaye, sedated, lying asleep on a makeshift bed, Clare and Reverend Lomas took Diana through the events of the afternoon. She sat in silence as they explained how Andrew's temperature had suddenly spiked and he had become restless, and when the doctors came into check they realised he was still losing blood internally and had also developed an infection.

He was rushed into theatre during which the bleeding intensified and then, one by one, his major organs started to close down. When the surgeons realised there was nothing more they could do for him, they brought him back to the room where Gaye was waiting.

There, the doctors explained that Andrew's life was slowly ebbing away. As Gaye argued with them that he could still recover, the doctor gently told her that Andrew himself knew that it was unlikely he would survive with the internal bleeding.

He held Gaye's hands and said in the kindest voice he could manage, 'Dr Harvey told me this morning that he was happy he had held on long enough to be married to you. It was the only concern he had, and we noticed a difference in him from the moment you arrived. Against all the odds, he survived long enough until the wedding was over. I know it's very hard for you … but it's time to let him go now.'

Within an hour, his breathing had slowed down, and shortly afterwards, with his wife holding his hands, Dr Andrew Harvey took his last breath.

Chapter Fifty

November 1940
Cheshire

Clare looked at her watch and sighed. She wouldn't have time to change out of her nurse's uniform before Mass. She had been late finishing her night shift, as the nurse due to relieve her in the morning at eight o'clock had been taken ill. There had been several cases of the stomach bug in the hospital already, and staff affected had been warned not to come on duty for fear of spreading it to the vulnerable soldiers.

It was another half an hour before someone arrived from one of the other wards to take Clare's place. She went over the notes of each of the men, and then when all was sorted, she grabbed her cloak and bag and set off running across the grounds to the bike shed, as she didn't want to be late for nine o'clock Mass. She found one of the women's bikes with a basket in the front, and she threw her bag and gas mask into it and then set off.

Discovering that the local village had a Catholic church had been an unexpected bonus when she arrived at the army hospital in Oaktown in the Cheshire countryside. It had been one of the only positive things to happen to her since Andrew had died and Gaye had suddenly decided to go home to her family in Newcastle-upon-Tyne. It was a small church, dwarfed by the larger Church of England at the other end of the village, and the young curate who said Mass there every Sunday covered

St Mary's in Oaktown and the church in another small village several miles away.

So far, she had been lucky to make most Sunday Masses, as she had volunteered for the late shifts or the night shifts at the weekend, which meant she was always free in the mornings. Most of the other nurses wanted the weekend nights off to attend dances in the village hall or to watch old films on a screen in the function room of one of the two local pubs.

The big attraction in the area was the Canadian army base, which was a mile from the hospital and perfect for the soldiers to cycle or even to walk into the village. From what Clare had heard, the soldiers were great dancers and had great manners, and they had charmed all the nurses and the local girls, and brought some much-needed glamour into their lives.

Had it been only a few months ago, Clare would have been every bit as excited as the other girls, but watching a young man like Andrew die in such a way, and then seeing the effect his loss had had on Gaye, had left Clare almost emotionless and empty. This had been compounded by the fact that Oliver had still not returned to work in Liverpool, although he had managed to write and call Diana on a few occasions, which kept them from fearing the worst.

As she cycled along, she went over the devastating weekend when everything suddenly changed. When they arrived back in Stockport, a hollow-eyed Gaye slept one night in her nurses' room and at seven o'clock the next morning she had knocked on Clare's door with her coat and hat on and said that she was leaving that morning for Yorkshire.

'I have to tell Andrew's family what's happened,' she told Clare, 'then we have his funeral to arrange. I think it's only fair to his mam and dad that it should be in Yorkshire, in his local church and graveyard. I'm hoping that they'll accept me and the baby; after all I'm a total stranger to them.' She had held out a wedding certificate. 'Mr Lomas gave me this. It's not the one we got when we were married in the hospital down in Watford, I have that safe with my personal things. It was the one he'd wrote out the morning when the wedding was supposed to be in Stockport.'

Clare looked at the certificate that stated that Andrew and Gaye had been married in Stockport back in June.

'He hadn't filled in all the details as me and Andrew still had to put our signatures to it, and then he had to sign and date it.' She took a deep breath. 'He said I might want to keep it as a memento, as he would only tear it up and throw it in a bin. He said Andrew had told him about the baby, and that it would make all the difference if people thought we were married back in June.' She shrugged. 'The vicar hasn't done anything wrong, he just gave me the certificate with the blank spaces in it. So I just signed it and copied Andrew's name and put June on it. I have enough on my plate without anyone going on about when we got married. As long as I know I have my real certificate, that's all that matters to me.'

'That sounds like a perfect solution,' Clare said quietly, 'and I'm sure no one will even think to ask you about it.'

Gaye had handed her a letter addressed to Sister Townsend, saying, 'Will you give her this, please? It's letting her know I won't be back for a while.' She had looked at Clare with tear-filled eyes. 'I'm going home to Newcastle after I've seen Andrew's family and made all the arrangements for the funeral, because I don't want to stay for a week in their house waiting for it to happen.'

'Would you not stay here?' Clare asked. 'I'll cancel the transfer to Knutsford, and Diana and I will look after you.'

Gaye gripped both her hands tightly. 'You've done more than enough – the pair of you. I couldn't wish for two better friends, especially you. I don't deserve you after the way I treated you at times.'

'Don't say any more ...' Clare put her arms around her. 'You've been a wonderful friend to me, and I want to help you.'

Gaye gave a weak smile. 'I've realised that I need to be with my family and I know they'll look after me and the baby, and they'll bring me down to Yorkshire for the funeral.' She took Clare's hands in hers. 'I know you and Diana and May would help me, but it wouldn't be right. I have a feeling a lot of things will have changed when I get back home, especially with Audrey. When I look back, when it came to arguments, it was six of one and half a dozen of the other. I think we've both grown up since then, and can respect our different ways.'

'You're doing the right thing,' Clare had told her, 'and we'll look forward to seeing you when you get back. If I'm still over in Cheshire, I'll make sure I get over to see you.'

In the days that followed Gaye's departure, both she and Diana had talked of nothing but the devastating experience they had all gone through. Both the factory and the military hospital were very understanding of the tragic circumstances of Andrew's death, especially since they were both to be bridesmaids at the wedding, and they were granted a few precious days' sick leave.

Each time they met up, they went over and over those two days again and again, each time one or both of them breaking down in gut-wrenching sobs, lamenting the loss of such a lovely young man and a first-class doctor. Then they cried for poor Gaye and her shattered dreams of married life with Andrew and their baby.

Clare's heart was also aching, worrying over Oliver and trying to console Diana. Trying to lift her friend's flagging spirits drained any emotional energy that she had left. Sensitive as ever, Diana realised the situation and somehow managed to pick herself up. When they met for a coffee the following Monday afternoon, she had announced to Clare that they both needed to get on with things. 'You need to go to that military hospital in Cheshire,' she said, 'and I need to go back to the factory and get on with my art work. I promised Oliver I would have a heap of sketches and paintings to show him, and I'm jolly well going to make sure that I have.'

As she rode along on the bicycle now, Clare enjoyed the fresh breeze on her face and even the chill of the autumn morning, as it kept her alert. The roads as usual were quiet, and as she turned into the churchyard she realised that she had not seen another soul along the two-mile journey.

She went into the church, grateful that Mass had not yet started. It was three-quarters full, mainly with mothers and children and elderly people. She went to a pew near the back of the church, which made it easier to get out without having to talk to anyone.

Since the weekend in Watford, Clare found it harder to make small talk with people, and her sense of humour and interest in talking about trivial things like fashion and make-up had disappeared. She found it easier to talk to the other nurses about work, and put all her energy into giving the care and attention her wounded patients needed.

When she had first arrived, she had found the young men's injuries – the amputations, the burns and facial surgeries – almost overwhelming, and she realised that she had not mentally prepared herself for the job she had volunteered for. All she did that first week was work and sleep. She then began to realise that in order to survive in the new hospital – or even back in St Timothy's – she needed to start living in the present again, and stop constantly worrying about how Gaye and Diana were coping. But that was easier said than done.

Ten days into her new post, she was given a day and half off to travel over to York with Diana for Andrew's funeral. It was a difficult day for them both, and worse for Gaye. The girls hardly had a chance to talk to her, but they could see she was being well looked after by her own family and Andrew's family, who were totally devastated at losing their only son.

From the short time they spent with her, Gaye told them that Andrew's mother had been initially shocked about their marriage and the baby. Having had a few days to think it over, she had then rung Gaye in Newcastle to say she thought that the baby was a gift from God as it meant that a part of Andrew would always be alive. She also said that she and Andrew's father were grateful that he had found someone who had made him so happy and had been there to comfort him in his last hours in Watford.

Back in Cheshire afterwards, Clare still didn't feel fit to

socialise, and felt bad refusing the friendly women each time she was invited to join them for a night out. She decided it was best to tell the truth, rather than be thought rude and distant, so she asked one of the other nurses to explain to the others that she had just lost someone very close to her and was still grieving. The girls were very understanding, and although they remained as friendly, they stopped pestering her to come out with them.

Gradually, as the days and weeks went past, she found herself less tired, and she had taken to walking down the country lanes in the evening or sitting in her room reading, which she found relaxed her and stopped her ruminating over things. She rang Diana twice a week, and wrote to Gaye and her family in Ireland regularly too.

She put her bag down on the pew beside her, then took her rosary beads out of her dress pocket. She knelt down, blessed herself with the cross on the rosary, then joined her hands in prayer for Andrew, Oliver, Gaye and then all the members of her family, and people who she loved and cared for.

When she was finished, she sat up on the hard wooden bench, and waited for the priest and the altar boys to come on the altar to start the mass. The main door creaked open and some of the other people in the seats around her glanced back to see who was coming in. Clare stared straight ahead, and then out of the side of her eye she noticed a young dark-haired man of medium build and dressed in Canadian military uniform slip into a seat in the opposite aisle. She had seen a few of the Canadian air force men in the church, but like everyone else, to her they just seemed to blur in with the pews, the Stations of the Cross, and the statues on the altar and dotted around the church.

When the Mass was over, Clare lifted her things and moved along to the end of the pew to get out of the door. The serviceman moved at the same time, and he stopped to let her out before him, then as she put her hand on the door, he said, 'Let me get that for you, miss,' and reached to open the door for her.

Clare thanked him and then she went outside and down to the steps, and over to the corner of the churchyard to collect her bicycle. In a few minutes she was on the road again, and looking forward to getting into bed, where she would stay until the evening meal in the canteen at six o'clock.

She was halfway along the road when she felt the bike go over a stone, and a few seconds later she muttered a curse to herself when she heard the telltale hissing sound and felt the tyre starting to quickly go down. Having to push the bike back to the hospital was the last thing she needed, but there was nothing else for it. There was no puncture kit in the basket, and she was so distracted rushing this morning, she hadn't thought to check when she had grabbed the first bike in the shed.

She climbed down and then set off, bumping the flat tyre along as she went. She had gone a few hundred yards when she heard a noise behind her. She turned around and saw the Canadian chap from the church cycling towards her.

'Got a problem?' he called, coming up behind her.

'A flat tyre,' she said, barely glancing at him. 'I must have hit something on the road.'

'Can I look at it for you?'

She thought for a moment, and then she turned towards him. 'Have you a puncture kit?'

'Yep,' he told her, with a beaming smile. 'I'm like the Boy Scouts – always prepared.' He went to his saddlebag and brought out the tin with all the basic equipment inside. 'I'm Steve Conway, by the way,' he said, holding his hand out to her. 'You can probably tell I'm one of the Canadian lot from the RCAF base just a mile or so from the hospital.' He smiled warmly at her. 'And I don't need to ask where you've come from with the uniform.'

'I'm Clare,' she said, stretching her hand out, and he shook it in a warm, friendly manner. She held the bike while he knelt beside her quickly assessing the damage.

'Okay,' he said, 'we'll get this fella upside down now and sort him out.'

Clare moved out of the way, her arms folded, silently cursing the bike and the fact she was stuck here with a stranger who talked too much. She watched as he checked the tyre and the inner tube and then got the pump to see exactly where the puncture was.

'By the looks of it, I reckon it was a small sharp stone or even a thorn,' he told her. 'I've checked and I can't see anything, so it must have fallen out.' He opened the tin and took out a piece of yellow chalk and marked the small hole. He then started to rub the area around it with a piece of sandpaper.

'It's very good of you,' she said. 'I'll make sure I bring the puncture kit next time I come.'

'Working with a mucky bike would spoil your clean uniform,' he said, lightly.

She felt she needed to say something, be polite at least. 'I don't usually wear it to Mass,' she replied, 'but I have just come off night shift and I didn't get a chance to change into my ordinary clothes.'

He looked at her. 'You must be tired.' He turned back to mending the bike.

'I am,' she said, her voice weary, 'and this is the last thing I needed.'

'We'll soon have you back in the saddle. Another few minutes and I'll be out of your hair.'

She wasn't quite sure what to say to his comment, so she said nothing. She felt her eyes closing, so she opened them wide and then turned and walked a few yards, moving her arms around to warm herself up.

'Do you go to Mass most weeks?' he asked.

She walked back towards him. 'Yes, when I can.'

'I don't get there that often, because we're often out and about.' He shrugged. 'I'm not overly religious, but with all that's going on in the world at the moment, it feels good to go in somewhere that feels familiar.' He paused. 'Your accent, it's Irish, isn't it?'

Clare tried to stifle a yawn, but failed miserably, and was embarrassed by the length it went on. 'Oh, I'm sorry,' she said, 'the night shift is catching up on me. Yes, I'm Irish, from County Offaly.'

'My grandparents were from Galway,' he said. 'It's a place I've always wanted to visit. See exactly where they came from.'

'Galway is lovely,' she said. 'It's not a big city, but it's nice.'

He stood up. 'I'll give the rubber solution a few minutes to get tacky and then I can stick the patch on.' There was a little silence and then he tilted his head to the side, studying her. 'I don't think I've seen you at the dancing or movies in the hall.' He smiled. 'I'm sure I would have remembered you.'

'I haven't been dancing since I arrived here,' she said.

'Don't you like it?'

She pursed her lips together. 'It's not that,' she said. 'I do enjoy dancing, but I've just not been interested in that sort of thing...' She was really tired now and finding it hard to even find the right words.

He bent down, checking the tyre again and then he applied the patch. His head still bent, he asked. 'Is it that you have a boyfriend back home or somewhere else?'

She shook her head. 'No, I'm just not really in the right mood for dancing or anything like that. I like reading and ... just quiet things at the moment.' She knew her reply was rambling, and she wished she could close her eyes and find herself back in her bedroom, tucked up in bed.

'Okay,' he said, 'I think we're all sorted here. I'll just put a little more air into it, to check it's holding.'

She watched with glazed eyes as he double-checked every-thing, then he lifted the bike up again into the upright position. 'Thank you,' she said again, 'I really appreciate it.'

'You're welcome, Clare,' he said, 'and I hope you get a good day's sleep.' He gave a small laugh. 'Don't mind if you see me following behind you to the hospital, I'm just checking the puncture gets you back safely.'

When she reached the gate of the hospital ten minutes later, she halted and shouted a thanks to him once again, and he gave her a cheery wave and cycled off.

She met him again the following Sunday at Mass, and when he followed her out of the church, she felt it would be rude not to acknowledge him after he had so willingly helped her out.

'I hardly recognised you without the uniform,' he said, smiling at her.

She told him that she had been on a late shift the night before, and had been in bed for ten o'clock, so had thankfully had a decent night's rest. 'Last week when I met you, I was literally sleeping on my feet.'

'I can tell the difference,' he said, 'and I'm glad you feel brighter. I'm not too good if I don't get my sleep either.' He paused. 'Do you mind if I ride back with you again? It would be nice to have some company.'

'No,' she said, 'I don't mind at all.' They wouldn't be able to chat much when they were cycling, she thought, and so she wouldn't be under any pressure to make too much small talk with him.

As they went along the road he positioned himself so he was alongside her, and then he asked her about her family back home in Ireland, and told her bits about his own family in Toronto. He had one younger sister and his father had died when he was twelve years old. 'It must have been tough on my mom,' he said, 'but she never let it show. She's a teacher in the local elementary school, and she also runs voluntary craft classes several evenings a week in the local church hall.'

'What sort of crafts?' He had caught her interest in spite of herself.

'Knitting, sewing, that sort of thing. What about you?'

'Yes,' she said, smiling. Then she went on to tell him about the evacuee groups she and the girls had worked with.

'That's an amazing coincidence,' he said. 'That's exactly what my mom is involved with back home. She helps with a group of ladies who knit blankets for babies and clothes for the children of all ages. They also fundraise and collect stuff every week and send parcels over to England for the Guernsey evacuees.'

Clare kept cycling, not sure if he was pulling her leg or just trying to think of something entertaining to say. 'That is a coincidence,' she said.

'When she's writing to me, she always tells me about the latest things the group have been up to.' He grinned at her. 'I know it sounds like a tall tale to impress you, but it's true. Check it out with some of the Guernsey organisers, and next time I see you, I'll bring you one of her letters.'

She looked over at him and he suddenly caught her eye and gave her a friendly wink. It reminded her of the boys back home in Ireland, and she found herself almost laughing.

'The last letter Mom wrote, she told me that some of the ladies' groups were collecting Christmas gifts for the kids, especially since it's their first year away from home. You're probably involved in doing stuff like that too?'

Clare explained how the groups had disbanded over the winter, and were now more involved with organisations such as Cubs and Guides in the Stockport community. 'It's better for them that they mix with the local families,' she said, suddenly thinking of her friend, May, 'although we do keep in touch with the children through the churches as well.'

He slowed down now as they reached a small incline about ten minutes from the hospital. 'Shall we walk for a bit?'

They talked as they walked along, Clare telling him about Gaye's choirs and Diana's art work.

'You must miss them being over here.'

'I do,' she said, 'but before I came it had all changed.' And then, she suddenly found herself telling him about the weekend of Gaye's wedding and what had happened to Andrew. As she spoke, she kept her gaze straight ahead, not once stopping to look at him to see his reaction. And as she described the last few hours of Andrew's life, it was as though she was hardly aware that Steve Conway was walking beside her.

When she finished, there was a silence, and she suddenly felt foolish for having opened up so much to someone who was really still a stranger. When she looked over at him, wondering what he must think of her, she noticed him wiping his eyes with the back of his hand.

'I'm sorry,' he said, 'listening to you just caught me...'

'Are you okay? I shouldn't really have gone on like that about something so personal. It's the first time I've told anyone here about it.'

He pulled the bike to a halt. 'No, it's me,' he said, giving her a watery smile. 'I understand more than you could ever know. Since this damn war started, I've lost so many good buddies.' He gripped the handles of the bicycle. 'God, it's hell even thinking about it.'

'I didn't realise the Canadians were so involved in the fighting.'

'Some are involved in the air fighting over London at the moment,' he said, 'and a few of us were out in Dunkirk.' He sucked his breath in. 'That was something, I can tell you... I still dream about it, that bloody long beach scattered with men's bodies from all different battalions and countries. And then the poor bastards who were so badly wounded they couldn't move and the water was coming in on top of them. Hell is the only word to describe it.'

He looked distressed now, and without thinking about it, she reached over and touched his shoulder. 'I'm so sorry, Steve,' she said, 'I had no idea.'

He nodded. 'Our plane was shot down, but luckily we made it out and parachuted down a few miles from Dunkirk, and managed to walk the rest of the way to the beach.'

'We have some of the Dunkirk casualties in the hospital here,' she told him.

'I'm sure a few of the Canadian lads will eventually turn up in your hospital, when they're finished treatment in the places further south.' He paused. 'God, I'm sorry, Clare, I didn't mean to get so heavy about this. I forget for a while when I'm busy working, and talking to a lovely girl like you certainly helps, but it always comes back to catch me out. I never seem to get away from it for long.'

'I know it's only one person, and you must think it ridiculous when you've seen so much death, but I've found it so hard to forget about Andrew. I think it was the circumstances – going from the happiness and excitement about the wedding to watching Gaye fall apart when she discovered he had been involved in a bombing in London, and then watching him slowly die a day later.'

'It doesn't matter whether it's one or a hundred and one,' Steve said, his voice hoarse, 'it still gets to you.' He looked at her. 'And you nurses are doing a phenomenal job. I should say you *women* are doing a phenomenal job looking after our wounded men and keeping the factories, hospitals, trains – keeping the whole damned country running.' He smiled. 'Tough women like you and my mom.'

Clare smiled back at him, and as their eyes met again, she felt something stir inside her that she had never felt before, and she suddenly realised that she liked him. She liked this handsome, tanned, dark-haired Canadian very much.

They started walking again, and this time – partly to take his mind off his horrific memories – Clare asked him about growing up in Canada, and he went on to describe the small town where he went to school, and how he had loved playing football and baseball. Like her, he had gone to church every Sunday and sometimes during the week. They then moved on to talk about books and films they both liked, and they had just started on music when Clare realised they were approaching the hospital gates. She felt a little pang of regret at the thought of them parting now, because she had enjoyed chatting to him

They stood for a few more minutes talking, and then he said, 'Well, I suppose I better let you go. Same time, next Sunday?' He rolled his eyes and she could tell he felt self-conscious. 'Unless I can talk you into accompanying me to the dance in the local hall next Friday night?'

She thought quickly about her shifts. 'I'm actually on an early shift and on a late Saturday, so that would be fine.'

'Really?' He sounded amazed. 'Are you sure?'

She smiled now, the first spontaneous smile in a long time. 'Yes – I'm absolutely sure.'

Chapter Fifty-One

December 1940

Diana opened the door to her aunt's house and went inside, feeling tired and sore from another gruelling twelve-hour shift at the factory. She glanced at the hall table to see if there was a letter for her, then she gave a little sigh and carried on down the hallway. She called out to her aunt that she was home, and was heading down to the kitchen to have the meal that Mrs Brown had left for her, when a bubbly, excited Stella came rushing down the stairs.

'Come quick,' Stella said, 'we have a surprise for you.' She took Diana's hand and led her towards the kitchen.

Diana took a deep breath, trying to summon up the enthusiasm for the cake or oat biscuits or whatever the latest creation the young girl had made to surprise her and cheer her up. She stopped at the doorway and stared in confusion at the small, blonde boy around ten years old, sitting at the kitchen table beside her aunt. Diana looked from Stella to her aunt, who was beaming at her.

'It's Gilbert,' Rosamund said. 'We got a phone call this morning to say he had been found in Scotland, and was on his way down on the train from Edinburgh.' She patted the boy's shoulder. 'He's a brave and clever boy; he travelled all the way on his own, and even managed to change trains at Carlisle.'

Gilbert stood up and held his hand out to Diana. 'I'm very pleased to meet you,' he said, with the same clear enunciation as his sister. 'Stella has been telling me all about you, and she said that you are a brilliant artist.'

As Diana shook the little boy's hand, a smile broke out on her face. 'And I am delighted to meet you too, Gilbert, and so very, very relieved that you've been found at long last. Stella and Aunt Rosamund have been writing to places and phoning the Red Cross. They never gave up on finding you.'

'We've been upstairs sorting out his room,' Stella said, 'Aunt Rosamund has given him the small one next to yours.'

'Gilbert doesn't like the dark,' her aunt said, patting his blonde head. 'And I told him you are up until all hours painting and drawing, and will only be in the very next room. We will soon get his room sorted nicely for a boy. I'm going to ask Mr Chesterton to put up a few shelves for him. The kind family he was with in Edinburgh are apparently sending on a box with all his books and piano music and his model aeroplanes.'

Diana look at her quizzically, and before she had a chance to say anything, her aunt said, 'Gilbert will fit in perfectly here, he's exactly the sort boy that I like. He's clever and sensible and adores books – just like Stella.' She shrugged. 'We couldn't possibly separate them now, could we?'

'That's wonderful news,' Diana said, 'and it will be lovely to have someone else here to keep us all busy, and especially for Christmas.'

Stella put her hands on her hips. 'Come on,' she said to her brother, 'I want to show you your room, and we can finish off unpacking your case.' She looked at Diana. 'The people in Scotland were very generous to him, they bought him a new case, and they have sent all the lovely clothes they bought him.'

'And my books,' he said, 'I'll write to them tomorrow and thank them, and tell them all about the nice big house I've come to live in, until we are allowed to go back home to Guernsey.'

'Do you think you will miss them?' Stella asked.

'Oh yes,' he said, his face solemn now, 'but I promised that I will visit them again in Scotland someday. They were very happy that the people found me, because they know it's important for our family to be together.' He moved beside Stella now and took her hand. 'She is my big sister and I know she will look after me, the way she has always done.'

Tears suddenly pricked at Diana's eyes and she rubbed them with the back of her sleeve. When the children went upstairs she turned to her aunt. 'Are you sure about Gilbert?'

Rosamund gave a little sigh and then she smiled. 'What sort of person would I be to turn the poor child away? And Stella is very settled. It would be criminal to turn them both over to the care of the WRVS, and goodness knows where they might end up.' She halted. 'Besides, the minute I laid eyes on Gilbert, I just knew he was our sort of little boy.'

A feeling came over Diana, something she hadn't felt in a long time. A warm, almost comforting feeling. She suddenly realised it was hope. Gilbert's long-awaited arrival suddenly filled her with hope. 'Well, that is the most wonderful news—'

Her aunt held her hand up, cutting her off mid-flow. 'News!' she suddenly said, 'there's a letter from London for you on the piano. I lifted it with my own mail and forgot to put it back on the table in the hall'

Diana rushed out of the kitchen and down the hallway to the drawing room. She opened the letter and quickly read down the first few paragraphs. Her heart soared. Oliver was coming home! He had finished the work he had been assigned to do, and all had ended successfully. She kissed the letter and then held it to her chest. Thank God, she thought. Thank God he was safe and she would see him soon again. Two weeks, he said, so just in time for Christmas.

She then went back to read the final paragraph.

I don't want to worry you, Oliver wrote, *but it's only fair to warn you that I spent the last two weeks in hospital with some injuries I received during an incident. I have a broken collar bone and some broken ribs and a row of stitches under my eye, but other than that I am well, and looking forward to seeing you again. Do you think it would be okay with your aunt if I stayed at the house? I don't think I am quite ready to look after myself just yet, and obviously I want to spend time with you. One of the perks of my injuries is that the newspaper does not expect me back until I'm well recovered in January.*

Diana closed her eyes and then tears started streaming down her face. She wept and she wept – overjoyed about seeing Oliver again, and then her tears turned to ones of sadness, knowing that Gaye would never experience the relief that she felt at this very moment.

Chapter Fifty-Two

Christmas 1940

When Rosamund heard that Clare was booking into the Bluebell Hotel a few days before Christmas, and planned to spend the festive period there, she looked at Diana in astonishment.

'Why didn't you ask her to come here?' she said. 'She is your fiancé's sister after all. We can't have her staying in a hotel.'

'I thought you had more than enough people here already with Oliver arriving, and Clare didn't want to impose. I thought she was staying in St Timothy's, but apparently they have given her room away and she's going to have to look for accommodation when she finishes in Cheshire and returns to Stockport.'

'Well, that's different,' Rosamund said. 'She can sort all that out later, but the girl is very welcome to stay with us here over Christmas. I like Clare, and she's always been very helpful with my health issues.' She smiled. 'It will be lovely to have her here with Oliver, just as it is lovely to have two children for Christmas. What a jolly houseful we'll have.'

Diana made a little face. 'I think Mummy and Daddy were disappointed when I told them I wouldn't be home for Christmas. I felt bad about it, but I explained the situation and how Oliver is still recovering. I've promised them that Oliver and I will spend New Year with them, and she's already organising a ball for us to attend while we're there. I don't know how she manages to keep these things going in spite of the war. Thankfully, Manchester hasn't been hit too badly so far, although the sirens are sounding constantly these nights. It won't be any surprise to Oliver, as he's used to them, having lived through the air raids in poor old London.'

'Forget about the war and everything else for a while,' Rosamund said. 'Enjoy Christmas and then go and enjoy a night or two with your parents over New Year. You've worked your socks off in that factory for months, and you all deserve a break, especially after all you and your friends have gone through recently.' She paused. 'Have you heard from your friend in Newcastle yet?'

Diana shook her head. 'No, I sent her a letter about the evacuees' Christmas Party in the town hall the day before Christmas Eve. It will be the biggest gathering of our groups since they all arrived from Guernsey back in the summer.' She smiled. 'Clare is coming and May, and all the volunteers will be there, so it will be a lovely chance to catch up with the children and the mothers we haven't seen for a while.'

The Friday before Christmas, Oliver rang to tell Diana he was now fit to travel and would be arriving on the train in Stockport the following day. She had worked long hours of overtime in order to have a few days over Christmas for the children's party. Phyllis had been understanding, and the girls in the factory had all clubbed together to buy jars of sweets and chocolates to put on the party tables.

They had continued to bring in donations of clothes and household things for the families, and during their tea breaks, some of her workmates now came to sit with her and ask about the evacuees and about her wedding plans for the following year. She still had a wariness around certain women at times, but on the whole the improvement in her work situation was remarkable.

As she stood on the station platform waiting for Oliver, she felt jittery and anxious, and slightly apprehensive about seeing him again after such a long time. The train finally pulled in and she scanned the groups coming off, and then she saw him.

She froze as he came slowly towards her, as she took in the strapped-up shoulder, and the wound on his cheek which looked much more obvious than he had described. Even with a dressing on it, the discolouring around it was evidence of the seriousness and danger of the situations he had gone through.

'Diana!' he called, and a smile broke out on his face. He put his case down and waited for her.

She moved slowly towards him, unable to believe he was actually there. Then, very carefully she wrapped her arms around him, and laid her head on his chest.

'Thank God,' she said. 'Thank God it is all over.'

They stood there for a few minutes, Oliver kissing her hair and whispering all the endearments he had written to her in his letters. Then Diana took his camera case and his gas mask and put them over her shoulder, and with his good arm he lifted the case and they made their way out of the station.

As they walked along she told him about all the work she had done, capturing every scene in paint or pencil to document the lives of ordinary people going through an extraordinarily horrendous period in time.

'I have all my photographs too,' Oliver told her, 'and one day people will look at them and it will help them understand what we and the people of this country have lived through.'

'Was it awful?' Diana asked him. 'The work you had to do. I know it was much more dangerous than you said.'

'Someday I will tell you everything about it,' he said, 'but basically, three of us were living in a house opposite another which was occupied by highly trained Nazi collaborators, and we had to chart their movements twenty-four hours a day. They were dangerous people who were trying to bring the city down in any way possible, and it took everything we had to finally pin them down.'

'I knew it was something serious,' she said, 'and I'm so glad it's all over. I'm glad to have you back up north where you belong.'

Clare arrived over at the house around lunchtime on Monday

in time for the party at three o'clock. Rosamund made her feel extremely welcome, and surprised them all by producing a bottle of champagne and a box of chocolates.

'This is the first opportunity we have had to celebrate the engagement of Diana and Oliver, and it's high time we did!'

The girls sat chatting together, drinking and catching up on each other's news, while Gilbert and Stella kept Oliver occupied, showing him Gilbert's toys and model aeroplanes that had recently arrived from Edinburgh.

'Have you heard from Gaye?' Diana asked. 'I haven't heard a thing from her since I wrote to her about the children's party.'

'No,' Clare said. 'I haven't had a letter since last week.'

'She does seem to be improving. She told me in her last letter that she had been back down to York to visit Andrew's family again, and that she had also started buying things for the baby.'

'Yes, I noticed that her last few letters seemed longer and a little chattier. She also seems to be getting on much better with Audrey, and says that she and her parents have been more supportive than she could have hoped for.' Clare joined her hands together and smiled, saying 'Thank God, thank God.'

'The only thing now we can do is look ahead,' Diana said. 'I know the war is still going on and terrible things are happening every day, but we have to keep going – and keep hoping.'

'You're right,' Clare said, 'I've only begun to feel like that again the last few weeks.' She took a mouthful of the lovely bubbly drink. 'I could get used to this.' She sat back in the sofa. 'I feel more relaxed now than I have felt in the last few months.'

'You look well,' Diana said. 'In spite of everything, you do look very well. The sparkle is back in your eyes.' She saw Clare blush and then a smile broke out on her face. 'Have you met someone?'

Clare grinned back at her. 'Is it that obvious?'

She then went on to tell Diana all about Steve Conway from Toronto, and how they met at church, and all about his mother and her friends who sent things over to London to be distributed to the Guernsey families.

The girls were still chatting as they walked down to the town hall, alongside Oliver and Rosamund, and Stella and Gilbert, who were hugely excited about the party and reintroducing Gilbert to his Guernsey friends. When they went inside the main doors, they all stopped to look in astonishment at the beautifully decorated ballroom and the rows of tables all laid out for over a hundred children.

'It's unbelievable,' Clare gasped, 'it's like a different place compared to the one we first arrived to with camp beds and babies' cots, and boxes and bags everywhere.'

They went inside and were immediately greeted by Reverend Lomas, Lance and Jack Fairclough and most of the other volunteers who had worked with the children back in the summer. There was a great hum of excitement in the air as the children began to arrive in droves and were shown to the various tables, eyes wide with delight at the balloons and crackers, and the bowls of sweets from the parachute factory.

When they were all seated, the ladies from the various church groups and the Women's Institute came around with plates of turkey and roast potatoes and, later, bowls of trifle, which were all washed down with endless glasses of lemonade. Afterwards, Santa came around and shook their hands and rang his bell as he went along. Then he came back to sit at the front of the stage, and each child went up to receive a wrapped present, bought from money donated by the kind people of Stockport.

Standing against the wall at the side of the stage, Clare and Diana watched the children with tears in their eyes, noting the difference in them from six months ago. They had all grown in height, and most of them had also grown in confidence, and bore little resemblance to the poor, shivering mites who had arrived off the trains into a strange town after their gruelling journey.

They were just watching Gilbert walking back with his gift when the girls felt a hand on their shoulder and they both whirled around to see Gaye standing there, a big smile on her face.

'I'm sorry I'm late,' she told them, 'the bloody train stopped outside Manchester and sat there for nearly an hour.' She laughed. 'Better late than never! I didn't want to miss this.'

For the next ten minutes, Gaye was caught up with children and parents and all the other volunteers coming over to say how wonderful it was to see her again. Those who knew carefully avoided any mention of her recent sad loss, and a few, like May, hugged her and congratulated her on the baby, which was now in full evidence. Stella proudly brought Gilbert up to meet her, and Gaye was immediately entranced with him, like everyone else.

Oliver sat with Mr Lomas, while the girls drank tea and tried to catch up with each other's news. At one point, while Diana was over talking to one of the mothers, Clare touched Gaye's hand and said, 'How are you really?'

Gaye looked at her and then gave a little shrug. 'I honestly don't know ... one day I think I'm up a little, and the next I feel I'm back down at the bottom again.' She looked around the room. 'Today was a good day. I managed to get up and dressed and get myself over here – even changing several trains – all by myself.'

'Good girl,' Clare said, patting her hand. 'Keep going and keep doing things.' She smiled. 'You'll soon be as good as little Gilbert.'

Gaye's eyebrows lifted in question.

'He travelled all the way down from Edinburgh on his own,' Clare said, and was delighted when Gaye gave one of her little whoops of delight.

The tables were all moved to allow the children to dance to the band which was now all set up on the stage. Then, Reverend Lomas came to the front of the stage and held his hands up for silence. At the same time, Jack Fairclough wound his way through the children to come and stand by Gaye.

'Before we start off the dancing and games,' the vicar said, 'we have a request for a very special lady to come to the front of the hall, along with all the children who attended her singing

374

classes.' He looked around the hall. 'Could you all please put your hands together for Mrs Gaye Harvey and Mr Jack Fairclough.'

Gaye turned to Clare with a petrified look on her face. 'I can't!' she said. 'I can't do it. Not with all these people.' Then, she felt Jack's hand underneath her arm.

'We'll go together,' he said. 'I'll play and all you need to do is stand and look at the children.'

She took a deep breath and followed him through the crowds and up onto the stage where all the children had gathered. The vicar came to speak to them and then Gaye and Jack turned to the children, and in a few minutes they were all gathered together into an orderly, if very big, choir. Normally, Gaye had taken them in groups of twenty or thirty, depending on their age, and seeing them all together for the first time was quite startling.

Gaye took her place at the front and then the hall went silent at Jack played the introduction to 'A Nightingale Sang in Mersey Square'. Then, Gaye lifted her hands, and the children all took a deep breath and sang the words with gusto.

When they had finished, the hall erupted in clapping and cheering, and before she knew it, Gaye was leading them in singing a medley of the other songs they had learned over the summer.

Clare stood watching and listening, her heart filled with a joy she had thought she would never feel again. She looked across the hall at Diana and Oliver and thought about the wedding which the couple had planned for the month of May, in order to give Gaye time to recover from the birth of her baby. She looked around all the groups of children, happy and looking forward to Santa arriving in a few days' time.

Then she thought of Steve, who she had left behind in Cheshire. Already she was missing him. She had finally found someone who had awoken the passion deep inside that she had not even known existed. Although they were still only at the early stages in their romance, she knew this was very special.

Even though they came from opposite ends of the globe,

they had so much in common. They talked non-stop together, sometimes about the silliest things; sometimes their discussions were more serious and at times even emotional. But any time spent with him was enjoyable and she always went back to work feeling better in herself.

There was nothing official about their romance as yet, and she was in no rush to make it anything more. Steve, like all the other servicemen, could be called up at any time. The country was still under siege from the Germans, although the British were not defeated and so far had fought back any threat of invasion. Every day, the air-raid sirens sounded and the blackout and rationing continued, and the families from Guernsey had still not heard from those left on the island.

In spite of all this, all Clare could see at this moment were happy faces everywhere. The faces of people who had been driven out of their own homes, and the faces of the good people who continued to help them, and the faces of the children all looking forward to Christmas. Even in the midst of this troubled time.

A tear glistened in the corner of her eye now as she looked over at Diana and Oliver, happy to be reunited again, and Gaye, who was happy seeing the children she loved and all her old friends.

Who knew what tomorrow might bring? For the moment, this happy day was all that mattered.

Acknowledgements

I would like to thank the Orion staff who were involved in the publication of *The Nightingales in Mersey Square*, especially my lovely editor, Victoria Oundjian, who worked closely with me on it from the beginning, and also Olivia Barber.

My lovely mother-in-law, Mary Hynes, was a terrific help with this book. She came to Stockport as a young Irish girl in the '50s to train as a nurse. She told me stories about her training, accomodation, daily routine, social life etc., which helped greatly with the authenticity of the book.

During my research about the Guernsey Evacuees in Stockport, I visited the Plaza, which features largely in the book. I was given a guided tour of the beautiful theatre by a kind member of staff. It has recently been refurbished back to the original décor, and it was wonderful to see it exactly as it was during WW2.

Thanks to the staff in the Air Raid Shelters Museum in Stockport. The shelters also feature in the book, and the visits were extremely helpful to my research.

The Imperial War Museum in Manchester was superb, and I was delighted to have the company of our old history college friend, Steve Hall, from Yorkshire.

Whilst on holiday in New Orleans, I visited The National WWII Museum which was amazing, and gave great insight into the American Experience during the war. I spent a memorable day there researching, accompanied by Mike and old friends from Annapolis, Page and Eric Anderson, and newer friends, Stephanie and Richard Lonsdale from New Jersey.

Many thanks to historian, Gillian Mawson, for reading the finished manuscript, to ensure that my account of the Guernsey Evacuees in Stockport was authentic. She is an expert in that field and author of several books, and I very much valued her stamp of approval.

Thanks to all my Stockport friends, especially my oldest friends, Helen Fahy and Alison Murphy, who are always there for me through the good times and not so good.

I am always grateful to my beloved son and daughter, Christopher Brosnahan and Clare Feely for constantly encouraging my writing, and for always being there through any difficult times.

Finally, loving thanks to Mike, who is the cornerstone in all areas of my life, and in our family. He fills all the gaps to keep the important things running, to allow me to concentrate on my writing. He also checks every chapter as I write, happily accompanies me on research trips, and helps finds any obscure information that I need. I didn't realise all those years ago, how useful marrying another student from my history class would be!